Wren and the Tarnished Tiger

Game of Gods: Book 1

E. M. Leander

Wren and the Tarnished Tiger

E. M. Leander

Cover design by Giessel Design and Gabrielle Ragusi
Brand typography and artwork by Gabrielle Ragusi
Cartography by Foreign Worlds Cartography
Developmental editing by Ben Gibson
Line editing by Leonora Bulbeck

ISBN (hardback): 979-8-218-07354-1
eISBN: 978-1-088-05151-1

Also by E. M. Leander

Space Camp:
The View from Ganymede
Daughters of Jupiter

See all books and learn more at:

http://www.emleander.com

For all those looking for a sign:

This is it.

OCRON
SB 2022

N
W
E
S
Roallac
Estana
School of the Silver Flame
The Isles
Aclines
Spit
As commissioned by His Majesty
King Leonidas II

Prologue

Their horses had been abandoned miles ago. They were too precious to risk on a swampy scouting mission, so the company continued on foot. How Stefan's robe remained pristine despite dragging over the ground was a testament to the powerful magic imbued in it. Perhaps if Aris cut up the robe and turned it into socks, his feet would stay as warm and dry as Stefan appeared to be right now. Their bond might have been closer than if they'd been born brothers, but Aris would do anything for dry feet right now. He pulled one boot from the mud with a long squelching sound, wincing as he stepped forward.

If Aris had to spend one more second slogging through the backwater muck of Aclines, he was going to go mad. As it was, the continuous onslaught of the mosquitoes and the leeches and the interminably soggy boots was far worse than any enemy troops they'd encountered. Patience had never been his greatest virtue—not that he was particularly virtuous in any sense of the word—but his mood was quickly becoming as foul as the sulfuric air around them.

"Stefan, if you don't stop that fucking whistling, I'm going to knock your teeth out," he growled, smacking yet another mosquito that dared to land on his neck. His toes squelched in his boots, making his feet blister, and they were freezing cold despite the hot sun on his neck—a sun that was setting rapidly. His feet, he knew, would be healed by morning—his mood would take a lot longer.

His Mage turned and looked at him, grinning cheerfully, the bright yellow of his robe a stark contrast to their swampy surroundings. A wolf's tooth, as long and thick as

Aris's thumb, hung on a leather strap around Stefan's neck, a trophy from the single worthwhile skirmish they'd had in this gods-forsaken country.

"Aw, do you have wet paws?" Dimitra asked, smacking his shoulder as she passed, an otherwise silent wraith in the fading light. Technically, she was leading this expedition, and she was not going to let anyone forget it.

Aris grunted a reply and watched her appreciatively—they'd shared a bed often over the past few years. The fading light glinted off the twin steel blades strapped to the round shield on her back, beautiful and deadly. She was more lethal than any other Shield on this pointless mission, besides him.

"Easy, friend," Stefan said, clapping him on the shoulder. "You can have your fun after we're done with this mess. You're not the only one looking forward to a warm bed." He glanced over at Dafni, one of the Water Mages. She arched an eyebrow, looking him over skeptically. Stefan grinned widely in response.

"There's nothing here," Aris grunted, shrugging off Stefan's hand. "We should go back." His feet were cold and wet, and he was going to have mosquito bites the size of copper coins all over his body by the time this was done, and all for this damned futile task. The past few months of Aris and Stefan's partnership had generally been the stuff of ballads—daring assignments, the kind that brought them glory and women in droves. Their current task, making sure the way was clear for King Leonidas's army to move through to the capital of Aclines, was the most lackluster job they'd had yet. There was no road, no path at all that they'd yet found through the swamp. The army was going to have to slog through, wagons and horses and everything. Aris was more than ready to turn back.

But then something moved in the grass.

A slight ripple along the tall blades, a new scent wafting on the breeze, as faint as an echo.

"Stefan," Aris growled, on alert.

His Mage came to him, his usually cheerful face now stern, his damned robe still spotless. "What is it?" he asked.

Out of the corner of his eye, Aris saw Stefan's hands twitch, readying. Aris drew his blades, the short gladiuses that his kin had used to defend their Mages over generations. He left his eponymous round shield on his back, ready to be deployed at a moment's notice.

"What do you see?" Stefan breathed.

Around them, Dimitra and the other dozen who'd been traveling with them paused.

Bullfrogs croaked. Far off in front of them, a crow cawed loudly before taking off, startling a whole treeful of birds into flight.

Aris scanned the horizon, practiced eyes looking for anything out of place. Dimitra and her Fire Mage came to his other side.

"What is it?" she asked, golden eyes flashing as she surveyed the swamp.

A prickle ran along Aris's spine. Something was out there. Something was lurking in the muck. Waiting.

The attack came from all around them, all at once. Where there had only been moss-covered trees and muddy bogs, men in leather armor now stood like ghosts, yelling and shaking their weapons. They didn't look like much of an army—they were ill-equipped, with broadswords and shields that had seen better years. Their armor appeared scraped together, mostly leather with rare bits of metal.

There were a damned lot of them, though.

The first wave was on them in between one heartbeat and the next, yelling like banshees as they ran—until a blast of flame twenty feet long and as hot as fabled dragon's breath cut a swath through them, sending curls of smoke and screams and burned flesh up into the evening air.

Dimitra's Mage, Rafael, had cleared a path back toward the king's army—which was miles away and of little help now.

Aris, though, was itching for a fight. They'd been on the trail for weeks now, with no sign of the Aclinese army, no resistance at all. Now, a horde a hundred strong was coming at them through the muck. They would be no real match for Aris, but he'd take this over another day battling mosquitoes.

"Let's go," Dimitra said, quickly dispatching a man who dared come too close, thinking a woman easy prey. His fatal mistake made the rest of the horde hold back for a moment as they watched his body fall. "There are too many."

A roar went through Aris, the primal surge of his own magic coming to the surface. He felt powerful, ready to take on the world if he needed to. There would be no retreating for Aris, no matter what Dimitra said. He felt Stefan's solid bulk behind him, back-to-back, as they'd always fought. Around them, Mages and Shields paired off the same way. Blasts of flame and earth and water took down men by the score, but still the enemy came.

"Ready for a little fun?" Stefan yelled over his shoulder.

Aris tightened his grip and lashed out at a leather-clad barbarian, severing the man's arm at the elbow. The man howled and desperately launched himself again at Aris, coming close enough that Aris could see the decayed teeth in the man's mouth, could smell his rank breath—before Aris severed the man's head from his shoulders with a single powerful strike. Blood sprayed across the ground, making the footing treacherous. Another man slipped in it—a fatal mistake, as Aris's sword cleaved his neck. Blood spurted, catching Aris across the chest. The coppery tang in the air was intoxicating.

"About time we had a proper fight!" Aris yelled back, baring his teeth.

They made their way toward Dimitra and the rest of their party, making steady progress back to dry ground and the road back to the Ocronian army. Still, on the rabble pressed.

"They remind me of those wolves back in Fremulon. Do you remember?" Stefan said, grinning. He shot out his hands, uttering a single word laced with power: "*Pull.*"

The three men nearest him fell to their knees, hands clutching at throats that would not allow air to pass into their lungs. One of them fell face-first into a puddle, scratching for the air that Stefan denied him.

"Those rabid fuckers were ten times the challenge that this lot is," Aris shot back. He gave the downed men the mercy of a quick death—a sword through their hearts—as Stefan gathered his strength for another attack.

The enemy was waiting now, their line receding a bit, seething like a boiling pot.

"What are you waiting for?" Aris yelled. Blood soaked his tunic, ran down the grooves of his swords, but his grip did not falter.

"Arrows!" one of the Earth Mages, Niko, shouted.

A moment later, mud was flying through the air, clods of earth deflecting each buzzing projectile with unerring accuracy. Niko's aim was flawless, and not a single arrow reached its target.

Until a hurled javelin caught Niko in the shoulder.

He fell, a scream of pain cutting through the chaos. His Shield, Thekla, roared. She stood over him as Rafael tended quickly to the wound, pulling the spearhead from flesh, which shredded as the barbed head came out. Niko screamed again as Rafael applied pressure, his fire magic cauterizing the wound. The smell of charred flesh permeated the humid air. Thekla bared her teeth, clanging her own javelin against her shield as she guarded her downed partner and roared out her rage.

When Thekla caught sight of the man who claimed the shot—a broad man reaching for another spear—she shifted, her cropped hair turning into black fur that rippled down and across her skin in the space of a breath. One moment she was guarding her Mage; the next, she was racing across the mud to the man, a blur of giant black cat. Before the man could comprehend what he was seeing, she launched herself at him. Teeth like daggers tore out his throat before he could even raise his weapon. Blood sprayed like mist across the swamp grass.

Knowing about Shields and their shifting magic was one thing—seeing it in action was another thing entirely. The enemy balked, retreating from the great cat, who bared teeth that now dripped with blood. She let out another roar that shook the air like a thunderclap. More than a few of the enemy soldiers fell to their knees, weapons dropping to the mud, their hands held up in surrender before her.

Aris whirled from the scene, turning his attention back to his own Mage. Stefan was breathing hard as he sent a blast of wind that toppled trees like a miniature tornado, splitting the remaining enemy forces in two.

The enemy was untrained, but they were as damned persistent as the mosquitoes.

Niko was being held upright by Rafael and another Fire Mage, who took turns shooting progressively smaller fireballs into the enemy as they limped backward with him.

Another volley of arrows was loosed, seemingly from all over the swamp.

"*Wall*," Stefan said, throwing out his hands.

Aris saw too late that Stefan was not as accurate as Niko, that he hadn't fully recovered from his last strike—

About half the arrows stopped in midair, deflected like they'd hit a stone barrier, and dropped to the swamp below like so many harmless flies. The rest fell around them unimpeded, a lethal steel rain.

The bond between a Mage and their Shield was one forged in the sands of the arena, a partnership that went deeper even than blood. Aris had always pictured that bond like a thread or a wire between him and Stefan. Even when they'd been just boys, before they'd ever been accepted to the School of the Silver Flame, they'd planned their claim. While Aris had learned his craft swinging with wooden swords and practicing his shifting ability, Stefan had pored over his books, all day and night. They had been determined to be the best—to lead the crop of Shields and Mages that the king deployed, to achieve glory. It was an honor that they had earned, together. That wire between them was forged stronger with each victory, each mission.

Now, the wire between them twanged and pulled, like a bowstring stretched too far.

Aris turned toward Stefan, but he already knew what he would see. He'd felt it, as surely as if the arrow had struck his own heart.

Stefan stood pale, the color leached from his ruddy skin, mouth open as his hands grasped the fletched shaft protruding from his chest.

Aris rushed to Stefan's side, his hands desperately applying pressure to the pulsating wound, which did nothing to stem the tide of frothy blood coming from Stefan's mouth.

In his desperation, he missed the man coming right at him, bringing down a broadsword with all the force of a lightning strike.

Chapter 1: Wren

The day starts like any other—at dusk. I head outside, braiding my hair back as I go, ready to get to work. Again.

But there is something different in the air today, something that has nothing to do with the strange weather or the superstitious townsfolk. I listen for a minute, trying to decide what is different, what has changed. I can still hear the crash of the restless ocean on the rocks, the howl of the wind along the unforgiving coast. But something is not right. It's like the whole world is holding its breath, waiting.

That's when I realize—the cannon fire has taken a pause. It's been going on pretty much constantly for days now. Instead, there is now a heavy pressure in the air, like the kind before a storm hits, the ebb before a tidal wave. The air feels thick, and the flag atop my lighthouse hangs limp.

I can feel him watching me before I see him—a prickle runs down the back of my neck, a ripple of gooseflesh along my arms. Anticipation clenches in my gut.

I turn, my back to the lighthouse, and gaze into the forest, trying to discern the source of the sensation. If there are enemy soldiers out there, waiting to ambush me, well, I guess it's better to face them head-on than to run and get an arrow in the back. I wonder if they'll let me keep working here, these Ocronian soldiers, if they are in fact coming here. I can't bear the thought of my lighthouse falling into someone else's care.

For a while, though, nothing happens. I scan the rocks and the trees—there is hardly any underbrush in the thin soil—looking for a sign of movement, for a shape that doesn't belong. Years of scanning the seas have given me an appreciation for those subtle signs. The way a fin barely breaks the surface, the brief flash of silver that indicates schooling fish. Before me, I see nothing now but scrubby pines and gray rocks.

Then, there, looking back at me, is a pair of predatory blue eyes. The prickling sensation down my spine intensifies, as does a vague feeling of wrongness. The eyes are so bright they seem to glow in the fading light, and they are definitely not human. No white surrounds them as they regard me.

As the rest of him emerges from the shade, I take a step back. The vision before me is impossible, and I wonder briefly if the lighthouse fumes or constant fatigue have finally pushed me over the edge.

The long feline shape coils through the edge of the trees, his movements slow, fluid, but ... arduous. I hold my breath, not daring to move, to do anything to draw his attention further, but the creature does not take his eyes off me. I've heard of rabbits having a similar response when frightened by a predator—they freeze, unable to move out of fear. The cold grip of it seizes me now, from my spine to my feet, and I couldn't move even if I wanted to.

But I don't really want to—even if I am about to die, I can't help but admire the animal before me. If this is a hallucination, it's a darn realistic one. The sleek shape, the play of black stripes over snow-white fur that camouflages him so well in the faded light, the ripple of muscle. He moves steadily toward me—but not in a pounce. His left shoulder dips as he walks, and I can see he is heavily favoring that paw. As he approaches, his injuries become clearer. I see that his left side is caked in dark blood, running from one or maybe several gashes down his side. His breathing is labored, coming out in short, sharp grunts.

I swallow hard. I've always been good with animals—they often seek me out—but this is a stretch. Was he caught in the crossfire of the battle somehow? Did some cruel person use him for sport? That's something the Aclinese nobility is fond of, for whatever reason, like it is some big accomplishment to kill animals. Usually it is large elk, for their racks of antlers, or sometimes bears or wolves, which are also found in the inner part of the country.

But how did a tiger get to this part of the world? There are hardly any animals at all here on the Spit, and certainly no large predators. Did he escape some convoy? Is he some prize of the king's for display? Is he a strange part of the invading army, like the fighting dogs and horses of Aclines?

So many questions, but right now the only one that matters is, what am I going to do with him now that he's found me?

The tiger pauses, either to catch his breath or to size me up. He has such remarkable blue eyes, though the fur around them is matted with dirt and probably more blood. He keeps those eyes fixed on me, lowering his head as if to say, *See? I am not a threat*. His ears are pricked forward, not laid back in warning.

I take a step toward him. Whatever has been done to him, whatever is going to happen to me, he is still the most magnificent thing I've ever seen. So out of place on my dreary peninsula.

He takes a step toward me, nearly stumbling as he tries to bear weight on his left paw. I extend a hand to steady him, without thinking, and as he rises back up, I realize my fingers—which look hopelessly small and frail now—are just inches from a mouth full of teeth like daggers. I take a deep breath and slowly pull my hand back, fingers shaking. Too fast, and he might think I am prey trying to escape, and bite. I have never been bitten by an animal, and this is not the time to tempt that record. My pulse pounds in my ears, too fast and too loud.

He moves suddenly, and I flinch, waiting for the pain, for the teeth to sink through the bones of my hand. I wonder if I'll lose it entirely.

But the touch on my fingers is soft, just the gentle nudge of a head as big as my chest against my cold skin. The trembling in my hand eases, and I let out a breath, slowly, letting my fingers sink into his fur, so soft and thick where it isn't filthy. He is still watching me, sizing me up. Somehow he knows I can help him. Animals always know—though this is the first time any kind of predator has shown up on my doorstep. Usually it is a rabbit with a broken foot, or a bird with an injured wing. I've only read about tigers in books, never expected to see one in my lifetime.

I smile, relieved and a little giddy at my good fortune.

"Come on, handsome," I say, scratching his forehead a little. "Let's get you fixed up."

I turn, keeping one hand on his head, and go to my lighthouse. He walks with me, as gentle as a lamb, his tread silent.

Getting a massive tiger into my lighthouse is no small task. He looks at me with something like skepticism in his eyes when I open the door.

"Come on," I say. "You can't stay out here, where anyone could see you, and I need the supplies upstairs."

The lighthouse was not built for tigers. However, it was built very sturdily. It needed to withstand two grown men carrying three-hundred-pound barrels of oil up its winding staircase. The stairs are therefore broad and shallow, winding around the walls of the circular rooms, and the tiger has no trouble navigating, save for his limp. I lead the way, slowly, not wanting to tax him. Outside, a roll of cannon fire starts up again. The tiger's ears twitch toward the sound, but he continues to follow me.

We make it to the kitchen, and I push the table back against the far wall. It's a sparse room, and I haven't spent much time here in years other than to store supplies or grab a quick bite. My latest attempts at bread making roll across the tabletop like rocks.

"Lie here," I say, and he needs no further encouragement to sink to the floor. He is so exhausted that his head thumps down against the weathered pine. He can't muster the strength to hold himself up anymore.

I gather the things I'll need without thinking too much. A bowl of water from my rainwater reserves near the sink, a rag. I grab the ancient sewing kit from its place in the cabinet—and blow a thick layer of dust from it. I've sewn up animals on rare occasions before, but there is a difference between a scrape along a rabbit's side and this kind of … carnage. Still, the principles can't be that dissimilar. Right?

I kneel by the tiger, and my supplies plop down beside me, the sewing kit popping open and a bobbin of thread skittering across the floor. I grab at it—I don't think he'd appreciate being sewn up with bright green thread—and he eyes me, barely raising his head.

"This is going to hurt," I warn, and I raise a finger in the air. "Don't you snap at me."

He lets his head fall back down and lets out a *whuff* of breath. *Do it*, he seems to say. *Just get it over with.*

I look at the expanse of striped fur in front of me. He has to be over five hundred pounds, all thick muscles covered with the softest, thickest fur I've ever seen. If it weren't for the gaping wounds at his shoulder, down his ribs, and into his abdomen, I'd want to bury my face in it and wrap myself in his warmth. I shake my head and dip the rag into the water, then dab at the first bit of scabbed blood I find. He winces, and claws longer than my fingers and as sharp as razors extend from his paws, the movement as fast as a lightning strike. I remind myself that he is in fact an animal designed for killing, not a cuddly bunny for me to snuggle with. My hand starts to shake. What in all the hells do I think I am doing? I take a deep breath. He trusts me; he knows I can help him. That gives me strength.

"I did warn you it would hurt," I say as I pick off the scab.

The claws retract, slowly.

I work my way around the wounds, wiping off the caked blood, throwing in a stitch here and there, making steady progress, sewing muscle and skin where I can. I don't notice that the light is dimming until I go to rethread the needle and can't make out the eye.

"Son of a …" I jump to my feet.

The tiger opens an eye to look at me, questioning.

"I have to go," I say, wiping my damp hands—I hope that it's water and not blood, but it's hard to tell in the dark. "I just have to light the lamp. I'll be back soon." I don't know why I'm explaining myself to a tiger, but I do know that animals seem to appreciate being told what's going on, just like people.

I fumble up the stairs, adrenaline making my movements jerky. I completely lost track of time and am in danger of breaking Rule #3. There are three rules I live by, three rules that were drummed into my brain over and over and over, passed down through generations of lighthouse keepers. *Eat when you can. Sleep when you can.* And, most importantly, *Light the lamp every night, and don't let the light go out.*

I go up to the lantern room, where the crucial workings of the lighthouse are installed. My family has worked this lighthouse for four generations, and my fingers trail over the worn wooden railings, the small door in the stone wall. Each divot, each crack, and each worn spot is a place I've touched a thousand times before, and I like to imagine my parents and grandparents and great-grandparents doing the same motions as they started their days. I swing the outer-wall door open and am greeted by a view of the town. The door itself leads to nothing. It is just a gap in the wall forty feet above the ground—but the view is amazing, especially now, with the glow of sunset to my right bathing the sea in radiance. The worn dirt path from the lighthouse spirals back, coiling through the gray rock of the spit of land until it meets with the main road for the town. Low stone homes sit in uneven rows, housing the two thousand-odd people that call this place home. People are milling about at this time of day. Smoke is curling up from stone chimneys, the sounds of donkeys braying and hammers pounding reaching me, louder than usual. There are fewer people today than I normally see—those who could afford to left weeks ago—but those that remain seem to be working in a fury, like a freshly kicked anthill.

And beyond the buildings are the small gardens the townspeople jointly farm, where they grow the famed Tamdosan roses. Past that is just gray rocky plains, reaching on for miles and miles, until they merge into the mountains to the far north. I've never been to the mountains—few people in Spit have—but I know they are harsh and inhospitable, especially this time of year, when the weather is turning cold. No one in their right mind would cross the mountains now; they look like foreboding sentinels, keeping the Spit in as much as they keep others out.

I fling open the door as wide as possible so I can get a little more light into the room, and I grab my flint and steel. I go up the last few steps to the wick, a massive twist of rope that dips down into the oil reservoir below. I kneel, grasping the steel tightly in my right hand and the sharp flint stone in my left, and strike. The most pitiful spark I've ever made flickers and dies in mockery. My hands are still shaking, and my next few attempts are not better.

"Come *on*," I say. I've never had trouble with this before. However, I've also never stitched up a wounded tiger or had my country invaded by enemy soldiers, so I'll just say it's been a strange few weeks.

Strike, spark, nothing. Strike, spark, maybe it will catch, and ... No, no. That one's out too. I am so eager to get back downstairs, so distracted, I worry that I'm going to scrape off a knuckle against the flint. It's happened before, and it wasn't pretty. My hands still carry those scars.

"Come on," I mutter, and I hit the steel against the flint again. "*Light*."

A shower of sparks pours from the steel like a swarm of tiny fireflies, and the wick roars to life, firelight filling the room and shining off the lenses like the light of dawn. I breathe a sigh of relief, and a little thrill flutters through me.

"Better," I say, standing.

In the light, I can see streaks of blood down my tunic, and dark spots on my knees and shins where I was kneeling in it. I wince as I think of how long it's going to take me to get the blood out of the kitchen floorboards.

Satisfied that the flame is going to be all right for a while, I go back downstairs and find my tiger asleep—or unconscious—on the floor of the kitchen.

All night, I work on his wounds, going back upstairs every thirty minutes or so to check on the flame, to refill the reservoir, or to add oil to my lamp. By dawn, I am done with both. My tiger is still a mess, but his wounds are more or less closed, and nothing seems to be actively bleeding anymore. He has a patchwork of stitches now, from a gash in his shoulder that nearly went down to bone to several shallower cuts along his ribs, into the muscle of his abdomen. An inch deeper, and he wouldn't have made it to me. He needs a good bath—and so do I, but it will have to wait. I pat his head, and he leans into the touch, but his eyes don't open. He breathes easily, though. I stand up, feeling suddenly ancient. My back aches. My knees are trembling from kneeling all night. And I'm soaked in blood and sweat - but I'm not done yet.

I hadn't planned on rescuing a tiger that day, or on being caught on the edge of a war, but no one ever asked me what I wanted. It had been that way for so long—I wasn't even sure if I knew what I wanted anymore. I pause for a moment, looking down at the tiger sprawling on my kitchen floor, and shake my head. For now, I just want to help him. For now, I have work to do. No time to dwell on daydreams.

Chapter 2: Aris

Lady Luck is a capricious bitch. One minute she's holding your hand, and the next she's twisting a knife in your gut.

I signal Kemp that I want another drink, but he shakes his head. He goes back to wiping down the bar with a rag.

"Another!" I yell at him.

He rolls his eyes, but he ducks behind his bar and a moment later brings me another ale. I down the lukewarm liquid in a long gulp, then wipe the foam from my mouth.

"Where were we?" I ask, looking back at the dice on the table before me.

"You were about to give me all your money," Vassilis says. I know it's probably just a trick of the dim lighting—or the drink—but I swear his eyes flash yellow. Vassilis is one of my oldest friends, but tonight I hate his filthy guts.

"I haven't rolled yet," I say, reaching for the dice.

His hand slaps mine. "You haven't rolled a win all night. What makes you think that's going to change now?" he says. "Besides, you owe me three weeks' pay already."

"Coward," I say, grabbing the dice. I rattle them in my hand. "What's it going to be?"

"It's going to be my head if I don't get to the arena now," he says, standing—mostly not swaying on his feet.

"What? No, it's not that time yet," I say, but I catch Kemp's eye, and he's shaking his head at me again, his bushy beard swaying, like I'm disappointing him, the same way I've disappointed everyone.

"It is," Vassilis says, picking his sword up off the floor. "Another all-nighter, old friend? Not all of us get to sleep the day away. Some of us have to work. The recruits won't train themselves."

"Well, we can't all be as good as you, can we?" I say, getting up. My chair tips over, and I reach out to steady it. I miss, and it clatters to the floor.

"You were better," Vassilis says softly, righting the chair.

We're the only ones in the tavern, the only ones besides Kemp. He runs a popular joint here at the edge of the school's complex, and lately I've been his best customer—but I won't continue to be if he keeps cutting off my drinks.

I hate Vassilis. I hate the way he's so sure of himself, of his place here. I hate that he's so good at what he does, at training, at being a mentor to the new Shields. But more than that, I hate that he knows me so well, and he knows I don't actually hate him at all.

"Get some rest. I'll see you later," he says.

"Rematch tonight?" I ask.

He grins, a sly look. "Nina's back in town tonight," he says, shrugging. "Sorry."

"Don't be," I say, waving my hand. "Wait, what about Sonia?"

He shrugs again.

I can never keep his women straight, even when I'm not stupefyingly drunk.

"Wouldn't be fair to play against you, anyway—not when all your blood's running to your cock instead of your head," I say, rolling my shoulders.

"Speaking of, I hear Dimitra's back, bringing in a new candidate tonight," he says, picking at his nails.

I shrug, considering. Dimitra is a Shield, like I am. Like I was. When she isn't trying to tear my head off in the arena, she's a wicked temptress wrapped in leather.

"You're right," I say, clapping a hand on his shoulder, then heading out into the bright sunshine. My knees wobble as I walk. "Can't gamble my life away every night."

Gods, I have to do something to break this cold streak. I can't keep gambling away wages I haven't earned yet—at this rate, I won't get paid for months. A romp with Dimitra might be exactly what I need to turn things around.

I sleep all day and wake to a blinding headache. I then spend an evening with Dimitra—while briefly pleasurable, it deteriorates considerably.

We're lying in her bed, sweaty and sated. She is curled into me, still naked, running a hand in lazy circles across my chest. I like that. I like that a lot.

And then her hand strays to the puckered scar on my shoulder. It sure is taking its damn time healing. I shove her hand off. That scar still aches; the memories ache worse.

She smacks my chest. "Don't do that," she says. "Don't shove me away."

"Don't touch that," I say, frowning down at her. At this angle, I can appreciate the broken bend of her nose from an old wound, the curve of her full lips. I stir, remembering what those lips can do.

"And these?" she asks, fingers tracing the other new scars, still red and tender, along my chest, determined, prodding. "It's a miracle you weren't eviscerated."

"I'm hard to kill," I say, pushing her hand off again.

She sits up, her dark hair wild around her face, her bare breasts small and round over her muscled chest.

I drag my eyes back to hers.

"Maybe you were once," she says, getting out of bed. "Have you even shifted since …?"

The question hangs in the air. I flop back onto her bed, letting out a breath. No. No, I haven't shifted into my animal form since Stefan died. I tell myself that there's been no reason to, but that really isn't it. In the times before, Dimitra and I would race through the valley in our animal forms regularly—the ability to shift is one of the many gifts given to us by the god of day. Dimitra is a great spotted cat, as sleek and deadly as she is in her human form, and she is wickedly fast.

"I haven't seen you in the arena lately either," she says, breaking into my thoughts. She bends to retrieve a shirt, then tugs it over her head.

"Haven't felt like going," I grumble. Usually I like watching her dress, the way her strong body moves. It is a major turn-on, though right now she seems intent on achieving the exact opposite.

"Haven't felt like doing much, I hear," she says, crossing her arms, already fully dressed, like she is impatient for me to leave.

I glare at her. Usually that look is enough to send even the toughest Shield running, but not Dimitra. She just glares right back.

"You weren't complaining ten minutes ago," I mutter, getting up. I dress quickly, the chill in the air having nothing to do with the approaching winter. I wanted her company, not her lectures.

"You know what I mean. You're wallowing. You're going to go soft," she says, jabbing a finger into my stomach. Her finger meets hard muscle, and I raise an eyebrow.

"You know what I mean," she says. "We're Shields. If we're not used, we rust. We fall apart."

I see a glimmer in her eyes then, and I hate it. She knows what happened to me. She was there. Gods, everyone knows now—most of the story, anyway. I don't need her pity, or anyone else's. The golden boy's fall from grace. Everyone wants to sneer, secretly grateful they aren't the one who has fallen so far.

They can all go to hell.

"Good seeing you, Mitra," I say after a moment. I walk past her and leave her room. Like mine, it's in the Shield dormitory, one room in an endless hallway of rooms.

She slams the door behind me. I don't turn back.

It's late. I think about going to Kemp's, but then I think about last night, how he cut me off, and I change my mind. I don't even know where my feet are carrying me until I find myself at the arena.

Even now, it's a daunting structure. At night, with a full moon bright above in a cloudless sky, it seems imposing. The training area for Shields. A place I was practically born in. My sandal scuffs the grains of sand, drawing a line I dare not cross.

The arena has row upon row of seats for spectators—usually empty, sometimes full for the games, when the Mages come to be picked by their Shields. At the bottom of the bowl shape is the arena, the massive stone training ground covered in a layer of sand. At night, the place is as silent as a tomb. At the far end, racks of weapons are neatly stacked, ready for the morning's workouts—wooden practice swords, steel swords, tridents, javelins, nets. The arsenal of a Shield. I take a deep breath, looking at it. Once, I dreamed of standing here. The day I won my games and picked my Mage was the proudest in my life—he was a Wind Mage, the strongest in a generation. And me, the golden boy, descended from a long line of Shields. I had trained from infancy with my brothers and sisters. My father had never been prouder. My Mage and I were going to do great things together.

"Did I miss the invitation to your little pity party?"

I turn, and Shield Commander Markos Drusus steps up beside me, hands clasped behind his back. I wait for him to say more—wait for him to tell me how disappointed he is, just like Dimitra, just like my father and everyone else. I've been back now for a while, and I haven't once seen him, or gone to the arena to train.

"Fine night," he says, gazing at the stars.

I roll my eyes and look at him. He is a Shield but has never served with a Mage. He, like Vassilis and a handful of others, was picked instead to teach, to carry on the tradition of the place.

An idea starts forming in my brain. He's never served with a Mage. Maybe I don't have to either. Not again. I see the same thought flickering in the Shield Commander's gaze as he looks over the arena, then back at me.

"I hear you like to gamble," he says, finally.

I cross my arms and nod. "If the stakes are right."

"Then let's wager," he says, turning to face me.

I am intrigued.

"It's been too long since you were last in the arena, Aris. In fact, I'm not sure if you even remember how to hold a sword."

"So you want to fight me?" I ask, holding back a laugh. The Shield Commander is ancient. He's over fifty by now, thick around the middle despite his years of training. I am the best swordsman in a generation. I've never been bested—not in the arena, anyway.

He doesn't smile, just waits for my response.

"What is the wager?" I ask.

"If you win, I'll keep you on the payroll, maybe let you knock some of the recruits' heads together a bit, let you call yourself a teacher," he says.

It's a fair offer. I could work with Vassilis, stay here at the school. A change of pace. A comfortable job with little risk, not like going out on the road.

"Let's do it, old man," I say, and move toward the weapons rack.

He puts a hand on my shoulder, jerking me back with surprising strength. "Don't you want to know what happens when I win?" he asks.

I laugh then. "That will never happen," I say.

He shrugs but doesn't move.

I roll my eyes. "Fine. What do you want?"

"When I win," he says, staring me down, his brown eyes nearly black in the dim light, making him look even more sinister than usual, "you get back in the arena for real. You train. You go to the games. And you pick another Mage. You get off your sorry ass and do what you were born to do. The gods only know why you didn't go gray, but you're doing a damn sorry job of repaying them."

His words hit me like a punch to the stomach. Never. I could never be with another Mage. No one would want me, anyway, a smaller voice inside me says. But there's not a chance in all the hells that the Commander is going to beat me in this arena, so it doesn't matter.

"All right," I say, extending my hand. "You have a deal."

"Choose your weapon," he says, shaking my hand.

"Swords," I say, and we make our way across the arena. The sand crunches under our feet, the sound carrying in the silent night air.

He grabs a pair of short swords from the rack and tosses one to me. My hand plucks it from the air, my fingers curving into the ridged grip like it's an extension of my own arm. I roll it in my hand, feeling the round pommel as I swing the sword around, getting the balance of it. Like all Shields, I am heavily trained in the gladius, and it's my personal favorite. Markos doesn't stand a chance.

But he walks to the center of the arena like he's out for a stroll.

I roll my shoulders, loosening up. It's been weeks since I fought, and it's hard to put memories of my last fight from my mind.

"Do you remember learning to ride a horse, Aris?" the Shield Commander asks, turning to face me, his sword pointed down.

I have no idea what he's talking about.

"You probably fell off," he says, rolling his head from side to side. I hear cracks and pops as he shifts, a sign of his age. This is going to be easy. I hope I don't embarrass him too much. It's probably a good thing we're doing this at night, when there isn't an audience.

"Rarely," I say, raising my sword.

"What did you do when you fell off?" he asks.

I roll my eyes for what feels like the hundredth time. "Are you going to talk me to death, or do you want to just go ahead and surrender now?"

He shrugs.

He moves with a speed I did not anticipate.

One moment he's standing in the moonlight, gazing at the stars, his sword hanging loose at his side. The next, he's on me with the fury of an enraged bear, and I am immediately on the defensive. His sword clangs against mine hard enough for sparks to fly. In my pride, I did not think to insist on the use of our leather armor. Perhaps I should have.

He rains blow after blow, hammering me from above, as I pivot and counter. Our feet shuffle over the sand, and the arena is silent except for our deadly dance and our panting breaths—or maybe those are just mine. Sweat pours into my eyes, but my muscles are rejoicing, alive with the movement. This *is* what I was born to do.

I push him back, and we circle each other, gauging weaknesses, but I've been trained well, and I mark the drop of his arm and make my strike.

It was a feint. He smacks my knuckles with the flat of his blade as my strike goes wide, and the sword flies from my grip. I watch it go, shining, end over end, an impossible sight.

And then the world tips. My feet are swept out from underneath me as if I'm a new recruit, and I'm flat on my back, looking up at the point of the Shield Commander's sword. He's not even out of breath, and I'm breathing so hard that I worry my next breath will impale me on the point that he's got poised over my neck. My hand throbs, and there are probably some broken bones there, though at least he didn't break the skin.

"When you fall off your horse," Markos says, dropping his sword to his side and offering me his hand, which I take with my good one, hauling myself up, “you get back on. Immediately. Otherwise, you’ll be scared of falling off again for the rest of your life.”

Chapter 3: Wren

I go back up and grab some clean clothes from my room, then get some traps from the storage room on my way out. When my tiger wakes, he's going to need to eat to regain his strength, and I don't want him to view me as his food source.

On the ocean side of my lighthouse, the cliff is all dark stone. Time and tide have worn a hundred small hollows into the surface, and at low tide, like now, they're a hundred small ponds. I strip and ease myself into the nearest one, the chill taking the ache from my bones, the water washing away the grime of the night. I unbraid my hair and let the curls float on the water, untangling them with my fingers as I go. The water is freezing cold, so I move as fast as I can and rush to get dressed. Washing the bloodstains out of my other clothes is harder, and I lament that my only spare pair of pants is now likely ruined. Then I set the traps, cones made of wooden slats that let the fish come in but not go out. I set several. I usually just use one for myself, but I have no idea how much food a tiger might need. Better to be safe than sorry.

The sun is already midway through its ascent as I finally make my way back to the lighthouse. When I get to the kitchen, the tiger doesn't move. He is absurdly large, and I have to skirt my way around him, careful not to step on his flicking tail. I stumble into bed and fall asleep before my brain can start wondering about all the crazy things that happened overnight.

It's only a short nap today, since there is so much to do. I can't remember the last time I actually felt well rested. Sleeping during the day is a lifelong habit—it comes with the job. Still, when the rest of the world is awake, it's hard to get uninterrupted sleep. Someone's always coming by with a delivery or news or a payment or, more often than not, complaints. There are fewer of those these days, but I expect that is because the townsfolk think I might bewitch them or something if they came too close, and not because the smell or smoke or mess has suddenly become less irksome.

I wake up around noon to the sound of gentle snoring. I crack open an eyelid and find a pair of dormice sleeping next to me, pillowed on a nest of my hair. I watch them for a minute, wondering how such a noise can come from such tiny noses. As if they hear my thoughts, their little noses twitch, whiskers ruffle, and two pairs of bright black eyes like jet beads blink sleepily. One of the cheeky creatures yawns widely, revealing his sharp little teeth, and the other runs a pair of tiny paws over his disproportionately large ears. I like these dormice. I see them a few days a week and have since they were just little things the size of a walnut. They are more considerate bedmates than some of my other friends.

"Well, good morning," I say to them, leaning up on an elbow.

The dormice get up and make their way down the worn blanket to the post of the bed. They skitter down and away, back to their little holes for the day.

I stretch, yawning loudly, feeling the kinks in my shoulders from the last day's work. Usually I'd take another dip in the cool ocean to soothe my muscles. But this morning, even the cool water wouldn't be able to remove the collection of aches I've acquired.

I stand up and stretch some more, rolling my shoulders and touching my toes. The motion startles the small screech owl who's decided he is going to sleep the day away on my nightstand. I generally leave the bedroom window open expressly for this purpose, and there is a makeshift perch on the nightstand. The birds can come and go as they please, though they do tend to make a mess. A small dusting of downy feathers swirls below the owl today, and he eyes me through slitted lids, as if daring me to comment on his shedding.

"Hey, grumps," I say, stroking the side of his brown face with a finger. He is so soft it's like petting a little brown cloud—a cloud with talons and a razor-sharp beak.

The owl closes his eyes in response, leaning into my touch.

"I suppose I should be thanking you for not eating my other friends."

The owl merely blinks his wide yellow eyes before settling himself back down, flapping his wings and preening briefly, as if he cannot believe that I would think he'd commit such an indecent act. He is right—he's usually very well behaved around my other little friends. A perfect fluffy gentleman.

I shake out my hair and braid it back into the long plait that will keep it out of my way as I work. Most women in Spit wear their hair long, but if I don't braid it back, my friends make a real mess of it. I pick a stray wing feather out of the ends, giving the owl a suspicious look. The owl, however, is already asleep. *Lucky bastard.*

I go down the stairs and find a pair of calm blue eyes waiting for me. He's sitting up, which is good, I guess, and he seems to have been in the middle of washing his face with his paw. It's strange to me how much he resembles a regular house cat. He stops and looks at me, his tail swishing. I swallow hard.

"You don't want to eat me, do you?" I ask, half-laughing.

He responds by stretching hugely, his claws leaving furrows in the bloodstained floorboards. Gods, I'll just have to replace the entire floor at this rate.

"Are you hungry?" I ask, coming down the stairs one by one, ready to bolt if he comes at me.

But he doesn't move. He just gets out of the way as I reach him and allows me to check his wounds. They're not pretty, but as far as I can tell, there's no infection yet, and no active bleeding. The sewing thread seems to be holding up, though there's so much dried blood it's tough to say.

"Come on," I say, and he follows me down the steps and into the afternoon sunlight.

I realize I have no idea what's going on with the battle, with the war, and I don't care. Here on the Spit, it's just me and the tiger, and that's just fine.

"I'll get dinner," I say, and he follows me expectantly down to the traps.

I have to haul them in on their anchor lines, since the tide is up, but they're nowhere near as heavy as an oil barrel, even loaded up, so it's not that bad. The first trap is full of fat silver fish, and when I toss one to the tiger, he snaps it from the air in a single bite. I get a glimpse of his teeth—six inches long at least—and shudder, tossing him another fish. He likes this game and continues through the whole trap. I reset the bait and toss it back, and he eyes it as it flies through the air. I'm just tying off the anchor line again, to the steel spike jammed into the rocks here for this purpose, when I hear a splash.

He's dived right into the water, and as I watch his broad head cut the waves, he dives down and comes back up with another fish trap in his mouth. He brings it to me, retrieving it like a dog retrieves a downed bird, and shakes the water from his fur in sparkling diamond drops. I can't help but laugh, and pull the fish out of the trap. I toss them to him again, and he snatches them up. We finish the whole second trap before he yawns, licks his chops, and walks away, barely limping at all. At least his swim has washed the rest of the blood and dirt off him. He's even more magnificent now, all stalking grace and beauty in the fading golden light. I think he catches me watching him, but he just yawns again and heads back to the lighthouse.

The life of a lighthouse keeper is a strange one, and it leaves little time, if any, for socializing, which is just fine with me. Anyway, there aren't that many people out here on the Spit. It is a gloomy little peninsula at the southeastern corner of Aclines. My lighthouse stands a little apart from the town of Spit, on the jagged strip of land here unoriginally called the Spit, and it is my job to keep the light going, to keep the ships off the rocky reef. There is no kind, sandy port here—the nearest landing is miles away, west, along Aclines's unforgiving coast. When the tide is very low, I can sometimes make out the thorny tips of wrecked ships' masts breaching the waves.

By myself, running the lighthouse is a grueling task. I run down the six flights of stairs multiple times a day, haul each three-hundred-pound barrel of oil up with the pulley system, swing it into the lantern room, and repeat the process. I am stronger now than I once was, but it still isn't an easy job.

The cannon fire gets louder for a minute. I pause, the day's first barrel just touching the floor of the lantern room. It thuds down when I release the rope, as loud as cannon fire itself. I stop and listen for a moment. The sea crashes on, relentless, outside. I hear the animals in the town and the grinding of metal on metal as people sharpen swords, axes, anything that might come in handy if Ocron attacks us. I twist the rope in my hands. Last week, when the whale oil was dropped off, there was hardly anything in terms of payment, just some flour and a bag of small apples. I wonder what another week might bring, if supply lines are so limited now. I can get along fine with the fish, seaweed, and shellfish that I gather from our cold but abundant sea—plenty for one person—but it's not ideal. I like bread and fresh fruit and generally things that taste less like brine. Spit's not really known for its creature comforts, but we do have plenty of fish.

I'm not really sure why we're fighting Ocron, anyway, and I don't really care. We're pretty remote here. All I know about Ocron is that it's big—really big. It takes up most of the continent already, and I guess their king wants to keep expanding. Must be a guy thing.

More cannons. No one thought that there would be any real fighting here—the fighting was going to occur farther inland, at the cities, just like usual. The ownership of the Spit has been transferred a few dozen times in its long history, without any real interruption in the town's daily activities. Still, some people have left, but not me. This lighthouse is mine, the last remnant of my family, and I have a job to do. Besides, I have nowhere to go, no people to turn to, even if I could get through the blockade the enemy army has put up. No other family. Once, I thought I was going to marry the baker's son, Zacharias. After my father died a few years ago, Zacharias started coming by regularly, somehow always making sure he was the one to deliver the weekly oil supply. Pickings are slim in Spit—either he didn't mind my skin tone or he was desperate. I'm still not sure which.

But then one day, his horses spooked—some snakelike shadow, I suppose; they were very silly animals—and I quieted them both with just a word. A seahawk dropped from the sky a few days later, during another of his trips, and landed on my shoulder lightly. He preened and ruffled my hair, flashing his sharp beak and talons. I remember the look on Zacharias's face, the wideness of his usually placid brown eyes, the pallor of his tanned face. The way his mouth gaped like that of a fish. Looking past my coloring was one thing—when he saw a future shackled to someone whom wild things obeyed … well, he didn't come back after that. I heard a while back that he'd married Elli, the blacksmith's daughter, and that they had a child on the way. After that, I pretty much resigned myself to being alone. It's better this way, anyway—no one to get in my way, no one that I have to answer to. I don't really see myself as the housewife type, but I do regret that this lighthouse, which has been in my family for generations, might have to go to new ownership when I die someday.

I shake the gloomy thoughts from my head and listen again. The cannon fire is undeniably closer. I go to the outer-wall door, grab the frame, and lean out as far into the air as I can. The wind whips through my hair, flinging curls into my eyes hard enough to make them water, and a passing gull screeches at me, maybe wondering what in the hells I am doing. I don't see any soldiers. I do hear the crack of the Aclinese flag overhead—and wonder if I'll be getting an Ocronian flag soon. The gold sun on a field of red is much prettier than our own green flag with a giant black diamond on it. I've always thought our flag looks dull. I don't have any real patriotism for my country, though I suppose the evil I know is better than the one I don't.

I don't hear any other signs of battle now, no soldiers or anything. Just cannons, like thunder, the sound rolling across the Spit. I let go of the door and get back to work. The tiger regards me calmly from a spot on the floor, where he's decided to take a little catnap, occasionally opening one eye to check on me.

By the time I've hauled the barrels up, refilled the reservoir, and polished the lenses, the afternoon is growing late. I barely note the stench of the thick, fishy oil anymore, though I'm sure it surrounds me like a foul aura. I wipe the back of my arm across my face and head back down the stairs—again. Through my bedroom, with its ancient wooden furniture and the mess of clothing and other things I keep meaning to organize, spiraling down to the kitchen, down through the storage rooms, and finally out to the entrance. I don't really cook anything, but I grab an apple on my way through—*Eat when you can.*

I watch the path for any sign of the delivery cart, but no one is coming. I can trace nearly the entire road from here—it curves past the small, thin trees, then leads into a sparse forest along the coast to the north. I shrug. Maybe tomorrow, then. The ground is hard and cold, and as the heat of the daytime sun leaches from the air, I shiver and pull my cloak closer. It will be a cold night up in the lighthouse, though I usually don't mind that. There is a serene peace about it that I rarely find in the company of other people. Not that the townspeople speak to me much—I am too different, too *other*, between my skin tone and my … well, general knack for handling certain animals. On the rare instance I do go into town, I can hear them, whispering behind my back, generally something mean about my mother's homeland. Then the dogs will start howling; cats will start yowling. And once, a whole flock of chickens went berserk, chasing after me like I was a hawk come to steal their chicks. I wasn't able to shake them for nearly a half mile back up the path.

If the townsfolk think I'm strange for upsetting their fowl, how will they feel when they find out I have a tiger?

I leave the doors open for him. We go back into the lighthouse, and I go about my usual evening routine. The reservoir must be refilled, the lenses cleaned of greasy smoke. The tiger watches me with curiosity—another trait that reminds me of the smaller cats I know—before yawning again and lying down once the lamp is lit. He's still except for his eyes, and the silent flick of his tail.

I go and peruse the books in my bedroom. There's an eclectic mix here, everything from romance novels to politics, whatever the townsfolk have tired of and donated to me as part of the payment. What grabs my attention today is a thick tome called *Animals of the Continent*. The spine is worn from my fingers tracing the embossed lettering over many years. Mostly it describes animals that are hunted for sport—and I think I remember seeing something about the big cats in the north in there. I flip through it as I go back upstairs. It's not much, but there is a page on tigers after all. The book says they're nocturnal, territorial, and deadly. They roam in the far northern regions, but there aren't many of them. No one really knows, because they're so hard to find. And probably they also eat anyone who gets too close.

"Where did you come from?" I ask my friend, scratching his ears.

He's seated next to me, content to watch as I flip pages. I wonder again if he's an escaped pet of some kind, from the troops who went through. The company is nice, though. He gets up a few times, and I hear him padding down the stairs to go outside and stretch or do whatever cats need to do, but each time, he comes back. He moves stiffly, but his wounds have healed far more quickly than I would have thought. There's nothing in my book about tigers' healing capabilities, but in another day, I'll have to remove the stitches before they become embedded. It should take a week or more to heal that much. I frown, flipping through the pages, adjusting the lamp as the night passes on in peaceful silence.

I've always liked the night. I know it's a part of my job, but the night always feels comfortable. I tell my tiger this.

"When I was little, I'd try to count all the stars," I say.

He lays his broad head on my knee, and I oblige him with more ear scratches.

"My father taught me all the constellations." From in here, through the window, we can see a sliver of the night sky. "That one's the Hunter," I say, pointing to a cluster of stars near the horizon. "And that's the Headless Lady."

My tiger grunts at that.

"I know. I never liked that one either," I say, grinning despite myself. "It's easy to find, though."

We sit in companionable silence for a bit. Then he yawns hugely and lies on his side near me, so I can keep one hand on him, and he goes to sleep.

I lean back against the wall of my lighthouse, watching the stars, thinking about my father.

"You'd have lost your mind if I'd brought a tiger home when you were here," I say into the night with a wry grin. I pat the predator now sleeping at my side, his tail twitching slightly. "I wish you were here."

The next morning, I again take my tiger to the fish traps and fill up his belly. He dives into the pools, and so do I, scrubbing off the sweat and oil of the night's work before getting dressed and going back to my lighthouse to sleep. It is probably my imagination, but I swear he looks the other way while I am getting in and out of the water. I've never known a cat to be courteous before. Then again, I've never known a tiger before, so who knows?

I clean up the kitchen as much as I can while my hair dries a little. I was right—scrubbing the floors is futile. Dark bloodstains mar the ancient floorboards, deep trenches from his claws with jagged little splinters try to catch my socks.

"Well, I'll just keep working on it," I say, putting a hand on my tiger's head. *My* tiger. That's how I've already come to think of him. One day with him, and it's like we've been together for years. I have no fear of him at all, nor he of me. I wonder if someone is looking for him, and my fingers scrunch into the nape of his neck. He bumps his head against me, nearly knocking me over.

"All right, all right, time for bed," I say, and head up the stairs.

He sits and watches me, the tip of his tail twitching across the floor.

"Are you coming?" I ask. I've never understood why animals understand me, but they do.

He sits there, and I swear he looks confused.

"Unless you'd rather sleep on the hard kitchen floor."

I continue upstairs, too tired to think straight anymore. I get into bed and pull up the blankets. They're ancient and threadbare, as worn as the rest of the room, but they are clean and warm, and I settle into them with a sigh.

A minute later, I hear his heavy tread up the stairs, the floor creaking under his weight. I see his blue eyes peek up over the side of the bed, and then he's up. The big bed groans as he turns around and settles himself next to me, the mattress dipping under him. He turns his sky-colored eyes on me.

"Just don't try to eat me while I sleep," I warn. Sharing my bed with finches and dormice is one thing—sharing it with a predator who could eviscerate me with a single swipe of his massive paw is another. But I have no fear. He's shown no sign of aggression at all. He stretches out beside me, and I can't help but smile as I fall asleep.

I sleep for hours. I meant to get up in the early afternoon, like usual, but when I wake, it is nearly dark, and I am so warm and cozy that it takes me a minute to figure things out. I am tucked against my tiger's chest, his head by my arm. His warm breath tickles the little hairs on my arm. I was right—he is the warmest, softest thing I've ever felt. I take a deep breath, feeling better rested and more content than I have in ages, curled in the predator's embrace.

Until someone knocks at the door. Pounds, really, is more like it.

My tiger jolts away, a growl ripping from his throat. Claws like knives dig into my mattress, shredding the blanket.

"Hey," I say, shoving him. "Quit it. This is the only blanket I have."

He looks at me, and my heart sinks. For the first time, I truly see him as the predator he is. His jaws are open in a snarl, fangs bigger than my fingers glinting, all his muscles coiled. He shifts, and I swear my life flashes before my eyes—it isn't a very impressive flash, I have to say—as I wait for his massive paws to snap my neck.

But a moment later his face calms, and when I put out a tentative hand, he closes his eyes and bumps his head against it, as if to say, *I'm sorry. I overreacted.*

The pounding continues, though. I get up and braid my hair back—it's mostly dry—as I run down the stairs. I hope it's the oil delivery and that they have some news for me about the battle. I hope this doesn't take too long—it's almost time to light the lamp, and I'm tremendously behind schedule.

When I get to the bottom, I see Delan, the blacksmith, waiting for me. He's my father's age—or the age my father would have been—and covered in streaks of soot, from his thick boots to his bald head. His dog is with him, and he barks when he sees me. He's a big hound, the fearsome kind that people use as a guard dog. He sees me, and his tail wags like a banner. He rolls on the ground so I can scratch his belly.

"It's over," Delan says, wiping his face, leaving more black smudges across ruddy cheeks.

"What?" I ask, standing. The dog whines for more attention, so I pat his head absently.

"The war, miss," he says. "The Spit belongs to Ocron now."

"Well, that's nice," I say, picking a white hair off my sleeve. The dog is sniffing me all over, the fur on the back of his neck starting to rise. "Were there any … casualties on the Spit?"

"No, miss, not that I know of," he says, wringing his massive hands in front of him. He clearly doesn't want to be here, telling me.

I wonder who put him up to it, to come out here. Does he hope that his hound will protect him from me or distract me or something? I struggle to keep from rolling my eyes. Spit is a superstitious place in the extreme—between my skin color and the way animals behave around me, I've basically been outcast for my entire life. I stand a little taller.

So now my little backwoods town is a part of Ocron. Doesn't change the fact that I still have oil to haul up, still have a lamp to tend to. I guess I'll need to change the flag on top of the lighthouse after all, but it seems like that's the only thing that will change. *Fine*.

"Well, thank you for the notice, Delan," I say. I start to turn, but his dog suddenly drops to a crouch in front of me, growling, and I hear an answering rumble behind me.

Oh.

Oh no.

Delan's eyes go as wide as saucers. I can see the whites all the way around them. He backs up, hand reaching blindly for the scruff of his dog's neck.

I turn, and there's my tiger, crouching on the steps. He's coiled, his teeth bared, his tail flicking back and forth. He stares down Delan and the dog, ready to pounce.

"Oh, come on," I say, shaking my hand at my tiger. "He's not hurting anyone, you stupid, territorial cat."

I turn back, but Delan and his dog are gone. I have to give the blacksmith credit—I didn't think he could run that fast. They are rapidly shrinking into the distance, sprinting down the path to town.

I turn back to my tiger. "You should be ashamed of yourself," I say, hands on hips. "Now he's going to tell everyone that you're here. You could get me into a lot of trouble, you know. Well, more than usual." As if the entire town didn't already think I am "touched." This goes way beyond a few crazed chickens following me home, though. They'll be coming for me with pitchforks before the night is over. I'll be driven from my lighthouse for sure.

My tiger lets out a *whuff* of air, unperturbed by my outburst. He pushes past me, walking calmly now, all trace of his prior aggression gone. He looks back over his shoulder, and I put a hand on his back.

"I know. You didn't mean it," I say, stroking his fur. He likes this, so I continue. "But people here already don't like me. I don't need to give them another reason."

He shakes off my hand and takes a few smooth steps toward the scrubby trees, where I first saw him. He's barely limping now, I note with a twinge of pride. He looks back over his shoulder, and I swear that his blue eyes shine in the dying light. *See*, he seems to say. *I'll leave, and then you'll be safe*.

And then he's gone, loping off through the trees. I lose sight of him in seconds, and it's like all the air has gone out of me. There's just a cold hollow in my chest where there was a warm, burning ember. I wait for him and try calling out for him, hoping the townsfolk won't hear, but he's gone, really gone, just as quickly as he came into my life.

I eventually head back to the lighthouse, and I've definitely broken Rule #3. I stumble in, feeling my way up the stairs by memory. The lighthouse, which usually feels cozy, even tight, feels somehow too big without his presence. I make my way to the lantern room and ignore the tear that somehow makes its way down my cheek.

Chapter 4: Aris

Vassilis is not expecting me in the arena the next morning. Hells, I wasn't expecting me either, but my word is my bond. I stroll into the arena just after sunrise, when the recruits are lining up to get their daily instructions from Vassilis. This bunch is mostly men, from all over the continent, and there is one towering fellow with such thick hair running down his arms and legs that it is easy to guess what his animal shift is.

"Come to help me get these knuckleheads into shape?" Vassilis says, striding up to me.

The recruits straighten as I approach, their eyes locked straight ahead. Suddenly I feel old.

"I've come to train," I say, and Vassilis smiles broadly and punches me in the shoulder—my injured one. I wince, but he doesn't seem to notice that he just made my arm go numb. I shake out the hand as he yells at the recruits to drop and give him fifty push-ups. I drop down beside them, cranking out the exercises.

At first my muscles burn, especially that damned shoulder. Dimitra was right—I am getting soft, and for a Shield, that won't do. So I keep pushing, another fifty, then another, before standing and stretching. My hand throbs where Markos smacked it, but the bones at least are already healed. All that remains is a greenish bruise, and even that will fade by the end of the day.

"No need to show off," Vassilis murmurs. "You'll intimidate the recruits. Go do your own workout. I'll come get you when it's time to spar."

"You better," I mutter, rolling my shoulders.

I did miss this, the morning drills, the camaraderie. Shields might not be gifted with elemental magic, like the Mages, but we have our own gifts—we are faster and stronger than the ungifted, and we heal quicker too. We can push ourselves harder than an ungifted ever could. I can go for days without sleep or food or water. I can run for miles at a sprint without tiring—or I will, once I get my stamina back up.

With that in mind, I take off at a quick jog, out of the arena. This early in the day, not too many people are up. The School of the Silver Flame is a massive complex, but my favorite running trails are the ones outside the ring of walls, the ones that go down the hill that the school rests on and along the river. It's a beautiful morning, and the exercise feels good. I push myself faster, my lungs pumping and my legs burning. I am made for this. I have to rebuild. There is no other option.

I make my way back up the dirt road to the walls of the school. It's really more like a city. The wide front gates lead to an array of buildings. I pass the library, the stables, and the arena. Both Shields and Mages are austere in their lifestyles, mostly by necessity, and the architecture reflects that. We do a lot of traveling, after all. Hard to leave at a moment's notice when you're burdened with belongings or relationships.

I pass the greenhouse for earth elementals, then the buildings for wind, air, and fire. A bloom of flame bursts out of a window on the second floor as I pass that last one, followed by frantic shouts from the Mages training within. I grin. My own magic comes as easily to me as exercise does. I don't envy the Mages the years of book learning and studying required, but I do admire it.

I try not to think about the link too much as I head back to the arena. I'm sprinting now and burst back into the sandy pit with a roar. It feels good. I stand there, probably grinning like a fool, catching my breath. Vassilis spots me and waves me over to the far side of the arena, where the new recruits are starting to spar. The games for which the recruits are training are coming up in just a few weeks. It's a series of elimination battles, one-on-one. Whoever ranks first gets their pick of the Mages, but it's a little more complicated than that. The best Shield doesn't always pick the most powerful Mage, the way I did. A lot of it has to do with compatibility.

I spy a few Mages in the stands, watching us. Their striped trainee robes flap around them in the breeze. The Shield recruits are probably fraternizing with them every chance they get, staking unofficial claims and feeling out possible alliances. They have me at a bit of a disadvantage there, as I don't know the current class of Mages. I haven't been present for their entire last year of training, and the year before that, I knew I was going to claim Stefan. I'll just have to ask Vassilis about the Mage class.

Vassilis tosses me a javelin, the weapon of the day, and pairs me up with one of the women. I don't underestimate her, even though she's smaller than me—the female Shields are just as deadly as the males. There isn't one of us who hasn't been knocked onto their ass by Dimitra. My grip on the javelin tightens as I think of our last interaction—but now, there's no time for distraction. Vassilis calls for us to start, and the girl lunges, as quick as an adder. My heart rate spikes, and my mood soars as the thrill of battle roars through me.

Sometimes the only cure for hard luck is hard work.

Chapter 5: Wren

They don't come with pitchforks. In fact, no one comes for days, and I am just starting to think maybe they'll just keep leaving me alone, but then I see two men making their way up to my lighthouse one morning at dawn. I was just about to head back in for a nap after my night working—I am always extra careful about keeping the beacon bright on moonless nights—and seeing them coming my way is not putting me in the best mood. I really want that nap.

I have plenty of time to observe them as I wait for them, facing the scrub trees. I look there for my tiger, a habit now. I don't see him, but a few intrepid porcupines and some songbirds do come out and wait with me.

Both men seem to be middle-aged, but there is nothing familiar about them. One of them is tall, lanky, and enveloped in a billowing hooded robe over plain travel clothes. The robe is bright yellow, as bright as the brightest dandelion. On the gray rocky ground of the Spit, he really stands out. He has long straight hair and a long straight beard, both gray. The other man is shorter, stocky, and bald. He wears leather armor, padded especially at the shoulders and waist. Across his tunic is emblazoned a round shield, like the one he wears strapped across his back. He bristles with weapons.

I have no weapons except my sharp tongue. I could barricade myself inside my lighthouse, but I have a feeling that would only delay the inevitable meeting, so I wait instead.

"Good morning," the lanky man says, raising a hand.

I glare at him.

"We're looking for Verena Harker, the lighthouse keeper. Are you her?"

"Who are you?" I ask. I stand between them and the lighthouse, arms crossed. My screech owl friend comes, perches on my shoulder, and nips my ear—in encouragement, I think. The owl draws the eyes of both men, who then exchange glances.

"And where is the white tiger?" the man in yellow asks.

I shake my head, glad that my furry friend has departed, and decide to play dumb. "There is no tiger here. Maybe you should try the king's circus."

The stocky, bald man chuckles.

"I see," the other man says, stroking his beard. "The townsfolk seem convinced that you are hiding a tiger in your lighthouse. May we take a look?"

"I'm not hiding anything," I reply. "And no. It's my home. You cannot come in. Whatever you're doing here, you've wasted your time."

My owl fluffs his feathers up on my shoulder, making him appear twice his size—which, to be fair, is still pretty small, but I appreciate the gesture.

"How long have you been able to control animals?" the yellow man asks, eyeing my friend.

I purse my lips. I don't need to tell him anything.

"Do you have any other magic?" he continues, pressing.

Now I'm confused—and that's when it occurs to me that maybe his vivid clothing isn't just a weird fashion choice.

"Where are you from?" I ask warily.

He grins like we're best friends. Not that I've had a best friend, but I imagine they'd look at me like that.

"Ocron," he says. "From the School of the Silver Flame."

"The … what?" I ask, and he repeats it. "Well, that sounds ridiculous."

"We're a school in southern Ocron, not far from here, as a matter of fact," he says, flicking a piece of grass off his sleeve, as calm and collected as if we were discussing the weather. "I was sent to bring you in."

"To do what?" I laugh. It sounds more like a bark. "I'm not going anywhere, least of all with some strange man in a silly coat."

Out of the woods slink a pair of weasels, and they hiss at the men, baring yellow teeth.

That's when the stocky man beside him stirs. "Do you have any idea who you're talking to, little girl?" he asks. Obviously, he doesn't like it when I talk back to Tall Yellow.

I shrug. "Two circus performers looking for an escaped tiger?"

He rolls his eyes and looks at his lanky friend. "You said we could do this the hard way if the easy way didn't work," he says, cracking knuckles.

I don't like the sound of that. I could probably beat them back to the lighthouse if I ran, but I don't think the door would keep this human battering ram out for long. Dread coils in the pit of my stomach, and then Tall Yellow starts talking again.

"My name is Darius Hall, and I am a Wind Mage," he says, tucking his hands into his sleeves.

I frown. I've heard rumors of Mages in Ocron, true, but I've also heard rumors of trolls in the forests and wolves the size of bears, and those aren't true. They are all just stories told to frighten little children into behaving. Right?

"Prove it," I say.

Baldie rolls his eyes. "How long are we just going to stand here?" he asks Darius.

He's really pissing me off.

"Oh, *shut up*," I say, and a thrill runs down my spine.

His mouth snaps shut.

"Interesting," the yellow Mage, Darius, says.

Baldie opens his mouth, but no sounds come out. He turns a very satisfying shade of red, though.

"Did you know you could do that?" Darius asks, drawing his spindly hands back out of his sleeves.

Baldie is positively fuming, and I cackle at his distress. Darius whispers something that I can't hear, and a choked croak finally comes out of Baldie's mouth. He rubs his jaw and glares at me.

"Do what?" I ask. I don't know what's gotten into Baldie, but I have nothing to do with it.

"We who practice magic—who are born with elemental power—are trained in the power of words. That is, using our words along with our intentions to bring about certain changes. For example," he says, flicking his fingers, "*wind*."

Out of nowhere, a huge gust knocks me onto my knees and whips my braid into my face hard enough to sting. Dust swirls around me, making me cough, coating my tongue with sand. My owl takes off, squawking loudly.

"*Calm*."

And the wind is gone. Darius and Baldie are standing, completely unruffled by whatever just happened. I push myself to my knees and stand.

"Nice trick," I say, and my throat burns from the dry dust that was just shoved down it. "But I'm still not going anywhere with you."

"Miss Harker—" the yellow man says.

"Wren," I interrupt.

He stops, cocking his head at my words.

"I go by Wren."

"Of course. Miss Wren. We are offering you an education, now that your town is a part of Ocron. We can teach you to use your magic, to control it, so that it does not control you. Head Mage Saroya Asprenas would be very pleased to meet you—we've never had a student from Aclines before."

"Who?" I ask.

"Head Mage Saroya is our elected leader, the leader of all Mages across Ocron. She is also in charge of the education of new mages at the school. She answers only to the king."

"I don't have magic," I say, but I'm wavering, and Darius tsks at this.

"First rule," he says, holding up a finger, "words have magic. Never say anything unless you want it to come true, until you've trained. That includes, but is not limited to, saying that you do not have magic, unless you truly wish it to be so."

"What are you saying? What, I can say, 'Wind, come forth!'" I throw my hands into the air. Nothing happens, but the yellow man looks nervous. I cackle. "Guess you're wrong about me."

"I'm saying that, as an untrained Mage, you could unwittingly burn your lighthouse to the ground with a single careless word," he says.

I think back to the other night in the lantern room, when a shower of sparks fell from my flint and steel. Did I command it to light? A shiver runs through me, and Darius sees it. He knows he's got me interested now.

"So … how long does this training take?" I ask. Not that I'm actually considering his offer.

"Oh, a few years, at least," he says.

"A few years?" I blurt out. "And who is going to take care of the lighthouse if I'm not here?"

"I'm sure we can find someone," Darius says, folding his hands back into his sleeves. "But really, you can't stay here. The townsfolk are afraid enough of you. It's a matter of time before you're forced out, or worse."

My heart sinks, but I know he's right. They've never liked me, and now Delan's fed them some vision of me raising vicious man-killers right on their doorstep. And I have to admit, part of me is enthralled. If this isn't my home anymore, what is?

"So, you two want to take me to this Silver Flame place and see if I have magic?" I say.

Darius nods.

It seems like a stretch, but hey, maybe there's something to it. And if not, well, I could start again someplace far away from here, where no one thinks my talents are weird. Not that I know much about the continent, but I do know what I need to do—get away from Spit before I am forced out.

"You have magic," Darius says. "That much is clear. But our great king, Leonidas, has supported our efforts to find and teach new Mages. Your room and board, your instruction, even your clothes will all be provided."

"Under what conditions?" I ask.

He smiles again—it's a patient kind of look, like he's explaining something to a small child.

"You will serve him after you've finished. Usually it's a matter of a few years to pay back the debt, but most of us stay with him after the debt has been paid."

"Your 'great king' just conquered my country, you know," I mutter, and I run a hand along my braid, thinking.

I look back at my lighthouse, my home. Where my father taught me to tend the lamp and to catch fish and to read, and all the other important things I needed to know. Where he taught me to identify the constellations and spot the great black whales that migrate past Spit in the spring and fall. Where he died, a shell of the vibrant man he'd once been. I think back to those long, lonely nights afterward—peaceful, but lonely—in the lantern room. My life has had purpose enough, but do I want to spend my entire life here, even if the townsfolk left me alone? I think back to the vision I had earlier, when my life flashed before me, and I find it wanting.

Baldie grunts something to Darius—he's impatient and taps thick fingers against his hairy forearms, over and over.

"All right," I say at last, surprising all three of us. "I'll go."

Baldie's name is actually Lennox, but when I try to call him Ox for short, the way people call me Wren, he glares at me. Apparently, he prefers "Len." Len and Wren. What an odd pair we make—add in the dandelion Mage, and we might very well have been a part of the king's circus after all.

We make our way down to the town, where three horses are tied up at the first house, saddled and ready to go. These men travel light.

"Can you ride a horse?" Darius asks.

"I prefer to walk," I say. I've ridden a horse before, but it feels wrong, asking them to bear my weight.

"You'll ride," Len says, and before I realize what he's doing, he's grabbed me around the waist and thrown me up over the saddle of a small brown mare. I scramble to keep from falling off the other side, and sit up with a huff. Len ignores me, mounting his own horse as Darius unties the reins, and leads us to the road.

No goodbyes, then. No farewell to the town that has been my home, more or less, for my entire life. I look back over my shoulder at my lighthouse. I don't have much in terms of possessions. The books are too heavy. The other clothes are still so stained from the tiger's blood that they're not worth taking along, and my one good blanket is shredded. I'm not much of a sentimental person, but I'd take the lighthouse itself with me if I could. It looks small enough from this distance, like I could just pick it up and put it in my pocket. I thought about taking the flint and steel, something my father and grandfather and great-grandfather touched over the years, but then what would the new occupant use to light the lamp? Instead, I leave empty-handed, with nothing but the clothes on my back, wondering who Spit will decide to install there in my stead. I get a little teary-eyed thinking that they might not give it the same care and attention that I did, that they won't know how the wick likes to tip if it isn't properly seated, or how to keep the pulley ropes from tangling, or how the second step always squeaks, no matter how much I tried to fix it. They won't know to leave food out for the dormice, and the window open for the owl. I wish I could have at least said goodbye to my animal friends.

Darius and Len are clearly used to traveling. They set their horses into a quick walk, and my mare follows obediently. I'm glad she does—I feel stiff and unsettled on her back, like I'm being rude by imposing on her. The jostling bumps my melancholy thoughts right out of my head, and my teeth are sore from chattering. The horse doesn't seem to notice, though, and after an hour or so, I finally relax a little. I'm exhausted from being up all night, but also full of energy from the excitement. The mare tosses her head in encouragement, like I'm more comfortable now for her too. The Spit is shrinking behind me, nearly hidden by the trees. I pat the side of my horse's neck, enjoying the warm softness, taking comfort in it. It's been a strange day, but at least the weather is holding. I've never been even this far from Spit, as we head toward the jagged mountains. Darius assures me there's an easy pass through them and that he'll make sure the storms leave us alone. That last comment boggles me a bit. I wonder if I'll have wind magic too. I wonder what a Wind Mage does, besides fetching promising students to the school, and I ask him.

Len rolls his eyes at me.

"Mages do all kinds of things, whatever the king commands," Darius says. He's proud of being a Wind Mage. That much is clear. "Some of the Wind Mages work on ships in the Royal Navy. Some study at the capital. Some of us are stationed along the mountain passes to make sure travelers get through without too much trouble from the weather. A few work as soldiers."

"And you each have a bodyguard?" I ask.

Len snorts.

"A Shield. And yes, most do," Darius says. He's riding behind me, and Len is beside me, as if to keep me from turning around and heading back to Spit. Like I would want to—there's nothing for me there.

"Why?" I ask. The prospect of having a bodyguard is strange. I like being alone. "Is he with you all the time? What about when you sleep?"

"The continent is a dangerous place," Darius says mysteriously.

Len grunts. "We protect each other," he says. "We are partners. Spells take time, and he needs to recover between them."

I eye the twin swords strapped to his back, the knives sheathed at his waist. There's a small throwing axe on his saddle, and probably a hundred more weapons I can't see. It doesn't seem like he'd need protecting from anything.

"The bond between a Mage and their Shield is strong. Think of it like having a brother or sister or a best friend with you. You trust each other, and you do important work. It's a good life."

"What makes it good?" I ask. I don't have any brothers or sisters or best friends. I can imagine it, though. I've read enough books to understand the importance of those relationships, at least a little, even though I've never experienced anything like them.

"Why do you ask so many questions?" Len says.

"Because I grew up in a country where magic doesn't exist, you dolt," I snap. "And I want to know exactly what I'm getting into."

"We have a long ride ahead of us," Darius says gently. "A week, maybe more. I promise to answer all of your questions along the way."

"Magic does exist in your country, you know," Len says, giving me a side-eye. "You're proof enough of that."

"What kind of magic do I have?" I ask.

"Earth, maybe," Darius says. "Control over the beasts isn't common, but I expect it's just an early manifestation of a proclivity for earth magic. You have some talent with wind too, but it's common for early Mages to show some strength in each of the elements—wind, earth, fire, and water. Your training at the school will help us figure out which is your strongest element, which one to hone."

"I don't control animals," I say. "They like me. They just trust me." I turn to look at Darius, and he's frowning.

"Have you ever been bitten by an animal, Wren?" he asks.

I frown. "No."

"And you don't find that odd? That never has an animal harmed you, no matter if they were in pain or afraid?"

I think back to my tiger, to the snarl I saw when Delan knocked on my door. Then I think about how he let me tend his wounds. It must have hurt enormously, but he never flinched. I don't like this train of thought, though. Animals just like me. People don't. I squirm in my saddle—my legs are starting to get sore—and think for a few minutes. I think Len is grateful for the reprieve.

Is it possible, then, that animals *don't* like me? Are they just being influenced subconsciously by my "magic"? I don't like this. I'd rather believe that animals actually enjoy my presence, that anyone does, rather than know I have been forcing them to do something against their nature.

We ride for hours and hours. I'm usually asleep this time of day, but now I'm wide awake. I watch the road pass through the trees and over a wide plain of rock. I have no idea where we're going, what direction we're headed in, nothing. We don't stop all day. Darius hands me some bread and cheese and a water flask around midday, but we keep going. The horses are quiet, steady animals. I learn that my mare is called Poppy, which is nice. She looks like a Poppy.

We finally stop to make camp as night falls, in the shade of the most massive trees I've ever seen. The trees on the coast are short and sparse, as gnarled as the landscape. These are towering, with long branches and soft green needles. Len gathers wood for a fire, and I haul up some logs for us to sit on.

Darius pulls some food out of his pack. I recognize the bread, from Long's bakery in Spit, with his crosshatching over the top. It sends a weird twist of emotion through my gut. I accept the piece Darius hands me—after all, Long is a pretty good baker—but it tastes off, like whatever is going on inside me is somehow souring the soft, yeasty bread. I realize I have no idea when I'll be back, or even if I'll be back.

I swallow and nearly choke on the dry lump, then cough a few times until the bread finally goes down. The men look at me but don't say anything, and pretend to focus on their own meals. I put down the food and instead stretch my legs out toward the small fire Len's made. We're sheltered by the trees overhead, and the warmth is nice. I can just make out a crescent moon above. My legs ache distractingly. I'm used to running up and down stairs, used to carrying heavy loads, but riding a horse uses muscles I didn't even know I had. I'm going to be stiff tomorrow.

It strikes me then that I'm alone here. I mean, I'm used to being alone, but this is different. I am somewhere in the wilderness, presumably on my way to a school in Ocron. I am trusting my safety—hells, my life—to these two men in front of me. How do I know they aren't planning on harming me? I must have been pretty desperate to get away from Spit if I was too stupid to think of that *before* I came all the way out here. I am too far away from Spit now for anyone to hear me if they do turn on me. Goose bumps prickle up my arms as the enormity of the situation comes crashing down on me. The men are silent, probably because they are exhausted from the day—but who knows what else they are plotting? I could probably outrun Darius, but Len? I think he'd enjoy chasing me down. I shiver and try to turn my attention back to the bread, picking it apart until it crumbles.

In the distance, I hear a wolf howl. I rarely heard them on the Spit—not a lot of animals live in the rocky terrain—and always it was so far off that the sound barely reached my ears.

This is different. This animal is just a few miles off. I hear another animal join the howl, and this comforts me somehow.

Darius and Len exchange a glance, and Darius puts a hand into his pocket to fiddle with something. I catch a glint of gray metal, but he doesn't take the item from his pocket. A knife, maybe. I thought Len was the weapons collector, but perhaps Darius has something of his own. I don't like that. A thrill goes through me, like a shiver. The howling starts again.

"Cut it out," Len says, glaring at me.

"What?" I ask. I'm just sitting here, trying to be as small and unobtrusive as possible, trying to sort out the strange events of the day and the motivations of my traveling companions.

"The wolves. Stop it," he says around a mouthful of food.

Darius holds up a hand. He's sitting up ramrod straight, looking into the woods. He takes his other hand out of his pocket, and I see the item he's been messing with. It's a slim silver hoop, hinged so it swings open in two crescents. He's absently opening and closing the thing in his hand.

"What's that?" I ask, pointing to the hoop. Darius looks down, seemingly unaware that he's taken the thing from his pocket.

"A manacle," he says absently.

The howling starts back up, and it's closer this time. It sounds like there are two or three voices now.

"What's it for?" I ask.

"Control," Darius says.

I frown. It helps him control his wind magic? Does he think he's going to need a lot of wind magic for some reason tonight? I don't like the sound of that.

"Cut it out," Len hisses again.

I hear something move in the trees, and a low growl.

"I'm not doing anything," I say, scrunching up, hugging my legs to my chest. I fear the men before me far more than whatever is lurking in the trees.

Movement again, and I see four hulking shapes break through the gathering night. They are wolves, and they are much, much bigger than I thought they'd be. I'm not that tall, and I'd wager that their shoulders are as high as my waist. They are gray and white and lean. Their teeth are bared, yellow eyes flashing in the glow of the fire.

Len draws his swords. I do not like where this is heading. I knew the continent was a wild place, but this? So close to Spit?

Len stands and goes to the far side of the fire, his swords glinting in the flickering light. The wolves are staring him down. They are massive, muscled beasts—I'm sure Len is good at whatever it is he does, but I wouldn't bet on him against a wolf pack. I guess Darius realizes this too, because he stands up, his yellow robe fluttering around him. I look back at the wolves—they're closer. The hair on their necks is raised, and they are growling. The sound vibrates through the still night air.

And I feel the kiss of cold metal around my wrist.

Darius has put the silver ring on my arm, clasping it shut like a bracelet.

"What?" I ask him, and I go to take it off with my other hand. A shock races through me as my fingers contact the metal, leaving a numb feeling in my hand.

"What in all the hells is this?" I say, standing. I'm afraid. I don't like this thing on my arm. I want it off.

I don't even notice that the wolves have left the clearing, disappearing like ghosts.

"Control," Darius says, taking his seat again like nothing has happened.

Len is standing guard, his swords raised, looking for a fight that isn't there.

"Take it off," I order him. I am no prisoner to be shackled. What's next? Chains? A dungeon? Is this how teachers at the stupid "Silver Flame" school treat their students? I am boiling mad—mostly at myself, for having agreed to this journey in the first place. At least back in Spit I knew where the dangers were.

Darius ignores me, picking up his water flask and taking a slow sip.

"Take it off!" I scream at him, stomping my foot.

Darius raises a finger to silence me. Len, finally satisfied that the wolves have left, circles back to his seat but doesn't take his eyes off the trees. I touch the metal ring again, and again it shocks me.

"The manacle takes away your magic," Darius says. "I was hoping it wouldn't be necessary, but … those wolves would have attacked, and Len would have had to kill them."

"There were four of them," I say, eyeing Len.

Len grunts. "I'm tougher than I look."

"I wasn't doing anything! Take this thing off!" I say, whirling on Darius.

He just shakes his head at me, like I'm some misbehaving child he's having to punish.

Tears jump to my eyes.

"Miss Wren, you have no idea how to control your magic. Until you do, the manacle stays on, for your safety. And ours," he says. "Or did you not notice how your wolf friends came to your aid when you were panicking, and left as soon as the manacle nullified your magic?"

He's insane. There's no reasoning with him. I plop back down onto my log. I don't like this. I don't like feeling like a child—or worse, like some … some monster that needs to be caged. Tamed. Broken.

"I'm sorry. I won't do it again. You can take it off now," I say, extending my wrist to him.

Darius shakes his head, and then the tears really do start falling. Angry tears. And I'm angry at myself for crying, but none of that makes any difference, because now I'm chained with this stupid zappy bracelet and alone in the woods with two men who don't give a damn. I consider grabbing Poppy and taking off—somewhere, anywhere. Len catches my gaze and shakes his head slowly, in warning. *Don't even think it*, the look says. I imagine I'll be chained by more than just this stupid manacle if I do.

I catch the bedroll that Len tosses down from Poppy for me. It's musty and smells like horse, but at least it's warm. I lay it out close to the fire, trying to ignore the fact that the manacle still feels like ice against my arm. I try wrapping my other hand in the blanket and using that to pop open the latch, but I get zapped again, and I think I hear Len laughing at me, so I don't try again. The manacle is just a slim metal band, lacking markings of any kind.

I hate it. I hate it like I've never hated anything before.

I don't sleep well. Whether because I'm mad or because I'm usually awake at night, it's hard to say. Also, the bedroll is scratchy, and I can barely turn over inside its constraints. I never thought I'd miss my bed, as threadbare and ancient as it was, but sleeping on the ground is a new level of discomfort. The bedroll is warm enough, but the ground is slightly damp and chills me down to my bones. I am using my arms for a pillow, and the left one has gone to sleep. I resolve to find some pine needles or leaves or something to stuff underneath me next time, or maybe I could use Poppy's saddle for a pillow.

Darius and Len rise around dawn, looking disturbingly refreshed, so I get up too. I'm stiff, but it's not too bad. My legs protest only a little as I stand up and stretch. I shake out my braid and comb out my curls with my fingers before braiding them back up. Even braided, my hair nearly reaches my waist, but there are no feathers in it today, no sleeping dormice. The thought makes me immeasurably sad.

I pester Darius all day long to remove the manacle. I try reasoning with him. I try begging. I try threatening him. But Darius ignores me, which makes me feel like a child, which then makes me even angrier. He still rides behind me, though, and even if I could somehow turn Poppy around and get away from them, where would I go? Back to Spit? Back to a town that didn't want me, with this stupid metal thing on my arm that I can't take off? *Good luck explaining that to a town full of superstitious ninnies.*

We spend a day traversing a mountain pass, a narrow path cut between the roots of two mountains. Being in the mountains for the first time does a little to improve my mood. The walls of the pass are surprisingly smooth, as if the rock were butter, and a single large, hot knife had made the cut. Len tells me it's the work of Earth Mages, that they make similar safe routes for trade and travel all over the continent. I view the rock striations with interest—the rock on the Spit is just plain and gray. This has stripes and strips and swirls of black and orange and white and gray, all tipped with frost. It doesn't snow—I wonder how much of that is Darius's doing, since it seems gloomy enough to do so—but it is bitterly cold, and we don't stop until the path starts heading downward again.

I spend that night huddled in my bedroll, too cold to worry about the manacle. The metal felt bitingly chill on a good night, and this is anything but a good night. I stay as close to the small fire as I dare, and conserve my energy for warmth. The next few days are the same—cold and miserable.

I learn we've finally traveled into Ocron—well, I guess all of Aclines is technically Ocron now, which I also learn from Darius. They weren't satisfied with just taking Spit and the lighthouse to guide their stupid navy; they wanted the entire coastline. Greedy bastards. Darius tries to convince me that the war was actually Aclines's doing, that King Tiberius had taxed the Ocronian navy so much to use our ports that Ocron had felt it had no other option. I roll my eyes at this and go back to ignoring him for a while. He returns the favor.

The country is sprawled out before us now, with rolling hills and dried brown grass as far as the eye can see, crossed by roads like scars, and only a rare plume of smoke indicated a fellow traveler's campfire. I realize now how vast and unsettled this country really is, and how small I am in comparison, how trivial my own woes are—until the damn manacle zaps me again, and I fall back into moping.

I wonder briefly if cutting off my arm would work. Or maybe just my hand. I must wonder this out loud, because Darius and Len change places around me so that I won't have easy access to Len's knives to try anything stupid. I stare at the back of Len's bald head and think about throwing something at him. I don't have much on me, though, so I settle for glaring. He wears two short swords sheathed over his back, and on top of them is a round wooden shield. It's rimmed in metal, and the knob in the center has a sun etched onto it. It makes him look like a turtle. Darius sees me staring at it and gives me a long-drawn-out explanation on the origin of the Shield-Mage pairings, and on why Shields are called Shields. To sum up, they guard their Mages, and they are all given a shield when they graduate their training. Somehow that takes Darius the better part of an afternoon to explain. Len, as usual, is silent.

This trip is taking forever. I want this manacle off now. So I whine. I complain. I figure I'll wear them down eventually—I have nothing else to do—but then Darius reminds me that he is, in fact, a Mage. And a powerful one.

He quiets me with the same trick that I used against Len, binding my throat with his wind magic. And this is how, days later, gagged and shackled, I make it to the School of the Silver Flame.

Chapter 6: Aris

A week later, and it's like I never left. My reflexes are sharper than ever. I haven't had a drink since my wager with Markos, and I'm certain that if he went up against me now, he wouldn't stand a chance. I am a weapon, honed and ready for battle. He was right about one thing—I was born for this.

It's midmorning, and I'm helping Vassilis put the recruits through another round of sparring. The games are just days away, and competition is getting fierce. A few of the recruits—there are ten in this class—might prove a challenge in the games, all vying for second place. It's not unheard of for a Shield to reenter the games, but it is unusual. Shields and Mages are usually paired for life. The claim makes them both stronger. It's a bond only broken when one of them retires or dies, but then often the other person fades too, becoming an echo of their former self. Sometimes these shells go on to become priests or do some other menial jobs, but sometimes they simply … stop. Stop eating, stop drinking, stop responding to life altogether until they, too, stop.

I guess I'm too stubborn to just fade away.

Vassilis and I have had a few discussions about the upcoming Mages, my potential new partner. Out of them all, the strongest choice would be Mariana, a Water Mage. I'm familiar with wind magic, from Stefan, so picking another element would be a good way to start off fresh. She comes from a long line of Water Mages, and she's not bad to look at either. I've caught her glancing my way more than once after we met, so the feeling's mutual. A lot of the relationship between a Mage and their Shield comes down to compatibility, to chemistry, and we have plenty of it.

I also think about Rubita, a Fire Mage from the far western part of the continent. She's a little prickly, and her family isn't as prestigious, but she's a real hellion, and I'm sure she'll be stationed with the king's regiment. The thought of seeing combat again makes my blood heat until I feel like I'll explode.

I have little time to decide between them. They'll both be graduating this year, which means I could be back in action in just weeks. I think some of the other recruits will pick Mages in the younger class, though none of those students look promising to me. Sometimes there just isn't a suitable bond candidate in the older class. One of the boys has a sister who's a Water Mage in the younger class, and I hear he intends to pick her. I make it clear, though, that Mariana and Rubita are mine, and whichever one I don't pick can be fair game for the rest of the recruits. They don't like this, but I don't care. As winner of the games, the honor of the first pick will be mine.

I'm facing off against the big, hairy boy, my mind still on those Mages. Victor looks at me glumly as Vassilis is instructing the others. And I was right—his shift form is a bear. However, shifting isn't allowed in the arena or during the games, so he's stuck as a clumsy human boy for now.

"Come on," I say.

I offer him a few pointers on his technique. He's not that fast, but he is strong. His favored weapon is the gladius, so of course I make him use something else, currently the trident. He jabs at me clumsily, and I smack the trident away with the flat of my sword. He growls.

"You don't need to totally demoralize him," Vassilis reminds me from across the arena.

I shrug, rolling my shoulders, relaxing the tension that is creeping in. There's excitement in the air, which is now cool and crisp. Perfect for fighting.

"Come on," I say again, bouncing on my toes. "You don't want to have last pick at the games, trust me. Move those feet."

He shuffles and jabs again. This time, I grab the shaft of the trident as it passes by and yank it from his hands. He stumbles forward, and I jab the point of my sword up. A trickle of blood appears where it pierces the fleshy skin under his chin.

"I yield," he says. His eyes are wide.

I drop the sword, handing him back his trident. "Do you understand what you're doing wrong?" I ask.

He nods, wiping the dribble of blood from his neck. "I'm distracted," he mumbles. "A lot on my mind, with the games." He looks up at me like he's bracing for me to mock him. I think maybe he's not that popular with the other Shields.

"Distraction will get you killed," I say. "Or get your Mage killed."

His gaze drops. He knows my story. He nods and raises his trident again.

I step back, rolling the gladius in my hand. I turn to face Victor again, and when I do, I see a flash of long blond hair in the stands of the arena. Mariana is coming down one of the aisles, leading a Wind Mage and his Shield, a few more first-year Mages, and another girl, who is not wearing a Mage robe. I'm glad Mariana is here, and I wonder if she's come to see me. I catch her eye and wave, and she gives me a little wave back. The other Shield recruits see it, and I grin. She's mine.

I turn back to Victor, and I might be ready to show off a little. Victor drops into his ready stance, and I nod at him.

Then I look back, and see the other girl, the new one, behind Mariana. She's short, with a long brown braid and a simmering gaze that I recognize immediately, and it feels like a punch to my gut.

And then Victor knocks me flat on my ass.

Chapter 7: Wren

I hate the school immediately.

Darius loosens my gag before we ride in, and after I swear at him for a few minutes, I pointedly ignore him for the rest of the ride. It's been a miserable time. For the most part, we slept on the ground at night, though once we got closer to the school, a farmer did offer to let us stay in his barn. The straw made a nice change for my aching bones. I didn't realize how vast and empty most of the continent is—we encountered barely anyone else on the way. Darius thought maybe I'd get used to being gagged and eventually stop trying to yell at him. Or I'd tire of getting zapped and stop trying to remove the manacle. He did not count on my perseverance—stubbornness, my father would say. As a result, we are all exhausted and grouchy by the time we finally arrive.

The school is immense. We see it from miles off, perched on a hill in a lush valley, its thick wall ringing the hill like a crown. I've never seen so much green vegetation in my life, and I wonder if that's got something to do with the Earth Mages. A lazy river cuts through the valley, and I'm glad to see it. I miss the ocean. The world seems quiet without the constant roar of waves and the screeching of the wind.

The gates are so wide that we ride three abreast through them, Len and Darius to either side of me, like they're still afraid I'm going to bolt. Darius tells me that the dorms are in the walls, long hallways running down the middle and rooms to either side, for the Mages, Shields, and everyone else who works here. Over the gate is carved something in giant block letters: LUCEAT LUX VESTRA. I try out the foreign words, but they mean nothing to me.

"We're here. You can take this off now," I say, holding out my wrist. The manacle glitters in the morning light.

"It will come off after you train, after you demonstrate control," Darius says.

"How am I supposed to demonstrate control if I can't use my magic with this thing on?" I counter.

He pinches the bridge of his nose, and Len sighs. They'll be glad to be rid of me.

"After you demonstrate discipline, then," Darius says.

The school is like a small city, bigger than all of Spit. I've never seen any place so busy. We head to a stable, where we drop off the horses. I say goodbye to Poppy—she was the only nice part about the trip—and follow Darius and Len.

In the middle of the massive ring of walls is a long, blocky building. The school might have been made for magic, but it wasn't designed for beauty. Around this blocky building are a few small buildings, each made of the same bland gray stone. It almost feels like being back in Spit. One building has a domed roof made of glass—a greenhouse, Darius tells me, for the Earth Mages. There's a squat tower for the Wind Mages, another building for the Fire Mages, which smokes like a blacksmith's forge, and a low building for the Water Mages, which he says has a pool inside. I wonder if they'll let me swim in it. I think I'd like that.

We pass a few other buildings, and Darius waves at a pretty blond girl who's leading a group of people in long robes like Darius's, except theirs appear to be made of undyed cloth, with just a stripe of color at the cuffs and the hem in red, yellow, green, or blue. The blond girl's robe is solid blue, like Darius's is solid yellow. I have no idea what that signifies.

"Mage Darius, Shield Lennox," she says, greeting them both with a bow of her head. The other people bow too.

I look at Darius and Len, and they appear used to this kind of greeting. Seeing this group of people in their robes, I feel shabby. My clothes are filthy—I've been wearing them for days straight, with no bath. I hold my head high, though. The blond girl glances over me before giving me a broad smile.

"I heard you were bringing in a new student, and just in time, too," she says, and she extends a graceful hand to me, which I shake. I think I must leave dirt on her palm, because she wipes it surreptitiously on her robe after releasing my hand. "I'm Mariana." She gestures at the people behind her. "These are the other new students. I was just giving them a tour, and we are going to finish at the arena. Would you like to join us?" she asks.

"No," I say.

"Yes," Darius says, at exactly the same moment.

Len perks up.

"The Head Mage will be meeting us there," she offers, her voice musical. "I'm sure she'll be pleased to meet you."

I wonder if this Head Mage will remove the manacle from my wrist, and I decide it's worth going along with Mariana after all. I glare at Darius one more time, then follow the group into a massive coliseum.

The stone structure is immense, bigger than any building I've ever seen. There are rows of seating surrounding a sand-covered pit, where a dozen people are fighting. I look back at Len—he's watching them intently, his hands clenching at his sides like he's itching to join in. I guess that these people fighting are Shields, then, or training to be. Darius told me a little about how Mages and Shields get paired up—the order of selection is determined by some games, and the Shield picks a Mage, and they are partners for life. If the Mage turns them down, they have to wait until everyone else has picked, which apparently is a rare event and seen as shameful.

I follow Mariana and the other new students, who are silent, into the stands. I steal glances at the fighters—they wear leather shoulder guards, a wide leather belt with a kind of leather skirt, sandals, and not much else. Seeing so much skin on display makes me uncomfortable. Mariana pauses to look at the fighters, and I wonder if she has a Shield or if she's "in the market," so to speak. My guess is it's the latter, because her eyes latch on to one of the men across the ring, and he waves to her.

The fighters have paired off. Mariana's muscular pick is near us, probably by her design, and going up against a large boy with a trident. I don't know much about combat, but Mariana's pick is faster and seems to be taunting the large boy, like he's showing off. He looks back at her, and then his glance shifts to me, and he freezes.

Time stops. He's staring at me, even though he's fifty feet away. I stare right back. His blue eyes are bright in a tanned face, and even at this distance, they make me feel flushed, uncertain. I feel Mariana fidget next to me—and then Blue Eyes is knocked down by the boy with the trident, and suddenly I can breathe again.

Mariana raises a hand to her mouth in shock, but Blue Eyes laughs, gets up, brushing sand off himself, and says something to the other boy. The boy grins, pleased. Blue Eyes claps him on the shoulder, and they walk away from us, to the far side of the arena. He looks back over his shoulder once—though at me or Mariana, it's hard to say.

"Is that your Shield?" I ask her, not taking my eyes off him.

Her lips form a hard, thin line. "Soon" is all she says. Then she turns and leads us down the row of seats to a dark-skinned woman in a yellow robe, who's seated with some others in the first row.

The yellow-robed woman is reading something from a scroll, talking to the others, and also watching the Shield practice, all at the same time. I fight back a gasp when I see her—I've never seen someone who looks like her, who looks like I imagine my mother did. Her skin glows like polished ebony, and her thick, curly hair is up in a full bun. I look a little closer around the arena, and I realize that there are other people here whose skin is as dark as hers, some mixed like me, some with reddish-brown tones, and some more olive-colored. In Spit, everyone looks pretty much the same, pretty much like my father—fair-haired, fair-skinned. It seems that Ocron's "great king" has made his country home to all kinds of people, and they are welcomed, not shunned the way my mother was, the way I have always been. This woman before me wears no marks, no crown or extra stripes on her robe or anything. And she doesn't need to. She exudes power. Looking at her is like looking into the sun. She turns to look at us, and I fight the urge to squint.

"Good morning," she greets us.

The other students mumble a greeting. Darius and Len strike their right hands against their chests with a short bow. I just look at her, and she looks right back. She doesn't smile. I like that. I get the sense that not much gets past this woman. Surely a woman with power like this, power that is nearly palpable, will be able to help me control whatever is going on inside me. She looks different from Darius and Len, looks "other," according to the people of Spit, but here she is, a queen in her own right. Surely she'll remove my manacle, and then I'll be on equal footing with the rest of the students with me. I feel hope swell within me like a rising tide.

"I am Saroya Asprenas, but you may call me Head Mage. We are blessed to have so many new students with us this year," she says, looking over all of us in turn. "Mariana has offered to act as your mentor these first weeks. She'll show you to your rooms and the dining hall. Your first class will be in the morning. For those of you without declared elements, you will be allowed to attend each of the classes in turn until you declare. Welcome, and may the Silver Flame guide you."

"May the Silver Flame guide you," Darius, Len, and Mariana repeat.

The rest of the students stumble to repeat the phrase. I bite my tongue. I have no idea what a Silver Flame is, and until I do, I'm not wishing its benevolence on anyone.

The Head Mage looks me over, and from the tilt of her head, she finds me wanting. Something inside me shrinks from that gaze, where a moment ago she seemed warm, inviting.

"That is all," she says, and returns to her scroll.

I open my mouth to interrupt, to ask her to remove my manacle, but I'm distracted by a sudden crash of metal across the arena. I look up to find Mariana's Shield in combat with some other Shield. I think it's the teacher of the group, a slim, redheaded man. For a moment, I am transfixed—we all are—as they slice at each other with short swords, like the ones Len wears. I know it's meant to be a deadly fight, but it's beautiful to watch, like a dance. I've never seen anything like it. Blue Eyes moves with feline grace, all muscles and tanned skin and leather as he whirls on his opponent. I hear Mariana inhale sharply as the teacher tries a jab with his left, but his blade suddenly goes flying, and then he's on his knees, laughing, a sword at his neck. Mariana's Shield helps him up and looks back at us. I have a feeling the entire display was for our benefit—or maybe just Mariana's. Mariana, however, just raises her head, like she's looking down her nose, and walks off. If he wants to impress her, he'll have to work harder.

"Come on," a redheaded girl says, plucking at my sleeve.

I have to tear my eyes away from the blue-eyed Shield, who is still watching me. The girl wears a blue stripe on her robe. I look to Darius, who nods, so I follow her and the rest of the group behind Mariana. I glance back over my shoulder once—but Blue Eyes is gone.

Mariana takes us to the dorms. There are three levels, and we're on the top, which means a lot of stairs. Fine by me—I'm used to running up and down stairs all day. The long hallways are draped in a darkness that is only occasionally punctured by intermittent wall lanterns. Each door seems pretty much just like the next, with a name written on a slate above it. We come to a row that's empty, and Mariana starts assigning rooms. Some rooms have a circle marked on the slate, and she pushes me into one of these.

"They're for undeclared students," she says, catching me looking at the mark. "If you figure out which element you have an affinity for, we'll make sure you get the appropriate gear, and add the stripe to your robe."

If. Not when. I'm not sure I like this girl. At least I've figured out that the solid-color robes are for Mages who have graduated, whereas a colored stripe on an undyed robe signifies someone in training. Gods, this is confusing. I remember hearing about Mages when I was a little girl—mostly ones who could speed ships along our coast, against the current, or ones who could clear a stormy sky. But those were just stories—I never expected to see any of those things in person, let alone be a part of it. I wonder, not for the first time, why magic found me, of all the people in Aclines. I wonder if there are more like me. Now that Ocron has swallowed Aclines up, I wonder if there will be more Aclinese Mages.

I wonder if they'll all be forced to wear manacles too. Is this stupid bracelet because of some sort of prejudice toward Aclines?

At least the room is nice. It's cozy, and I have one of the rooms on the outside wall. This high up, I have a view of the river, which makes me very happy. There's a bed, a desk, a bookcase—empty—and a chest of drawers. Hanging on the back of the door is a robe of undyed wool, no stripes. I guess this is going to be my new home, then, for as long as I can stand it. Or until I graduate, whichever comes first, though I expect it will be the former.

I unconsciously reach for the manacle—*zap*—and then lie on the bed. The walls are the same gray stone as everything else, but I don't mind. Lying on a bed for the first time in a week feels amazing, and I doze off immediately.

Mariana comes back a few minutes later, or maybe an hour later—it's hard to say. She has me gather my things, including my new robe, and takes us down the halls—there are staircases every few hundred feet—and down some stairs to a building near the Water Mage building. It's also squat and square. We enter, and a blast of steam greets us.

"These are the baths," Mariana says. "Men on that side, women here. Wash up and change. I'll meet you back here in ten minutes and take you to the dining hall."

I follow the redheaded girl who spoke to me earlier, since she seems pretty comfortable with this place. We go into a separate chamber, and there's a large tiled pool sunk into the floor. I look at it suspiciously, and my anxiety spikes when I realize the other girls are stripping down and getting in. My face heats up.

They don't seem at all perturbed by the nudity. They go to their separate corners and wash, chatting away while they comb out their hair and lather up. I plaster my back to the wall, hugging my robe. Washing in the ocean is one thing—no one was around for miles. Washing here, where everyone can see me, is making my breath start to come too fast.

"Aren't you coming in?" the redheaded girl asks.

I see way more of her freckled breasts than I want to and avert my eyes. "I'm fine," I say.

"You are *not* fine," she says, wrinkling her nose. "You stink of the road."

"Thanks," I mutter.

I back into a corner, assessing my options. I need to get clean, desperately. Maybe I can just jump in with my clothes on.

"What's your problem?" the girl asks. It's not meant as a barb—she's genuinely curious.

I realize that none of these girls have ever been told that their skin is something to be ashamed of, something to hide. That their heritage is shameful. Hells, their Head Mage is as dark as squid ink herself. One of the other girls in the bath looks at me—she's got an olive tone to her skin that I've never seen before. She has no qualms about her coloration either. I take a deep breath—I guess this is one thing the country of Ocron has done right, but it doesn't wash away the nearly twenty years I've been covering up around others.

The redheaded girl watches me, and I bet I look like a cornered animal. She frowns and then gestures back toward the bath. "Come on. I'll send up some steam for you."

"You'll what?" I ask.

She spins her finger across the surface of the water, whispering, "*Steam.*" A trickle of steam from the warm water becomes an opaque cloud, and with a flick of her hand, she sends it my way. It hovers in a corner, and she nods at me. "Go on. No one will be able to see you over there."

I'm not sure why she's helping me, but I appreciate it. The steam wraps me like a towel. I strip, then get into the water as quickly as I can. It's blessedly warm, and I can see layers of dirt drifting away from me. The steam stays, though, hovering around me, and I feel a surge of gratitude toward the redheaded girl. I scrub quickly, trying not to moan in bliss as I become clean, truly clean, for the first time in days. I scrub my greasy scalp and let my hair float around me like seaweed for just a minute. The other girls are finishing up quickly. I grab one of the towels along the edge of the room and wrap myself in it, covering as much as I can, and throw a second towel over my shoulders. The other girls are rubbing themselves dry, and I turn my back so I don't have to look at them. They all brought clean clothes to change into. I only have the clothes on my back, and while it felt awful to put them back on, I didn't really have a choice.

I get dressed in a flash, and we all file back out to Mariana.

"Thank you," I whisper to the redheaded girl.

"No problem," she says, giving me a smile. "I'm Agata."

"Wren," I say, and we shake hands.

She's taller than me, and her eyes are brown and crinkle up as she smiles.

"How did you … you know?" I say, making the twirling motion I saw her do, with my own finger.

"Oh, my whole family are Water Mages. I've been doing small magics for years," she says airily, like it's not a big deal.

I frown.

"You're undeclared?" she asks.

"Yep."

"You're not from here, are you?"

"Nope."

"Haven't seen much magic?"

"Haven't seen any," I admit.

Agata's eyes widen. "Really?" she breathes. "What rock have you been living under?"

"Aclines," I say, and she startles.

"Oh" is all she says, and she is silent the rest of the way to the dining hall.

We grab plates loaded with food in the dining hall—yet another squat gray building—and sit at long tables with the other students. The food is good, especially after eating on the road all week—roasted chicken and greens and fresh bread. I listen to the other students chatter—about their magic, about which element is better. They've come from all over the continent but mostly from Ocron. I listen to them talk and talk and talk, and I miss the company of my screech owl. His conversation was infinitely easier on the ears.

"And make sure you watch out for Mage Eleni," one of the boys—Elias, I think his name is—says around a mouthful of food. He's a second-year Mage, which makes him feel infinitely superior to new students. He wears a band of blue around the cuffs of his robe, marking him as a Water Mage-in-training. He's even dyed his hair blue somehow, and he wields his spoon like a sword when he talks, punctuating his words.

"Why?" Agata asks. As a fellow Water Mage, she's completely entranced by everything he's saying—and I also note a spot of pink on her cheeks as she speaks.

"She's one of those Black Water Witches," he whispers, and Agata's eyes go wide.

A few of the other students near us turn, suddenly interested in the conversation.

"What's a Black Water Witch?" I ask.

Agata shushes me, and I smack her hand away.

"A story to scare little children," a dark-haired girl says, sniffing, and she turns away from us.

Agata rolls her eyes. "Of course she'd say that. She's a Wind Mage. They don't know anything about water magic," she says.

Elias nods. "They're a group of Mages that operate outside Head Mage Saroya's influence. They come from the Isles, maybe, or the north. They don't answer to Saroya or the king, and some say they can send tidal waves and typhoons, the big ship killers."

"I heard their Shields are shark shifters," another boy says. He's a burly boy named Argyris, a to-be Earth Mage whose smirk deepens as he speaks. He seems like a bit of a ringleader, a bully that the others leave alone.

Agata clutches my arm, her fingers tight enough to bruise me through my robe.

"Or worse," Elias says ominously, raising his eyebrows, clearly enjoying the attention and spooking us.

I pry Agata's fingers from my arm. "There are groups of Mages that don't answer to the king or Saroya?" I ask.

Agata shrugs, trying to pretend she's not frightened by the talk of the Black Water Witches. I start to wonder about all those fairy stories I heard as a child, and how many of them might actually be real. I try not to shiver.

"They're just rumors," Agata says. "Most Mages work with the king. We can choose to go out on patrol or work with the navy, or in academics. It's really up to you." She stirs the untouched food on her plate.

Argyris is launching into an argument with Elias about whether or not sea serpents are real, and Agata's face has gone from white to sickly green. Well, I've lived on the coast my entire life, and I've never seen a sea serpent, so I figure these boys are just making things up at this point to scare us. And in Agata's case, it's working. I make up my mind.

"Are you done?" I ask, standing. I'm ready to leave, and clearly she is too.

We head toward the dorms. She shows me that the stairs go up one more level from our rooms, to the top of the wall. The gray stone path is smooth from generations of booted feet, and from up here we can see the whole valley. We can see the whole school too, but it's just a bunch of boring buildings. Agata points out a pair of wolves—Shields—racing down the slope to the river, and the color returns to her face as we take in the fresh air and scenery. Up here, it's not so bad. Up here, it's easy to feel hopeful. The river sparkles in the light. My chest tightens as I think of the way the sun would strike the sea back home, how I could see nothing but water all the way to the horizon, instead of grass.

We're given free rein for the rest of the afternoon and evening. There's a curfew at nightfall, and we're supposed to be back in our rooms by then unless accompanied by a full Mage or Shield. I planned to stay in my room for the rest of the day, but after a few hours, I get antsy and decide to go down to the river. I miss the ocean as much as I miss my lighthouse, which makes me wonder if maybe I have some water talent. The river will just have to do.

When I head down to the gate, a guard in leather armor stops me.

"Students aren't allowed out," he says.

I frown. "Why not?"

"You're just … not."

"Are you worried I'm going to run away or something? I just want to go down to the river. I promise," I say, putting a hand over my heart, "that I will not drown myself. I'll be back by nightfall."

"I've got her, Tarso," someone says behind me.

The guard nods and steps aside.

I turn, ready to say something snarky, that I don't need anyone's supervision, but the words die on my lips.

It's Mariana's Shield.

Up close, he's dazzling. His dark hair is damp, reaching his shoulders, with some of it pulled back from his face. His cheekbones are sharp, his jaw strong, and I find myself staring. He's over six feet tall, which means he practically towers over me. He's changed from that scandalous leather thing into loose pants and a shirt like mine, with sleeves rolled up to his elbows. He gives me a smile and gestures for me to walk on. My feet seem to remember how to do this after a few moments, and we leave the walls of the school.

It's midafternoon, and I'm glad I have my robe. The sun isn't warm today, though nowhere near the chill that we usually get in Spit. We head down the hill, and to the right is a path that leads down to the river. He doesn't say anything as we walk, but it seems something is on the tip of his tongue. He opens his mouth a few times like he's going to say it, but he doesn't.

The river itself is a broad, slow-moving thing, brown with sediment and lined with sandy shores. Tall, thin-bladed grass borders the road—now a path, really—and we pass only a few other people as we walk.

"What's your name?" he asks, finally.

"Verena," I say, and he nods, like he's been given the answer to some burning question. "But I go by Wren."

"Like the bird," he says.

I nod. Obviously, like the bird. Small, brown, unremarkable. Just like me.

He holds back a clump of grass to reveal another path, along the sandy shore. It's nice. It's quiet, and actually kind of private. I'm surprised by it. If I'm going to stay at this school, I feel like this is a place I'd like to visit again.

"Aren't you going to tell me your name?" I ask.

He smiles, a little rueful, like he expected me to just know him, like maybe he's someone important, or thinks he is.

"Aris," he says. "I'm a Shield."

"You're Mariana's Shield," I say.

He looks sideways at me. His blue eyes are very bright, the brightest I've ever seen, and I know I'm staring at them. No one in Spit has eyes like those.

"Maybe," he says. He bends to pick up a stone and skips it into the river. "The games are in a few days. Then we'll all decide."

I consider this. I don't know a lot about the games, or how all this pairing off gets decided. I guess I have a lot to learn. Darius and Len weren't the most forthcoming conversationalists.

"Well, Aris, maybe Mariana's Shield, thank you for helping me get out of the school. You don't have to babysit me, though. I'll head back in a bit."

He shrugs, like he has all the time in the world.

"Is it true you control animals?" he asks. He picks a spot on a bit of driftwood and sits. I can feel the weight of his gaze as he waits for me to answer.

"Not with this thing on," I say, raising my hand. The manacle glints in the sun.

He stares at it for a minute, like he can't believe what he's seeing. "Is that a manacle?" he asks. There's a heaviness in his words. He's disgusted by it, and I like him even more for that.

"Yep," I say, fighting to keep the flush from heating my face. I strive for levity. "You don't know how to take it off, do you?"

He shakes his head.

I kick a pebble with my shoe. It was worth a shot, anyway.

"Why are you wearing it?" he asks.

I look at him warily, but it doesn't seem like he's trying to mock me. I sigh and choose a seat a few feet away. I like being close to the water again. I wonder whether it will respond to me if I try to make it do something, like it did with Agata, but with Aris watching, I don't want to try. Having him watch me is doing all kinds of funny things to my stomach. No one has ever watched me the way he is, with interest rather than fear or scorn.

"I maybe set a pack of wolves on Darius," I say, and at this, he bursts out laughing, and I can't help it—a few seconds later, I'm laughing with him.

"Well, he seemed to be in one piece," he says at last.

I nod, wiping my streaming eyes. "Yeah. He put this thing on me before they actually attacked. I don't know how I did it, to be honest," I say. "I tried for days to get Darius to take it off, begged him, even—so then he gagged me."

"He … did what?" Aris asks. All traces of humor are gone. His jaw is set, and the tone of his voice sends a prickle up my spine, and not in a good way.

I did think we might be on the way to becoming friends. Now I'm not so sure.

"Um, he did some kind of spell thing," I say, mimicking the motion with my hands, "and told me to be quiet. He called it an air gag. I couldn't talk at all. He left it in place for days until we got here."

Aris doesn't say anything, but he's furious. He was shocked by the manacle, but this has tipped him over. I mean, I'm mad too, but there's nothing I can do about it. Aris has a piece of grass in his hands, and he twists it around and around until it breaks. He stands up suddenly, looking down at me. I have some inkling then of what it must mean to go up against a Shield in battle—right now, he's terrifying. His hands are clenched, flexing. I'm grateful not to be on the receiving end of his wrath.

"I'm … sorry," he says at last. Those words sound rusty, like he hasn't said them in a long time. "That's no way for him to treat you."

"Thanks," I say, and I mean it. "The way Darius and Len looked at me sometimes … it made me feel like I was some sort of monster in need of taming."

I look at him and realize I'm waiting for him to refute this claim. He doesn't, but his jaw tightens, a vessel pulsing in his neck. He looks back up at the school, at the high walls ringing the hill.

"You sure you'll find your way back all right?" he asks.

I nod, and he turns his back to me. Without another word, he disappears into the tall grass, and I'm left alone.

Chapter 8: Aris

I find Darius and Len near the stables, asking about some horses for their next trip.

"You *gagged* her?" I fume, coming to a halt in front of them.

Darius looks at me quizzically, but Len moves immediately, getting in between us. My hands are itching for a weapon. To strike a Mage or a Shield in anger—I'd be disowned in the same instant, and probably thrown into the king's prison to rot for a few decades. But consequences be damned; that was the wrong thing to do. She does not deserve to be treated like that.

"I did," Darius says at last. "Why does it matter to you?"

I clench my jaw so tight that my teeth start to ache.

Darius seems unfazed by my outburst, but Len isn't taking his eyes off me. Darius sighs.

"We were trying to find you, you know, down there in that hellhole," he says.

I blink, taken aback.

"We didn't find you, obviously, but we did find her, conveniently in time for her to be a part of next year's class," Darius continues. "You know that words carry power, Aris." He turns to walk toward the dorms and gestures for me to follow.

The gesture irks me, but I go after him. It reminds me that, as I've reentered the games, I'm now considered a recruit, and therefore beneath him, able to be ordered around. It chafes.

"Obviously," I say, each syllable feeling like it's being dragged out of me.

"Did she tell you that she silenced Len first?" he asks.

Well, no, she didn't. That's a surprise. I guess Darius sees the shock on my face. I look at Len, who nods but doesn't take his eyes off me. He doesn't trust me not to do something stupid—which is fair.

"It was unintentional, I believe. But words have power," Darius repeats. "This girl Verena … there's a lot of power there."

"And you shackled her," I say. She is being treated like a criminal for acting out of ignorance. It isn't fair.

"Because a pack of wolves was about to attack us," Darius counters calmly. "And I don't have to explain myself to you, Shield recruit," he says, and the rebuke stings. It is not my place; I know that. "But if you must know, I was worried for our safety," he says. Another surprise. A senior Wind Mage, afraid of an untrained girl. "She's strong. I don't know how her power will manifest, but when it does, we'd all better be ready."

"If her tongue doesn't get her into trouble first," Len rumbles.

Darius nods.

"I still don't think it was the right decision," I say.

Darius sighs. "Honestly? Neither do I," he says. "But I couldn't think of any other options."

I don't like this at all. His admissions have me on edge, and I can't stop thinking about the manacle. How powerful must she be, that she has to wear it? And how is she supposed to learn anything that way?

Len has his arms crossed, as still as a stone. He's staring at me, so I glare right back.

"*Vires, honos, fides*," he reminds me, the code of the Shields. *Strength, honor, faith.* I've heard it so many times it feels like it's tattooed on my skull. Have faith, he's saying.

Faith in the system that binds us, trains us. Faith in king and country, faith in each other. Honestly, it's a stupidly vague motto, open to many interpretations.

"*Vires, honos, fides*," I mumble automatically, rolling my eyes.

I leave them, thinking I'll head toward Kemp's. I could use a drink after today. Wren has unnerved me. I need to do something, maybe play a game of dice, or run a few miles. I feel antsy, cooped up.

And that's when I see Mariana across the courtyard.

I leave her room before dawn, closing the door quietly. She's still sprawled on her bed, sound asleep, and doesn't stir as I dress and leave.

Ignoring whatever other nonsense is going on around me, I decide to get back to work. The other Shield recruits—soon to be new Shields of the Silver Flame—and I knock out our calisthenics before going on a ten-mile run. I usually lead them down to the river, but I don't want to go down that path today. I take them the other way instead, which loops down the road and around some boulders before coming back. I'm back in fighting form, and it feels fantastic.

My mind keeps going back to Wren. Today is her first day in classes. I wonder what good she'll get out of it with the manacle on. I haven't ever heard of another student having to wear one, and I wonder how long Saroya will make her wear it. If it's not safe to remove it here, surrounded by Mages, then where?

I see her twice, though. The first time, she is turning red after a handful of the Shield recruits have been talking to her. I head toward them, but when she sees me, she turns and leaves. The second time I see her, she's leaning over the top of the wall, her hair streaming behind her like a banner, her eyes closed. She looks like she is going to take flight.

I head down to the smithy in the afternoon. I need a new helmet, armor, everything. After the last time I was in battle, I shifted. There are a lot of benefits with using our animal forms, but the downside is that our clothing and armor don't shift with us. When we shift back, we're as naked as the day we were born. In my case, that time I was also a hundred miles from where I'd started. That stung. I really liked my helmet.

But I am getting sick of wearing borrowed leathers. The smithy is run by a few Fire Mages and their Shields. Tulliano is my favorite. He's ancient and as massive as a bear, but he makes the finest swords on the continent. His mastery over fire is present in everything he does—his forges maintain a constant temperature and never need to be relit; he doesn't even need bellows.

I look around as he takes down my order. I eye a helmet cooling on a stand by the front of his forge—the steel is crafted to look like the head of a wolf with its jaws open, the upper canines extending down to protect the wearer's face. It's more than just a protective head covering—it is a work of art.

"You know, when I make one of those," he says, pointing a massive finger at the helm, "I expect it to last a lifetime."

"I'm sure mine is still lasting, somewhere," I say, giving him a grin. "I just don't know where. Someplace down in an Aclinese swamp. Who knows?"

He grunts, but he'll do it. I hope to have it done by the end of the games. He rolls his eyes at this but doesn't say no. I like that about him.

As I'm turning to go, I see Mariana coming toward me, a shaky smile on her full lips. Gods, what she can do with that mouth. Being her Shield would come with some serious perks.

"Hi," she says.

I say goodbye to Tulliano and walk with her. She tries to make small talk, but again I'm distracted, thinking about that damn manacle. It's nightfall, and since Mariana's technically still a student, she's under curfew – unless I'm with her.

"I'll be up awhile in my room, studying," she offers, putting a hand on my arm.

I consider, before something else that's been itching my brain all day finally surfaces.

"I've got something I've got to take care of tonight," I say, but I give her a smile.

She seems to accept this.

I don't want to upset her—she's the best chance I have at salvaging my career, after all. Her whole family has been entwined with Ocronian royalty for generations.

And then she's off, blue robe fading into the dark, and I'm left wondering about the risk I'm about to take.

Chapter 9: Wren

My first day in classes is abysmal. I am shunted from building to building, loaded up with more books than I can carry, and asked to attempt some small magics, like lighting a candle or opening a flower bud. With the manacle in place, nothing happens. Hells, I'm not sure anything would have happened anyway. I feel like a fake. The instructors purse their lips at my restraint, but none of them offer to remove it. "Just read up on this," they each say. Between classes, I have to dash back to my room just to deposit all the reading material.

Around lunchtime, I head toward the dining hall. Agata said she was going to meet me there, and I have been looking forward to seeing a friendly face. I see a pair of unkempt men by the stables and stop to watch them for a second. One wears a faded blue robe over threadbare clothes. They move slowly, like each step is a great effort. They shuffle over to the side of the barn and drag a bale of hay around. One of them looks like an older Shield, still strong but bent now, withered. Even their skin tone is off, like all the color has been leached from them both.

"They've gone gray," an older student says in passing as he catches me watching. "You push too hard or you lose your claim, and that's what you get. Something to look forward to." The student shrugs and wanders off.

I shake my head—what a contract to consider. I can join with a Shield, but if they die, or if I push my magic too far, I'll "go gray," too? I feel a chill run down my spine—the one in the blue robe is staring at me, but his eyes are glazed, almost cloudy, like he's already dead. I avert my gaze and hurry off. He's like something out of a nightmare, already a ghost.

I stop on my way to the dining hall, though, when a badger appears in the middle of the courtyard. He stops too and looks at me. I've only seen a badger once before—this one is larger, hefty and sleek. I look around, but no one else seems to notice him, or care that he is there. I wonder about my supposed gift, about the way that animals seem to respond to me. This one, at least, seems to be fixated on me, so I decide to try something stupid.

I walk up to him slowly and extend my hand. He sniffs at it but doesn't bite. So far, so good.

And then, suddenly, he is gone, and in his place is a very naked, very fit blond boy who is laughing so hard at me that tears are running down his face. He's about my age, but I feel like a foolish child next to him, the subject of his prank. I've heard something about shifts—the animal forms that Shields are able to take as a part of their magic—but to see it in person is something else entirely. One minute there is a badger in front of me; then a split second and a whirl of air later, there is a boy.

Plus, he is naked. He doesn't seem to care about that, but I do. I care an awful lot. My face heats up, and I try to avert my eyes, try to come up with something clever to say to hide my embarrassment, some way to get out of this predicament. Some of his friends are coming over, and they clap him on the back as they hand him some clothes.

"I can't believe—did you think I was a real badger?" he wheezes, trying to get dressed but laughing so hard he keeps missing his pant leg with his foot and nearly falls over. "Was I that impressive?"

My face feels melting hot. I look him up and down, pointedly pausing below his waist.

"You're not *that* impressive," I mutter.

His friends think that's funny, and I'm glad to have deflected their attention for a minute.

That's when I see Aris, fuming like a thundercloud, coming across the courtyard. Gods, I do not want to see him. I don't want to have to tell him what happened, have him laugh at me too. I turn, ignoring all of them, though I hear the laughter continuing, and flee back to my room. I'm no longer hungry.

The afternoon isn't much better. I ask the Fire Mage instructor to take off my manacle. She's a pretty lady with strawberry-blond hair that's almost pink, but unlike the fruit, she's sour and sharp, a rule follower to the extreme. She tells me that she was specifically instructed not to remove my manacle, and that if I insist on pursuing the matter further, she'll be happy to help me find a more suitable career path with the ungifted, perhaps in mucking out the stables. I decide to seek out the Head Mage, but when I finally find her office, I'm told by a really rude secretary that she's too busy to see me, and to check back in a few weeks.

I skip dinner too. If I keep this up, I'm going to be as thin as Mariana soon. Instead, I head up to the top of the wall again. The stone is warmed by the afternoon sun, and I lean over the edge, eyes closed, drinking in the sunshine. Up here, the memory of the stupid badger boy is already fading. Up here, it almost feels like I'm back home, back in my lighthouse. I can almost hear the crash of waves in my mind, almost smell the brine.

Someone clears their throat.

"You're not planning on throwing yourself off, are you?"

I open my eyes and see Aris standing a few feet away. Twining around his feet is an orange cat, his fluffy tail winding around Aris's legs. I fight back a groan. I'm already over Shields and their stupid shifting and their stupid pranks, and I've barely started here.

"Not today," I say, standing back up. I look at the cat skeptically. "Friend of yours?" I ask.

Aris cocks his head, studying me. The cat leaps up onto the wall, precariously close to the edge. He purrs loudly as Aris strokes him. His large, strong hands move skillfully, making me a little jealous of the cat. I clear my throat.

"No," Aris says slowly, holding my gaze. "I mean, yes, I guess. But he's not a Shield, if that's what you're asking."

I flush. If there's some way to tell Shields from regular animals, I have no idea what it is. I'm so out of my depth here that I'd laugh if I weren't so frustrated.

"His name's Geoff," he says, scratching the cat behind the ears. "And he's good company. Better than most people."

The cat meows loudly in response and then pads down the wall to me. He's a very brave cat—one gust of wind would send him right off the edge of the wall here, down thirty feet to the ground below. He seems unbothered by the height and butts his head against my hand until I rub his soft tawny fur. I've missed my animal friends, and I can feel tears prickling in my eyes. He lets me pick him up, purring loudly as I hold him close, rubbing his head against my face. With animals, I've never felt lonely, not like I have since coming to this place. I can feel Aris's eyes on me, questioning, but I can't look at him. I sniffle instead and focus on Geoff, and the sunshine, and the feel of the breeze in my hair.

"You know," Aris says, and I look up at him. He's studying me openly, and it makes me fidget.

"What?" I spit out after a moment.

He shakes his head, like he's forgotten what he was saying. "Most people can't tell the difference between a Shield and a true predator at a glance. It's their actions that reveal who they really are."

I think about this, petting Geoff until my robe is coated in orange fur. I keep my gaze fixed on the fields of grass rolling away like waves from the school all the way to the horizon, on the river winding like a brown ribbon through it all.

Eventually, Aris leaves me alone, and Geoff and I spend an hour cuddling in blissful silence, warm on the top of the stone wall.

Ultimately, though, I have to go back down to my room. Someone's left new clothes for me—apparently, locks and privacy are not allowed either—and they fit all right. The shirt has some laces up the front, and I have to tie them up tight so my breasts don't show. But still, the new clothes are clean. I can't remember the last time I had two new sets of clothes, so I decide to go down to the bathhouse to scrub again.

This time, Agata's not here. I'll have to tackle the group bath by myself, without any protection. *All right. No big deal. I can do this*. My skin is not something to be ashamed of here. My lack of declared element may be, but at least my appearance is not. I look again for Agata, hoping she'll somehow materialize out of thin air. She does not. Instead, I take a deep breath, square my shoulders, and head for the baths. I can't rely on her steam cloud to hide me forever.

A crowd of boys is pushing in at the same time I get there—it seems some sort of study group or something just ended—and I don't like the way they look at me. I'm grateful, at least, that the men and women bathe separately. There are only a few other girls bathing. I go to the far corner, strip as fast as I can, and slip into the water. I feel less exposed here and take my time scrubbing and rinsing out my hair until it floats around me. I feel kind of good and start to relax a little.

All right, so today wasn't great. But I have at least one potential friend in Agata, and a stack of books waiting for me in my room. I've always liked reading. I think about spending the rest of the day flipping through those ancient tomes and feel the stress leaving me. Maybe I'll open the window, catch a breeze coming up from the river. That would be nice. Maybe I can convince Geoff to visit. I make a note to sneak some chicken out of the dining hall next time for him.

The few other girls in the bath are other Mage students, I think, but they don't talk to me, so I don't talk to them either. They whisper to each other but otherwise leave me alone. When they get out and walk past my corner, I duck underwater so I don't have to make small talk.

When I surface, I'm alone. Thankful for small mercies, I get out of the tiled bathing pool—and realize that my new clothes are gone. I wish I had taken a closer look at the other girls in the pool—so I could remember their faces and ask them exactly why they thought it was fun to steal my clothes. It's a low, sneaky trick, and I struggle to remember exactly why I'm putting myself through all this.

My hands clench. I've never felt so helpless. I'm all alone in the bath now, and I go over my options. There aren't many. I can stay here and wait for someone else to come along, and ask them for help—but with the number of assholes at this school, I could be waiting a very long time.

My only other choice is to wrap myself in a towel and dash back to the dorms.

And of course, the entire crowd of boys I saw earlier is waiting for me to emerge, since apparently they were planning this with those stupid girls. The catcalls and laughter ring in my ears as I push my way through them. I've wrapped a towel around my body and another around my shoulders, covering as much as I can.

Argyris reaches out to grab one of my towels, and I slap him hard across the face. He steps back, a little stunned, and after that no one tries to grab me anymore, though they continue to heckle me. The badger boy chases after me, telling me to drop the towels, to give them a show, and positively howling with laughter. I'm acutely grateful for my job at the lighthouse, because I sprint up those stairs fast enough to finally leave my crowd of admirers behind.

I make it back to my room, and I'm too shaken to get dressed quickly. My fingers slip on the laces of my old shirt and I nearly burst into tears. Why are they picking on me? Is it because I'm new? From Aclines? I think that if I had this manacle off, maybe I could actually do magic, and then they'd be too afraid of me to try anything. Then I think maybe that's why Darius put the damn thing on me in the first place.

My fingers slip again, so I just leave the laces alone. My hands are shaking—from embarrassment, from rage, from a feeling of impotence so severe it leaves me breathless.

I stare around my room, which is starting to feel like a cell. Then I figure if I'm going to stay in my room the whole day, I might as well take a look at the books I was given. Maybe I can glean something from them, some way to bring my magic to the surface, something—anything—to make the other students back off. The first tome is heavy, dusty, the pages yellow with age. It creaks open, and I realize it's going to be too dark to read soon. There are some fat candles in a drawer. I set them out on the desk and try to strike a match to light one. My hands are still shaking so badly that I break the first one, and the second.

"Damn it!" I yell, slamming my hands on the desk. "Why won't you just *light*!"

A thrill races down my spine, and every candle lights instantly with a cheery flame.

I stare at them for a minute, my jaw wide open. I look down at my hand, a broken match still lying in my palm. The manacle glitters softly in the candlelight. I shouldn't have been able to do that, right? The manacle is blocking my magic. I try to remove it—and get zapped again. It's still working, still active. Still a pain in my ass.

I look down at the book in front of me—a toddler's introduction to wind magic, complete with alphabet-centric pages. *A is for Air. B is for Breath.* It's a struggle not to throw the stupid thing across the room. Still, if I made an air gag without meaning to, I wonder if I could do something intentional with it, and if this means I have a proclivity for wind. The first few pages here are all about harnessing your breath—basically, blowing out a puff of steam or cold air. I try it, and nothing happens. I try again and again.

"Hot," I say, and blow. "Cold," I say, blowing again. Nothing happens. I blow and blow until I think I might faint, but I achieve nothing. I'm wondering if there's some way around the manacle's binding—like maybe it only blocks wind magic. I try some water magic then, try to condense water out of the air. Agata has told me this is something most children are able to accomplish.

And again I accomplish nothing. Was making the candles light just a fluke? Did I once do the same thing at my lighthouse, that day my tiger showed up? Am I a Fire Mage, and that's why the wind and water magics aren't working now? I blow out a candle and spend a stupid amount of time trying to get it to light again, until my eyes hurt and my tongue feels heavy from uttering "Light" a million times over.

It's late, and I'm exhausted, and hungry, and grumpy. My head is pounding. I blow out all the candles—there's enough moonlight streaming in to see well enough by—and get into my bed. It's comfortable, at least. And there, in the quiet, dark stillness of my room, I realize how far from home I am, how alone. A few people here have been decent to me, but the majority either ignore me or seem to go out of their way to humiliate me. I'd like to go find Geoff, but I don't want to leave this room right now. I wish I had the company of my animals—I'd settle for a mouse or a pigeon, but there aren't any around. I miss my little dormice. I hope that whoever is taking care of my lighthouse is being nice to them. I should have left them a note.

I sniffle. My eyes are burning. I toss and turn for an hour, but sleep eludes me. Years of nocturnal work and daytime sleep schedules are hard to break. The ceiling is stone, like the walls and floor. All stone. It is two blocks wide and three blocks long. There are smaller ones for the walls. I count each stone many times.

Sometime around midnight I feel a shiver pass over me, like a cold wind just blew through the room. I sit up to close the window, wondering if someone is playing another trick on me.

But the breeze isn't coming through the window. It's coming from the open door.

And standing in the doorway, twitching his tail, is a massive white tiger with blazing blue eyes.

This is impossible. I'm hundreds of miles from home, in a different country, in a school surrounded by massive walls. The manacle won't let me call any other animals, but somehow, against all the odds, my tiger has found me. I let out a choked sob and open my arms. He crosses the room, and I sink to the floor, burying my hands in his soft fur. He is warm and solid and here. I can't believe he's here. Tears drip from my nose onto his neck where I'm holding him, and I don't even care. I'm crying hard. My breath is coming in ragged gasps. He butts his big head against my chest, and I sit down, forehead to forehead with him, trying to slow my breathing. I run my hands down his face, feeling his prickly whiskers, the soft spot behind his ears. He likes this, and when he lets out a rolling sound like a *whuff*, I start giggling, and then I can't stop. I'm laughing. I'm crying. My tiger is here, and everything … everything is better.

This has to be a dream, some hallucination brought on by exhaustion and hunger and fear. There's no way he's actually here. He feels real, though. I put a hand on his big chest, and I can feel his heartbeat. I wipe my streaming eyes on my sleeve and sit on the bed. He lies down beside me. The bed isn't as big as my bed back home, and I have to curl up right against him so I don't fall off the side. I'm exhausted, and he feels so good. It's like having a piece of home here with me. He's wedged up against the wall and doesn't seem to mind being squished.

I wonder if he missed me. I wonder if the manacle is still shielding my magic, or if I somehow called him to me, across miles and miles of forests and hills—then I realize I don't care. I'm too happy to see him. The tip of a rough tongue swipes against my cheek, and a heartbeat later, I'm asleep.

Chapter 10: Aris

I leave the Mage student dorms before dawn for the second day in a row. Vassilis sees me and meets me in the courtyard.

"Everything all right with Mariana?" he asks.

I shrug.

"I hear a couple of Shields are coming in from the capital tomorrow to compete," he says, arms crossed.

"Anyone we know?" I ask, accompanying him to the arena.

"Nope. They've been out a few years. One Shield's Mage left the king's service to settle down, and I think the other pair just kept butting heads, so they're getting reassigned. Might give you a run for your money."

This adds an element of the unknown to the games—tomorrow. Tomorrow is the most important day of my life—again—and I am going up against unknown opponents. I feel a thrill in my gut—if they are any good, it will just make my performance that much more outstanding.

"Will your family come?" Vassilis asks.

I shake my head. At my last games, my entire family came—my Shield father, my three older brothers, and my two younger sisters. My father's chest swelled when I came in first—just like he had years ago. Then I claimed Stefan, the most powerful Wind Mage in years, and I thought my father might actually explode with pride. I glowed under his praise.

I haven't heard from my father now in months. I don't even know if he is aware that I am reentering the games, and I don't care. I am practically dead to him, and the rest of my family haven't been much better to me—those that are left, anyway. Adriana, my youngest sister, takes after our mother the most. I've always felt close to her for that reason. But even she has been distant lately.

I didn't mean to sleep as late as I did. My body feels calm, rested, but my mind is spinning. A run seems like a good idea. I head out, down the path, and I avoid the river again. I don't want to wear myself out today, just loosen up, rest up for tomorrow, but my thoughts are racing, and before I know it, I'm sprinting down the last half of my run, flying like a spear.

Mariana is the obvious choice. I haven't spent as much time with Rubita, though I hear she's been asking about me. We could be headed to the capital days from now, to receive our assignment from the king. I itch to be back on the road, like a snake shedding skin that's now too small. As much as I hate to admit it, Markos was right—I belong out there, not here in the school.

Around dusk, I see Wren across the courtyard, a couple of books in her arms. She walks quickly, her robe swamping her and dragging in the dust. She's not making eye contact with any of the other students, not talking. There's a rush of people here, leaving the dining hall and going about their business, but she might as well be invisible for all the attention anyone pays her.

And then I see her stumble. The books go flying, and she hits the dirt hard. A couple of Shield recruits start shifting in front of her—a wolf, a hawk, a leopard. They bark and roar at her, while the others laugh. She pushes herself up, and now I'm close enough to see that her strange gray-green eyes are blazing. She's standing as straight as an arrow, hands clenched. I can see the manacle glinting on her wrist.

And that's when things get really weird.

She's shouting something at them that I can't hear. I can't hear, because there's a roaring in the air, and the wind howls like an animal itself as it spins around her, forming a dust devil that whips her hair behind her like a flag. The wind pushes against the other students, until they're shielding their eyes and backing off.

But she doesn't stop. The ground around her quivers, and soon rocks are peeling away from the surface and spinning around her like cannonballs. Overhead, a thunderhead appears out of the clear evening sky, and the fading light dims further, until the only light is an eerie green glow coming from Wren herself.

She's got the attention of most of the senior Mages now. A few of them are standing at the periphery of her storm, chanting spells and raising their hands. Darius is standing at the front, robe flapping, lips forming frantic spells. For a moment, the tornado shrinks. Then it blows up again, pushing everyone back a hundred feet. Jade-colored lightning crackles down in a blinding flash, striking the ground in front of Wren. A stone clocks Darius in the cheek, and he drops. Len is at his side in an instant, and his face when he looks back at Wren is murderous.

Wren doesn't notice. She's too far gone, too caught up in the magic, magic that she has no business wielding. I've never seen this kind of loss of control before. I've heard of it, though—Mages trying spells beyond their capabilities, getting so wrapped up that the magic consumes them, leaving just a husk of a human behind. It's something Shields are taught about, warned about, something we have to keep our Mages from.

That can't happen to Wren.

I try to get closer, but the wind is moving so fast it's like pushing against a solid wall, and then I almost get clobbered by a flying rock.

So I do the only other thing I can think of.

I shift.

I like my animal form. I feel powerful in it. There are stories about Shields who get so wrapped up in their animal forms that they never shift back—and I can understand why. I've been there, so lost in the animal's mind that I lose all track of what it means to be human. But now that I understand that, now that I've experienced it firsthand, I know what it feels like, and I can push past it.

The wind tears at me, but in this form I'm faster, lower to the ground, and my reflexes are heightened. I dodge a few rocks that whip by, and then I'm in front of her.

We're in the eye of the storm. She's standing with her arms raised, and she's screaming, but I can't hear her over the wind. Her eyes are closed, streaming tears, so I get close to her and stand, putting my front paws on her shoulders, trying to get her attention, to snap her out of the storm she's caused.

Her eyes fly open, wide and jade green and furious. It takes her a minute to register that I'm here, in front of her.

Then she crumples, and I have to move fast to catch her so that her head doesn't smack the ground. The wind around us dies, and the rocks and dust fall. The sky clears in a heartbeat, and the courtyard is eerily silent. Now that the roaring of the tornado is gone, it's like the world is holding its breath. Students, Mages, and Shields flood the courtyard, but no one is speaking. No one is moving.

Wren is conscious, but barely. Her eyelids seem heavy, and I nudge her with my face to keep her awake. I could shift back, but I think if she saw me naked right now, it might be more traumatizing, so I stay in my animal form. The form she knows, the form she trusts. She raises a hand to my face, stroking it, and a ghost of a smile appears on her lips. Her hair is a tangled brown-and-gold mat behind her, and dark purple circles ring her eyes, but still she smiles at me.

Head Mage Saroya pushes through the crowd that's encircling us. In her hand glints a silver ring—another manacle.

No one has ever worn two manacles. Saroya clasps it over Wren's right wrist, and Wren doesn't even protest. She can't. They're smothering her.

Wren pushes herself to her feet, and the crowd backs up, like they're expecting another outburst. But she just puts a hand on my back. It feels heavy, like she can't support her weight on her own.

"*Go* to your room," Saroya says, and there's a pressure behind her words. She's using her magic on Wren, making Wren do as she says. That kind of manipulation isn't a common gift—but Saroya's not a common Mage.

Wren nods and trudges away without a word, her feet shuffling in the dirt.

I walk with her, letting her lean against me when she needs to, and when Darius comes to talk to her, I bare my teeth. There's a scrape along his cheek where the stone struck him, and it's already swelling. Len tries to push past him, to put himself between us, but Darius just backs up, one hand raised. He doesn't try to come up again.

The crowd parts, silent, as we pass. She makes it up one flight of stairs before her eyes roll back, and she loses consciousness. I have to shift then, to carry her the rest of the way. She doesn't stir as we move, and for a moment I'm afraid she's stopped breathing, but a strand of hair flutters in front of her lips, so I keep going, not stopping until I've got her settled on her bed. I grab a towel from her desk and wrap it around my waist—no sense upsetting her further if she wakes up—and then tuck her blanket around her.

She looks so small, so frail. It doesn't make sense that such a small person could unleash such a torrent of magic. I run a hand through my hair, which is now coated with dust. None of this makes sense.

"Why did she respond to you?"

I turn, and Head Mage Saroya is standing in the doorway. This close, she's like a small sun contained in this little room, all yellow and gold and practically simmering with magic. The air feels thick and warm.

I shrug. "I thought the manacle was supposed to keep her from doing any magic," I say.

Saroya purses her lips. "It should have," she says. "There are documented cases of Mages being able to push past them, but not recently."

We watch Wren like she's sleeping. She's breathing easily. I don't know if she's done any permanent damage to herself with this display, if she'll wake up and just be a gray, washed-out shell of who she was. When she wakes, we'll know. I've heard of Mages wasting away, forgetting to eat or sleep or even move unless someone makes them, once they've burned out. Like the way Shields sometimes do when their Mages die. It must have taken an enormous amount of magic to bypass the manacle, let alone generate the storm. She doesn't look like a husk, though. Her skin is still a deeper brown than my own tan, and she's a little flushed, like with fever.

"Tell me about your bond," Saroya says.

"We have no bond," I say. "The Mages just didn't seem to be having any luck stopping her, so I stepped in."

Saroya considers this for a minute, but I don't think she believes me.

"You should go," Saroya says.

I growl, forgetting I'm not in my shifted form.

She raises an eyebrow, and I realize that growling at the Head Mage isn't really a great idea. She could toss me out the window with a single word.

"I'll keep an eye on her for a while," I say, struggling to keep my voice even.

"You have a big day tomorrow," Saroya says.

I cross my arms. I'm not going anywhere.

"She'll be fine," Saroya says. "Out. Don't make me *tell* you."

And she could. She could order me out of this room, order me to cluck for days like a chicken, and there'd be nothing I could do about it. I consider this. Probably, defying the Head Mage the day before I'm going to claim her prize pupil as my Mage isn't the best decision, and I seem to be making a lot of bad decisions lately.

In the end, Saroya doesn't have to order me out. I leave after I reassure myself that Wren's breathing fine and that she doesn't seem to be in any immediate danger.

The courtyard is mostly empty, and I find Vassilis waiting at the bottom of the stairs with my clothes. His eyes are wide, and dust is caked on his bright red hair, dulling it. He waits for me to dress.

"Want to tell me what happened?" he asks.

I shoot him a glance, and he shrugs.

"Mariana's upset, in case you wanted to know," he says, picking at some dirt under his nails.

I didn't see her in the courtyard during Wren's episode, but even if she wasn't there, I'm sure word traveled fast. It isn't every day that a student makes an elemental storm in the middle of the school's courtyard.

"I've made no promises to her, or anyone," I say.

Vassilis sighs but doesn't say anything.

Tomorrow I'll make my claim. It's rare that a Mage rejects a claim, but it's not unheard of. I can't let that happen with Mariana. I'd never live down the shame of a rejection.

"She's your best chance at getting your life back, remember?" Vassilis says, clapping me on the shoulder. "Don't fuck this up."

Chapter 11: Wren

I can't remember ever sleeping so long.

I get up once and find two Mages standing guard outside my door. They escort me to and from the bathroom. If I didn't feel like a prisoner before, I certainly do now. I can't help the flush that I feel spreading up my cheeks as we walk along, one stone-faced guardian to either side, but mercifully, we don't encounter any other students on our way. Then I wonder if that is an intentional thing, if someone's keeping the other students away from me—if they think I am a danger to them.

I don't think I hurt anyone. The memory of whatever happened is a little hazy, like a memory of a dream. I start to piece together a new theory about my magic now—maybe when I get really emotional, the magic finds a way around the manacle. I'm not sure why. I've tried looking up the manacles in the books I have, but I can't find anything. I'd like to visit the school library, since nobody feels like giving me a straight answer about anything, but I'm too damn exhausted, and I don't want to talk to anybody right now. I can't even summon the energy to have any emotions besides exhaustion. I ask my guards why Saroya is forcing them to watch me—I'm just sleeping. Seems like a giant waste of their time. They look down their noses at me—one is particularly large and bent, like a hawk's beak—and regard me like I'm simple.

When I sigh and throw my hands up, though, they flinch.

I think about the storm, the rocks and the wind and the lightning and clouds. All the elements were there, but wind was first. Maybe that's my element. Maybe that's where I should focus. But then I think of the thrill that ran down my spine when the green lightning struck the ground, of the way my blood rushed through me like wildfire when the clouds started to spiral into the funnel. I wonder if Mages sometimes pick more than one element. There might be something in the books I've been given, or in the library. I suppose I could just ask one of the Mages, but seeing as they've unanimously decided to be assholes to me, that's not my first choice. I'd rather spend days digging through old books than face any of them again. Still, I wonder what I can do, what I'm capable of. What it will mean when I'm done with training—if I ever start, that is. Most Mages apparently get out of here in two years. I'll be lucky to be done before I'm old and gray at this rate.

I'd like to see my tiger again, though. I thought maybe he was a figment of my imagination, some sort of spirit guide awakened by the stress of the situation, but there were white and black hairs on my blanket when I awoke. I gathered them and stuffed a few into my robe pocket, like a good-luck charm. I vaguely remember walking back to my room after the storm, my tiger at my side. I remember being tucked into my bed, but I can't recall by whom.

Someone brings in a plate of food during one of my naps, and I devour it. I ask my guards if anyone's come to see me, and they say no.

I look at my twin bracelets. They're pretty, but they're still chains. I've never owned or even seen anything so fine as these bits of silver. Sometimes I even think they glow a little. Both of them zap, though. I tap them against each other, to see if their magic will cancel out or something, but nothing happens.

I flop back on my bed. Why am I even here? I can't go back to Spit, but it's a big continent, and it's mostly one country now. There are dozens of other towns and cities

I could go to where no one will care who I am. With my doubled restraining devices, no one has to know I have magic—unless knowledge of these stupid manacles is common in Ocron, though I get the impression that not even most Mages have seen them used.

At least I can read and write, and I know a thing or two about lighthouses and the sea. Maybe I could find another coastal town, get another job. Get away from these people who seem intent on holding me back, all under the guise of "teaching" me. Away from students who are so competitive that they'll sabotage anyone else who they think will get in their way. I wonder if they'll ever be punished for tormenting me. I doubt it.

When I think about competitions, I realize that the Shield games will start in a few hours. Even if I somehow get through the next two years of training, no one will want to be my Shield. It would be humiliating to get through all this and then not get picked. Maybe I could be a Mage without a Shield. I know the teachers here are, but no way would I want to stay here and teach. I want to get as far away as possible.

I haven't decided that I'm staying, but I haven't decided to go yet either. At least I can go see the games and find out what the fuss is all about.

Chapter 12: Aris

I go to my room intending to spend the night alone.

Traditionally, the Shield recruits go down to Kemp's and get roaring drunk the night before the games. It's kind of a dumb tradition, given that we're all going to try to kill each other the next day. Usually a brawl breaks out. Sometimes someone gets bloodied or stabbed. Everyone leaves in the company of someone or two someones. It's a last chance to get the nerves out.

I'm not nervous. I've been through this before. There's an element of pageantry to the whole thing—the roar of the crowd is deafening. My first games were a rush. I was so intent on impressing my father, who glowered at me from the stands, that I nearly botched my first match. After that, I settled in and rapidly dispatched the next several opponents until, finally, I won. Emotions run wild during the games—the thrill of victory, the hopelessness of defeat, seeing the rest of your life rolled out like a giant golden carpet before you. I breathe deep, relaxing my body, preparing for sleep. My mind refuses to follow suit, though, and instead spins for hours.

I haven't seen Wren since the evening. I went by after dinner, but the two guards at her door wouldn't let me in. They said she was resting, so I didn't force the issue. I don't know how long she'll sleep after an episode like she had—I can only hope she comes out of it intact. I picture her burned-out, gray, and gaunt, a mockery of her former self, and something clenches in my chest. I've seen people go gray, after one of a Mage-Shield pair dies, or when a Mage overextends. The first time I saw one, I was a child—and I had nightmares for months.

Gods, I really can't sleep worth a damn. I decide to go to the library—I haven't been there in a while, but I can find my way around. This time of night, it's mostly deserted. It's got shelves and shelves of books and scrolls, probably more than any other place on the continent, save the palace at Estana. I take a small candle and am directed to the back corner by one of the ungifted humans who staff the place.

I pass rows and rows of books in orderly stacks. Most of them haven't been moved in ages, and dust lies thick upon them. When I come to the end, I find one of the books—the one I am interested in—has been disturbed recently, the dust on it cleared away. Someone else has been reading it.

I take the tome and find myself a table. The spelled candle doesn't offer much light, but given how valuable and flammable everything is here, I won't be allowed anything else.

Apparently, manacles have been around for ages. I read further—they offer the wearer a potent zap if they attempt to remove them. I'm positive Wren has tried this, which makes me pause. I think of how any other animal might feel being shackled, having pain inflicted anytime they try to escape. A passing bear might not bother you in the wild, but once you corner it, once you threaten it, watch out. I keep turning pages, oblivious to the passing time.

I should be sleeping, but that's one of the benefits of being me. I don't need much sleep. And even if I'm tired, I'll be fine. We're trained to be alert and fight even on days of no rest or sleep. You can't predict when an attack might come; you don't always have the luxury of a good night's sleep or a full meal beforehand. You take what you get and keep going.

I keep reading until nearly dawn. I have something like a vision, or a premonition. I see my future laid out in front of me like a book. I can claim Mariana. It will be easy. We'll go to the capital, get assigned somewhere, work together. We'll be good together. Good, but not great, not epic. Not worthy of remembrance. Not like my time with Stefan.

I keep reading. I'm not really sure what I'm looking for, and if anything, my mind is now more wound up than ever. I've got to get my head on straight. I roll my shoulders, working out the kinks. I need to focus. I force thoughts of Stefan out of my head.

It's time to chase my destiny.

The arena is buzzing when I arrive. The other Shield recruits are already there, along with two men I don't recognize, who must be the new arrivals from the capital that Vassilis mentioned. We all wear the leather shoulder and waist guards with the skirted belt, which are traditional, and our chests are bare. Well, the women wear cropped leather tops, but they don't cover or guard much. Nothing screams "Shield" like going into a fight without chest armor. It's the ultimate declaration of strength.

I enter through the long stone tunnel that cuts through the stands. Along the wall, which has been worn smooth from generations of passing hands, are engraved brass plaques. Each plaque bears the names of the Shields who have likewise passed through these halls and entered the games. The oldest plaques are worn with age but kept to a high polish by the ungifted who care for the school and the arena. The names on the oldest ones are barely legible—the years of polish meant to preserve them have ultimately begun to erase them. My fingers trail over them as I pass, the roar of the crowd building, like a storm growing inside me. As Shields fall, their names are struck through. I pass the plaque for my father's year—his name at the top, as the winner of that year's games. I find my brothers, each name likewise at the top of its plaque.

I find mine. Or the plaque for my last games. My name gleams at the top of it like a challenge. I cannot fail today. To be less than the best is to sacrifice my gift, my heritage. I breathe deeply, savoring the scent of rock and heat and sweat. My blood pounds through my body, readying my muscles for battle. I am ready.

It is time.

As I enter the arena, I size up the competition. One of the newcomers is a mountain of a man who looks capable of snapping me in half with his bare hands. The other is just as tall but lean, quick, with shifty yellow eyes. Both have the calm, focused looks of warriors. Both will give me a challenge, and that sends a thrill through me. As the sun crests the top of the arena, a horn blasts out, and Head Mage Saroya steps into her place in the stands, accompanied by the Shield Commander and a phalanx of other senior Mages. The arena is packed with Shields, Mages, students, families, and the ungifted. The place is completely awash with color and noise. Everyone has come to see us fight. Wages are being placed, on who will best whom, on who will pick whom. It's the event of the year, and I'm the star.

"Hey, pretty boy. Aren't you the one who got his Mage killed?" the mountainous man asks.

I flash him a broad, feral grin—I want him to see that I'm not afraid of him, that I look forward to hearing him yield to me in the ring. I don't bother denying his words. He's right. It was my job to protect Stefan, and I failed. I failed, and then I ran. My animal instincts fought me, and I let them. I was wild.

But I came back. I am back.

I stretch out my arms, my back, my legs. My shoulder twinges—even after all this time, even with my enhanced healing, it's not completely back to normal. I go over to the weapons rack and pick up two gladiuses. The weight of them feels good in my hands, like they belong there.

"You really think Saroya will let you get another of her students killed?" Mountain Man continues.

He's starting to rankle me. I sheathe my weapons and continue to stretch. In the stands, I see Mariana, seated a few rows back from the Head Mage. She's wearing her blue Water Mage robe, and she is surrounded by a group of blond people I can only assume are her family, and most of them are in blue robes too. She smiles at me, but I only nod back. Her smile wavers.

The arena is divided up into half a dozen rings. Victory is declared when one of the Shields yields, or if he or she goes outside the circle drawn in red on the sand. Rarely, Vassilis or another Shield will step in if serious injury occurs. Otherwise, the rules are pretty simple. The winner advances to the next round. Once you lose, you fight some of the other losers to determine where in the lineup you'll fall.

"That pretty blond one yours?" Mountain Man asks, jabbing a finger toward where Mariana is sitting. "Nice. I look forward to getting to know her better. A lot better."

I shrug. I know this game. I've played it a thousand times myself. He's decided I'm the only real competition here, so he's trying to get under my skin. He'll have to try harder than that. My silence is starting to irritate him, and he gives me an obscene hand gesture. I give him one right back.

The drum beats, and we're paired off.

"*Vires, honos, fides*," we chant in unison, thumping our left hands against our chests. Markos is watching me like a hawk—waiting to see if I'm going to embarrass him again, no doubt.

My first battle is against the small adder-like girl, and she's even faster than I remember, fueled by desperation. She's sweating before we even start, and she does well.

The fight lasts a whole minute. She yields quickly, my gladius glinting at her throat.

And I'm just getting warmed up.

By now the crowd is warming up too. They cheer at each victory; they hiss at each draw of blood. My pulse thunders in my ears. The air is cool, but the sun is warm on my skin. I feel like Odall the First Shield himself, drawing his strength from the god of day.

I'm paired with Victor, the bear man, next. Honestly, I'm surprised he made it past his first round. He's not thrilled to be paired up with me, and he doesn't try all that hard. It's a quick match, and he yields easily.

The time passes in a blur. I gulp down ash water between rounds and stretch to keep my muscles limber. The sun is warming the cool air. Most of the Shields are sweating heavily, the moisture making them irritable and prone to error. Shouts go up as someone draws blood, a scratch down a recruit's leg that makes him crumple, his opponent's gladius poised to go for the throat. The boy doesn't give in, though. He barely pauses. He sweeps out his uninjured leg, catching the attacker behind the knees. He goes down, and the boy leaps up, his spear at the other's chest. Victory is declared as blood pours down his injured leg. He stabs his spear into the sand and offers a hand to the loser, to help him up. *Now there's a true Shield.* I forget his name, but I decide I like him. The crowd does too. He is bandaged up and gets back into the arena with Mountain Man.

I go up against the other returning Shield, the tall, lean guy. I expect his shift form is a wolf from the way he moves. He's decided on a pair of gladiuses too, and I'm glad. It might make for a more even match.

The drum beats again, and we begin. The man has yellow eyes, narrowed and sharp. We dance, circling each other, watching for an opening, for someone's gaze to falter, perhaps distracted by the crowd or by nerves. He's got experience, more than any I've gone up against. I feel a rush of energy, like I'm gaining strength with each fight instead of wearing out.

He feints, and I dodge. He whirls on me, swords wielded like claws. Metal clashes against metal, and sparks fly. We dance apart. He's grinning, and I realize that yes, he has to be a wolf with those elongated canines. His grin is way too wolfy to be anything else. I decide that I can use that to my advantage—a wolf will usually wear its prey out, biding its time. I need to be quick, decisive, and end this match fast.

I forget that wolves are also very, very clever.

While I'm looking for an opening, he brings one sword in low, one high. I block the blow to my torso—just in time to see his other sword head for my injured shoulder. I whirl, but not before the hilt of the blade slams into the puckered red scar.

I fall to my knee, and the crowd draws in a breath. My vision narrows, the edges blackening from the surge of pain.

The wolf comes at me again, fast, to capitalize on my vulnerability. My left arm hangs useless, stunned by the blow, the hand tingling as sensation fights to return. I hold it close to me, and as he makes a lunge, I explode. I leap up from my knees and whirl around him, my elbow slamming into his back—and then he's down, and my sword is at his throat, his yellow eyes wide. He's panting hard. He drops his swords.

"I yield," he says. The only thing I've heard him say all day. The only thing I care about hearing him say.

I turn my back on him and leave the ring. My arm burns. I clench and unclench my fingers, but my left hand feels sluggish. He might as well have cut it off, for all the good it will do me now.

I hear another roar from the crowd, and I look up. Mountain Man has beaten his opponent—blood is streaming down the other Shield's face—and he has his hands raised, egging the crowd on. They love this and roar back at him.

He turns to me and points his sword at my chest.

"You're next, pretty boy."

As I expected, it all comes down to Mountain Man and me. We take a few minutes' break, during which frantic wagers are made in the stands. I swing my arm—and pain shoots down my shoulder. I'm going to have to rethink this next battle.

The drum beats, and we step into the red ring. A hush falls over the crowd. My world shrinks until it's just me and Mountain Man. He's the one obstacle between me and my prize, and I will not be beaten.

He laughs at me.

"You think a shield is going to protect you?" he says.

I've chosen a small round shield—from which we take our name—for my left arm. It is light, and I can't raise that arm to use a sword, anyway. It's not my preferred way to battle—I'm usually all offensive—but I don't really have a choice. Whatever Wolfy did to my shoulder, I was not prepared for it. Still, injuries happen. A Shield knows how to work with them, work past them. I ignore Mountain Man and his taunts. He thinks he can distract me, bait me, get me worked up. I will not fall to his pathetic attempts. Nothing can get between me and my prize.

Then I look up, and suddenly I can't breathe.

Chapter 13: Wren

I don't make it for the early matches, but I sneak into one of the less popular parts of the stadium, far away from the Head Mage, for the semifinals. My guards escorted me part of the way, but then I snuck behind a crowd and lost them. I stifle a giggle when I think of how Saroya will scold them for losing me, and then I get swept up in the tide of bodies in the stadium and forget all about my grumpy guards.

Most of the other Mages and Shields are seated close to the Head Mage. I'm with a bunch of other people here, whom I've seen working around the school—ungifted, as they're referred to. Stable boys and cooks and laundry women. They're surprised to see me, and I get some strange looks, but no one jeers at me; no one tries to trip me. They just quietly make a spot for me near the front, so I can lean on the barrier and look out at the fights.

There are two fights going on. One is with a huge man against one of the Shield recruits. The recruit looks like he might faint from fright. He has a bandage wrapped around his leg that is stained red. I don't expect that fight to last long.

The other fight is between a tall, lanky man and Aris.

I don't know a lot about fighting. They seem to just kind of watch each other for a while, sizing each other up, before exploding into a series of swings and jabs almost too fast for the eye to follow. They're impossibly swift and agile. I've heard that Shields have enhanced strength and speed, but hearing it and seeing it are totally different things. It's like trying to follow a lightning strike with your naked eye, and potentially just as destructive.

Aris falls to one knee, and my breath catches in my throat. But then he's up and spinning, a whirlwind of leather and tanned skin and muscle and grace.

The other man falls and yields.

Behind me, people are taking bets. The last fight will be between Aris and the large man, named Zale. Aris is tall, but this other guy is massive. His biceps are as big around as my waist. He's lifting his hands to the crowd, grinning ferociously as they roar back at him in response. The wagers are evenly split, though—a lot of the ungifted are pulling for Aris. They say things about his bloodline being strong, that it will carry him through. Other people spit back that he's already failed once, that it's a miracle he hasn't turned gray. I want to hear more of the story, but the drum starts beating again, and then Aris and Zale are in the ring. Aris is wearing a shield on one arm, while Zale wields a sword in both hands. They are talking, stalking each other around the ring.

And then, Aris looks up.

He's a hundred feet away, but he looks right at me and freezes. My heart skips.

Zale bellows and attacks. The world stops—we're all holding our breath.

At the last possible instant, Aris whips up his shield, and Zale's swords slam into it. I can feel the reverberation across the arena, can hear the air leave Aris's lungs in a grunt of effort. It's so quiet now; I can hear their feet scuffling in the sand.

Then they're whirling around each other, a deadly dance. Aris is faster, but Zale is going at him with sheer power. Their leather armor seems pitifully inadequate. Zale chops at Aris like he's chopping wood—a single blow from him could take off a limb.

I try not to dwell on that thought too much.

They parry and strike, back and forth. Zale's swords clang against Aris's shield, and Aris keeps just out of his reach. Biding his time, I hope.

And then Aris strikes. Zale's arms are somehow now locked around his shield, and they're stuck, face-to-face, unable to use their arms to strike. Zale's bearing down on Aris with the sheer weight of his massive body, and I can't breathe.

Aris's gaze flicks back in my direction.

A sound like a roar tears from his throat. Zale seems to tumble—no, Aris has pivoted and heaved Zale over his shoulder. Zale soars, then lands hard on the sand on his side.

Completely outside the circle.

The crowd goes berserk. People around me are screaming and clapping, swearing at lost bets and cheering over their wins. Mugs of ale are clanked and spilled and drunk—but my eyes are fixed on the dark figure in the arena. His chest is heaving, sweat gilding his skin. He looks like a god reborn, shining in the sunlight. Then he raises his sword, and the crowd falls silent. I shoot a glance at Mariana, in the stands by the Head Mage. She's standing and beaming at him, glowing, even.

He lowers his sword, pointing it at his choice.

Chapter 14: Aris

Things haven't gone exactly as planned.

The sight of Wren in the stands—whole, not a burned-out husk—nearly undid me.

Mountain Man took advantage of my distraction. I thank all the gods for the quick reflexes that saved me from that first blow. I believe he would have taken my head off if he could have gotten away with it.

But I emerged victorious. There was never an alternative.

I close my eyes for a moment, reveling in the moment. I've won. I went to the depths of despair, into a darkness no Shield ever wants to see, and I came back from it when most don't. I have another chance. A chance to fulfill my destiny, to fulfill the promise of my bloodline, to bring honor to my family name and to the realm. *Vires, honos, fides.*

And as usual, I fuck it up.

Chapter 15: Wren

His sword is pointed at me.

I'm not really sure what's going on, but the people around me cheer and shout, clapping me on the shoulder, hugging me. Across the arena, Aris is still staring at me, his arm outstretched. I look over—Mariana's slumped in her seat, her face white. The people around her are still, whispering to each other. Then I'm swept away by the crowd, down the aisle to the stairs and to a room underneath the stadium. It's a dark stone area, and it feels disturbingly like a dungeon. Torches are lit on the walls but do little to warm the place up. Goose bumps ripple over my arms.

What's going on? And what in all the hells is Aris thinking? Anger replaces trepidation, and my hands are clenching so hard that my knuckles ache. I'm not even a student yet, not even sure if I could be a Mage even if I wanted to stay here and try. I think about him standing there in the arena, victorious, undefeated, raising his arm. There is no way he made a mistake, that his movement could be misinterpreted—his motion was intentional. It said, *She's mine*.

He'll regret that. I expect it will be sooner rather than later. I wonder if he can take it back or if he can change his mind about his claim. If he can claim Mariana instead. If she'll even still have him after being humiliated by not being his first choice.

I hear the roar of the crowd above me again, and a few moments later, Aris enters the room. He's without his sword and shield, but he still looks fierce, dangerous. He's gleaming with sweat, and sand is stuck to his muscular legs, to his chiseled torso. Seeing so much of him brings a flush of heat to my face, but I try to look anywhere—anywhere except at his eyes.

I hear another roar above us, and I unconsciously raise my gaze to the ceiling. Of course, I can't see anything, but I imagine that Zale has made his choice. I wonder if they'll be joining us, or if this is meant to be a private moment between Aris and me.

And then I can't help it. I look at his face, at his eyes, blazing blue in the flickering torchlight. He's staring at me, so I clench my hands tighter and stare right back.

"Do you understand what happened?" he asks.

I blink.

He runs a hand through his sweaty hair, like he's searching for the right words. We're just a foot or two apart, and I can feel the heat rolling off him in waves as he moves. His eyes meet mine again, and there's no uncertainty there, no regret. He's clearly not fighting the roiling battle of emotions that I am.

"Wren, I claimed you," he says evenly.

A thrill runs down my spine at his words. "I don't know what that means," I say. The words come out quieter than I meant them to.

He nods—he expected this. "It means I want you," he says. "I want to be your Shield. I want to go where you go, to protect you from whatever comes our way. To be beside you as we work to help and protect this country." He pauses. "For most of us, it is a lifelong commitment."

At those last words, there's a flicker across his face, but he doesn't elaborate. He's waiting for me to say something. My mind is reeling. This makes no sense. Nothing about the past few weeks makes any sense. I suddenly miss the peace and solitude of my lighthouse, the predictable, if boring, nature of it all, and I pinch the white and black hairs in my pocket, rolling them between my fingers.

"I'm barely a student yet," I say, my mind feeling strangely unmoored. "Why would you pick me? I'll be here two more years at least, two years you could be off saving the world."

"I can wait," he says, crossing his arms, like he's never been more certain about anything in his whole life. "I'll wait for you."

"You're crazy," I say.

He grins, and it's a predator's grin.

I wonder suddenly what his animal shift is. I realize I know next to nothing about him, nor he about me. The space between us has narrowed, and it makes me acutely uncomfortable, but I don't step back. He could have had his pick of anyone—he could have had Mariana, or that Fire Mage girl, or anyone, anyone else. I haven't even declared an element yet. I'm not even sure I still want to be here at this stupid school. When I tell him this, he frowns, like it's something he hasn't considered.

"You can't really go back," he says.

I glare at him.

"Wren, can you really look me in the eye and tell me that you'd just go back to that lighthouse for the rest of your life? Let those manacles stay, binding you, forever?"

When did I tell him I lived in a lighthouse? The idea that the school is gossiping about me makes my blood boil. I wonder what else they are saying.

"Look, it's in a Shield's nature to be protective," he says. "You've been mistreated, from the moment Darius met you. I won't let that happen anymore," he says, and then he smirks. He smirks at me. "You do seem to need more protecting than most."

"It's not my fault this school is full of competitive assholes," I mumble.

"Well, speaking from the perspective of a competitive asshole, I agree with you." He lets out a long breath. "Have you heard anything about my history?" he asks. That's a loaded question. He shifts his weight from foot to foot.

"You claimed a Mage once before," I say. I pieced the story together from the roaring crowd earlier—that these were Aris's second games, that he had the experience in the arena to emerge victorious, which is why so many bet on him to do so.

He nods, his lips pressed into a hard line.

I force my gaze back up to his eyes.

"He died," Aris says, and the shadow is back in his eyes. "We were scouting in Aclines, and we were ambushed. I let my guard down, and he paid the price."

I take a moment to process this. Aris isn't exactly my enemy, but he was part of the army that conquered my home country. And he's failed once before. Is this the kind of person I want to swear myself to? I want to ask about Mariana, but I bite my tongue.

"A claim doesn't have to be accepted," he says, gently, like he's reading my thoughts. "You can think about it, for as long as you want. You don't have to decide right now."

"What's in it for you?" I ask.

He cocks his head to the side. "You're the strongest Mage I've ever seen," he says. "And you haven't even gotten started. I want to be the one at your side, making history with you."

I consider. So, losing a Mage has made him a pariah. He thinks that somehow I can restore his shredded honor, and he believes it so strongly that he's willing to bind his life to mine. He believes in me that much—so much that I start to believe in me a little too.

"Think about it," he says, and turns to go.

Without thinking, I reach out to put a hand on his arm.

He stops, looking down at my hand. He's staring—no, glaring at the manacle there. He's as furious about it as I am, and that's when I realize my mind is made up.

"Aris, I claim you too," I say.

A thrill that has nothing to do with the manacle races down my spine as his eyes hold mine, blazing.

He covers my hand with his. "Let's go make history."

Chapter 16: Aris

As I expected, there are repercussions.

Wren and I leave the room under the arena. The claim has been made, the invisible bond between us settling into place, like it has always been there. Not a wire or thread this time—a sound, clear as a silver bell. I'll be able to hear that, to feel it in my marrow, and find her, no matter the distance. She is mine. It's a gamble, to be sure, a calculated risk, but when it came down to it, to choosing between her and Mariana, well, it wasn't that hard a choice at all.

As we exit the underground, there are pairs of Shields and Mages all around us, all newly claimed, most grinning and being hugged and congratulated by family members. I catch Mariana staring at me—she's standing next to the wolfy Shield, the one who injured my shoulder. I flex my fingers just thinking about it—the sting of his blow is only now starting to fade. Then she turns her back on me.

With Wren, this is not going to be easy. One more episode like her little tornado, and she might even be imprisoned or exiled. But if she soars, if she overcomes the restraints that are being piled on her, she will go down in history as one of the strongest Mages of all time, and I along with her. There will be no limit to what we can do together.

It was a gamble I was apparently willing to take. This girl has been dealt a winning hand, and I want in.

"We've got to set some ground rules," Wren says.

I arch an eyebrow. "Rules?" I ask, incredulous.

"Yes," she says, pursing her lips. "Conditions. Boundaries. Our partnership is contingent on you thinking I'm some sort of prodigy. If I don't live up to your expectations, what will you do? Can you choose someone else?"

I shake my head. "No. No one's ever gone back to the games a third time."

"Why not?" she asks.

We make our way through the crowd of Mages and Shields, who part uneasily for us, cramming themselves against the walls to give us space.

"Because … well …" I shake my head. "It doesn't matter. I don't need your stipulations."

She thinks about this for a second. "You're awfully cocky," she says, glancing at me.

I shoot her a smirk. "Princess, you have no idea."

"Don't call me 'princess,'" Wren mutters as we exit the underground.

"Why not?" I ask. "You lived in a lighthouse, which is kind of like a tower. You talk to animals. Ergo, princess. Like in children's stories."

"I don't talk to animals," she grumbles. She keeps close to me, like she's afraid of what's coming as we reenter the courtyard.

Relief at her response to my claim sweeps through me, making me feel a little light-headed, and a lot like teasing her. "Whatever you say, princess," I say.

She smacks my arm, and I grin down at her. She bites her tongue to keep the smile off her face, but she doesn't succeed. Vassilis sees me then, and the fury on his face wipes away any relief I am feeling about Wren's response.

"What in all the hells do you think you're doing?" he asks, his voice raised enough that the people around us turn and stare.

I glare right back at him. "I'm a Shield. I claimed my Mage, and she claimed me. What's the issue?" I ask. I know full well what the issue is, but his attitude is grating. As a

Shield who's never claimed a Mage, he has no right at all to question me.

"She's *not* a Mage!" he says, pointing at Wren.

She shrinks back, and I slap his arm away.

"She will be," I say, though it's an effort to keep my voice level.

"She can't be controlled! Everyone says so!" Vassilis bellows.

"She doesn't need to be controlled!" I roar back, fed up. "You tell me how easy it would be for you to stay calm and quiet while someone chains you up." I hold up her wrists, the manacles glinting. Wren grabs her hands back from me, shoving her arms into the sleeves of her robe so no one else can see them. I see Saroya coming toward us then, her yellow robe flaring behind her like a pair of giant wings.

"You've made a mistake," Vassilis says, frowning, his hands out in supplication. "Saroya might yet let you change your mind. Maybe you can enter next year's games. Markos would vouch for you."

"I don't need to," I say. My jaw aches from clenching my teeth so tight.

Saroya hears this last bit and arches an eyebrow. Vassilis throws his hands up and leaves, muttering.

"You've both made your decisions, then," Saroya says, looking from me to Wren and back.

Wren nods solemnly, and I feel a jolt of pride at that. Saroya has no idea what it's like. She's never been claimed—she was chosen for leadership early on, before even becoming a full Mage. She has no idea what the bond is like, so I don't really give a damn what she thinks.

"So be it," Saroya says. She continues past us.

Wren turns to watch her, but Saroya doesn't look back.

We make our way across the courtyard. No one else stops us, and no one tries to talk to us. We get a lot of strange looks, though. Wren holds her head high, walking beside me, like she doesn't even notice, though her cheeks are stained pink. A princess indeed.

"So what happens now?" she asks, a little breathless, as we reach the edge of the crowd.

"Now we're a team," I say. "We do whatever we need to do to help you identify your element, master it, and get these manacles off. Then we go wherever we need to go, wherever we're needed."

"And how do we start doing that?" she asks. Her tone is sharp.

"Well, we'll move your things into my room. Then—"

"Excuse me?" she chokes out. Her skin changes from smooth, soft brown to pink, all the way to the roots of her hair.

I raise an eyebrow. "How am I supposed to protect you if you live in a dorm across the courtyard?" I point out. "Besides, I have a great view."

I can hear her teeth grinding.

"I was not aware that moving in with you was part of the deal," she says at last, each word carefully articulated, her temper barely controlled. She's glaring at me like she's seriously reconsidering the claim.

I fight back the urge to roll my eyes.

"Are there any other … caveats I should know about?" she asks.

"It's a big room. You'll have all the space you could want," I say. "It's not like we can share the bed in your little room."

She flushes darker.

Teasing her is a little fun, I'll admit. She kind of reminds me of my little sisters in that way. It's easy to get them all riled up too.

"Come on. Let's go get your things, and you can tell me about your plans," I say.

She seems placated for the moment and leads me to her room in the students' wing. She has nothing in terms of belongings other than a change of clothes, a hairbrush, and the books that she was given here.

"You travel light," I say, running a hand down the doorframe, where generations of students have carved their initials. Some are blocky, some etched deep. I trace them as Wren gathers her things. I don't miss these little cages, so cramped—particularly when one has company.

"Didn't really have time to be sentimental when my choices were getting chased out of my home with pitchforks or kidnapped by a cranky Wind Mage," she says. She puts a hand in her pocket as she speaks, though, fiddling with something in there.

I shrug.

We go the long way, walking the hallway all the way around the ring of walls to the far side instead of cutting across the courtyard. It feels strange, bringing her here, when I did the same thing with Stefan not so long ago, though personality-wise, they couldn't be more different. I swear I feel his ghost walking beside me.

I open the door and let her in.

I wasn't bragging—it is a nice room, as far as rooms at the school go. It's several times the size of her old one, with a row of windows overlooking the river and surrounding green hills. My bed is on the far wall. The one for my claimed Mage, nearest the door. There are two of everything—and it's felt strange, only one person living in this room. Maybe that's one of the reasons I have spent most nights in other places. Bringing anyone else here felt … wrong.

Wren is silent. I gesture toward her side of the room, and she stacks her books on the desk, puts away her clothes. I sit on her bed while she arranges things. It doesn't take long. Her gaze lingers a moment over a phrase carved above the window, which Stefan carved there not so long ago in blocky letters: NON DUCOR DUCO.

"So," I say, lying back, ripping my eyes from the window. My bed's much more comfortable than hers, but maybe that's just the twinge in my shoulder talking. I tuck my hands behind my head, trying to get comfortable, and take a deep breath. "What's your plan?"

"I don't have one," she snaps, banging a drawer shut. "I've been here for less than a week. I'm not even sure Saroya won't have me kicked out for making that storm yesterday."

"Yeah," I say. "Let's try not to do that again."

"I wasn't trying to do it in the first place!" She slams a book onto the desk.

I raise an eyebrow. She is a noisy little thing.

"Look," she says, sitting in the chair, keeping her distance. "I don't understand magic. I grew up where none of this exists, so this is all new to me. They tell me I'm out of control and a threat and give me these things"—she holds up her wrists—"and don't tell me what I can do to get control!"

"Well," I say, watching her. Her chest is heaving, but she seems to be done shouting for the moment. "You scare Saroya because you don't fit her little mold of what a Mage is supposed to be. You're supposed to come to this school with your element already declared or close to it, tied up in a neat little bow, ready to be trained in service of king and country."

"So what element am I? Wind?" she says, looking at the candles on her desk. "Fire? Can I be more than one?"

"No," I say slowly, noting her gaze. "Have you been able to make any magic on purpose yet?"

She frowns at the candles.

"Not really," she says, stroking the wax tapers. "I think I've made sparks a few times. And I made Len mute when he was irritating me, so that's wind, right?" She shoots me a glance.

"I heard about that," I say, and she sighs.

I get up and head to my side of the room. I take off my leathers and then look for my sandals.

"Oh, for the love of …" she says.

I turn back to find that she's turned around, facing the far wall, resolutely not looking in my direction, which is strange. Women like looking at me, especially when my clothes are off.

"Kind of a prude, aren't you?" I say, pulling on my pants. I bend to get my other sandal and feel a smack against the side of my head.

A shoe. She's thrown a shoe at me. I have just defeated every single Shield recruit in the School of the Silver Flame in combat for the *second* time, a feat that no one else in the history of Ocron has ever managed, and my Mage has thrown a shoe at me.

"I want a privacy screen," she says at last. She's positively fuchsia now and trembling with fury. It's kind of cute.

"Whatever my princess commands," I say with a bow.

She raises her hand, her other shoe poised.

I put up my hands. "All right!" I say. "We'll get you a screen. Happy?"

"Yes," she mutters, putting down her shoe.

Satisfied she's not about to attack me again, I finish getting dressed and pour myself some water—mixed with the ashes of burned plants—from the pitcher on my desk, then down it. After so many years, I barely taste the ash anymore. Markos swears it helps us heal faster after exertion, and my own family had me drinking it since infancy. I offer it to Wren, who takes one look and wrinkles her nose.

"Ugh, no, thank you," she says. She peers into the pitcher on her side of the room, seeming relieved that it's just plain water.

"You don't have to worry, you know," I say.

She looks at me quizzically, and I take another sip of ash water.

"I promise I won't look—unless you want me to."

Her gaze flicks to her shoe.

Fine, she doesn't like this kind of teasing. Noted. I raise a hand in mock surrender. "All right, I'm done. Come on." I set down my glass. "Let's go to the library. I found a book about your manacles last night. We should go through it."

"What were you doing looking up my manacles?" she asks, blinking in surprise.

I shrug, heading out the door.

"It just … seemed like picking me in the arena was kind of an impulsive thing," she says.

“Maybe it was,” I say, heading for the stairs. “Come on. We’re going to give this a shot. If you decide you hate me and want another Shield in the future, that’s fine. That’s your choice. But we’re a team for now, and it’s in my best interest to help you—so I’m going to help you.”

She nods and follows me across the courtyard to the library. Most of the other spectators have left. A few families are headed to the stables to get their horses and carriages, so it’s crowded over there. We go the long way around to avoid any unnecessary interactions.

“Do you have any family?” she asks when she sees me eyeing the groups by the stables.

“None worth mentioning,” I say, not adding that my father will probably disown me once he hears about what happened today. That’s all right, though. He’ll come around once he sees what Wren can do, when he sees what I see.

“Me neither,” she says.

I shoot her a look, but she doesn’t elaborate.

The library is a two-story building that actually goes pretty deep underground. It’s roughly circular, with shelves that go on for miles. The more popular stuff is kept on the first floor, near the door. A few ungifted work the library, organizing the books, handing out spelled candles to those reading so that they won’t burn the place down. It’s dark and oppressive inside, and not usually my favorite place. I prefer the wide-open space of the arena, but the library is the only place we might find answers.

Wren is quiet now, thoughtful. I guess she’s been through a lot recently, but there’s no time to waste, not for either of us. We get to work.

Chapter 17: Wren

I'm in way over my head.

I wait at a table in the heavy darkness of the library, flipping through the book Aris was reading, while he goes in search of some other texts. The library feels oppressive—the narrow aisles between shelves, claustrophobic. I'm grateful for the relatively open space he guided me to. I feel like I can breathe a little easier here, though each breath feels like I'm pulling dust into my lungs. We're deep in the building, and it's so quiet and dusty that it feels abandoned. There are no spiderwebs, though, no book corners with tooth marks from mice. I wish there *were* mice here—it might make the place feel a little less like a tomb.

The candle he's left with me is interesting, so I try to focus on that instead—the flame doesn't flicker or waver. I put my hand near it, and it's not even warm. My fingers go through it like a real flame, but it gives off no heat, no smoke. I wonder if I could learn to make candles like this. It would have been nice to have them back home—I wonder if my lighthouse could be made to do this, and avoid the use of whale oil altogether. I briefly fantasize about taking an axe to the pulley system.

My lighthouse. I have to face it—I'll never go back there.

I flip through the pages of the book, trying to forget the smell of the sea in the dusty tome. It's ancient, the paper thick and brittle, and the writing is small, like the author was trying to fit as much as possible onto each page. There are whole paragraphs about what the manacles can contain—hint: pretty much everything. They're not common—that much I gather. It also doesn't seem to be commonplace to subject students to them. It feels like Darius and Saroya recognized I was a little different than expected and immediately branded me as being in need of containment.

I think back to the morning—was it only this morning?—to the arena and the games and the roar of the crowd. Aris, the victor, invincible. Picking me, the unknown. He is taking a pretty big risk, but he is the only one who seems interested in actually helping me. He believes in me, even if it is to further his own agenda. And I don't want to admit it, but having him as my Shield made sense too. I wonder what it will feel like, to have someone like him watching my back. I've been alone for so long; I don't even know if I can let him. I'd like to see someone try to steal my clothes now. I bet those pricks who were taunting me in the courtyard with their shape-shifting won't dare pick on me, not after their golden boy has staked his claim.

That's when I realize that I have no idea what Aris's animal form is. I figure Shields are mostly predators, which makes sense. A badger, a wolf, a hawk. I could see him as a hawk. Sharp-eyed, sharp-tongued. Maybe he hasn't told me what his form is because it is something silly, like a shrew or a weasel.

"You're smiling, so I guess you found something," Aris says, coming back with an armful of books. Another man is with him—he's older, and I remember seeing him with the Head Mage. Though his hair is gray, his arms are corded with muscles carefully honed over a lifetime of training.

"No," I say to Aris. "Just thinking."

"All right," he says, and drops the books. They hit the table with a loud thump that seems to echo through the entire floor. He shuffles through them, and little clouds of dust rain down on the table, briefly flickering in the candlelight.

"Markos," the older man says, and he extends me a hand. I shake it—his massive paw envelops mine in a tight squeeze.

"Wren," I say.

He holds my eyes for a moment longer than necessary. I feel like he's trying to look inside me somehow, glean some sort of information there. He settles himself at the table with us. He doesn't bother to look at the books.

"Shield Commander Markos Drusus has been in charge of the Shield training here since before I was born," Aris says by way of introduction. "I figured if the Mages weren't going to help you, at least I could ask the Shields."

"No doubt, you have power," Markos says, leaning back in his chair. He lets out a long breath. "I've had this cub under my wing for most of his life. I can't say I approve of the gamble he's taking with you."

Aris shoots him a glare that would make most grown men flinch. Not Markos. And I do not fail to notice the word cub—it helps me narrow down Aris's shifted form a little, but not much. Fox? Some sort of cat? Bear?

"What's done is done," Aris says, taking the top book off the stack, blowing off a thick layer of dust. "You said you could help. If you're not going to, feel free to leave."

The Commander raises an eyebrow but doesn't otherwise acknowledge Aris's tone.

"The manacle. May I?" he asks.

I look at Aris, who nods, so I give my hand back to Markos. He runs his massive fingers over the metal—it looks impossibly delicate next to his hands, like he could snap it as easily as a twig.

"If you're thinking I could break it for you, think again," he says, reading my mind, and he sits back in his chair once more. "Saroya likes things neat. Uncomplicated. She's under a lot of pressure here, to turn out more students. It's a dangerous time, Wren—more threats, especially from the west. Dark things stirring. Not a good time for the country to run low on Mages." He leans back, letting out a long breath. "Someone like you … complicates things for her. She was hoping we'd get more students from Aclines. Admissions have been dwindling over the past decade. She's looking for fresh blood, but she's not entirely sure what she's found in you. I've never seen a student have to wear a manacle to keep their magic in check before."

"Great," I mutter. I open my mouth to ask about these "dark things" he mentioned, then close it—I'm not really sure I want to know right now. I miss my lighthouse with a sudden pang in my chest, like a throbbing wound. How did I ever imagine my life in Spit was dull? At least there I knew my place. At least there I was safe. I look to Aris, who is staring at me.

He clears his throat. "In the meantime, I asked a librarian for some help. They love being asked for help. It's weird. Anyway, he's off getting a dozen more books for me right now. He said to start with this one." Aris hands me the book, and I open it. The title is scrawled in neat curling handwriting—*The Books of Bronze, Silver, and Gold: A History*.

"The Book of Silver is the mythical tome that granted Mages and Shields their powers, passed down by the gods at the creation of man," Markos says. "Three books, out of which three lineages sprang. Bronze for the ungifted, Silver for the magic—that's Mages and Shields—and Gold for the king's family. It's a story all Ocronian children know."

"There is a literal silver book here somewhere? Is that what all that 'Silver Flame' stuff is about?" I ask, confused.

Markos shakes his head. "Not literally, no," he says. "The whole Silver Flame thing was someone's idea of incorporating the myth along with the 'flame of knowledge' or some such. The history's a little hazy, but the Book of Silver is more of a cult now, a religious sect that still worships the old ways. I hear the capital even has a silver sculpture in the palace as a nod to the real thing, but not even our librarians here have ever set eyes on one of the books, if they were even real to begin with."

"So I have my magic because of a book the gods sent down ages ago? I get my magic from a book?"

"So the stories say," Markos says, shrugging.

"And you want me to read about these myths?" I ask Aris.

He nods. "Got to start somewhere," he says. "We grew up on these tales. You didn't. We have a lot of ground to make up."

"I'll leave you to it, then," Markos says, and gets up. He starts to leave but then turns back to me. "I'm sorry I don't have more help to offer you, Wren. I do wish you the best, for his sake." He claps Aris hard on the shoulder. It's his injured one, and he winces, just a little. I pretend not to notice.

"Thank you," I say.

"If the Mages here can't help you, though," he says, his eyes flicking to the stack of books on our table, "or if the librarians can't, you might want to consider the capital. Mage Panos is an old friend of mine. A bit batty, but I'd wager there's nothing about magic that he doesn't know by now. Even more than our Head Mage. The king has a team of Mages at the capital that do nothing but study magic—waste of talent, if you ask me," he grumbles. "But it might be that someone there can help you, if Saroya cannot."

I thank him again, and he leaves us to our task.

For hours we work our way through the stack without finding much, but we press on—until my stomach rumbles loudly.

"Time for a break," Aris says, standing and stretching.

I close the book I've been reading. We've found a lot about early magic, about how young children start to manifest, about how subtle the signs can be. We haven't found anything else about the manacles, though, or how to make a Mage's element manifest in the first place. It would be a hell of a lot easier to know which element I should start focusing on, if I could just get these damn bracelets off.

We head to the dining hall, and I'm startled to realize it's way after dark now.

"I think I have a curfew, right?" I say.

He shakes his head. "You're with a Shield. You're my responsibility now, so no, no more curfews," he says.

We make our way across the school.

"What were you smiling about earlier?" he asks.

I shrug, but he wants an answer. "I don't know what your animal form is," I say.

He smirks. "You haven't figured that out yet?" he asks.

Pompous ass.

"I've been thinking, since you haven't told me, that it is probably something embarrassing," I shoot back. "Maybe a rat. A scrawny one with yellow teeth and a crooked tail."

He laughs at that, and it rings out across the courtyard. A couple of people turn to look at us before going back to their own business.

"No, princess," he says, still chuckling, like he's pleased that he's holding this secret over my head. "I'm not a rat."

We eat in silence, and I flip through another book. Aris offers no further hints as to his animal form, and he looks alternately amused and a little concerned that I haven't figured it out yet. I ponder this, taking my time eating, realizing I don't really like the idea of going back to his room, our room, afterward. I shift on the bench.

"What are you eating?" I ask.

The dining hall is nearly empty this late in the evening. A pair of Water Mages sit by the large stone fireplace, sipping from mugs and vehemently discussing something. A couple of Shields have just left, so other than them, it's empty. My words ring through the open space without the usual hundred or so bodies to muffle them.

"Food," Aris says, raising an eyebrow.

I fight the urge to roll my eyes again—my eyeballs are already feeling sore, and it hasn't even been a full day yet.

"Obviously," I say, gesturing toward his bowl with my spoon.

His bowl is full of mushy-looking grains and miscellaneous veggies. It does not look appetizing. For the first time, I realize that we were given different meals. The pair of Water Mages stand and take their plates back to the entry and deposit them in the receptacle there—plates, like mine. Not bowls of mush like Aris's.

"Is that some sort of special Shield diet?" I ask. If I were a religious person, I'd be thanking the gods for not making me a Shield, if I had to subsist on mush.

"Yes," he says. When he realizes I'm waiting for more, he sighs and puts down his spoon. He leans on his elbows, folding his hands on the table.

"We can go longer without food than Mages or ungifted, so when we do eat, it has to be food that is high in energy. Grains, beans, that kind of thing. Mostly vegetarian. The ungifted sometimes call us *hordearii* because of it, which means 'barley eaters.'"

I snort, and he stops his lecture, cocking his head to one side, waiting for my commentary. Then, out of the corner of my eye, I see Darius and Len enter the dining hall. Darius has a fading scrape along the side of his face, the bruise under his eye a sickly greenish hue. He looks at us and makes his way over.

"You do see the irony there, right?" I ask Aris, deliberately ignoring Darius.

Aris picks up his spoon, putting a giant heap of mush in his mouth. He chews for a long time, staring me down as he does so.

"It's just … you're all predators, and yet you're vegetarian," I say, and out of all the ridiculous things I've learned today, somehow this is the one that makes me laugh.

He raises an eyebrow again, and I think he looks amused.

"A month ago you'd never heard of Mages. Just think of what you'll know in another month," he says. His spoon clatters into the now-empty clay bowl, and he sits back, stretching his arms, rolling his left shoulder.

It's a sobering thought. I chew my own meal—which is decidedly nonvegetarian, and I don't really care, because at least it's not fish—and look at my book, my food, the hall, anywhere but at the sardonic Shield sitting across from me.

"I suppose congratulations are in order," Darius says, coming to a smooth stop near our table.

I glare at him. This whole stupid ordeal is his fault. If it weren't for him, I'd still be in Spit, without these stupid manacles.

"For what?" I ask.

He regards me like he would a child. "Your claim," he says. "No doubt you both considered this pairing carefully. The consequences of your actions, of course, will reverberate throughout your lifetimes. A poor claim leads to a poor partnership."

Len grunts. It is evident that he feels he and Darius are the model pair—hardworking and rule-following and overall righteous assholes.

"You're just sore that she hit you with a rock," Aris says lightly, but I see the clench of his jaw.

I look at the fading bruise on Darius's face—I did that? I vaguely remember seeing him yesterday when I was in the courtyard, with the elemental storm. I remember him trying to hold me back—again. I snort. Serves him right.

"Fortunately, the healers assure me that nothing is severely injured but my pride," Darius says. "I assured Head Mage Saroya that the injury was unintentional on your part, of course. An accident."

"Of course," I echo. I swallow, suddenly feeling a lump in my throat. I did not intend to hurt anyone—what consequences will there be? He is certainly implying that he has the ability to cause trouble for me. Back in Spit, squabbles were brought before the mayor, and punishment was doled out according to his whims. I have no doubt that if Saroya were involved, such a ruling would not bode well for me.

"Still, one would hope you will not be making a habit out of such things," he adds. He picks at an imaginary piece of dirt on his immaculate yellow robe, then discards it.

Aris starts to get up from his bench, but I put a hand on his arm. Surprised, he sits back down, though slowly.

"I'm so glad that you were not gravely injured, Mage Darius," I say. I try to sound bored, but my voice shakes. "I'm sure that Head Mage Saroya's manacle will be effective."

Darius sniffs at the implication that his manacle was not, but he otherwise leaves it alone.

"Just keep her on a leash, will you?" Len tells Aris.

Aris bares his teeth at him, but I still have my hand on his arm.

They leave after a moment, after Len and Aris stare each other down for a few heartbeats.

"You're stronger than he is," Aris says after a moment. He's settled back down.

I realize my hand is still on his arm and snatch it away, feeling my face heat. "What?"

"He's jealous. He knows we're going to eclipse him, and he's pissed because his manacle wasn't strong enough to hold you," Aris says. He fixes that blue stare on me, and for a moment I forget to breathe.

"Yes, well," I say, fiddling with the plate in front of me, averting my eyes. "Um, I'm tired. Can we …?" Anything, anything to get out of this awkward conversation.

He gets up and nods his head toward the door.

Just eating a meal with someone else is strange—how about sleeping in the same room as someone else? I'm so used to being alone. I like it. I realize that I'll never really be alone again, and that makes me feel funny. Like somehow it's nice and also not, at the same time. Like too much is changing too fast. I wonder if Aris would object to sharing the room with my dormice and screech owl friends, and that makes me smile as we walk.

We get back to the room to find a paneled screen folded on my side of the room. Opened up, it makes a nice partition, behind which I can change into my sleep shirt and pants without being seen.

When I come out, I find Aris has shed his shirt—again—and flopped onto his bed. He might already be asleep. I guess he's had an even longer day than I have. I get under my covers, trying to tune out the steady sound of his breathing. It's strange—the snoring of my animal friends never bothered me, but try as I might, I can't stop thinking about the fact that I'm sharing a room with this man, that he's bound himself to me. I'm sure I don't understand the depth of that oath, what it must mean to him, someone who's grown up knowing that this is what is expected of him. I worry that I'm going to let him down, that he's thrown away his second chance on me. I toss and turn for what feels like hours—but finally I sink into sleep.

I wake up in my bed back home. The day is late, and I realize I've overslept, that I'm about to break Rule #3. I scramble up the stairs to light the wick. The door in the wall is open, and through it I hear shouts.

My hands tremble as I go to it. It seems to take an inordinately long time to cross the floor. The sun is setting, and Spit is dark. I see a glowing trail leading up the path to the lighthouse, and it takes a while to come into focus.

It's a stream of people, practically everyone in town, from Delan to Long, the baker, to the farmer whose chickens I traumatized. They're glowing because they're all carrying torches in one hand—and in their other hands are pitchforks, and axes, and swords.

They're coming for me.

The breath catches in my throat. The lighthouse is on a rocky little peninsula, and that road is really the only way in or out. I can try to reach the tree line before they get here, but I'll have to move fast. I can probably lose them in the trees.

I turn, and the oil drums behind me fall, the lids slipping off, the oil spilling in a greasy wave across my feet, across the floor. I watch in horror as it reaches the wick, which is already burning, burning higher than it has any right to. The oil catches, and I can't move, can't breathe, as the flame races across the oil slick, up the walls of the lantern room, across the roof—then I'm surrounded by flames, the thick smoke choking me, forcing its way into my nose and my lungs, until I can't scream, can't breathe—

I wake and realize that I am in fact surrounded by flames.

I roll from the bed and hit the floor, and then I'm being dragged across the room by my shirt. I scrabble and kick—

My tiger. He's here. He's pulling me from the flames, now trickling across from my pillow to the blankets, a flicker of jade green before burning orange and yellow. I see the glimmer of the fire reflected in his eyes. He butts his head against me, satisfied that I am not in danger of combustion, and roars back toward my bed—

Shifting into Aris as he leaps.

He grabs the water pitcher from my desk and douses the flames before folding the blanket in on itself and smothering the last little sparks.

The room goes dark. He throws open a window, and in the moonlight, I can see the smoke trailing out into the night air, the soggy black mess that was my pillow, the scorch marks on the blankets—and the very naked Aris standing in front of me.

I bury my face into my knees and wrap my arms around my head.

"What?" he says.

"Put something on. It's distracting," I mutter, though I peek a little anyway.

He looks down at himself, like he's not sure why I'm so offended, then rolls his eyes and grabs a pair of pants. He does nothing to conceal his bare chest.

"Better?" he asks.

"Not really," I say. I smooth the hair back from my face and look up at him. He's leaning back on my bed. I'm sitting with my back braced against it. Everything is so backward about this situation that I want to laugh or cry, and apparently, my body decides it's just going to do both, and I end up giggling and sniffling and burying my face back into my knees.

Aris is my tiger. My tiger is Aris. Why the hells didn't he tell me? That's how he knew I lived in a lighthouse—it wasn't from gossip; it was because he'd been there. With me. In my bed. Comforted me. Pulled me out of the tornado of my own emotions.

Oh my gods.

“So, are we going to talk about what happened?” he says. His arms are crossed. His jaw is tight. “Or do we expect this to be a nightly occurrence?”

“When were you planning on telling me that you were my tiger?” I counter.

He cocks his head. “*Your* tiger?” he says.

I roll my eyes. Yes, I thought of him—the tiger, not Aris, never Aris—as mine. I have since the day he came into my life. A crazy, miraculous beast who somehow just showed up at my door. *Oh gods*. It’s all coming together now.

“You were wounded, after your Mage died. I sewed up your wounds,” I say.

He nods, and my gaze snags on the jagged scars across his shoulder, marring his muscled chest.

My tongue feels thick from the smoke, and my mouth is dry. I swallow, trying to coax some moisture into my throat so I can speak. “You came to me when I made the storm thing in the courtyard,” I continue. When I was completely out of control, at my lowest, at my worst.

Again he nods.

“Why?”

“No one could get near you,” he says, shrugging. “I knew that the tiger was a form you would trust.”

He was right. I hate it.

“Gods, I hate you,” I mumble, my face in my hands. How did I not see? Those eyes, as blue as the heart of a flame, are the same, whether he is a tiger or a man.

A second later, and his calloused hand is under my chin, gripping it hard, forcing my face up, my eyes to meet his own blazing blue ones.

“No,” Aris says, stern. “No. Words have power, Wren. Until we know what yours is, you will be careful of what you say. Don’t you remember when Saroya ordered you to your room?”

I nod. He’s all Shield now, and not a little intimidating.

“When you say something, even in jest, without control, without knowing whether your magic is active, you could make it true. You could say you hate me; you could make it true, make yourself believe it."

"How do you know I don't?" I say, wrenching my chin from his hand.

He doesn't back up, though. In fact, he smirks, his eyes not leaving mine. "You don't," he says. Then he sits next to me, not quite touching, his arms draped over his knees like mine are. He smells like sweat and smoke. The fire didn't do all that much damage, but my pillow is ash, and my bedding will have to be replaced. Somehow my clothes and my body are untouched. As much hair as I have, I would have expected it to at least be singed, but it's all fine. I pull my braid over my shoulder and toy with the end as I consider everything that just happened.

"We can't tell anyone," I say quietly.

He nods.

I mean, it's not like they can put a third manacle on me, right? I'd have an armful by the end of the month. Not that they seem to be doing much good.

"I know," he says. "We'll say you fell asleep reading and your candle tipped over or something. We'll come up with some excuse."

I stare at my manacles, glinting softly in the moonlight. The room is growing a little lighter, and I guess it will be dawn soon. I stare at the blackened spot on my bed—I shouldn't have been able to do that. It makes no sense.

"What were you dreaming about?" Aris asks.

I look at him—at the puckered red scar on his shoulder, the smaller ones on his ribs, nearly reaching his muscled stomach. The wounds I stitched. I did such a shitty job. I can't believe I didn't see it. It makes me cringe inside, how badly I missed my tiger, his company—how much I wish he were just a tiger and not this infuriating man beside me. How I cried, holding on to him for dear life, that night he came to me here. My face burns. Why *did* he come to me?

"Fire," I say, looking at my hands, at anything instead of the man beside me. "The town where I lived, the people coming to force me out, with torches, and the lighthouse catching fire."

"The fire was green," he says. He frowns. "It was green at the base, before it caught. Like there was an accelerant on your bedding or something."

He leaps up and inspects the bed, the frame, the sheets, and the pillow. He sniffs them, runs a finger over each surface, trying to detect a hint of fumes, a trace of powder, but comes up with nothing.

"Has this happened before?" he asks.

I feel like combusting myself, like I really might just explode. I'm so pissed at everything. What will happen the next time I feel like taking a nap? Will I cause an earthquake? A monsoon?

"No," I say. My voice cracks. "None of this has happened before. Is this how magic normally manifests? Is any of this normal?" The volume in my voice is going up and up, and I stand. I can't be in this room anymore. I need air, and space, and I can't, I can't, I can't be in the same room as him right now. I want my tiger, not Aris.

"Where are you going?" he asks, jumping up.

I grab my shoes and my robe and head for the door. "Out!"

He grabs a shirt and runs after me, dressing as he goes.

"You are not coming with me," I say, whirling on him.

"Yes, I am," he says.

"No," I say, and turn. He grabs my arm, and I wrench it away. "No!"

"I am your Shield!" he thunders. He's close now, so close that his breath heats my face. "Where you go, I go."

"I don't need you to protect me!" I shout back. And that may or may not be true. I reach the courtyard and feel like I want to run.

"What did I just tell you about watching your words?" he yells back. "Maybe everyone else needs protection from you!"

I whirl on him, and he nearly runs into me. He's mad, seething mad, and normally, he'd be intimidating, but now I'm mad as all the hells too.

"Argh! You're infuriating! I cannot believe I let you sleep with me!" I scream at him. And I realize, belatedly, that we're not alone in the courtyard, and that maybe my words may be … misinterpreted.

There are a few other Shields around, getting ready for early-morning exercises. One of them stops and stares at us. I think it's one of Aris's friends, the one who yelled at him for picking me yesterday.

"Lovers' quarrel?" the "friend" says.

I throw my hands up and scream again.

This time, when I head for the gates, Aris doesn't follow. This time, the guards don't stop me.

Chapter 18: Aris

When she screams, the air shakes. When she stomps her foot, the ground trembles.

I'm in way over my head.

And Vassilis's smart-ass comments are really not helping my mood right now.

"I have to say, she's not your usual type, but her curves are just so …"

I glare at him, and he stops. For a second. His hands are paused in midair, outlining an hourglass shape. I mean, he's not wrong, but that's beside the point. I turn and watch Wren vanish into the dawn beyond the wall, practically trembling with fury.

Shit.

"Look," Vassilis starts, putting a hand on my shoulder. "Let's grab a drink tonight. You can tell me about what's going on here."

I shrug him off. "No more alcohol," I say. My body tingles, feeling a pull, hearing a bell chime—I need to go after her. I should go after her. She doesn't want me to, but I should. Her power seems to overwhelm the manacles when she's emotional, and she's very emotional right now.

"Wow, one night with her, and she's got you whipped, huh?" Vassilis says.

I've had it.

I turn and punch him in the jaw.

It knocks him off-balance, but he doesn't go down. Vassilis is a natural fighter, and he sinks into a crouch immediately. We circle. I'm so worked up; beating up Vassilis seems to be a good outlet for all the pent-up energy that's surging through me. He doesn't seem to mind—he's grinning like a fool. Somehow that smug look on his face just makes me madder.

Vassilis jabs. I feint. And we exchange a series of blows as the sun rises over the walls. After a moment, I get him into a headlock, and he raises a hand, yielding.

I'm panting hard, but the exertion feels good. I release him.

"Better?" he asks, rubbing his jaw.

"Better," I say, wiping a thin sheen of sweat from my face.

"So … what? No more drinking?" Vassilis looks over at Kemp's.

"I can't do anything that might slow down my reflexes with her around," I say, looking in the direction Wren went. I need to go after her. "No alcohol."

"All right," he says, shaking out his shoulder. "All right. I get it. You've got a Mage now. Things are different."

"Everything is different," I say. I clap him on the shoulder. Vassilis might be an ass, but if I could claim anyone as a friend, it would be him.

"No gambling either?" he asks, looking hopeful.

I shake my head.

"Well, go on then, killjoy." He nods toward the gate. "Go do your Shieldly duty."

I find her sitting next to the river, where I took her a few days ago. She's sitting and tossing a handful of pebbles into the slow-moving water, watching the ripples disperse before throwing another one. The air seems to quiver and vibrate around her, but I still feel the tug, the claim, pulling me toward her.

I shift.

Chapter 19: Wren

Thoughts are screaming through my head, whirling like the tornado I made. I throw rocks into the river, each one another thought, another crazy thing spinning through my brain.

Toss.

Aris is my tiger. He is my Shield, and I'm barely starting to grasp what that means. He thinks I'm going to save him somehow, restore him to his former glory. The only upside to this is that it means he'll help me, because it'll mean helping him too. I feel a mix of frustration and anxiety about this. I realize I don't want to let him down. I realize that he's been my friend for a while.

Toss. Splash. A fish jumps, probably pissed that I am throwing stones instead of breadcrumbs. The water ripples from his movement before the current sweeps it away.

So I have magic. I don't know why it's decided to rear its ugly head now, and I don't really comprehend what this is going to mean for the rest of my life. I wonder if it's because I grew up in Spit. Like there wasn't anyone else with magic there, so my magic just isn't going to manifest the same. Like it didn't have anyone to learn from, so it's just a little wild. I like the idea of having magic, I think. It means I can learn to protect myself, and maybe other people too. There's a whole world I'm just starting to uncover—maybe I can make candles like the ones in the library. I feel a tingle of anticipation as I wonder what other things I'll be able to do. I can't even begin to imagine. It kind of feels like I'm standing back in the lantern room again, at the outer-wall door of my lighthouse, looking down and down at the ground below. Like I'm about to fall—or fly.

Toss.

I just hope I don't keep setting Aris's room on fire. It's hard to think of it as "our" room. At least I have a screen now. I don't know if I'll ever get over how the people here are so open about nudity, like the body is nothing to be ashamed of.

Toss.

I hear four heavy paws tread through the grasses behind me. I feel like he's intentionally making noise, since he's usually so silent, so sneaky. Like he doesn't want to scare me. My tiger is my friend. Aris is … I'm not sure yet.

Toss.

I sigh and turn. He's sitting in the grasses a few feet behind me, tail switching. He's a magnificent tiger, sleek and powerful and beyond beautiful. His eyes, though—they're Aris's eyes, as blue as the sky. I pat the ground next to me, and he comes to me. I lean on him, enjoying the warmth, the softness of his fur. I realize that I feel like they're two separate entities—I'd never, ever lean on Aris this way, never seek comfort from him like this, but it feels natural with my tiger.

"I like you better this way," I say.

He lets out a rolling *whuff* sound.

"Also, you can't talk right now, which is a nice change."

He looks at me and bares his teeth. I smack his foreleg lightly, and he stops. This close, he smells earthy, woody, a little like pine. I breathe it in. Then he stretches and lies down beside me, his massive head by my knee. I stroke his head, scratching lightly behind his ears. He likes this. The motion soothes me too, and for a long while, I just watch the river and hold my tiger, and I feel the anxiety and frustration leaking out of me like water through a sieve. I stretch my legs out, just enjoying the moment, the winter sun warming my face, the sound of the river in front of me. My tiger lets out a long breath, like a sigh, rolling his head against my thigh in a very catlike way, as if to say, *Please keep going*.

"What, do you want me to rub your belly too? Get you some string or something to play with?" I ask, but the bite is gone from my voice.

He rolls over and wiggles, offering an expanse of fluffy white stomach.

I roll my eyes, but I can't keep the smile from my face.

"I'm sorry," I say. "About earlier."

He flips back over and dips his head, as if to say, *Me too*.

After a while, he gets up and goes back into the grasses. A moment later, Aris comes back, fully clothed. He sits by me, but not nearly as close as he did before. I think about reaching out to see if he likes me playing with his hair in this form too, and I feel heat rising to my face.

"Why didn't you shift back to your human form after you were injured?" I ask. I keep my eyes on the muddy water in front of me. I wrap my arms around my knees, to keep my hands out of trouble.

"I don't think I could," he says.

I sneak a glance—he's frowning.

"I think I tried, at first," he says. "I … I went a little wild."

"What's that mean?" I ask. I hear his breath hitch in his chest.

"When Stefan died, I couldn't think straight," he says after a minute. "After the battle, I was … just overwhelmed with the emotions. I could feel our bond snap, and I don't remember much after that."

He's clenching his jaw. His body is tense, like he's ready to jump up and run.

"A lot of the time—most of the time, a Shield can't handle the loss of a bond. We just … fade. But I could feel your magic, even then," he says, looking at me. "I was miles away, but I felt it. You were just … hemorrhaging magic. Whatever magic you have, it called to me, in my animal form. The tiger in me just took over, like it knew what to do, how to find help, how to find you."

I picture my lighthouse, picture my magic leaking into the air around me, like blood in water, dispersing. I shudder.

"Once I was with you, your magic was … overwhelming. It wasn't until I started healing that I could exert control over my animal form, and by then … well, I figured shifting back would traumatize you, with your prudish ways."

He's teasing me.

I roll my eyes again, which seems to satisfy him.

"So I left," he says. "The farther away I got, the clearer my mind became. I could feel your pull, though, for miles. And then, when I saw you here … After I saw you had the manacle, I tried shifting one night, to see if I could still feel your magic. I hadn't shifted since I'd left you. I didn't trust that I wouldn't go wild again, that something wasn't … broken, inside me. Like letting the tiger take over was a way to keep me from feeling the shame, the impotence, to keep me from missing Stefan."

"You came to me," I say.

He swallows and nods. "Even with the manacle, I could feel it. I could barely resist it. I didn't mean to come to you then, but you were crying, and emotional, and I think that the manacle just somehow couldn't contain you."

My face warms. I was emotional that night. Is it my emotions that somehow trigger the magic? I'm not sure. I do know that my tiger has seen all my sadness, my vulnerability, all the things I keep inside. I don't know how to reconcile Aris and my tiger in my head. I don't know what to do with the fact that he saw me crying like a hysterical little girl—and didn't run away.

"With two manacles," he continues, "it's a lot less strong. I don't know if the other Shields feel it when they shift, if they understand that it's coming from you."

"So … when my manacles come off, and you shift, what will happen?" I ask.

He shakes his head. "I have no idea. I might not be in control—if I shift, and your magic is out, I might be forced to come to you, whatever else I'm doing."

I've got to get this under control. Aris could just not shift—ever again?—but that isn't really an option. I need these manacles off.

I stand, brushing the sand off my pants. He watches me, cocking his head.

"Well? Let's get to work," I say.

He grins, and I swear his canines look longer than usual. He jumps up, all feline grace. I can't believe I didn't see it before.

"Whatever you say, princess."

We go back to the library. Technically, classes are in session, and I should be learning about the history of the school with all the other new Mages—but since none of the teachers seem to give a damn, I want to go back to the books. We go back to the table we used the day before, and I settle in to read while Aris goes in search of more material. He returns with yet another book, and a small bag.

"What's this?" I ask, but I can smell the warm bread already, and my stomach roars in response.

"Breakfast," he says, and he takes bread, cheese, apples, and a flask of water—at least, I hope it is water—from the bag.

I munch away happily for a minute while he glances through the book he's brought. He props his feet up on the table, leaning back in the chair.

"Did you already eat?" I ask around a mouthful of apple. Gods, the food here is so good, even the simple things. Or maybe the food on the Spit was just that bad, which is entirely possible.

"Don't need to, remember?" he says, flipping a page.

I chew, considering. "Is that a Shield thing or an Aris thing?" I ask.

Aris glances up, one eyebrow raised. I stare back.

"A Shield thing," he says.

"What else?" I ask, taking a sip of water. Thankfully, yes, it is water. I was worried it was going to be his ash drink or something.

"What else?" he asks. "I don't need to sleep as much as an ungifted, or a Mage. I can run for days without needing to stop. I'm stronger than you, faster than you. I heal faster."

"All Shields do?" I ask.

He nods.

"Why didn't your shoulder heal better?" I ask.

He frowns. "It's fine."

"It's not," I counter. "You favor it. Is it because of my stitches?"

Aris realizes then that I'm asking because I feel guilty about it, not because I'm questioning his healing ability, which would be like insulting his ego or something equally fragile.

"I heal faster than you, but not perfectly," he says, carefully. "It was a bad wound. Without your help, I could have bled out. Without your help, I might have gone gray."

It's not a thank-you, but I think it's the closest I'll get.

"How did you know you were a Shield?" I ask.

He frowns. "The gift typically runs in families," he says, but doesn't elaborate.

"Are your family all tigers too?" I ask.

"You ask a lot of questions," he grumbles.

"You'd better get used to it," I say. I open my mouth to—yes—ask another question, but I'm interrupted when a librarian comes to our table with some more books for us.

Aris seems relieved.

But he's got me thinking. If magic runs in families, then where did mine come from? I never really knew my mother, but I think my father would have mentioned if she'd had magic. And he didn't have any … right? I think back. I try not to think about him too often—it kind of feels like ripping a scab off a barely closed wound. Valeri was a lot of things, but magic he was not. He was quiet and funny and hardworking. He was kind. He liked to read and taught me how—I think just so I'd be quiet for a little bit and give him some peace. He was fair-skinned—nightlife suited him, since he was always getting burned by the sun—with light brown hair and my greenish eyes. My mother was dark-skinned, and their complexions blended in me like cream in coffee, so my father always said. I have a single memory of her—or maybe it was a dream. It's hard to say. Whenever I think of her, I always picture her surrounded by silvery light, glowing like the moon.

She was from the Isles, the islands to the northeast of Spit. I don't know much else about her—my father didn't like to talk about her. I have her curly hair. I know that. But is it possible she had some magic in her blood? Do I have magical cousins out on the Isles somewhere?

I think about my parents for a while, then fight back a sniffle and return to my books. I eventually find some chapters on magical families. Aris is right. Not every child of a Mage or Shield inherits their abilities, but most do. It is rare for a new gift to emerge from a previously nonmagic family, and this is usually attributed to infidelity, but it does happen occasionally. There doesn't seem to be a rhyme or reason for it. One of the chapters talks about it being "the will of the gods," which I've never been much of a believer in. Another chapter talks about magic like it is its own being, has its own sentience, and chooses whom to bestow powers on. The chapter gets very esoteric from there, so I flip through the next bit.

After a while, the librarian comes back. Aris looks up from the book he is reading. The librarian glares at his booted feet, propped up on the table. Aris raises an eyebrow but otherwise doesn't move.

"The Head Mage requests your presence—immediately," the man says. He is older, wearing a dark robe, like he wants to blend in with the dim library.

I look at Aris, who shrugs.

He takes his feet off the table and gestures for me to follow him. "Saroya is not a patient person," he says.

"*Head Mage* Saroya Asprenas," the librarian hisses quietly.

Aris doesn't acknowledge him. "Unless you want to spend the next year quacking like a duck instead of talking, we shouldn't make her wait," he says.

I can't tell if he's joking, but he's walking fast, so I chase after him.

Chapter 20: Aris

Saroya's office is imposing—just like her—but the similarities stop there. Two massive doors bar the entry and are guarded by two Mages. They swing the doors open as we approach.

I've never particularly liked her office. The school is not one for pageantry. We're used to a certain sparse lifestyle; we don't care much for material things. We move too much to be weighed down by anything that isn't weapons or armor.

Saroya's office makes my room feel opulent by comparison. It's all gray stone, down to the carved desk she sits behind. There are no cushions on the chairs, no drapes to keep out the drafts from the windows, no fireplace. It's like she wanted to make the room as uncomfortable as possible, so that people wouldn't want to linger. I have no idea how she spends all day in here.

I enter, Wren trailing behind me. She's quiet, which at first seems nice. Her mouth is set into a hard line, like she's holding something back. I wonder how much of my time as her Shield will be holding *her* back, rather than protecting her. It's an interesting thought.

Saroya gestures to some chairs opposite her desk, and I sit. I nod at Wren, who reluctantly sits as well. She's sitting ramrod straight, her back not touching the back of the chair, like she might bolt at any second.

Saroya's presence is nearly overwhelming in this space. With her bright yellow robe, she seems like a sun, at odds with the gray of her office. The very air feels thick, hot.

There's a letter on her desk, with a thick red wax seal, broken. I recognize it immediately. She sees me looking at it and nods.

"I have a letter from King Leonidas," she says, resting her hand on the paper.

Wren squirms a little in her chair and tucks her hands into her pockets, obscuring the manacles.

"The Shield Commander has apparently written to his friends at the capital. They want you there, for … testing," Saroya continues, like it's nothing, like she's sending us on a minor errand instead of miles and miles across the continent to the Golden City.

Wren looks at me, but I am at a loss. Is *this* Markos's idea of helping? I regret ever going to him.

"You're sending her away," I say.

Saroya turns the force of her glare on me, and I feel like I might melt, like ice under a hot sun. I don't like the feeling.

"The king commands it," she says, lightly, like she's not ready to smite me where I sit.

"You want to send her, untrained, to be in the presence of the most powerful man on the continent? How is this a good idea?" I ask.

Wren shoots me a glance, but I don't look at her.

"Whether I agree or not, the king doesn't need to explain himself to me. Neither, apparently, does the Shield Commander," she says. She touches the letter, and whips of wind shred it into pieces so small they form a pile of dust on her desk. She waves her hand, and a breeze whisks the dust out the window.

Wren has no idea what she's capable of—none of us do. The school at least has walls and can provide some protection while she figures this out. The road to the capital is long, and not without dangers. People die on the road all the time. And what if she makes another tornado—or something worse—when we're in the capital? Saroya might put her in cuffs, but the king could put her in a dungeon. This is a terrible idea.

I look at Wren. A faint tremor goes through her, but she's just staring at Saroya. I wonder if she has any idea what we're getting into.

"When do we leave?" she asks, like she's hoping the answer is going to be a week, a month. Longer. Time to spend in the library, time to formulate a plan.

"In the morning," Saroya says. "A caravan is headed that way, and you can travel with it." She rests her hands on the desk. In the absolute silence of this stone room—one that is feeling more and more like a prison—the sound of her fingers drumming is deafening.

My pulse thunders in my ears. In one fell swoop, Saroya is getting rid of both of us. It's probably a dream come true for her, to get us out of the school. The tarnished Shield and the undeclared Mage, blights on her otherwise spotless record.

Wren just nods, her face impassive and pale.

"What does the king want with her?" I ask. My hands ache from clenching so hard. I don't like the road to the capital. I don't like traveling with a caravan. Just me and my Mage, fine—if that Mage is trained so I don't have to babysit the entire time. Stefan and I traveled the road just fine. We encountered bandits, trolls, and wolves but didn't get so much as a scratch. The caravan, while possibly affording Wren some minor amount of protection, will slow us down and make us easier targets. But like all the hells am I going to let Wren take this journey alone.

"I'm sure I have no idea," Saroya says. Then her face softens. "King Leonidas has Mages from all over the continent at the capital. It may be that one of them is more … suited to the task of helping you," she says to Wren.

Something lights up in Wren's eyes, making them glow like jade.

It's hope.

Saroya might be kicking us out, but she's also offering hope—which is suspicious, like dangling a carrot in front of a surly mule. Either Saroya is unimpressed with Wren and therefore has no problem kicking her out—unlikely—or she has no idea how to handle her and wants to palm her off to someone else.

"All right," Wren says. Her mind is made up. She'll take that bait instantly, that shred of hope that Saroya's offering. She wants answers. She wants control. And I will go where she goes. She has no desire for glory, like I do, no reputation to rebuild, like I do, but I feel that we're headed in the same direction.

She looks at me. "Let's go."

Wren wants to go back to the library, to soak up what she can before we hit the road. I don't think we'll be able to smuggle more than a few books in our saddlebags without being noticed, so I tell her to be discreet. She gives me a sly smile as she slips away.

I head to Tulliano's forge. He hasn't had time to make my helmet yet, but I have new leathers and a pair of gleaming gladiuses waiting for me. He shows them to me like they're his newborn children. The swords are light and sing when I swing them through the air, cutting the very breeze with their razor-sharp edges. He has scabbards for me too, and a round shield. I settle it into place on my back through its strap, feeling whole again. To be a Shield without a shield has just felt wrong.

The rest of the day is a blur. I have to get some warmer clothes for both of us for the trip, have to go to the stables and make sure we have horses to take us. I pick out a placid mare for Wren, unsure of her horsemanship. I keep busy with the preparations, trying not to think too much.

Trying not to think of the last time I made this trip, with Stefan.

Besides the fact that the weather is notoriously unpredictable most of the year, we were also set upon by a pack of Fremulon wolves, beasts larger and meaner than their common cousins. It is not an experience I want to repeat. It was a story Stefan loved telling the women at the palace, though, and they ate up every word.

I make it back to our room around dusk. Wren is there, and she's bathed. She's unbraided her hair, and it forms this cape of partially dried curls down her back. She's got books, maybe dozens, all over her bed, opened to various pages.

"This is discreet?" I ask.

She grins and reaches for a candle. "I asked the librarian for one of these too," she says, and I realize she's holding one of the spelled heatless candles from the library. "You're right—they like to be helpful."

"So," I say, settling myself at her desk. "You're all right with all this? Going to the capital? Being summoned?"

She shrugs. "I've been kicked out of my lighthouse. I'm being kicked out of this school. Do you want to bet that they won't kick me out of the capital too?" she asks. She's grinning, but she's not laughing about it. There's fear there, uncertainty. She wants to belong somewhere. It's a hunger that I understand.

"I won't be taking that bet," I say, trying to keep the mood light.

Her face falls, and she looks down at the tome in her lap. "What's the road like?" she asks.

I cross my arms, considering. "Bad" is the word that I settle on. "Probably a week of riding, maybe eight days if the weather turns, which it usually does. We'll be with a caravan of some ungifted on their way to a different town, so we'll have company except on the last day or two. The worst bit is in the middle—most of the continent is pretty wild, you know, so all kinds of things like to hide out in the forest there. Bandits, trolls, wolves."

Her face pales.

"Can you handle a weapon?" I ask.

Wren shakes her head and looks down at her manacles, gleaming in the light of her spelled candle. She'll be worthless on the road as far as protection goes.

"Do you want to learn?" I ask.

She looks up, surprised.

I shrug. "Until you get your magic under control, you're helpless," I say.

She narrows her eyes at me.

"Don't deny it. It's true. Other Mages can defend themselves plenty by the time they make this trip. I don't think throwing your shoes counts."

She eyes the gladiuses on my bed, but I shake my head.

"Oh, no," I say. "We'll get you a dagger or something from Tulliano in the morning, and I'll show you how to use it. And a shield, maybe. We can practice on the way."

She considers, then nods.

Wren keeps reading as I get our packs organized. I head down to the baths, and I don't take long, but by the time I come back, she's sound asleep, a book on her lap and another open in her hand. A curl has fallen over her face and flutters when she breathes.

I go to blow out the spelled candle, but it won't go out. I realize I have no idea how to turn the damn thing off, so I just leave it burning on her desk. I move the hair off her face so she won't suffocate in her sleep, and go back to my side of the room.

Sleep does not come easily. I'm not sure what Wren will be like on the road, what to expect from her magic. I think of the swamp in Aclines, and the sudden volley of arrows that bounced off Stefan's wall of air. Wren has no such technique. I figure the best thing to do, since I can't teach her magic, is to at least teach her to defend herself. My next thought keeps niggling at my brain—*In case I fail again.*

I want to get out of this room, maybe go for a run, or see if Dimitra's forgiven me yet. Then Wren turns over in her bed, snuggling down under the blanket, an uneasy sigh escaping her.

What if I leave and she catches fire again?
So I stay, and I watch, and I wait.

Chapter 21: Wren

I wake up to the sound of Aris throwing things around. I thought he was a morning person, but maybe not. It feels strange to me, sleeping through the night instead of through the day, but I guess that's not the only thing in my world that's turned completely upside down lately.

Dawn light is streaming through the windows, and I stretch, letting it bathe my face in warmth. It's going to be a beautiful day. I can't wait to leave this place, with its stone walls that make it feel more like a prison than a school.

Aris has changed. He's wearing pants, instead of that ridiculous leather thing that shows off just how muscular his legs are, and a long shirt and a vest. He sees me assessing him, assessing his new clothes, and he tosses me a bundle—nearly identical clothing for me, in greens and browns instead of black, like his, albeit in a smaller size. He comes over and deliberately, gently, places a pair of boots on my bed. I look at him, and he smirks, drawing my attention to his mouth.

"Thought these might hurt if I threw them at you," he says.

I roll my eyes and go to my privacy screen to change, only briefly considering chucking a sock or two at him.

We otherwise get ready in silence. I stash a few books in the pack he gives me and put a finger on the wick of my spelled candle, like the librarian showed me. It doesn't burn me, but the candle immediately snuffs out, and I put that in my pack too.

Other than that, I have nothing. I assume the school will let me keep my undyed robe, and it seems it could be cold on the road, so I put that on too and braid back my hair. Aris tosses me an apple as he heads out the door, and I take a big bite as I follow.

The courtyard is still pretty quiet this early. A few Shields are headed to the arena, and Geoff meows loudly at us before racing off somewhere. Aris points me in the direction of the stables, while he heads to the forges. I wonder what it will feel like, fighting with a dagger. I think about how he moved in the arena, all molten grace and strength. Physically, I guess I'm strong enough, but I've never hit a thing in my life. I've never feared for my life. It's a sobering thought.

I swallow the chunk of apple that seems suddenly lodged in my throat and head to the stables. A man has a pair of horses saddled and ready to go—a tall dappled gray with feathering on his legs for Aris, a sweet-looking brown mare for me.

Then there's some shouting inside the stables. They're big enough for dozens of horses. I've seen some of the Shields training on them, big war stallions that are weapons themselves. I stroke the nose of the brown mare, and she smells the scent of apple on my hand. Her lips tickle my palm as she looks for the source.

And then the shouting intensifies, and I hear a thud of metal and a rattling chain, and out of the stable thunders a massive black horse, charging like an avalanche, his shoes clanging against the stones so hard they send up sparks.

He's not just black; he's as dark as night, without a trace of white on him. A crowd of people is chasing after him, rattling bridles and chains. If he takes off, who knows when they'll catch this beast? I bet he'll crash right through the school's gates, maybe take a portion of the wall with him.

So I step in front of him to stop him. I raise my hands, and the manacles glint in the early sunlight. I realize, belatedly, that I have no power over animals anymore. No strength in me that calms and gentles them, not with my shackles on.

I'm about to get trampled by two thousand pounds of angry black stallion. At least this time, when my life flashes before my eyes, it's a little more interesting.

But then, the horse stops.

He stops so suddenly he nearly sits down on his haunches to keep from bowling me over. He looks down at me, huffing and snorting, tossing his head, like I'm a barrier he can't cross. His shoulder is taller than me, and his feet are the size of plates, stomping and pawing.

"It's all right," I say. I see the men chasing him slam to a stop too, watching him, watching me. I think I hear someone calling my name from far away, but I keep my eyes on this horse.

His ears prick forward, catching my words. He dips his head, and I pull the half-eaten apple from my pocket. He accepts it, crunching it, his breath warm across my hand. I put my hand on his nose, stroking the swirl of hair up and up until my palm is between his eyes, as black and depthless as the sea. He closes his eyes and butts my chest with his head. I'm glad I'm holding on to his neck, because otherwise I would have fallen from his gentle nudge.

"What in the name of all the gods …?" someone says.

I look around the stallion, at the man speaking. He's covered in straw and has a bridle in his hands. When he moves, it jingles, and the stallion flattens his ears against his head again.

He doesn't want to be chained either. And he's willing to fight for his freedom. I like this about him.

There's a large bucket a few feet away, and I lead him to it, one hand on his nose. I step up and slide onto his back.

He tosses his head, sending his long black mane flying as he prances beneath me. He's magnificent, the embodiment of freedom. He should be flying across a wide-open field somewhere, not stuck within these walls with these men, who only want to tame him.

I swear he can hear my thoughts. I feel his muscles bunch, and then he's rearing up, striking out with his hooves, a challenge to the men who are still standing there, watching him. I clench my thighs against him and grab his mane so I don't slide off, and I can't help it—I laugh.

Chapter 22: Aris

I send Wren to the stables as I head to Tulliano's to see if he's got a knife or something I can get for her, something so she can learn some basic self-defense. I'm just tucking the dagger he's given me into my belt when I hear a commotion, shouts and a thundering of hooves across the courtyard.

I spent all night watching her, and she didn't so much as spark. I gambled that she couldn't get into much trouble in five minutes without me.

As usual, per my shitty run of luck, I bet wrong.

I turn and see one of the warhorses bearing down on Wren, a literal ton of menacing horseflesh intent on trampling her into the dirt.

I've seen men bigger and stronger than her, in full armor, fall to those hooves. It's not pretty.

I'm halfway across the courtyard before I realize the horse has stopped.

He's stopped, and he's eating an apple from her hand like he's a damn bunny rabbit.

I stop. The men chasing the horse stop. The whole damn world stops.

I can see Wren's manacles from here, glinting silver on her wrists. She has no access to her magic. When I shifted the other day, I could feel the pull, but it wasn't as strong as it had been at the lighthouse, certainly not strong enough to bring a charging warhorse to heel.

I see the next sequence of events like it's slowed down, like time itself is taking notice of her now and wants to savor every second. She gets up on the horse's back, and the animal prances beneath her, like he's trying to show off. She's smiling, and then he rears up, his front hooves striking at the sky.

The rising sun chooses this moment to break over the walls of the school. The beams hit her and the horse, bathing them both in morning radiance. He's neighing out a challenge, like he's screaming it to the whole world, and she's clinging to him, her head thrown back, and she's laughing, laughing like it's the most exciting thing in the world, and I realize she's not at all afraid of him, has no idea that he could kill her with a single hoof strike. Or she just doesn't care.

He calms, and she's still smiling, stroking his neck and talking to him like he can understand her, and maybe he can, because his ears are flicking back, heeding her words. I approach, and so do the stablemen, with something like awe on their faces. I recognize it, because I'm sure I have the same look on my face.

Wren sees me, and her smile melts away, the gleaming radiance fading into normal, cool morning sunshine.

"What?" she asks, her hand still on the stallion's neck.

I clear my throat. This is going to be a long, long trip. We aren't even out of the damn school yet, and she's turning everything upside down.

I extend a hand to help her down, and she takes it, sliding off the warhorse. She doesn't take her other hand off him, though. She strokes his neck, and he tosses his head, enjoying her touch. I can't help the growl that escapes me. He snorts, eyeing me, and a front hoof paws the dirt, as if in challenge.

"Competitive asshole," Wren murmurs, shooting me a glance.

"Mage, I'll be taking over from here," one of the stablemen says, approaching the stallion.

The stallion's ears flatten onto his skull. He does not like this man.

"I don't remember seeing this one in the arena," I say, and the stableman flicks his gaze to me only briefly, like he's afraid the horse might bolt any second.

"He's new," he says. There's sweat running down his red face, but his hands are white where they clench the bridle. "Name's Obsidian."

"Obsidian," Wren whispers, still stroking the stallion's neck.

He snorts, tossing his head, as if to say, *Yes, yes, that is my name*.

"It suits him."

"Aye," the man says. "Black as all the hells and dangerous to boot. Now, Mage, if you'll step aside, I can take him from here. I appreciate you … catching him."

Wren's hand lingers on the black velvet of the stallion's neck. Obsidian looks at the man like he'll turn the stable fence into matchsticks if he tries anything. I've got to get Wren out of here before she attracts any more attention.

"Why is he here?" she asks, looking at me. Her eyes are round and shining, pleading, in ways that she will not give voice to.

"Training," I say after a second. "The king sends us horses a few times a year. We train them for battle, and we send them back to the capital. It's good for the Shields to learn to break a horse."

It is the wrong thing to say. I know as soon as the word *break* leaves my mouth that I'm in trouble. Her mouth settles into the hard line that I'm beginning to recognize.

"We're headed to the capital," she says, looking at the stableman. "Can't we take him with us?"

I roll my eyes. No way. I have an unpredictable girl to look after; I am not going to take some half-wild warhorse with me too. I will not allow this.

"No," I say, shaking my head. "Absolutely not."

Which is how, a half hour later, I find myself riding out of the School of the Silver Flame, headed for the capital, me on my gray stallion, and Wren on Obsidian, smiling like the sun.

Chapter 23: Wren

Aris doesn't talk to me for a long time.

But it's a glorious day, and I refuse to let his broodiness ruin it. It's one of those rare mornings when the air is cool and crisp but the sunshine is warm, and a light breeze ruffles my hair with fingers as soft as owl feathers. I'm leaving the musty old school and its rules and scary-ass headmistress, and I'm headed toward the capital—where, maybe, someone will help me get these damn manacles off and figure out how I am to wield my magic. I fight the urge to fling my arms wide and embrace the whole world.

Obsidian is a perfect gentleman. He doesn't wear a bridle, but he follows Aris easily. He did let me put a light saddle on him, though, so he can carry my pack, and so I have less chance of accidentally sliding off. I call it a compromise. Aris called it something else, whispered under his breath in a pissy tone.

The road winds out of the school and down the hill, and I feel like I can breathe again. We head down the road a few miles before we meet up with a caravan of horses and wagons and carriages, maybe twenty people in all, coming from the south. I note uneasily that there are no children in the caravan.

A short man on a tall, leggy roan comes up to us, raising a hand in greeting. He wears a long leather coat, with a thin saber at his belt. He introduces himself as Gaspar and reassures us that he's made this crossing hundreds of times and has only lost a handful of travelers. I don't find that particularly comforting.

"I'd appreciate it if you'd ride at the back, Shield," he says, and looks at my undyed robe. "Some folks get nervous around magic, especially with an untrained Mage. And I could use a good set of eyes there." He looks admiringly at Aris's sheathed swords, and his hand drifts to the hilt of his own.

Aris nods, and we take our place at the rear of their dusty procession, our horses walking easily at the slow pace. I get a few strange looks from the other travelers, who gawk openly at Obsidian and my undyed robe. I do my best to ignore them. We could go faster alone, but Aris has said it isn't safe. I'm not really sure what to expect, but if it has Aris scared, I guess I should be too.

The passing countryside is all smooth, rolling grassy knolls as we leave the valley. Long grass as far as I can see, interrupted only by the ruts of the road.

"Are you going to give me the silent treatment the whole way?" I ask Aris after a few hours of stalemate.

"Depends. Are you going to keep doing stupid shit and putting your life in danger?" he spits out.

I frown. "I wasn't in any danger."

He pulls up his horse, sidling up until his horse slams into Obsidian, his thigh pressed against my leg. "He is a warhorse!" he shouts, unleashing his pent-up anger. He stabs me in the chest with a finger. "He could have killed you!"

"But he didn't," I say, pushing down his hand.

Obsidian bobs his head, as if in agreement. He seems unperturbed at being pushed around by Aris's horse, Flint.

"How did you know your manacles wouldn't work?" Aris asks. He's a little quieter now and pulls Flint apart from me.

"Maybe I am just good with animals," I counter.

He rolls his eyes. I stick out my tongue at him.

"And when we get to the capital? He'll go back to the royal stables to be trained. He's not a pet, Wren," he says. His blue eyes are flashing.

"Maybe he'll be happier there too," I counter.

He rolls his eyes again and doesn't talk to me for another few hours.

I wonder if Aris is going to strain something in his eye sockets, the way he keeps doing that. I think he's starting to regret this arrangement of ours, and that's fine. I'm used to doing things on my own, in my own way. I've gotten by for years without help—no reason for me to start needing it now. I've got a plan, which is what matters. Make it to the capital, meet the Mages there, get my manacles off. I don't need him. If I think it enough, maybe I'll even start to believe it. Maybe I should say it out loud and see if my magic makes it come true. I purse my lips tightly and focus on the road ahead.

We make camp around nightfall. We keep back a little from the caravan, make our own fire. I think Aris is afraid that I might go up in flames or something again and doesn't want the others to get in the way.

Making a fire is something I'm pretty good at, at least. I've had a lot of practice with the lighthouse. Aris gathers some logs, and I clear a space in the grass. It's open here, out on the grasslands. I like it after the oppressive school, even if it is a little monotonous.

I grab the flint and steel from my pack and get a fire going. Aris is clearly used to this kind of travel—he's efficient and moves quickly. I mimic his steps. There's a lot to do, with taking care of the horses and getting settled for the night, but after a while, things quiet, and it's just us, sitting on opposite sides of the fire, lost in our own thoughts.

A little brown bird flits down from the sky and lands on my knee. I don't recognize what kind she is, but she reminds me of the finches back home … back on the Spit. She regards me with bright black eyes and offers a chirp of greeting. She's a cheeky thing, and I like her. I stroke her soft breast, and she trills.

"Aren't you pretty," I say to her.

She agrees.

"Do you always talk to animals?"

It's the first thing Aris has said to me in hours beyond "get that" or "take this" or other such orders.

"I do," I say, meeting his eyes over the embers. His eyes reflect the firelight, like the flame is inside him. Something is building in the air over the fire. Like the air there has become sharper, clearer, different. I clear my throat. "She says your boots are going to catch fire if you keep your feet that close to the flames," I say, shifting my eyes from his. It's a lie, of course. She's not saying anything, other than "*Chirp-chirp*."

He raises an eyebrow. "What? My feet are cold," he says.

The night air is crisp, and I can tell it's going to be a chilly one. He can burn up his damn boots if he wants to. I pull my robe tighter around me, and my little bird friend flies off. Aris is leaning back against his pack, arms crossed, looking relaxed, but the flames continue to flicker in his eyes as he regards me. I wonder what is going through his head, then decide maybe I don't want to know.

"I'm tired," I say after a moment, and get my bedroll. I lay it out near the fire, and Aris does the same, on the side opposite. Close, but not too close.

"I'll stay up a bit," he says. "The horses will warn us if anyone approaches."

Obsidian stamps a foot. He and Flint aren't tied up, but Flint is well trained, and Obsidian is … well, he's not trained, but he doesn't seem interested in leaving.

The sky overhead is clear and full of stars. I lie on my back, because if I curl up toward the fire, I'll see Aris still watching me. It's unnerving. So I keep my eyes on the stars and try to go to sleep.

It's different, here with Aris. Despite it all, I do feel safe with him. I mean, it's in his best interest to protect me, and I believe him when he says he wants to get my manacles off. It's not at all like traveling with Darius and Len. With them, the newness of everything had me feeling uneasy—frightened, if I am being honest. I guess that's what summoned the wolf pack to protect me. Here, with Aris, I've only called up a finch. I don't feel like I need more protecting.

Obsidian snorts, and I grin—I guess I have him too, at least for the trip. How much safer could I possibly be than with the school's best Shield and a massive warhorse looking out for me? I smile up at the night sky, at the fluffy white clouds scuttling along, bright streaks of silver under the nearly full moon. It's a beautiful night. And soon we'll be at the capital, and I'll get my manacles off and start training for real, and …

With all these hopes running through my head, I fall off to a deep and dreamless sleep.

I wake up in the morning snug and warm in my bedroll. I crack open an eyelid—the fire is just glowing coals now. A pair of rabbits have decided to keep me company, sleeping with their little fuzzy bodies against my chest, and I grin at that. I stroke their soft dust-colored fur, and they stretch awake, whiskers twitching. They creep silently out of my blanket and, in a moment, bound off through the grass.

Manacles or not, animals seem to like me, no matter what the Mages and their rules say.

And then, a moment later, I hear a shout, and Aris is leaping out of his bedroll. His swords are drawn—I'm not certain exactly where he kept them overnight—and he's glaring at something.

His blanket moves, an odd lump at the foot of it creeping up and up until a pair of grumpy groundhogs emerge. They chatter angrily as they disappear into the grass.

Aris scowls at me, his chest heaving. "Did you do that?" he asks, pointing. He sheathes his swords and runs a hand through his dark hair, now wild after sleep. He pulls some of it back absently, fixing it with a tie as he looks out at the grass where the groundhogs went.

"Do what?" I ask, perplexed.

His gaze snaps back to me, cold as ice. "That! They were keeping my feet warm!" he says, and I can't help it—I laugh. I laugh and laugh until tears are running down my face and I'm struggling to catch my breath.

Aris is not amused.

I'm still chuckling as I grab a drink of water from my pack and greet Obsidian. He's in a good mood too, and he prances like he's ready to get back on the road. The caravan is waking up. The sounds of people packing up and horses snorting fill the early-morning air. Aris puts Flint's saddle on, and I see the hilt of something poking out of a saddlebag.

"What's that?" I ask.

Aris glares at me for the hundredth time already today.

"Is it a knife? Is it for me?" I ask.

"It's a dagger," he says, exasperated. "Dagger. Not a knife."

"Whatever. Is it for me? Are you going to teach me?"

"Maybe tonight, barring any other developments," he says.

"Can I hold it?"

"No."

"Why not?"

Aris picks up a stick from the ground. He breaks it so it's roughly the same length as the knife—sorry, dagger—in his pack. "You'll use this until I say otherwise," he says.

I frown down at the little stick in my hand.

"Let's go."

Chapter 24: Aris

I wonder if it's really true that no Shield has ever gone through the games a third time.

Not seriously, but … I entertain the idea.

Mages I can handle. Women I can definitely handle.

But groundhogs as bedmates? No way. I'm not even sure it was completely unintentional on her part.

Wren and Obsidian ride ahead of me today. This girl is something special—the gamble I'm taking sure as all the hells better be worth it. She glares at the stick I gave her every so often, but she doesn't let it go. The caravan moves so slow. I could go faster on foot, but soon we'll be approaching the forest, and we're better off together. Wren will be damn near useless in there, but Obsidian at least will provide some measure of protection. I don't want to admit I'm glad that she wanted to bring him along. He's as much a warrior as any Shield.

A couple of birds appear and zip around Wren's head for a minute, chirping at her. She waves at them. They swoop a bit, like they're talking to her, and then continue on their way.

What in all the hells?

The manacles are defective. They have to be. Maybe they are just so old their magic has worn off. She has been able to make fire, though—but it was green. Perhaps the manacles are blocking out only elemental magic, and Wren is something else entirely. I consider this as we ride, but I don't like it. There's a reason this academic shit is better left to Mages. It's giving me a headache.

About midmorning we come across the temple ruins. Despite the caravan, we're making good time. Gaspar is a decent leader and keeps the group moving. He seems at home in these endless grasslands. A lot of the other travelers look like mice caught out in the open—one balding man looks up so often that I think he half expects something to come out of the sky to grab him. A few of the others nod or greet me when we pass, and I catch whispers of "*Hordearius*." I don't bother learning their names. Generally, people are grateful to have a Shield with them on this sort of crossing, but Wren's lack of a colored robe throws them, makes them nervous.

"What is that?" Wren asks, looking over the ruins as we pass.

The temple itself was a fairly large building once, nearly fifty feet across the front. Now the columns jut up at irregular heights, like so many broken teeth. There are not a lot of landmarks out here—the grass is as constant and featureless as the sea—but the temple can be seen from a mile away. It's ancient, a white stone building ringed with columns and a pitched roof, all of which have largely collapsed. Grass covers most of the marble floors. I never could figure out why a temple would have been all the way out here, in the middle of nowhere. There used to be some smaller buildings surrounding it, like housing, maybe. Sometimes Mages will come out here to study them, trying to decipher the words carved on each pillar. I have no idea what they mean. They're in the long-dead language of the gods which no one really speaks anymore.

"It was a temple," I say.

Most of the people in the caravan aren't talking. They hold their breath as they pass the ruins—an old superstition.

"For what?"

"The old gods," I say.

One of the men from the caravan shoots me a dirty look for talking, but I ignore him.

"What gods?"

"Don't you worship the gods back in that hellhole you come from?"

Wren glares at me. "It's not a … well, it wasn't that bad, anyway," she says.

I guess if the only other place she's been is the school, then Spit probably doesn't seem that bad.

"You need to get out more," I say.

She shrugs, looking at the ruin.

"So, no gods in Spit?" I ask.

She shakes her head. "Just the sea and sky. It's not like … well, we don't worship it or anything," she says. Obsidian's hooves clink off some of the smaller chunks of marble strewn in our path. "The sea just … is. It provides food. It sustains us—and it can be brutal too. Indifferent. The sea is female, the sky is male. Together, they were our gods."

I consider this. I'm not really a religious person—I've never seen the gods. I believe in my own strength. If a god comes down someday and bests me, then I'll believe in him. Or her.

"Who are your gods, Aris?" Wren asks. She's looking at me now, not at the temple anymore.

"Some people say there are six gods," I say. "The god of day and the god of night are the main ones, the lesser gods being those of the elements—fire, earth, air, water. The ones who gave gifts to mortals, making the first Mages."

"And the Shields?" she asks.

I perk up. I like this legend. Mostly because I'm in it. "They say that the first Shield was made by the god of day, Lord Rigrasil," I say. I've heard this story a million times. "To protect the gifts the lesser gods gave the first Mages. My family can trace our lineage back to Odall, the first Shield." I can't help the pride that comes into my voice with this story.

"And who's this temple for?" she asks. We've passed it, so she looks back over her shoulder at the structure, now abandoned for generations.

"I don't know if anyone remembers," I say. "The old gods aren't that popular anymore. I mean, they haven't been seen in generations. There are still some old temples in Estana. Some retired Mages and Shields end up working there." Burned-out Mages and Shields who have lost their way, mostly. Broken, derelict shells of what they once were. I avoid those areas at all costs. I guess they try to find redemption in religion, find some purpose in their empty lives. I saw the temple "priests" once, years ago, when I was traveling with my family. Their hollow, empty eyes, their listlessness, haunted my nightmares for months afterward.

We stop only briefly at noon, to stretch and eat, and then get moving again. If Wren is sore from the ride, she doesn't say anything. Obsidian is much too large for her—he's meant for a fully grown Shield with weapons and such, not a short, curvy Mage with a stick. She swings the stick through the air as she rides, though, stabbing at imaginary foes. I shake my head—Vassilis would laugh at me. He'd be much better at this. I'm no teacher.

Still, when we break for camp at dusk, she approaches me soon after we get a fire started and holds out her stick. She's picked all the bark off it, so it's a clean, smooth piece of wood.

"Ready?" she asks.

I turn and catch a glimpse of the forest a few miles off—at this time of day, it's just a dark, ominous smudge on the horizon. Like a predator crouching just at the edge of your field of vision, waiting to strike.

"All right. Rule number one," I say, headed for the wagon that's carrying firewood. I select a stick and break it down to size. "Do not fight to win. Fight to stall. Fight to gain time to get away from your attacker, or to wait for me to arrive. You're strong, but you're small, and against a trained warrior, you will lose."

"Great motivational speech," Wren snorts.

"All right, princess, arms up. No, no, not like that. And get your feet apart—yes … no, like … yes, like that," I say, guiding her through a basic stance. I adjust her grip, tilting the "blade" away.

"Rule number two: keep the blade pointed away from you, at all times."

"Got it," she says, gripping the stick so hard her knuckles blanch. "Step three?"

I spend an hour or so showing Wren how to do a basic block and where to find weak spots in an opponent's armor. There's a move we call "defanging the snake," a move to disable your opponent's grasp, to get them to drop their blade, and I show her this as well. She's barely keeping up. She's strong, but her movements are clumsy, uncoordinated.

"I wish Vassilis were here," I say, running a hand through my hair. It's slick with sweat, and it's slipped from its tie. Stefan always said I was going to go bald running my hands through my hair like this—but Stefan is gone, and I still have my hair. My stomach clenches with bitterness as I reknot the tie. I have to keep reminding myself Wren is not Stefan. I'm trying to teach her too much, too quick, and we're both getting frustrated. "He's the teacher, not me."

"I've learned more from you in an hour that I learned from the Mages at the school in a week, so, you know, you're not doing a terrible job," Wren says.

We eat that night in silence, regarding each other over the fire. The night falls quickly out here, and soon the blackness surrounds us, pierced with innumerable glittering stars. I wonder if I can find the Headless Lady constellation, and Wren points it out to me, along with the Shark Fin and the Anchor.

"So … are there any groundhogs in these parts I should know about?" I ask as she stands and stretches. Behind us, the caravan is so quiet we might as well be all alone out here.

She laughs and heads for her bedroll. "Not here," she says, then shoots me a wicked smirk. "Too many snakes."

With that comforting thought and her subsequent chuckle ringing in my ears, I stretch out and prepare to rest. I need to be completely alert for the next two days.

Fortunately, I do not wake up with any serpents sharing my bed. I do wake up cold, and my shoulder is stiff. I have to work it out for several minutes before it feels limber again. I shave my face as best I can with one of my smaller knives, and we set out.

This morning, we approach the forest. It's a massive swath of ancient trees, and it will take us two days to cross. Arguably, this is the worst part of the journey to the capital. The trees are large enough to conceal all kinds of predators—animals and humans alike—and the weather can be unpredictable.

Wren is silent as we approach the forest. The trees are so tall, their canopies so broad, that the sunlight is absorbed before it has a chance to reach the ground. As a result, the road is soft from moisture and smells of rot and fungus. People think of forests as whimsical, enchanted places—this one is something out of a nightmare.

"I like it," Wren says, peering up at the trees.

Of course she does.

"It's different. I've never been in woods like this," she says. She looks as delighted as if she were looking at a daisy or something equally innocuous. It's hard to tell if this is genuine reaction, bravado, or sheer ignorance of the danger of the situation—maybe a mix of all three.

"Let's hope you never have to be again," I say, frowning. "Keep your eyes open."

The caravan creaks along the road. Even the horses are subdued, quiet. The only sounds are footfalls and creaking wheels as we go. I think it starts to get cloudy, and I worry about rain, but it's hard to tell with how thick the canopy is.

We stop only when it gets too dark to see. I make our fire closer to the caravan tonight. Wren hasn't had any episodes since that first night she slept in my room, so I'll have to risk it. If something comes for us at night, I need to have her protected.

The horses are restless. Everyone eats in silence, and Wren heads straight for her bedroll afterward. She just looks at the fire for a long time, not speaking.

I think about my first trip here, with Stefan. We were traveling with the other newly paired Shields and Mages and thought that meant we were invincible. We were not careful. We lit big fires and laughed and talked loudly, practically inviting trouble.

That first night, we were attacked by a pack of massive wolves. The second, a band of trolls. Stefan was always an easy-going, cheerful kind of guy, with a personality to match his sunshine-yellow Mage robe. People—especially women—liked him instantly, which he capitalized on at every possible opportunity.

Seeing him fight, though, truly fight, wielding the air around us like I wielded my swords, made me regard him in a totally different way. He was no longer my cheerful childhood friend. He was a Mage now, a trained warrior as much as I was. He used his powers to choke the air out of the trolls' lungs, to create a shock wave that knocked the wolves back a dozen feet. He didn't have the depth of magic that some others did—he approached burnout after just a few potent moves—but he did have imagination and style. It was one of many things I admired about him. He could look at an impossible scenario and find a way out. He'd been drilled in strategy, just like I had. He just wielded air instead of swords. It made us an unstoppable team.

"Aren't you going to sleep?" Wren asks, breaking my reverie.

I shake my head. "Tonight I'll keep watch," I say.

She nods and shrinks further into her bedroll. There are no fuzzy creatures here to keep her company, only the smells of rot and decay, the sound of creaking tree limbs. I watch the firelight dance in her eyes for a long, long time until, exhausted, she finally falls asleep.

I don't like this place. Every twig cracking, every snort of the horses has me on edge. The trees aren't like normal trees either—they grow boils and tumors, festering, rotting appendages that sprout fungus like hair. Their presence borders on sentience, and I don't like it. I keep my swords in my lap and sharpen them to a razor's edge, just to give my hands something to do as my mind runs in circles. Wren is not Stefan. To be honest, I'm actually not sure what she is. She's untrained, though. That much is certain. I won't be able to depend on her to watch my back if something happens here.

The hours pass, and though I hear some far-off howls of some animal I can't identify, nothing otherwise happens. Wren continues to sleep soundly.

The ambush waits until we're all awake, when people are fumbling for saddles and pots and pans, and their weapons are temporarily put aside.

It is not a well-planned attack, but neither are we a battalion of trained Shields. The first hint of trouble comes from Obsidian—he starts pawing at the earth, nostrils flaring, and then rears, striking out at the air with his hooves. Wren runs to him, and I rip the gladiuses from the scabbards on my back.

The trolls come out of the forest, screaming and flailing their battle axes. Wren is pinned between Obsidian and a wagon, which means she is momentarily protected. Good. I yell at her to grab my shield, and she does, hefting it clumsily.

There are at least a dozen of them—massive, warty creatures with boar-like snouts and tusks to match. They fight like men, but when they see me and my bristling steel, they turn and go for weaker prey.

The horses. And Wren.

I throw myself into the battle, fighting to keep myself between them and Wren. A few other men and women have grabbed whatever weapons they have and are more or less making a ring around everyone else.

"Look out!" Gaspar cries, rallying his men to his side. They shout bravely and rattle swords against their old, dented shields, though their faces are turning white with fear.

A troll lurches toward me, some sort of leader of their raiding party, I'd guess, with rotted tusks protruding from his lower jaw. His skin has that strange green cast that all trolls have, and his skin is covered in lumpy growths. Even this far, I can smell the stench on him, like death.

He raises his arm, ready to bring down a rusty axe and cleave my head from my shoulders.

So I go low and slash him across the gut.

He howls, blue blood spurting from the wound as his entrails fall to his feet. The sight seems to spur the rest of them on, because after that comes a barrage of attacks, a frenzy of movement. The trolls aren't coordinated or particularly skillful, but they are very large—most at least six and a half feet—and very, very strong. One misstep, one miscalculation, and death comes on swift wings.

I spare a moment to glance back at Wren—Obsidian is guarding her, slashing at the one troll fool enough to approach. The great black horse rears, and the troll falls to the earth, his skull caved in by a massive hoof, brain matter splattering on the ground. Wren retches at the sight, a trembling hand covering her mouth.

I turn, jab, parry, strike again, keeping Wren and Obsidian behind me. A single thought rolls through my head, over and over—*Not again. Not again. Never again.* I part limbs from trunks when I can, and aim for arteries when I can't. I fight with a desperation I've never felt before, but not for myself. I have to get to Wren. In the fury of the fight, I've been lured away from the caravan, and now there are many large, stinking bodies between me and my Mage. I yell, throwing myself at them, the heat of battle blazing through me as my gift comes fully awake. The magic of the Shields sings through me, the bringer of death. Troll after troll falls in my path, until it is all over, and they are all dead, and the forest floor is awash in a stinking heap of blue-stained flesh.

"Wren!"

I hear no answer. In the chaos—wounded men and horses, piles of dead trolls—I cannot see my Mage, cannot see Obsidian anywhere. I cannot hear her over the screams and moans and clatter of the caravan. My pulse pounds in my ears like a drum—*Not again*.

"*Wren*!"

"Here," a quiet voice finally answers.

Relief floods through me, so strong that I nearly go to my knees.

I find her behind Obsidian on the other side of the caravan, her hands fisted in his mane, hanging on for dear life. It looks like she'd fall to the ground if he weren't supporting her, and she's pale as a ghost. I look her over, which makes her scowl at me, but don't see any obvious signs of bleeding. I let out a breath and pat Obsidian on the neck, grateful that he protected her.

"Good boy," I say.

He snorts derisively, shaking his massive head. He paws at the earth, like he's daring anything else to come for him, to come for her.

"Is it over?" Wren asks. I can barely hear her over the screaming coming from the others.

There is wailing, a keening as the ungifted mourn their dead. Two of their men have fallen to the trolls, and a third is probably going to lose a leg at least. Gaspar is kneeling next to him, wrapping a tourniquet around the leg and yanking hard to apply pressure. Blood, dark in the filtered light, oozes from a gash in his thigh. I recognize him as the balding man, the one who kept looking to the sky for trouble—when he should have been looking to the trees.

I change my mind. The man with the gash is dying, and quickly. Wren shoots a glance toward him, her eyes wide, starting to panic, her breathing becoming fast and ragged. I grab her arms and force her to look at me instead.

"Breathe," I tell her. I can feel her trembling, and tighten my grip.

It will not do to have her lose control now, for her magic to surface now. It would attract the attention of every predator in the forest. Her gaze flicks to my face, my hair, my shirt, and I realize she seems afraid of me, and that will not do either. Finally, though, she looks at my eyes, and I don't move, don't blink. I keep eye contact with her, like I might with a scared or wounded animal. I don't let go of her until her breathing slows to a normal pace, and she gives me a silent nod.

The balding man is quiet now.

I release Wren.

"Are you hurt?" she asks, wrapping her arms around her stomach.

I shake my head. Injured? Me? It's an amusing thought. I am covered in blue troll blood, though, and there is a small scratch on my arm from one of their blades, but it's already starting to heal.

"Can you ride?" I ask, saddling Flint. I've had it with this damn forest.

She bites her lip but nods.

I help her onto Obsidian, and then I get us the hells out of there, leaving the caravan behind.

We gallop through the forest, putting miles and miles behind us. The horses are fierce. They've been kept to a walk for days, and they relish the chance to stretch their legs. We run all morning, breaking only when the horses are lathered with sweat, and then only long enough for them to catch their breath. We keep going due west. I let Obsidian lead, and Wren clings to him like a drowning woman clinging to a piece of driftwood, but she hangs on. My head swivels as we run, checking for any sign of further trouble, any hint of trolls or worse. My blood sings through me, readying my muscles for another battle—but none comes. Every brush of a tangled vine against my back, every branch that cracks and creaks in the wind has me on edge, tensed for another attack.

By noon, we emerge from the forest, and the horses drop to an exhausted walk. Even Obsidian is spotted white with sweat, and as the breath blows from their nostrils, it's flecked with blood. I don't start to relax until there are another few miles between us and the trees.

We stop and prepare to wait for the caravan to catch up. Maybe I should have stayed with them, but my obligation is to Wren. If staying with them put her life in further danger, then it was not an option.

She dismounts, and her knees nearly buckle. She grabs Obsidian's mane, hanging on, taking a few deep breaths before she tries to walk. We've reached a small stream, and she cups her hands in it, drinking eagerly.

"Is it safe here?" she asks. Her eyes are so wide I can see the whites all the way around.

"Safer," I say.

Wren accepts this and slumps, sitting in the grass. She's in shock—she doesn't move, doesn't do anything other than sit and stare, unseeing. I've seen the same expression on many soldiers after their first battle. Like they had no idea how harsh and cruel the world could be until that moment. I used to laugh at them.

I don't laugh at Wren.

"I'm going to bathe," I say, gesturing at the blue blood dried on my clothes, my skin, my leathers. "If you're that worried about safety, feel free to keep an eye on me."

The teasing works. She flushes bright red, and the spell of fear seems a little alleviated.

But she turns her back to me, watching the forest instead.

Chapter 25: Wren

I try to process what just happened. I've been trying to all morning, but the thoughts scatter, like the way shards of glass do when … well, when a glass hits the ground. Shards everywhere, sharp as blades and nearly invisible, intangible.

I've never even imagined anything as terrifying as those trolls. I've never actually been in fear for my life before. I've never even seen a dead man before, or a dead troll, and now I've seen both, hacked to pieces, bleeding and screaming as they die. And the way Aris moved—calm, calculating, with a cool, detached fury and the speed and strength of a tiger. I've never seen anyone move like that. His swords cleaved limbs and heads without pause, moving faster than I would have thought possible. Blue blood spurted through the air, sparkling in the dim sunlight, like an obscene rainfall.

Obsidian's had his fill of water, so I go to check on him. I rub him down and inspect his hooves for damage. He flicks my face with his tail, as if to tell me he's fine and that I should stop fussing.

I think about the sound Obsidian's hoof made when it caved in the skull of a troll with a crack like thunder, splattering gray brain matter across my boots. He had gotten close, so close that I could smell his fetid breath, and his rusted blade had swiped at me, tearing my shirt, before Obsidian had reared up. I wonder if I'll ever get their stench out of my nose.

My side burns as the memory comes back to me, like I blocked out all the pain in some sort of self-protective instinct. I check over my shoulder—Aris is still splashing around, not paying me any attention—and put a hand to the rent in my shirt. It comes away red. Still bleeding, but not a lot. I'll take a closer look later. It hurts to breathe deeply, when the skin stretches, but it's not that bad. I think.

I hear Aris stop splashing, and a few minutes later he's back at my side, cleaner at least. There are dark stains on his leathers, but he's changed his clothes, and the blood isn't caked on his face anymore. When I first saw him after the battle, his blue eyes blazing, his face was a dark mask, covered in drying blood. He looked terrifying, like a monster himself.

"You can take a turn, if you want," he says, nodding toward the water. "I won't look."

My face heats up, but I nod. I turn gingerly to grab my pack and some clean clothes.

And then his hand grabs my wrist like a vise, hauling me back upright.

Aris is holding my arm out from my side. His jaw is tight as his other hand lifts the bottom of my shirt, which is now stained with fresh blood from my reopened scratch.

I smack his hand away from my shirt. He raises a finger in warning, closing his eyes and taking a deep breath.

"What happened?" he asks evenly. It's like he's got this other personality, like his shift from arrogant bastard to Shield is just as dramatic as his transformation from man into tiger. And he's all Shield now—cold, pissed, deadly.

"Just a scratch," I say, but my voice wavers. I do not want him touching me, but I also do not like having him go all scary on me.

"Show me," he says.

I start to shake my head but stop when I look at him. He's not teasing. He's not asking. And he will not stop until he gets what he wants.

Fine.

I lift the edge of my shirt just high enough so he can see the scratch. It has bled more than I thought, and the cloth is stuck to it in places. Aris probes it with his fingers, the motion clinical, assessing. The edges of the thin cut ooze as they split apart at his touch. It's not deep, but it's a long scratch, along the left side of my ribs and nearly to my navel.

He tears a piece of cleanish cloth from the edge of his bloodstained tunic and uses it to wipe away the dried blood. This makes the damn thing start bleeding again.

"Go wash up," he says, nodding toward the stream. "I can't do anything with it until it's cleaned."

"I'm fine," I say.

Aris levels those icy eyes at me, raising an eyebrow. "Don't make me come in there with you," he says.

All right, yes, that would be worse. I picture him dunking me in the stream kicking and screaming, just to make sure the damn cut gets clean, throwing me over his shoulder like a petulant child.

Then I picture something quite opposite—and my enjoying it.

"Fine," I say again, clenching my hands, and I do as he asks.

The water in the stream is only about three feet deep, and very cold, but it feels good to get some of the grime off. I feel like I'm washing away the fear from the morning. The wound makes the water run red for a while, but it feels good to get the dried blood off too. The edges of the wound gape a little as I move, which makes my breath hitch, but it's tolerable. I caught myself on a fishhook once, which pulled clean through the skin and muscle of my calf. That was much worse. I consider old injuries, anything to keep my mind off the trolls, and manage to rinse my hair out, more or less. When I dress, it makes a cold, damp strip down my back. I comb it out with my fingers as I go back to the horses, where Aris has set up a small fire.

"Sit," he says.

He's arranged some makeshift bandages—pieces from his ruined tunic—and when I sit and lift the edge of my shirt for him, he winds them around my torso. His calloused fingers rasp over my skin lightly, smoothing the cloth into place. It affects me more than I care to admit. My breath catches for a second as he presses a dressing over the wound itself. He looks up at me, and the mask breaks—no longer scary Shield Aris. His brow is furrowed, like he's concerned about the pain. He holds my gaze for a moment, then looks back down at the bandage, tying it off.

"The caravan should catch up to us by tonight," he says abruptly. "We can camp here and meet them."

"All right," I say.

He stands, graceful as a cat, and tends to his swords. He takes some time cleaning his weapons of every last speck of troll gore, and I get a small pot and some water and heat up some food. After a while, I hear a splash and turn to see the white tiger emerge from the stream, a fat silvery fish in his mouth. He drops it on the bank and turns back for another. He's remarkable to watch like this—the way he crouches, just the tip of his tail twitching. The way his muscles coil and spring as he pounces. He's breathtaking, and for a moment, he distracts me from thinking about the caravan and the trolls.

I avert my eyes when he emerges again, and a few moments later, Aris is back at my side, a pair of fish in his hand. I borrow one of Aris's smallest knives and in a flash have the fish gutted and prepared. I may not be the ideal traveling companion for him—I may be useless as far as fighting trolls goes—but I do know my way around a fish. A hot meal and a bath can really make you feel nearly human again, no matter what has happened. We brought some supplies, and I found some wild onions growing nearby, so I'm able to cobble together a reasonable stew. With barley and legumes, of course, for my Shield. The ache in my chest starts to ease a little as we eat, seated side by side, watching the shadow of the forest together.

Aris thanks me for the food, but now that the adrenaline has worn off, he's pretty morose. I wonder how often this kind of attack happens. I didn't think I'd miss the School of the Silver Flame, but I'd take bullies over trolls any day. A chill runs through me, and goose bumps rise on the back of my neck. A breeze stirs the little hairs there, and I shiver.

I glance back toward the forest. I wonder what else lurks in there, what else might be preying on the caravan at this moment.

"We should have stayed with them," I say.

His blue gaze snaps to me, lingering over my side for a moment. I wonder if it's bleeding again, so I look, but nothing is seeping through.

"They are not my concern," Aris says. "You are." His words are harsh.

I realize then that this is what it means to be a Shield. Protecting not those most in need but those you're bound to, above all else. There are no warriors in that caravan, not like Aris. If something else came after them, they'd need him.

I look at the forest again. I feel like they should have joined us by now.

"So if I go back in there to find them, you'll be duty-bound to come protect me?" I ask.

He growls and glares at me, unblinking, until I start to squirm. "Don't even think about it."

I do, but I don't move.

After we eat, he grabs some sticks and tosses one to me. I grab at it and miss, and it falls to the ground.

"What, we're having a lesson now?" I say. After all that's happened today?

"Unless you want to be defenseless the next time something like that happens," he says, pointing his stick toward the forest.

I grumble, but I pick it up. I guess this is his way of distracting me from running back toward the caravan, maybe his way of maintaining some semblance of normality amid the chaos. He proceeds to put me through a series of blocks, making me think about my foot placement and hand placement and my core and my stick, and so much so that I nearly get frustrated and quit, but I don't. It does take my mind off the scratch on my side.

By the time dusk falls, Aris calls our training session to a halt, and the caravan is starting to emerge from the trees. Relief floods through me. They make their way to us before camping, a more somber crowd than before. Several of the horses are limping, and two of the wagons are splintered, their wheels damaged. No wonder it took them so long to catch up to us. Guilt tugs at my chest anew. We should have stayed with them.

Aris goes to talk to the leader of the caravan for a bit, and I go about some small chores mechanically—getting my bedroll out, gathering a few more sticks for the fire, packing up the clothes I washed in the stream, which have dried by the fire. Obsidian and Flint are grazing quietly, which sets my heart at ease. I wish I had some apples to give them. I promise myself that as soon as I can, I will spoil Obsidian with treats until he is fat and happy. I owe him my life.

Night has fallen, and out here in the wilds, there's no light except the stars, the moon, and our small fire. Everything is black around us, darker than I've ever seen. Back on the Spit, even on the darkest, stormiest night, the sea would reflect something, even if it was just the light from the lighthouse. Out here, it is easy to feel very small and alone. The whisper of the wind through the grasses is spooky. I'd take the crashing of waves on rock any day.

I feel restless. I couldn't sleep even if I wanted to, so I get the spelled candle and a book from my pack and settle down by the fire to read for a bit. Aris comes back. I'm used to seeing a smirk, a hint of laughter on top of his usual broody expression, but tonight there's nothing. He moves stiffly, mechanically.

"Go to sleep," he says.

"You go to sleep," I say, holding up my book. "I'm going to read for a while."

"You need your strength," he says. He folds his arms, frowning at me.

"So do you," I counter, turning a page. "Besides, I've got my stick to protect me." I hold up my makeshift dagger.

He grudgingly relents. If he's too tired to be grumpy and argue with me, then he's definitely exhausted.

He crawls into his bedroll and turns his back to me and the fire. Within seconds, I think he's asleep, the broad width of his chest rising and falling in slow, steady movements, like waves on a shore.

I read for a bit, but I don't find much of use, just some gibberish about how to access your magic in your core, which is apparently somewhere behind the bottom of my breastbone, how to tap into it. When I look inside me, I see nothing. I close my eyes and try again, trying to picture my magic like a glowing ball, but again I see nothing, just the darkness. I open my eyes and see the firelight glint off my manacles.

Damn them.

I guess we have another few days until we reach the capital, where maybe I can convince someone to take them off. Then I can start putting all this reading into practice. I stare off into the darkness, watching the full moon shine on the grass. In the dark, the grass ripples with the breeze, and despite the lack of brine in the air, I can almost imagine I am looking at the sea again.

Perhaps an hour has passed, and Aris starts to stir. His body twitches, and his breathing grows ragged. He rolls onto his back, and I can see his chest rise and fall in irregular gasps. He's dreaming, and it doesn't seem to be a good dream. His eyes roll behind his lids, like he's searching for something. I grip my book tightly, wondering if I should wake him up.

Before I can take any action, he jerks, like he's been hit by something, and he sits bolt upright, awake, his eyes open and frantic and wild, unfocused.

"Hey," I say softly.

He snaps at the sound, coiling, like he's getting ready to pounce. His eyes flick toward me, and it takes a moment for them to focus, but that icy glare softens, like he's reassured. He seems to realize where he is, and he lies back down, running a hand over his face, smoothing back the long dark strands plastered to the sweat that has gathered there.

"You all right?" I ask. Whatever he was dreaming about has him in a panic. I don't really want to know what makes Aris this scared.

"Fine," he says, and rolls back onto his side, ending the conversation.

I'm not sure if he goes back to sleep. It seems he's awake, staring out at the darkness beyond our small circle of light. He twitches and fidgets a lot, and every so often he lets out a sigh.

I give up on reading and go to bed, my head pillowed on my folded robe. The weather is mild, and I'm fairly comfortable.

I feel even better when a little brown night snake joins me, curling up on my robe like a folded blade of grass.

Chapter 26: Aris

After that rude awakening, I don't sleep at all the rest of the night. I get out of my bedroll a few hours before dawn and decide to work out some of my nervous energy. I glance at Wren, but she's sound asleep, wrapped up tight. There's a snake on the robe she's using as a pillow, and it regards me with sharp brown eyes, like it's watching over her, daring me to disturb her peace.

I leave it be. At least my own bedroll was empty of critters this morning.

The attack yesterday was not unexpected. I mull over it in my mind. Trolls are not organized or intelligent, but they are strong, and they've amassed a wicked trove of rusty weapons from their quarry over the years. The caravan lost three men to their dozen. Wren's words echo through my skull—what if we'd stayed? What if she'd wanted to go back and help them?

I told her no, that my responsibility was her, not them. They are not untrained—they aren't Shields, but they did well enough—and they were fine.

But that isn't the whole truth. I got her the hells out of there because I was scared.

The attack, seeing her cowering, at risk like that—suddenly I was seeing Stefan there, seeing his eyes wide with shock and pain as an arrow pierced his chest. Seeing the blood pour from his mouth and nose as he died.

Small wonder I had dreams about it too. Dreams that felt real. I could feel the warm blood on my hands, the sting of the arrow against my palms as I pulled it out, trying to stem the tide of blood that followed. The rage roaring through me as I felt the bond between us thin, then snap.

And then it was Wren's face, not Stefan's—Wren lying in my arms, her lifeblood pouring out of her.

I relived it all in my nightmares. It was Wren's voice that called me out of it, when I woke in a panic. I nearly shifted right there and went to her, like the tiger in me wanted to be near to her, to feel her touch and reassurance, since she won't let me near otherwise.

Gods, I'm an idiot.

I can't go for a run—I don't want to stray far from our campsite—so I put myself through a barrage of calisthenics instead, until the heat in my muscles, the thrill of my strength, banishes the impotence of my nightmares from my mind. Another dip in the freezing stream, and I feel ready to take on another attack with my bare hands if needed. Once again I am the invincible Shield, the guardian of Mages and the terror of trolls.

By the time I am done, Wren is awake, and dawn is breaking. The caravan gets ready in quiet solemnity, like they are afraid a single misstep will call down another horror on them.

I check on Wren's wound. She rolls her eyes, but at least she doesn't smack me this time. I unwind the bandages, noticing the way her smooth skin pebbles in the cool air. The dressing is stained where it touched the wound, which is …

Gone. The wound is gone.

What in all the hells? She heals like a Shield, too? There's not even a scar. I run my thumb over the unblemished skin, where there should have been a scabbed-over wound.

This time she does smack my hand. She does not like being touched by me. All right, fine. Weird, but fine.

"What happened?" I ask.

Wren looks down at her skin and pulls down her shirt. She shrugs. "No idea," she says. Like it's not a big fucking deal that she healed that quickly.

I wonder if there's Shield magic in her lineage, something that would account for her healing abilities. I'm not sure I'd have healed so fast.

"Has this sort of thing happened before?" I ask.

She stares at me. "I don't make a habit out of getting filleted, you know," she says.

"Do you … I mean, never? You don't have any scars?" I ask. I look over the skin that I can see, which isn't much, just her face, her hands.

"Maybe it's an Earth Mage thing," she says. "They can heal people with their magic sometimes. Some of the Water Mages too. I read about it." She glances toward the saddlebag where her books are stashed.

I frown. I don't like this, but at least she's not bleeding or injured. I add it to the mental list of crazy things she's capable of.

"I wonder if you're some sort of Mage-Shield hybrid," I say, turning the idea over in my mind as I ready Flint. She could be something like the way a mule is a hybrid of a horse and a donkey. Maybe not the most flattering analogy, from the way Wren sticks her tongue out at me when I mention it.

"No one in my family is either," she says, "so how could I be a hybrid? Doesn't magic run in families?"

"There have been cases of Mages and Shields being born to ungifted families," I say, thinking. "I think usually it ends up being a case of infidelity with someone magical, but not always."

Wren gets Obsidian's saddle, which looks ridiculously small on him, and she looks equally ridiculous trying to get it set up. But she does do it and mounts up. He kneels on his front leg to let her get up, like a damn trick pony.

"My father definitely did not have magic. I never knew my mother, but I don't think she did, either, so how could I heal the way a Shield does?" she asks.

"I have no idea," I say. "I can get a cut during battle, and it closes almost immediately. The scars fade, and most don't entirely disappear. But piercings or tattoos—our bodies get rid of them almost instantly. Believe me, I've tried."

Wren fiddles with an earlobe, which I realize is unpierced, like she wants to try something stupid. She catches my gaze and drops her hand, urging Obsidian after the caravan. I grunt and urge Flint after her.

The day is quiet and gray, and we ride through the rolling hills without much of anything interesting happening. I feel taut, like a pulled bowstring. I wonder what other stunts Wren is going to pull. Will she suddenly develop the strength of a Shield? Breathe fire like a damned dragon? I can't anticipate her next move, which is frustrating to a degree I've never felt before.

When we camp that night, I burn off some steam exercising and show Wren a few things with her stick dagger—she isn't the worst student I've ever had, but she is pretty close. At least I know she hasn't manifested any other Shield talents—yet. That makes me feel significantly better, for some reason.

Tomorrow the caravan will be breaking off in the morning to head to another town, while we'll have one more night of travel to reach the capital. This isn't a bad part of the continent—too populated for anything dangerous to lurk. And if we are lucky, we'll make it to the Golden Crown Lodge, where we can spend the night in a bed, with four walls around us. Keeping watch all the time is making my neck ache. It's not the palace, but it's a far cry from sleeping on the cold ground another night. As we camp for our last night with the caravan, I feel relief trickle through me. One more night in the wild with Wren. If we ever need to do this again, she'll be better trained and better prepared. At least this time we came through unscathed—sort of.

And then, after one night in the modest comfort of the Golden Crown, we'll be at the capital—the Golden City, Estana. It is the largest city on the whole continent, and not my favorite place to be. I like open spaces, not crowded streets, and certainly not the confines of the court. I have no idea what the king wants with Wren, unless he knows something about her, something about her power, that we didn't. If nothing else, the library there dwarfs the school's. We will find something there that will explain all this. We have to. Satisfied that I have a plan, I feel marginally better, more settled.

That morning, we leave the caravan and continue west. The road is wider, the dirt compacted by a steady stream of wagons and carriages and animals. We pass some people heading toward the city and few leaving it, mostly peddlers and farmers and merchants, no large groups. Wren attempts to read as we ride, periodically being interrupted by a chatty bird or a curious rabbit, and once a farmer's ancient mule, which leaves a trail of drool down Wren's shirt as she rubs its nose.

Despite its name, the Golden Crown Lodge is a dark, dreary wooden structure in the middle of nowhere, though the crown on the sign probably used to be gilded. Now it's faded to a dingy yellow. Shields have been coming here on their routes to and from the city for decades, though. It's not the most respectable place, in general, but the reputation of Shields means a lot here, and the staff and guests usually keep their distance. We don't have to worry about pickpockets or bedbugs here, at least.

Wren is wide-eyed as we approach and ride through the gated courtyard. We leave the horses at the small stable to the side of the main building. The boy working there has a fit when he sees the size of Flint and Obsidian, but the horses are tired and eager to eat, and they don't give him too much trouble.

The main room of the inn is large and dark, with scattered tables and a smoldering fireplace. Black soot covers the brick there, and a thick layer of dirt and grass covers the floor no matter how often they sweep it. After paying for a room, a meal, and access to the bath, we follow the owner up the narrow staircase at the back. Wren is exhausted, nearly stumbling up the stairs, her robe pulled tight around her, accenting that curvaceous body she is so intent on hiding.

The room is drafty but big enough, with a fire going and two small windows that let in the evening light. I glance over the room, automatically taking note of possible escape routes, possible points of entry—there aren't many. I also take note of the bed.

The one bed.

I turn to the lodge owner and glower.

His red face blanches. "I'm sorry, Shield. It's the only room left, and I assumed ..." He looks between me and Wren.

I raise a hand, and he stops, his mouth gaping like that of a fish as he struggles to come up with some excuse.

"Then bring up a cot," I say.

Wren is silent, her face flushed. She's also noted the fact that there's only one bed. I think that if I mention sharing it—it's big enough that we wouldn't even touch—then I'd wake up with her snake bodyguard on my face, or worse.

We head down to the bath while the incompetent owner is scrambling to accommodate us. I hear him shouting at someone to find bedding and bring it up, followed by a string of threats and curses. We make our way down the narrow hallway to the bath, Wren clutching her clothing and towel to her chest. There's just the one bath, a large tub of lukewarm water in a small room on the other side of the kitchen, so the fires can keep it warm. Wren goes first, resolutely shutting the door in my face.

"How am I supposed to guard you if I'm stuck out here?" I ask. Not that that's too much of a concern—this place is relatively safe. I'm just not supposed to leave her alone, ever. Rule number one in Shield training. But my modest Mage has other ideas. She doesn't deign to answer me.

"You know I've already seen you naked!" I say, rapping my knuckles against the door.

Another lodge patron eyes me as he passes, curious, but continues without comment.

Something clatters to the floor inside the bathroom, and she squeaks. "*What*?"

"At the lighthouse. Remember swimming in the ocean?" I say, grinning at the memory, her strong brown body cutting through the water—and at picturing how red Wren's face probably is right now.

She doesn't say anything else for a minute.

However, the door to the bath might be shut, but the slats of wood that form the walls have gaps. I can keep an eye on her if I need to. She realizes this at about the same time I do, and I find myself eyeball-to-eyeball with her.

"If I catch you peeking in here again, Aris, I'll set every flea and cockroach in this place on you," she warns.

I sigh and put my back against the door. "You don't have that kind of control," I counter.

"Try me," she says, her tone flat.

I roll my eyes. "Fine, no peeking," I say. "But if you're getting murdered in there, you'll have to let me know. Give me a whistle or something. Hoot like an owl if it's one assailant, or howl like a wolf if it's more."

She ignores me.

I hear some movement, then a small splash and a grateful murmur.

I mean, I peek a little. I'm a Shield, not a saint.

When Wren is done, she's a happy little cloud of clean contentment, and I take a quick turn, satisfied that she can't get into too much trouble in the room by herself for a few minutes.

I'm toweling off my hair as I enter the room, and find her seated on a cot by the fire, a book in one hand and a mug of some kind of soup in the other. Someone's brought food up, and it's laid out on a rickety table by the bed. Night has fully fallen now, and the fire has been built up.

"What are you doing there?" I ask.

She looks up, confused, and raises the book, like that explains everything. It's *The History of Ocron: Lineages*.

"No. I mean, *there*," I say, indicating the cot. I wonder whose lineage she's looking at, if she's tracing magical heritages back in time, trying to locate someone with a gift similar to her own.

"Oh," she says, folding up her legs. "I'll take the cot. You're bigger—you take the bed. Besides, I need the firelight to read."

I run a hand through my damp hair, praying to the old gods for patience—I mean, I know I don't believe in them, but I'll pray to just about any deity right now. If there were a deity that protected Shields from insanity, I'd be down on my knees in an instant.

"That's not how this works," I say after a moment, looking the cot over. It is just that, a cot. A thin straw pallet suspended on some wooden poles. "You're the Mage. I'm your Shield. I'll take the cot."

"Don't be ridiculous," she says, turning her attention back to the book.

Gods help me. This woman is going to drive me crazy.

Chapter 27: Wren

I know that being one-half of a Mage-Shield combo is new to me and all, and that Aris takes his duty very seriously, but it is a little bit fun to antagonize him.

He's still standing in the doorway, his hair dripping, fuming at me. I can see him turning the scenario over in his mind, like he's struggling to find a way to convince me to change my mind and coming up short. I turn back to my book and try not to let a satisfied smirk make it to my lips.

I think I fail. And he's done talking.

Two strides, and he's across the room, picking me up in arms that feel like hewn stone, and then he tosses me onto the bed. There's a moment, a fleeting heartbeat only, when I'm sinking into the downy mattress, his arms still around me, and our eyes meet. I feel the breath catch in my chest, and he stops, his face suddenly a breath away from mine, his eyes bright and shining in the firelight despite the frown on his face. If he bends just a fraction of an inch lower, his lips will brush mine. I can smell the harsh soap on his skin. Droplets of cold water fall from his hair and land on my arms, sending a tingle through my skin. I wonder if he knows that I peeked in on him in the bath, that I watched the way the suds sluiced down his muscled back, down his carved stomach, and then had to rush back to the room so he wouldn't catch me. He is an arrogant, preening peacock most of the time, but gods, he is beautiful.

And then he's gone, away from the bed, turning his back on me, the moment broken. He stalks to the cot, grabs up my things, and deposits them unceremoniously at the foot of the bed.

"Use the candle to read. And you sleep here," he growls, not looking at me. He sits on the cot and flops back, a long breath escaping him. "And I'll sleep here," he says, softly, like it's mostly himself he's talking to.

Something has shifted, like suddenly the world has tilted on its axis, just a hairbreadth, but enough that it's impossible for me not to notice. A thrill runs through me, a heady mix of cold and warmth both at once. I'm just tired, I tell myself. I'm tired, and he's being kind, sort of, taking his job very seriously. That's all. That's all it is. I let out a shuddering breath, and he tenses, like he can hear it. I don't even consider asking him to share the bed with me—it is pretty big. At least, I can't consider asking without feeling a little light-headed. I've never shared a bed with a man, in any sense of the phrase. I mean, I shared a bed with him when he was a tiger. Twice. But that was before.

I get under the blankets, suddenly chilled, and fish out my spelled candle from the pack, along with another book, this one on earth magic. Aris sits for a while, staring at the fire, while I surreptitiously watch him and try to read about all the things earth magic can be used for. I think this element might be my favorite—everything from growing plants to tunneling to reducing a mountain to gravel. My eyes widen as I come across a passage describing how to cause an earthquake. From then on, I get absorbed into the book like I've never been before.

Aris sits by the fire for a long time, his feet stretched toward it to be warmed. I wonder if he's fallen asleep sitting up, but eventually he moves, organizing his pack automatically, like he's not really thinking about it. I wonder about all the other times he's been on the road, what it must have been like. He's still not looking at me, and I feel the tension in the room start to grow, like the way the air crackles before a lightning strike. I don't know if this is due to our proximity to the capital and some anxiety, or the heat that coursed through me when we touched, or both of those things. I swallow and put my book down.

"What's the capital like?" I ask, trying to defuse the tension, to bring some semblance of normality to this crazy situation, to make small talk so that I don't feel so cold and alone.

He stills and answers without looking at me. "Big. Noisy."

"And the king?" I ask. I'm not sure what to think of him summoning me. After all, he did kind of just conquer my home country, absorb it into his empire. I picture him as a ruthless warrior bent on having the whole world bow to him. If I stay, if I become a Mage in his service, what will that look like? I don't think I'd like being indebted to a despot, having to work for him to pay back my education.

"He's … more politician than soldier," Aris says, pulling some of his hair back with a tie. The rest hangs damp, making little spots on his shirt where it touches his shoulders. He's looking resolutely into the fire, like he can read something in the flames.

"What do you think will happen tomorrow?" I ask.

He shrugs. "We'll present ourselves to the court—probably stay at the palace until he has time to meet with us. Sometimes it's a few days' wait."

I realize then that he's thinking about the last time he was here, which must have been with Stefan. I picture him with another man, all puffed up with pride and self-importance, ready to slay dragons together.

He keeps staring into the fire, keeping some kind of silent vigil. I try to keep reading, but my attention drifts, and the bed is so warm and cozy that before long, I can barely keep my eyes open.

The next morning, Aris is coiled as tight as a spring. I'm not even sure he's slept. We rise with the sun and retrieve our horses. Aris remains silent, brooding, and people give him a wide berth as we pass. The stable boy has given Obsidian the best grooming of his life—the stallion's black coat is as smooth and soft as velvet, his long, wavy mane and tail brushed and sleek. He knows it too, the big goof. He prances in his stall when he sees me coming. I get some odd looks when I lead Obsidian out without a bridle, just the small saddle. I wonder if whatever glamour or charm I have might wear off at some point, but he seems just as eager to please as always and doesn't give me any trouble.

We mount up and head into Estana with a trickle of other travelers. Aris seems to fold into himself as we approach.

I can see why it's referred to as the Golden City. Unlike the faded yellow crown on the lodge's sign, this place truly gleams. There's a wall around it, like at the school, but it's twice as high and made of a pale golden stone that shines with flecks of quartz, like the whole thing is studded with stars. There are towers placed throughout the wall, where red flags with a golden sun whip in the breeze. The gate we head into is wide enough for six horses and manned by soldiers in gleaming metal armor.

It's a far cry from Spit. In my wildest dreams, never could I have imagined a place of such magnificence, holding so many people. We ride down what seems to be a main street, flanked by shops of all kinds, from bakers to weavers to metal workers, with roofs of copper-red tiles. After so many days in the quiet of the open plains and Aris's taciturn company, it's almost overwhelming. The air is warm with smoke, filled with smells of unwashed bodies and ale and baking bread and everything in between. Obsidian and Flint—and probably Aris too, with his swords bristling like spikes from his back—seem to have an effect on people, and no one approaches us as we make our way through.

After about a mile, the road turns into a massive stone bridge, as wide as the gate we entered and nearly a quarter mile long. It spans a moat that's more like a river, before ending at a drawbridge.

If I thought the walls and the city were impressive, they are nothing compared to the building before me. The spires are three times as tall as my lighthouse, with peaked tiled roofs. The central building soars above us, and it's crafted with arched windows and scalloped dormers—if the School of the Silver Flame's architecture is the definition of austerity, this palace is the definition of elegance. We ride through manicured rose gardens, pass small orchards full of lemon and olive trees, and then through a long row of tall cypress trees before reaching the palace.

We're greeted at the massive, open carved wood doors by a pair of men in gold-and-red livery, who are there to take the horses. The one who helps me down from Obsidian seems confused that there's no bridle for him to lead the horse by. He recovers quickly, though. He puts his hand on the stallion's neck, and Obsidian follows him easily enough. I wonder belatedly if this will be the last time I see him, and my chest feels tight.

And then Aris is next to me, one hand on my back, ushering me into the golden palace.

The inside is light and open and airy, and I have no idea how a stone structure can achieve that. I wonder how much of this place is architectural genius and how much is just sheer magic. There's a long main corridor that is several stories high, hung with tapestries and portraits. Everywhere the hallway is decorated in red with gilded accents.

A few people are in this space, headed into various rooms off to the sides. The first thing I notice about them is that the fashions here are very different than I'm used to. At the school, clothes are simple, austere, practical. In Spit, again practicality takes precedence. I only ever saw Aclines's royalty once, at a distance as they passed, and even their clothing was loose, easy to move in.

I have no idea how these women breathe, or even walk. Their waists are cinched so tight, their hair piled so high, and their breasts pushed up so far that it's a wonder they don't tip over. They wear gowns in dazzling colors, jewels dripping from ears and wrists and fingers like raindrops, their faces painted with bright eyelids and lips and cheeks. They look confident, worldly, sophisticated. The men are slightly more conservative, but only slightly, in loose shirts and brocade vests and shiny, tall leather boots that have never known a scuff.

In my dirty clothes and undyed robe, I feel very small and very shabby. Like a wren among swans. I find myself fiddling with the end of my braid—a nervous habit, so I flick it back over my shoulder and hold my head up high. Aris walks beside me, hands clasped behind his back. His pose is relaxed, but his eyes flick to the corners of the hall, always assessing. The people passing assess us too, the women's eyes lingering on Aris. I glare at them.

We reach the end of the main hallway, and a man in livery stops us. He's older, with a shock of neat white hair. He's trim and sprightly and bounces on the balls of his feet, like everything is a dance.

"Mage Verena, Shield Aris, welcome," he says.

Aris stands tight-lipped but nods his head at the man. "Tolis," he says.

I'm not sure what to say, so I say nothing. I am a little unnerved that this man knows who we are. I'm not sure how I feel about my reputation preceding me.

"Safe travels?" the man asks.

Aris snorts, his attention briefly caught by a brown-and-gray puppy—no, a wolf pup, running down the hallway, being chased by a woman in leathers. A Shield, then, running after … a child? The pup has shifted and is now a boy with tousled brown hair, maybe five years old, running naked down the hallway, howling in laughter as the woman chases him down, her face red. I smother a laugh, wondering briefly what Aris was like as a child. A tiger cub must have been adorable. He catches my eye, a slight curve on his lips, like he knows what I'm thinking.

"Well, I am sure you are both exhausted," Tolis says, recapturing our attention with flawless courtesy. "We have room prepared for you in the west wing. I must warn you, though, Aris." The man leans in, like he's telling a secret. "Your father is waiting there for you."

Aris tenses. A muscle flickers along his jaw, but otherwise, his pose remains relaxed. His brow furrows, though, and he looks down at me. He hasn't mentioned his father to me at all, and I don't think he expected that he would be here. Given that his father was not present at the games and the claiming, I wonder what that first interaction is going to be like.

The man—Tolis—must have a similar thought. "If you aren't too fatigued by your journey, Mage Verena," he says, turning a charming smile on me, "I'd be happy to show you to the library. We are renowned for it."

I'm exhausted, and I want nothing more than to flop down onto the nearest soft surface, but that will have to wait. Aris doesn't say anything, but his eyes say plenty. He's not looking forward to meeting with his father, and it will probably be best if I am not there when he does. Besides, the library is one of the main reasons I'm here. Why waste time?

"Go on," I say, shoving his shoulder.

The contact startles him.

"How much trouble can I get into here?" I say, raising my wrists, letting the sunlight streaming in through the windows glint off my manacles.

He raises an eyebrow in response.

"I'll behave. Promise," I say.

Tolis beams and claps his hands.

Aris rolls his eyes but looks down a hallway, toward what I assume is the west wing.

"I'll meet you in the library as soon as I can," he says, his eyes still looking down that hallway. His hands flex at his sides, like he's missing the feel of his swords.

"Shoo," I say, and he chuckles but relents and stalks off, like he's headed to battle.

Tolis claps his hands again in eagerness, bringing my attention back to him. "Wonderful," he says, and ushers me down the hallway opposite. "Mage Verena, if you would follow me, I'd be ever so pleased to show you to the library."

As we walk, he tells me the history of the palace. He's obviously proud of it, and his polite cheerfulness is pleasant. It's like listening to a bird singing.

The palace was built three hundred years ago, by the current king's great-great-something-grandfather. The current king, King Leonidas III, recently widowed—at this, Tolis's face droops, and I get the idea that the queen was a beloved figure—has made bringing peace and prosperity to the continent his life's work. I try not to roll my eyes at this—the man just conquered my country. It seems like empire building is more his legacy, but I miraculously manage to hold my tongue.

And the palace is beautiful. The people are beautiful too, and I try not to stare at them, though my head swivels so much I begin to envy an owl's range of motion.

After about fifteen minutes of walking down marbled halls, we come at last to the library.

Calling it a library is like calling Aris a house cat. It's a massive space housing a towering atrium with a glass ceiling in the center, from which hangs a glass chandelier twice my height and covered in candles, which I imagine are spelled, heatless. The floors are marble, and the shelves are polished golden wood. There are couches and armchairs covered in red and gold velvet strewn strategically around, and some of them are occupied by people reading alone or quietly chatting over a book. Around the atrium winds a grand carved marble staircase, leading up to another floor of books. Tolis leads me up the stairs, and we find a table near a tall window overlooking lush, manicured gardens, where more people are strolling, even in the cool weather. A stack of books is waiting for me.

"We took the liberty of pulling a few things that we thought might be of interest," Tolis says, gesturing toward them. "But please, while you are here, the library is yours. Most of the books on magic are in this quarter, with history down the other side, and politics and novels on the first floor. If you are in need of assistance, just ask anyone in livery, and we'll be pleased to help."

"Thank you," I whisper, completely overwhelmed. This place is a far cry from Spit, or the school. I feel out of place but at the same time bursting with hope. "Will I get the chance to meet some other Mages soon?"

"I will inform them all immediately that you are ready to meet with them," Tolis says, and he bows to me.

Heat rushes to my face. "That's really not necessary," I mumble.

He stands and frowns. "But it is," he assures me, lifting his chin high. "It is my honor and privilege. If you are ever in need, ask for me, and I will help."

He disappears silently, like he was no more than a figment of my imagination.

I sit at the table for a moment, too stunned to move. Tolis was kind—more than kind, he was considerate and helpful and made me feel … well, not like some sort of monster that needed to be shackled. It was a nice change.

I look at the books that Tolis has pulled for me. *A Brief History of Magic*—this one is thicker than my hand, so clearly not that brief—*The Interactions of the Elements*, *The First Shield*, and *The Gods: Mighty and Magnanimous*. A broad overview, then.

I realize I'm too wound up to sit and read, and I really want to see the rest of the library, so I get up and wander through the stacks. I bet I could read a book every day for the rest of my life and not begin to make a dent in the collection here. There are shelves and shelves of books, for what seems like miles. I drift through them. Many are in languages I don't recognize, and some are so old the titles have been nearly worn off. Some are fat, some thin, some bound in velvet or leather, and I realize I can't wait to get started. This place feels warm, inviting. Magical. Something like hope flutters through my chest.

I must have drifted out of the magic section and into another part. There's an open area here, with a large round table in the middle. Spread on the table is a map nearly ten feet by ten feet, and I realize I'm looking at the continent.

I see my corner of the world, Spit, down near the bottom right. When viewed like this, it's a small, stubby little peninsula, no more than an appendix to the sprawling landmass before me. I see the School of the Silver Flame, and then Estana—and I realize then just how massive the continent is. I see someone's outlined Aclines, my own country. It's less than a tenth of the size of King Leonidas's empire, and I wonder that he even went through the effort to claim it. We have no real wealth that I am aware of.

Most of the map, though, is just … wild. Blank, open spaces, especially to the west of the capital. There are labeled mountain ranges and lakes, but no large towns, just a few mines and temples. I knew the continent was vast, untamed, but to see it like this is something else. And everyone is clustered in the east, unconsciously or maybe consciously avoiding whatever is in the west.

"I like looking at the whole continent like this," a voice says behind me. "It gives an interesting perspective, don't you think?"

I turn, and my faces flushes. I wonder if I'm not supposed to be here, if I'm intruding on some private space, but the man before me doesn't seem to be scolding me. If anything, he seems pleased that I'm here.

He's tall, taller than Aris, leaner, with thick golden-brown hair and the beginnings of a beard, like he's been too busy recently to shave. His eyes are deep brown, and his face is handsome, smiling. He's dressed finely, in dark pants and high, polished boots, and a crimson shirt with the sleeves rolled back, exposing muscled forearms. He comes over to the table and looks down at the map.

"What do you think?" he asks, gesturing at it.

I frown. "It's not what I expected," I say.

He laughs, and it's a warm, rich sound. "And what were you expecting?" he asks, like he's genuinely interested.

I size him up—I wonder at his motives, or if he's just making polite small talk.

"Of the map? Or Estana?" I ask.

Obviously, he can tell I'm not from here. He leans back against the table and crosses his arms, amused, like he's playing a game with me. "Estana," he decides.

"Honestly?" I ask.

He nods, gesturing for me to go on, so I do.

"Chains."

He frowns, and the room feels colder, like it was warmed by the strength of his smile alone. I hold up my wrists in explanation. I wonder if he knows what they are, but before I can explain myself further, he takes my hands in his, turning them over to look at the manacles. It's an unexpected gesture, even though it's gentle, and I jerk my hands back from his touch, rubbing my hands where his were.

I expect him to be upset, but he just looks at me, assessing me with those warm brown eyes, like he's trying to figure something out.

"What?" I ask.

"No one should ever be chained, especially not for simply being who they are," he says.

"Some very powerful people would beg to differ," I mutter, thinking about Head Mage Saroya.

He laughs at this, and the room feels warm again.

I decide that I like this man. "I'm Wren," I say, and hold out my hand, an apology for jerking away from him earlier.

He pauses for a second, bemused, but then takes it. "It's a pleasure to meet you, Wren. And you can call me Leo, but only when we're alone," he confides.

He's still holding my hand, and my palm begins to sweat. I wonder if he can feel it.

"Why's that?" I ask, but I'm getting a sneaking suspicion that I know the reason why, and I can feel the weight of it, like the start of an avalanche. My mouth feels suddenly dry, and the words barely make it past my stunned vocal cords. I might be the world's biggest idiot.

"Well, in public, my courtiers get antsy unless I go by 'sire' or 'Your Majesty,' or sometimes just 'King Leonidas,'" he says with a sly smile. He's still holding my hand. The King of Ocron is holding my hand and not letting go.

"You are not what I expected either," I manage to say.

He smiles widely, and it's like the force of the sun, warming me all the way to my toes.

"Neither are you," he says.

He's still standing there, still holding my hand, when Aris walks in like a thunderstorm.

Chapter 28: Aris

My day has gone from bad to very bad to catastrophic in the course of half an hour.

Bad was walking the halls of Estana again, feeling echoes of Stefan everywhere. Bad was being greeted by Tolis, just like I was last time, making me relive the pain of the past.

Going to confront my father, that was very bad.

But going to the library and finding Wren with the king, holding his hand and beaming up at him like he had hung the stars in the sky …

Catastrophic.

The girl has no idea whom she's dealing with, the forces at play in this court. I begin to wonder if Tolis had a hand in setting up their meeting, since he oh-so innocently offered to escort her.

The visit from my father was a surprise. After his Mage retired to spend time with his family, Nestor was set adrift. I figured he'd be home—which is many, many miles away—raising his horses. He was always better with his horses than he was with his children.

After I failed Stefan, my father refused to talk to me. I was officially the outcast of the family, the one who had let his Mage die, while he lived. I didn't even have the decency to go gray and commit myself to religion or some other esoteric pursuit.

Which is why it was such a big fucking surprise that he had bothered to come see me at all.

The rooms here at the palace for the Mages and Shields are opulent by any standards, more so when considering the austerity we're used to at the school and in our travels. It's nice for a time, but after a while, it feels like a gilded cage. A mere hour before seeing Wren with the king, I was directed to the quarters that had been prepared for us, and when I opened the door, my father was standing in front of the large fireplace, like he'd only been waiting for a few minutes.

My father is an imposing man. It's a trait that all his sons inherited, and, well, one of his daughters, anyway. He's massive, with limbs as thick and unyielding as tree trunks, and eyes as black as all the hells. He doesn't smile, ever. He's not a warm man, not affectionate. I have wondered what it was that my mother ever saw in him. I have her eyes, which might be another reason he dislikes me. He looks at me and sees the ghost of his dead wife.

"I hear you continue to drag my name through the dirt," he says by way of greeting.

I push past him and deposit my packs on a couch. "Hello, Nestor. It's nice to see you too," I say.

I see the slap coming, but I don't try to stop it. That would just make him more pissed off. His palm connects with the side of my head, and the force makes me stumble, but I don't fall; I don't cry out. He hates that even more.

"I won the games. Again," I say, ignoring the blow, ignoring the fact that it feels like he damn near ripped my ear off.

"And instead of picking a proven Mage, someone to bring pride to the family, you pick this girl who, what, talks to animals?" he says.

"Be careful how you speak of my Mage, Father," I say, turning back to him. I let him see that he's gotten my hackles up. "You know how protective Shields can be."

"Is that a threat, cub?" he says. I've always hated that term. "In that case, I hope you've learned a thing or two about how to protect your Mage since last time."

I let out a breath. My heart is racing, preparing my body for a fight. Brawling with another Shield—not to mention my father—is not taken lightly in our circles. And fighting this man? It's a battle that I'm not sure I'd walk away from alive, let alone win.

"Did you just come to hear yourself speak, old man, or was there something you wanted from me?" I ask.

"I came to see for myself what my wayward son is getting into," he says, crossing his arms. Muscles bulge on top of muscles. His shifted form is a great dark-maned lion, and it's not hard to see why.

I have three older brothers who are off doing great deeds with their Mages—it's little wonder Nestor views me as a failure now. All of that is going to change, though. It has to.

I shrug. "I'm sure Saroya has kept you well informed as to my actions," I hiss.

He narrows his eyes but doesn't deny it. "I'll be in the capital for a few more weeks, training the horses," he says. It sounds innocent, but it's a threat. He'll be here, watching me, watching us. "I look forward to meeting your Mage."

I picture Wren chucking a shoe at him and smile. "I'm looking forward to that too," I say.

We have a momentary standoff, and then he leaves, without any further insults or blows. I let out a breath and touch my ear—but it's already healing, the bruise already fading. By the time I reach the library, the searing pain is only a memory.

Replaced immediately by the shock of seeing Wren with the king.

I can't decide if I should bow or punch him. I guess I take a little too long to decide—Wren jerks her hand back and rubs it on her pants. Her face goes bright red.

"Shield Aris, I'm glad you're back," the king says. He offers me his hand, and I shake it, belatedly bowing, but not an inch lower than required.

"Sire," I say.

I don't know the man well, but he's charismatic, the kind of person who inspires confidence in others. Kingship sits lightly on his shoulders. He leans back on the table, where a map is laid out. He's completely at ease here, or at least appears to be. If I were in my shifted form, the hair on the back of my neck would be up. Maybe it is anyway.

"Why don't the two of you join me in the main hallway after dinner tonight? I'll have my Mages meet us, and we can get those shackles off you," he says to Wren.

She is already nodding her acceptance.

"Great," he says, beaming. "Now, I'm afraid I do have to run, but I look forward to seeing more of you. Of both of you," he says, glancing back at me.

Wren nods again.

He leaves, and she watches him go until he's disappeared down the stairs. Then her gaze finally flicks back to me.

"He's … unusual," she says.

I nod.

Her gaze flickers to the side of my face, where I guess my rapid healing has not completely erased the evidence of my father's blow. The pink flush fades from her face. "What happened?" she asks.

I shake my head. "My father."

"I didn't know your family would be here," she says, frowning, and she makes her way through the stacks, to a table laden with books on magic. She doesn't need to ask if he hit me. She knows.

A growl rumbles in my chest. "Just him," I say, picking up the first book and flipping through it, but not really seeing the words. "And I didn't either. He's just here to make sure I don't besmirch the family name even more."

"No pressure," she mutters. "He sounds like a real bastard."

"You just focus on you," I say, nodding toward the books. The last thing I need is Wren getting distracted—and it's not like *I* need *her* protection. I've been on guard against Nestor since the day I was born.

"What do you want to start with?" I ask. If her manacles are going to come off tonight, I'll need to be on guard more than usual. A casual word, a nightmare, and she could unwittingly bring down this palace around us. The thought doesn't scare me, though—after what we've been through already, I'm confident that I can pull her out of any destructive magic.

Wren obliges me, running a finger down the spines of the stack of books, but she's not really focusing.

A helpful librarian tells us we're free to take whichever books we like with us, so Wren grabs an armful, and we head back to our rooms.

Chapter 29: Wren

Once the shock of meeting the king wears off, I realize how completely exhausted I am. I'm not sure what went on between Aris and his father, but the right side of his face is red, so I'm assuming blows were exchanged. I expect that I'm the reason behind it—but I didn't expect their meeting to be violent. My own father never raised a hand to me, ever. Aris accepted this altercation like it was to be expected—what kind of childhood did he possibly have, with a man like that as his father? The thoughts tumble through my mind, uneasy, as we walk. It seems to me that with a role model like that, Aris had two options—to emulate him or to run in the opposite direction. Aris has never raised a hand to me, despite his profession, which by definition involves a certain amount of violence, and despite me throwing tantrums—and shoes—so I expect he chose the latter option. It's hard to imagine, a lifetime under a tyrant like that.

Aris leads me down to the west wing of the palace, where Shields and Mages stay. I ask how many are at the palace, and he's not sure. Most don't stay long. The king dispatches them all over the continent based on the needs of the people. There's a drought in the south? Send out the Water Mages; install some wells. A hurricane is threatening the northern ports? Let the Wind Mages see if they can minimize the damage there. Bandits along the Western Road? Send a battalion, which usually involves a lot of Fire Mages.

The "room" we're to stay in is actually several rooms. We enter into a sitting area that's so fine I don't even want to touch anything for fear of dirtying it. There's a massive stone fireplace, with a couch and several chairs and small tables scattered throughout, all tastefully decorated with throw pillows and oil lamps. To the left are two doors, to two separate sleeping areas. Aris nods toward mine, which is also attached to a private bathing area. There's even running water. This is a completely unimagined luxury, and I can't wait to try it. I miss my daily baths in the sea. Also, I stink.

The sleeping area has a large four-poster bed hung with red-and-gold drapes, with the fluffiest pillows I've ever seen. The mattress feels like a cloud when I throw myself onto it, reveling in the fact that I will not be spending another night sleeping on the ground. The rest of the furniture is simple but finely crafted, all made from polished golden wood and decorated with red velvet and gold accents.

I settle my books onto a table in the sitting area and spend a minute unpacking. It's not like I have much. I do lament the state my clothing is in and ask Aris if there's some way I can launder it.

"There should be clean clothing in the wardrobe," he says, nodding to the large carved oaken thing dominating the far side of my room. Since my room is on the hallway side of the suite, I realize there are no windows, and I wonder if Aris chose that intentionally.

He's right about the clothes, though, so I realize this room is especially for me. I shoo Aris off and spend a moment admiring the bathing room—the white-and-gold decor is lush, decadent, and beyond my wildest imagining. There's a mirror here too, which occupies nearly one entire wall, and when I see what a mess I am, I flush to think that this is the first impression Leo got of me. I look so out of place here. I realize I want to make a good impression on Leo, and not just because he's the king. Exhaustion flees from me at the excitement of getting clean—really clean—and at the thought of seeing Leo again.

The bathing room is floored in white marble, culminating in a freestanding tub that is big enough to completely submerge in—which I test out. I spend the next hour luxuriating in the massive marble tub, scrubbing off all the dirt and grime from the road, and I dedicate several minutes to getting all the tangles out of my hair, working assorted products through it. I love it long, but the traveling has not done it any favors, and my scalp is sore by the time I'm satisfied with the results. I leave it down to dry, and it surrounds me in a cloud of lavender-scented curls.

I take my time rummaging through the wardrobe, looking for something appropriate to wear when one is going to see a king. Something that would erase that disastrous first meeting from his mind. There are some gauzy, low-cut dresses in jewel tones that I pass right by, and I settle at last on leggings and soft leather boots, over which I belt the softest tunic I've ever touched, in a deep twilight indigo. Maybe I spin around in the bathroom's mirror a few times, enjoying the feel of the fabrics.

I spend the rest of the day going over the books from the library. Aris comes in at some point to check on me before going back to whatever exercises he's doing. Then he comes in to use the bath, and when he emerges with a towel draped around his waist, I do my best to keep my gaze on my book.

I fail, and he catches me looking. He smirks, and I glare at him while trying to keep from blushing. Gods, he likes to strut. He's gorgeous, and he knows it. He seems to be in a better mood, though, after burning off some steam with those calisthenics he likes to do.

My eye snags on his scars—he's got a lot of them, thin pale lines on his back, his arms, his chest. The ones I sewed up are less red now, though still thick and puckered. Sometimes I think that shoulder still pains him, or stiffens up—not that he'd admit it, but I catch him rolling it sometimes, swinging his arm to loosen it up. This gets me wondering again about the Earth Mages and some Water Mages who also have healing powers. I make a mental note to look into it. If something happens to him again, I don't want him to end up with a permanent disability due to my own incompetence. I guess a Shield's healing magic only goes so far. I realize I can't bear the idea of something happening to him. He's the closest thing to a real friend I've ever had.

Food is brought to our rooms as the sun sets, but I'm too jittery to eat, and then we're off. My pulse is racing, like I've just run a mile flat out rather than just walked sedately down a marble hallway. I can hear it hammering in my ears.

Will Leo keep his promise? Will my manacles be removed? And how should I even greet him, anyway? Should I bow, like Aris did? Or curtsy or something? I mean, I'm wearing pants. Can one curtsy wearing pants? These are the kind of mad thoughts echoing through my skull when we turn from the west wing back into the main hallway. Aris knows where he's going, and I'm grateful, because this place is so huge it feels like a city unto itself.

He stops at some point in the main corridor, and we settle in to wait. A few courtiers and men in livery pass us. I twirl the end of my braid — but we don't have to wait long. After just a few minutes, a group of people leaves a door down the hallway and heads toward us, led by Leo. King Leonidas. He's wearing a crown now, a thin gold circlet on his head. He greets us with a sincere smile, and I can't help but smile in return.

"Mage Wren, Shield Aris, I'm glad to see you," he says.

When he looks at me, I feel warm all over.

Aris bows, so I copy him. That seems to satisfy the people with the king. There are five or six of them in his entourage, and two are Mages, one Earth and one Water.

"Are you ready?" Leo asks, and extends his arm to me.

I realize he means for me to take it, to walk with him like I'm some great lady. I look at Aris, who looks like he just bit into something sour, and then slip my arm through Leo's. I can feel solid muscle beneath my hand, and I hope he can't tell that my hand is shaking. Being invited to touch him like this is mind-blowing. He does not fear me. He does not approach me like I am something to be studied, to be contained. I find myself squeezing his arm a little, to memorize the texture of his shirt under my fingers. He gives me a reassuring smile in return and covers my hand with his other one, like he thinks I'm nervous. But I'm not—I am in awe.

We don't go too far. There's a short flight of stairs down a magnificent marble staircase, another hallway, and then we end up in an empty stone room with just the one door and no windows. It looks like some kind of study, with a long table in the middle and some strewn quills and pieces of paper. I look up at Leo questioningly.

"I hope you don't mind the relative seclusion here," he says. "Head Mage Saroya was … concerned about the strength of your gifts. I thought that a closed, quiet space might be better than a public spectacle while we get those chains off."

I nod. He hasn't forgotten about his promise to remove the manacles. I am no one to him, but he makes me feel special. It's a heady feeling.

He releases my arm and gestures for the Earth Mage in the green robe to come forward. She's a broad, middle-aged woman with red hair and skin splattered with freckles. She's been talking quietly with Aris, who still glowers. She gives me a wide smile, though.

"Hello," she says, and I swear I can feel the ground below rumble in response to her presence. "I'm Ismini. We're very pleased to have you with us, Wren."

I'm not sure how to respond to this, so I just nod. Aris moves to stand close behind me, his arms crossed, and I feel my heart rate settle. He won't let anything happen to me. I notice Ismini seems unintimidated by his presence, which makes me realize she's probably someone quite powerful herself.

She puts out her hands, and I place my palms in hers. Aris draws in a breath. The manacles glint on my wrists, those malevolent bracelets. I wonder if my magic has changed since they were put on me—if I'll lose control immediately once they're removed, if I'll feel any different. Ismini gives my hands a comforting squeeze.

"This may feel a little strange," she says, holding my gaze with eyes as green as seaweed.

For a long time, nothing happens. My nose itches, and I fight the urge to take my hand from Ismini's and scratch it.

Then the manacles heat up, just shy of being uncomfortable, and they give off a glow like far-distant stars. I feel a thrill rush down my spine, a torrent of heat and cold and pleasure all at the same time, like something is settling into place where it always should have been. The sensation makes the breath leave my mouth in a moan—and then the bracelets just snap open and fall to the floor with a light clink.

I stare down at them. They look so benign, just lying there. Jewelry, nothing more.

I don't feel any different. No tornadoes form out of thin air; no sparks fall from my fingers. I look up at Ismini, and she's smiling at me, still holding my hands in hers.

"We're so excited to see what you're capable of," she says, practically vibrating with energy.

"What do you mean?" I ask.

King Leonidas clears his throat.

"How do you feel?" Aris rumbles.

I turn and realize he's close behind me, like he was ready to jump in if things got out of hand. The proximity sends a shiver down my spine, and I turn back to Ismini.

"The same, pretty much," I say, other than the fact that my heart is hammering in my chest like a hummingbird's wings. "Should I try to—"

"No," Ismini interrupts, but not unkindly. "If you don't mind, I'd like some privacy the first time we try to manifest your magic, and the king should not be there, for his own safety," she says.

Leo shrugs.

"I understand," I say, and I do, but that doesn't mean I like it. She's aware that my magic might get … messy. Does this mean that I can't see Leo until I have complete control?

That won't do. I'd like to see more of him. A lot more, if I'm being honest. King or no, the attraction I'm feeling is undeniable. Warmth floods my face, and I feel my stomach flip-flop. Leo's watching me carefully, but he still doesn't seem afraid of me. That gives me confidence too. "So when can we get started?"

Given that no tornadoes or earthquakes or firestorms immediately flared up after the manacles were removed, everyone around me is breathing easier. Ismini makes Aris promise to keep a close eye on me overnight, and she promises she'll send for me in the morning so that my training can begin in earnest.

"So I won't be going back to the school?" I ask, looking at Aris.

He looks at Leo.

"Wren, there's something different about your magic," Leo says. I like his honesty, his straightforward approach. "We don't know why it's behaving the way it is, but Ismini and Panos"—he gestures toward the quiet man in the blue Water Mage robe—"are two of our finest scholars. They'd like you to stay here with them to train and find out more, if that's what you want."

"What I want?" I ask.

Leo nods.

This feels like the first time in a long time that I've had a choice about anything. It feels like a trap.

"What you want. No one is going to force you to do anything you don't want to," Leo says. "Although"—he gives me a sheepish grin—"I do hope you'll stay."

"So, if I want, I can go back to Spit and my lighthouse now?" I'm pushing it now, but I have to. I have to know how far their promises will go, or if it's all just for show.

"If that's what you really want, of course you can," Leo says, and I believe him. He says it like it's such a simple thing.

Aris bristles behind me. He knows I won't go—it's no longer my home, and I'm too invested now. I need to know more about my magic. Still, he doesn't like me even saying it.

I turn to Ismini and Panos. I vaguely recall Markos telling me about Mage Panos, that he knows everything there is to know about magic. I feel more hopeful than I have in forever. “Thank you,” I say, and Ismini grins at me. “I’ll behave tonight. I’m sure my Shield will see to that.” I glance sideways at Aris.

He scowls.

“See you in the morning, then,” Ismini says, like we’re making plans for tea or something equally mundane.

Chapter 30: Aris

Damn right she's going to behave. I don't care if I have to watch her all night. Nothing is going to happen. No fires, no groundhogs in my bed, no nothing. I need to prove that she's not going to cause a problem, and that I can do my job.

I like Ismini. She and her Shield, Aleka, traveled once with Stefan and me. They treated us like errant sons. Aleka is a force to be reckoned with, a seasoned Shield with a network of scars across her body, marks from a long time spent crossing the continent with her Mage. Ismini's maternal facade is just that—I once saw her cause a rockslide that buried an entire tribe of trolls, with only a single word.

We make it back to our rooms. Wren was quiet the entire walk, which is a little disconcerting, but she is smiling to herself. I hope it is because of the manacles being gone, not from seeing the king again.

Now the real work can begin. She can finally start to explore her power, to hone it. Being tutored by Ismini and Panos is an immense honor. People everywhere will soon know her name—and mine along with it. The Shield who was so certain of his Mage's gifts that he claimed her when she had barely begun her studies. I wonder about where our first deployment will be. To the Roallac coast? To the Isles to deal with pirates? To the mountains to defeat whatever evils are brewing out there? Even here we've heard the rumors, of monsters prowling in the night.

My body thrums with anticipation. I will be ready. I will train as I've never trained before, honing my abilities until people whisper that I'm Odall the First Shield himself, reincarnated. And I will make sure Wren is just as ready.

But she just picks up some books and heads for her room.

"What about practice?" I ask, incredulous.

"What practice?" she asks. She doesn't turn back, just goes into her room, otherwise ignoring me.

I storm after her, my daydreams slipping away. "*What practice*?" I ask. I don't believe what she just said. I'm holding on to the doorframe, gripping it tightly to keep the irritation from my voice. I don't succeed.

"My manacles are off, Aris," she says, pleased. She's busy organizing her books. "I don't need to learn to use a knife anymore. That's what I have you for. You can be the brawn; I'll be the brains, right? Isn't that how it works?" She gives me a smile, but her eyes are unfocused, her attention elsewhere.

"And, what, you think you're safe here, protected by these four walls?" I ask.

"Am I not?" she asks, finally looking at me. She crosses her arms and glares at me for a moment, then relents. "I don't see any sticks here we can practice with."

Fine. I get it. She's pleased that she's free of her manacles. Hells, I am too. That means we'll get to see what she's really capable of, if my gamble has paid off. But training takes years, and I'll be damned if I leave her defenseless during that time.

My gaze falls on a gilded letter opener on her bedside table. She sees me looking at it, and her eyes go wide. She makes a grab for it, but I'm far quicker. She goes to pry it from my hand, and I mock a slow, deliberately slow, jab at her with it. She puts her arms out straight, using her body's momentum to knock my arm aside, even though I'm bigger, stronger. It's a move I taught her days ago, and I'm pleased she's remembered it. She is too, but I'm not about to let her feel confident yet.

I grab one of her wrists and spin her so that she's pinned against me, one arm locked behind her back, the other stuck to her side. I place the blade of the letter opener under her chin, tipping her face up to look at me. Her jade eyes are narrowed with fury.

"You're not invincible yet, princess," I say.

She stops struggling against me. I realize abruptly this is a woman whom I've only ever touched, other than fleetingly, in my shifted form. She's never wanted me to. I realize this as the awareness of our contact, the press of her body against mine, her breasts heaving against my chest, cuts through my irritation. I realize that seconds are ticking by. I realize finally I'm still holding a blade against her throat, and I ease off, clearing my own.

She steps back, and I don't stop her.

"I like you better as a tiger," she says, rubbing her neck. There's not so much as a red mark from the blade against her smooth skin.

"Liar," I say.

She snorts and holds up a finger. "One hour. You get one hour," she says. "And don't touch me again."

"I would never touch a woman who doesn't want me to," I say, and it sounds almost gallant.

She gives me a sideways glance, and I have to smirk.

"Arrogant ass," she says. "One hour. Don't make me change my mind."

"Every day," I counter.

Her lips press together tightly, and I have to drag my gaze back up to her eyes.

"Fine," she says, then puts out her hand for the letter opener. "Now show me how you did that."

Chapter 31: Wren

Aris is in a foul mood. Since my manacles came off, he's been watching me like a hawk.

I am not about to let him ruin my own good mood. I was planning to read up on everything I could before meeting with Ismini tomorrow. I know most Mages my age are already accomplished, have been working on control since they were toddlers. I have a lot of ground to make up.

And then Aris grabs that damn letter opener.

Even after an hour of instruction with my letter-opener makeshift dagger, I am distracted. During that hour in our mutual sitting room, he did not touch me at all, did not come within several feet of me if he could help it. He demonstrated the blocks from a distance.

Even after we've finished, and he's retired to his room, satisfied, I cannot focus on my books at all.

I try to shrug it off. I fidget at the desk, trying to get comfortable, trying to put the whole thing out of my mind. I tried to pretend that I was interested in his letter-opener stunt and the mechanics of disarming an opponent. All the while, my body hummed with the memory of being pressed against him, the hard planes of his body molded to mine, while his blue eyes blazed with an intensity I did not understand—but oh, do I want to.

I give up on the desk and climb into my bed instead, bringing a book and my candle with me. If there is indeed a well of magic within me, I wonder that the blankets do not spontaneously combust with the thoughts raging through me. He is my Shield, I tell myself. Again and again. I could potentially be spending a lot of time with him over the years, if he doesn't decide to move on. I will have to come to terms with this … whatever it is.

I realize then that I don't want to move on, don't want him to claim another Mage, even if I turn out not to be what he hopes. When did that change?

I flip through a few more pages, not really absorbing anything. I am thrown out of my daydreams, though, when Aris stalks back in, a book of his own in hand, along with a spelled candle. He settles himself into an overstuffed armchair across from my bed without a word.

"You have your own room, you know," I say, irritated. Being irritated is better than whatever other emotions are running through me.

"Wren, you set your pillow on fire, while you slept, with two manacles on. If you think I'm letting you sleep alone without them, you're a fool."

A fool? The arrogant bastard. I can't believe I was getting so worked up about him, about being held by him. It was just a lesson, nothing more.

"And, what, you're just going to stay up and watch me sleep all night?" I ask, hugging my knees to me.

"Yes," he says. It's a simple reply. Yes. Because he's my guard. Because he's not worried about me or my safety, but whether or not I'll burn the palace down and wreck his chance at restoring his precious honor. I have to remember that he's using me, for one thing and one thing only—no matter how strongly my body seems to be responding to his.

I grumble and bury myself under the blankets. The bed is massive and warm, and if I weren't so pissed, I'd be reveling in it. I settle myself in and expect a long night of tossing and turning, trying not to think about the man sitting guard in my room. Exhaustion wins out, though, and I fall asleep quickly, dreaming of clouds strewn across a star-studded sky.

I don't set anything on fire, so that's a good start to my day. I wake up and stretch, feeling warm and cozy and rested—before remembering Aris. He's sitting in exactly the same spot, though he's finished his book and has moved on to a second. He looks disturbingly well rested despite his vigil.

"Good morning," I say, smoothing the hair back from my face.

He glances up but otherwise doesn't say anything. I wonder suddenly if I talk in my sleep—or worse, snore. He holds my gaze, and I can feel warmth creeping up my neck. I break eye contact and jump out of bed.

I go to the bathroom to change. The wardrobe is full of dresses in bright colors, finely made—though not nearly as ornate as some of the ones I saw women wearing yesterday. I settle on pants and a soft, loose shirt the color of amethyst. I expect to do some hard work today, and those dresses, though lovely, are simply impractical.

By the time I get my hair brushed out and braided, there's a knock on the door.

"I'll get it!" I shout, but Aris is already up, like he's expecting an invasion or something.

But it's just a girl wearing the colors of Estana. She passes a note to Aris before dipping into a short bow and rushing off.

"Ismini's ready for you," he says, waving the note.

I grin—the sun's barely up. I wasn't expecting to hear from her for a few more hours, but I'm so eager that I'm tripping over myself as I lace up my boots.

"Here," Aris says, and he makes me eat something and drink a cup of juice before I go. "Magic will take a lot more energy out of you than you expect. You have to fuel up, or you'll pass out, and I'll be stuck carrying you all the way back here."

"You're so thoughtful," I grumble before downing the juice. "Can we go now?"

We go back to the room we were in the night before, and I'm glad Aris is with me—I don't have a clue how he can find his way around this stone maze, but he has an unerring sense of direction. His confidence is soothing, and we walk through the palace in a comfortable silence. The room is quiet, private, out of the way. I can see why Ismini picked it. No distractions. Also, not much I can destroy in here if things get out of hand.

Ismini's waiting, along with a petite female Shield with cropped blond hair.

"Aris," the woman says, greeting him with a firm handshake and a feral grin. "Glad to see you."

"Aleka," he says.

She looks him over, appraising him. "You look good. I was worried you'd go soft without a Mage," she says.

He shakes his head.

I think he likes this Shield. She fusses over him like I imagine a relative might, like an aunt, maybe.

"Let's go down to the arena, and I'll show you just how soft I've become," he says.

She laughs, her hands on her hips. "Issi, you won't need him around, will you?"

Ismini shakes her head.

Aleka claps Aris on the shoulder and steers him out. He shoots me a glance—*Behave*, it says. I roll my eyes at him, and he smirks before he disappears through the door.

"She was worried about him," Ismini says. She's staring off at the doorway, like she can still see our Shields. "After Stefan died. Those boys were like brothers. The death of a claimed is not something that many survive. For him to have found you, well," she says, looking at me with a kind smile, "you must be something."

Something good or bad, she doesn't say, which I suppose is fair. I'm beginning to realize that I want to succeed. I don't want to disappoint him, not when he's risking so much for me.

Ismini settles me into a chair and sits opposite me. She asks me what I've been able to do so far, and I tell her about everything, from the air gag to the tornado to Obsidian to healing after the troll attack. She doesn't interrupt, but I can see emotions and thoughts flickering on her fair face.

"And what of your family?" she asks.

I blink. "What about them?"

"Do any of them have magic? Magic families in Ocron are carefully monitored, their progeny noted. We know nothing of those in Aclines," she says.

I frown. It kind of sounds like she is talking about breeding dogs or something.

"My father's family is … was from a place called Spit. They'd been there for three or four generations, and as far as I know, none of them had magic," I say, thinking of him. The illness that ravaged him was quick, but not painless. He wasted away in front of me, but his eyes remained clear and focused until the last. It wasn't until after his death that animals started responding to me. At first I thought it was my father's way of reaching me from beyond the grave, a way to offer me comfort. Now I wonder if the trauma of his death somehow cracked something open inside me, unleashed something. I shake my head, clearing the image away.

"Siblings?" Ismini asks.

I shake my head again. "None."

"And your mother?"

"Died before I was a year old," I say. "Fever. She was from the Isles."

"I see," Ismini says, pursing her lips in thought. "A lot of strong Wind and Water Mages there. Do you know her family name?"

"No," I say. I don't even know her first name. My father never talked about her. I kind of know what she looked like, but only because of the differences between my father and me. She must have been short, and probably curvy too, with curly hair. My father used to tell me a story about how her ship was wrecked on the reefs near Spit during a storm, and she found her way to the lighthouse through the choppy sea, clutching only a single board to stay afloat. My father found her washed up on the rocks, and the rest, as they say, is history. She never returned to her homeland. My father said she was some kind of trader, making her way along Aclines. She didn't speak about it much—I guess because it was too painful—and he was not one to pry or question his good fortune.

I used to dream of a love like theirs, the sea pulling my true love to me. In my dreams, though, his form was foggy, indistinct. My mother was real, solid. Her presence caused a stir in sleepy old Spit. Her skin was dark, like Head Mage Saroya's, an oddity and therefore something to be feared. At the thought of the Head Mage, a shudder goes through me. Ismini notes it and changes the subject.

"We're going to start with the basics," she says briskly, settling herself back into the chair. "I want you to picture your magic inside you, here." She points to a spot just below her breastbone.

"What does it look like?" I ask.

"It differs. The Fire Mages will say a flame or a spark, for example. I picture a seed. Whatever it is, root that image firmly in your mind. This will be the well from which you draw your power."

I close my eyes and try, and the image flickers from a seed to a water droplet to a flame to a cloud. I sigh and try to settle my mind. I picture the calming waves of the sea, the way the starlight sparkles on the water like jewels. It is a soothing scene, and one so familiar that I can smell the salt on the air, can hear the voices of the gulls over the crash of unforgiving waves.

I take a deep breath and search—but find only darkness. I frown, looking deeper, but then I realize the darkness has edges—wispy things, like bits of shadow or smoke. I realize that the darkness I envision in my core has nothing to do with an absence of magic. Rather, the darkness there is the magic. Gods, perhaps I am a monster after all. My lips feel dry, and when I try to swallow, my throat feels like sand.

"From this core, you will draw your magic outward, like a wisp of air or a vine," Ismini says.

Her voice is comforting, and my fears recede. The nights at my lighthouse are a safe memory, a time when I knew who and what I was. I will have that peace again. I breathe deeply. I wonder why the teachers at the school couldn't be more like her.

"For now, I want you to picture yourself pulling inward, not out," she says. "If you see vines, pull them in, wrap them around your core. Wrap and pull until nothing leaks out. This is control. This is a way you can regain control, no matter what happens. Breathe deeply, in and out, like waves on a shore, and pull in."

I picture colored light, like the beacon of my lighthouse, streaming back toward my center, being wrapped in the darkness, becoming a part of it. I feel warm, and a little light-headed. The shadows pulse and writhe, like a snake, but as I breathe, they settle.

I'm not sure how long I do this, with Ismini's gentle instruction, but when I eventually open my eyes, I realize I'm sweating profusely, and parched from thirst.

"It gets easier," Ismini says, and passes me a glass of water.

My arm shakes as I accept it. The fact that I'm tired at all makes me realize that I'm actually doing something, not just sitting here breathing. I'm working with my magic, and that thrills me.

Then she hands me a small clay pot filled with black soil.

I look at her quizzically.

"I want to see what you can do," she says. "Intentionally. Let's grow a flower."

"What kind?" I ask, looking at the pot.

"What's your favorite?" she asks.

It doesn't take me long to decide. "Tamdosan roses," I say, smiling. As far as I know, they only grow in Aclines, and are prized in Spit. I tried to grow them a few times and failed miserably. They are notoriously hard to cultivate.

"What do you like about them? The blooms? The fragrance?" Ismini asks, but she's grinning. She knows.

"The thorns," I say, wickedly.

She laughs.

Tamdosan roses are beautiful, true, in shades of deep violet-red, and fragrant too, but their thorns are over an inch long and needle-sharp. In times of trouble, the stems have even been used as makeshift weapons.

She has me fix an image of the flower in my mind, thinking about every single detail, from the color of the leaves to the texture of the petals. Then she has me try to project a wisp of magic into the pot in my hands, with the command "Grow."

We try for the remainder of the morning, but nothing happens. I've said the word "grow" so many times that it starts to sound funny to my ears, like I'm warping the word or like my tongue is going numb. If Ismini is disappointed, she doesn't show it. I wipe a damp curl out of my eyes. My fine purple shirt is dark with sweat.

"I'm glad I have a private bath," I say, accepting another glass of water from Ismini. "Why do I feel like I just ran twenty miles?"

"Think of it like flexing muscles you've never used before," she says. "You'll get stronger."

"I hope my wardrobe is up to it," I say. I'm glad I didn't wear any of the fine dresses—they'd be a mess.

"If the clothes in your room don't suit you, you can always go shopping in town. I could show you around sometime."

Like this Earth Mage, this senior Mage in the king's court, has nothing better to do than go shopping with me.

"I don't have any money," I mutter, embarrassed. I've never needed any before. I feel heat rush to my face, and I look down at the clothing I'm wearing, finer than anything I've ever owned by a hundredfold.

Ismini blinks her leaf-green eyes. "Of course you do. Didn't anyone tell you about your stipend?" she asks.

I frown. I definitely would have remembered that.

"While training, and after too, you'll be provided a monthly stipend, for as long as you're employed by the king. It's enough for the basics, and some fun too," she says, her eyes twinkling. "I'll see to it that you're given access. At most shops, simply signing your name is sufficient. The shopkeeps then come to the palace for payment."

I've never really had any money before. The people in Spit gave me supplies and things in exchange for keeping the lighthouse working. I bartered for things I needed, like thread or soap or clothes. Money is an interesting idea, and one I guess I'll have to get used to.

"Well, I'm not sure I'd be able to navigate the fashions here, anyway," I say with a rueful grin. "I have no idea how the women can take a deep breath in those dresses, much less walk."

"They don't do much of either," a voice says from the door.

I look up to find Leo—King Leonidas—lounging against the doorframe, looking elegantly amused, and I wonder how long he's been there. Heat rushes to my cheeks, and I smooth a wayward curl back from my face.

"How's it going?" he asks.

I feel like the question should be addressed to Ismini, but he's looking at me. I realize that a lot more time has passed than I thought—it is dusk, the hallway outside dim.

"It's not," I say, and he chuckles.

"She's doing very well," Ismini reassures both of us.

"What's with the pot?" Leo asks.

"She's going to grow some Tamdosan roses," Ismini says.

His eyes go wide. "Interesting choice," he says lightly.

I wonder if I should have picked something plainer, simpler, prettier—like a daisy. But then again, that's not really my style.

"Well, don't let me stop you," he says. "I just wanted to check in."

"We're fine, Your Majesty," Ismini says with a smile. "Now shoo."

He throws up his hands in a show of acceptance, shoots me a grin, and vanishes down the hallway.

"Sometimes I think of him like one of my own boys," Ismini says wistfully.

The admission shocks me. "You have children?" I ask.

She beams. "Three boys, about your age," she says. "They work the farm with my husband mostly, though the oldest will be married soon."

"You're married," I say. For some reason, I pictured Shields and Mages as … dandelion fluff on a breeze. Not belonging anywhere, not setting down roots. Belonging to each other—which made me think of that damned letter opener and my own damned Shield and his double-damned disregard for clothing—but belonging to no one else.

"That surprises you," she says.

I nod.

"Aleka and I have been working together since, oh, before you were born." She stands, stretching. "We had our fill of adventures and wanted to settle a bit. Estana was a good job for us both. She is still my Shield, but she also fills her time working as chief of the palace guards. I have my family. This world, being a Mage," she says, looking at me, "it can be whatever you want it to be, despite what Head Mage Saroya might teach at the school. It's why I stay here, why I settled here instead."

But what did I want it to be? For so long, my life was simple, laid out before me—my father worked the lighthouse, as did his father and then his before that. I thought maybe I'd get married someday, though prospects in Spit were slim. Have a family, raise them to be the next lighthouse keepers.

And then all this happened, and I am just taking the next step, trying to figure out my new life. What do I want? I'm not sure. Ismini makes it sound like the world is at my fingertips—a thrill goes through me at that thought, all the way down to my toes. I can do anything I want.

I look down.

In my hands, a perfect violet-red rose blooms on a stem of needle-sharp thorns.

Chapter 32: Aris

Leaving Wren alone, historically, hasn't been a great idea—but I'm leaving her with one of the most powerful Earth Mages on the continent, inside a room of stone. Ismini could contain a hurricane inside that room if she wanted to—though I hope it won't come to that. Wren's magic seems to be tied to her emotions, especially negative ones. And she's been all sunshine and rainbows since her manacles came off.

I go to the arena with Aleka, where some of the other Shields are getting in some workouts. I haven't had a proper workout in days, and my muscles sing with anticipation.

"Well, kitty cat, fancy a match?" Aleka says, grinning.

She tosses a gladius toward me, and I nab it from the air. It's a practice sword, the blade nicked and beaten, but it will do. I whirl it in my hand.

"Do you want to put some leathers or a chest plate on first?" I ask her. She's in loose pants and a long-sleeved shirt—it's cooler here than at the school.

She grins, flashing white teeth as she thumps her chest with her free hand. "Chest armor? That's what a rib cage is for!"

And then she's on full attack mode. And she's good. She's got nearly three decades of experience on me, but I've got size and strength on my side.

"You're getting slow, old lady," I say.

She responds with a flurry of jabs and kicks that would put most Shields to shame.

The other Shields are stopping to watch. I recall Aleka is something like a captain of the guard here, and probably doesn't get her ass kicked too often.

To be honest, I drag it out a little. I like the spectacle. She doesn't like it when I do this and goes on the offensive even harder.

When I sweep her legs out from under her, and her back hits the packed sand of the arena, the other Shields cheer. She glares at them, and the cheering is abruptly cut off as they all go back to their tasks, pretending they haven't been watching.

For a minute, Aleka lets her head fall back to the sand, chest heaving.

"Not bad, kitten," she says, lifting a hand.

I grab it, pulling her upright. "Not bad, granny," I say.

She laughs, smacking my arm. "Oh, I missed you," she says, and wipes the sand off her pants. "Come on. Show me what else you've learned since I saw you last."

I run drills with Aleka for a while. Then she's off to beat up some new guards, so I spend the rest of the morning on calisthenics before going on a run through the city. It's fine, I guess, as far as cities go. I go out through the gate and into the fields for a few miles before turning back. The exercise feels good. I grab food in the guards' hall with a few other Shields, and the camaraderie feels good too. One of them remembers me and offers to deal me in on a card game later that night, but I turn him down. I can't afford distractions. Somehow it's like nothing has changed since I was last here, even though everything has.

My good mood vanishes when I get back to our rooms. Night fell an hour ago, and I expected Wren to be ready for a training session when I returned. Instead, she is standing in our shared living space, where a massive bouquet of dark red roses has been placed on a table. The smell of roses permeates the room, as thick as fog, and I fight back the urge to gag. She's grinning down at a piece of paper in her hand, her cheeks pink.

I don't like it.

"What's all this?" I ask, like I don't know.

"Oh," she says absently, looking at the flowers. "Don't touch them. Those thorns are wicked."

She's right. You can barely see the stems for the thorns. The flowers are nice enough, I guess. Strange choice, but she doesn't seem to notice that. I mean, I'm not really the flower-giving kind of guy—I've never needed to be.

"Leo … um, the king has asked us to dine with him tonight," Wren says, fluttering the note at me. "Isn't that … unusual?"

"Not really," I lie, collapsing into the nearest couch.

Something flickers across her face. I turn away.

"He'll get you to like him, and then like his cause and believe in him and it so firmly that the cause becomes yours too. Every Mage that works with him goes through this," I say, waving my hand through the air dismissively.

However, the king never sent Stefan flowers or anything, or showed any particular interest at all in him, or me. Not that we needed any encouragement. We'd been born into old families of Ocron, raised with loyalty to country ingrained in us from birth. We served gladly.

"Well, I hope you're planning to bathe before dinner," Wren says, wrinkling her nose at me.

"Why? You miss seeing me with my clothes off already?" I ask.

She turns dark red, glaring at me. I swear the room feels colder, and the moon has vanished behind clouds in what was a clear night sky ten minutes ago. Maybe I shouldn't antagonize my Mage.

"Be ready in an hour," she says, and she takes a book to the far side of the room, where she sits and begins to flip pages, pointedly ignoring me.

I feel like pointing out that the book she picked up is in a language I know she doesn't read, but I don't feel like having fleas in my bed tonight—if I even sleep tonight—so I manage to hold my tongue.

My eyes flick to the paper on the table, and I pick it up.

Dinner tonight?
—Leo
PS Bring your Shield, if you must.

I crumple the paper in my hand before throwing it into the fire.

An hour later, we're standing before the king's private apartments. There are four guards at the door, meant to be imposing, though none of them are Shields. I can't hold back a smirk.

Inside is a sitting room larger than most houses, with a dining table set for four. By a stone fireplace nearly ten feet wide, King Leonidas stands talking with a Mage in a blue robe, I think the one that was with him last night.

The king lights up when we enter, greeting us like we're old friends. It's hard to tell if this is just showmanship, a part of his political savvy, or if he truly believes it himself.

"My little Wren, this is Panos, the finest Water Mage you could ever hope to meet, and chief among our researchers," he says. He has a hand on Wren's back, ushering her toward the other Mage. I wonder at how easily he touches her, and how easily she lets him.

She's changed into a loose green dress and wrapped her braid around her head like a coronet. Next to the king, she looks effortlessly regal, and not at all like a lighthouse keeper from Spit, or even the ornery Mage I knew on the road. She shifts as easily as a Shield.

"Hello," she says, shaking the man's hand.

He's older, solemn, quiet, like a deep, still mountain lake.

"It is my pleasure," the man says. His voice rumbles like soft thunder.

He's a few decades older than me, and stooped, with a long gray beard to match his long gray hair, and blue eyes that seem to shift color in the firelight. It's like he's the embodiment of water itself. He doesn't look at me, and that's fine. Shields are trained to fade into the background, but always be ready to pounce if needed.

"I understand you are having some trouble manifesting an element," Panos says, leading Wren toward the table.

"You could say that," she says, making a wry face.

"And you were able to perform some unintentional magic with a manacle on?" he asks.

They sit at the table, leaving the king and me at the fireplace. King Leonidas looks at me with a gleam in his eye.

"Yes," she says. "And I don't understand that. I thought they stopped magic."

"They do," Panos says, accepting a glass of wine from a server.

Wren politely asks the man for water instead, as do I. I am not about to do anything to dull my reflexes here, in this room, with Wren and the king.

"There are very few objects which can block magic in such a manner. We have a few here, at the palace," Panos continues. He's an academic, and he drones on about the history of the manacles for a while.

"So, Head Mage Saroya told you about my … lack of control?" Wren says, with only a slight wince.

Panos shakes his head. "Markos, my old friend, wrote me through a messenger Shield—ah, that's a Shield who chooses that sort of employ rather than claiming a Mage, usually a raptor of some kind. This one was a particularly speedy falcon who—" He stops when he realizes the king is staring at him, one eyebrow raised in amusement. Panos clears his throat. "Anyway … yes, the Head Mage did message our king about you, which is why we thought it best to bring you here."

Wren looks at the king, who shrugs, and I note there is some redness in his face that I can't entirely blame on the wine he's been drinking. He still has nearly a full glass in his hand.

I tap my fingers against my leg. I am not comfortable here. This isn't some state dinner; this is a private affair, in the king's own chambers. The significance is not lost on me. He wants Wren to feel comfortable, at least. I wonder to what end. Either that, or he doesn't want to risk her accidentally causing a scene in front of a large audience. I get the feeling that this is the less likely option.

The dinner feels interminable. Panos and Wren discuss magic for a while, and the king and I listen. Then the topic turns to Wren's home. She shoots an apologetic glance at the king after calling her home country Aclines, as it's now technically all Ocron.

The king doesn't seem offended. If anything, it's like he's been waiting for an opening to talk to her, to steal her attention. It's odd to think of a king making such an effort.

"My dear Wren, my skin is not so thin," he says, smiling. "Aclines is a welcome addition to Ocron. I begrudge its inhabitants nothing. They are not to blame for their king's poor decisions."

Her face lights up. I know she's not all that invested in the politics of her home country—Spit was too far removed from its capital to be much more than an afterthought—but she does seem interested in him, in the king, and in his reasons for the invasion, like she wants an excuse to change his label from "villain" to "hero" in her mind.

"What poor decisions?" she asks.

Panos sucks in a breath, but the king doesn't mind.

"There were several, besides the decision to declare war on Ocron," the king says, with a wry smile. "I wanted access to the coast. Aclines controls a large part of the southern coast, and my ships will be able to travel faster to the western part of the continent if they can use it, rather than having to go north, if you'll recall from the map."

Wren nods, enraptured.

"He wouldn't grant me access. Now a ship can make it to the western continent in half the time."

"Why is that important?" she asks.

"Oh, all kinds of reasons," he says, sipping from his wine and leaning back in his chair now that he has her attention. "For example, last year there was a terrible drought in the west. The Water Mages could have gotten there earlier, maybe saved the fall crops. And then the southwest was having a hard time with a band of mountain trolls. We could have sent troops more quickly, saved some of the towns there. That kind of thing."

"Mountain trolls?" Wren asks, catching my eye. She pales a bit, remembering our encounter with their milder cousins in the forest.

I nod.

"Among other, nastier things," King Leonidas says, rubbing his temple, like a headache is forming. "We've been sending scouts to the western mountains for months now, but the travel is hard, and slow. One more reason I wanted Aclines's coastline."

"And what will happen to Aclines now?" she asks. Her eyes are shining.

I want to kick her under the table, but my leg won't reach. She's in his clutches now, completely at his mercy. He's got her snared, and he knows it.

"The same thing that happens to the rest of Ocron," he says, leaning forward conspiratorially. "Better infrastructure. Roads. Better schools, maybe even another one for gifted students. Whatever is needed."

"And my part in all this is …?" she asks.

He winks. "Yet to be determined."

Panos coughs, sputtering on a sip of wine. The spell is broken, and Wren goes back to chatting with Panos about all the things water magic can do—reroute rivers, heal, influence the weather, speed ships on their way. I'm grateful for the distraction, and for the look of dismay on the king's face now that he's lost her undivided attention. He tries to hide it, but I see it. I smile into my water goblet as I take a sip.

The strength of the magic, Panos is saying, depends on the strength of the user. Each Mage is limited by their own well of magic—some have more; some have less. Some can do little more than heat water in a teakettle, while some can change the very tides. Stefan was a pretty powerful Mage, but even he would get worn out after a few heavy spells. It could take him days to recover sometimes.

"And some burn out?" Wren asks, glancing at me.

Panos frowns. "Yes. Some do," he says. "When you overreach, you can deplete your magic so completely that it is never restored. You 'go gray,' as they say."

"How do you know your limits, then?" she asks.

"Practice," Panos says, with a patient smile. "Lots and lots of practice."

"Why is magic only in Ocron?" Wren asks.

I raise an eyebrow, but Panos loves her questions, and his eyes shine silver in the firelight as he talks.

"It's not, but it does seem to be more common here," he says. He takes a quick bite of his food before continuing. "The Isles seem to have more wind and water magic, and to our knowledge, Aclines had next to none. It has been said that it is because Ocron worshipped the gods, built them temples, sacrificed to them, honored them, that the first Mages and Shields were from Ocron."

"The gods?" Wren asks, shooting me a glance. "For the elements?"

Panos nods excitedly. This is clearly a favored topic of his. The king stifles a smile.

"Lord Rigrasil, god of day, and his brother Lord Caladrius, god of night," he says. "Their temples shone bright as the sun and were flooded with worshippers, so the legends say." He shoots a furtive glance at the king, who nods. "They have … fallen into some disrepair over the last few decades," he says. His lips tighten. "After giving their gifts of magic, the lesser gods have been silent, and their brothers too. Some say they no longer exist."

He leans forward, hooking a finger at Wren. She leans toward him, like they're sharing a secret.

"But some of us still study the old ways," he says, and again looks at the king. He straightens. "For academic reasons, you understand. It's a major part of our country's history."

"Of course," Wren says, smiling.

King Leonidas takes this opportunity to dazzle Wren with his grand plans to restore the temples, to make sure that their history is not lost in the crumbling, derelict ruins that they are otherwise sure to become. She's listening intently, but I'm bored. It's late, and I don't try too hard to contain my yawns.

At the end of dinner, Panos kicks us out. "We have a big day tomorrow. I want you well rested," he says kindly.

The king takes Wren's arm as we turn to leave.

"I realize this might come across as a bit … in poor taste," he says.

She's looking up at him, and she's not pulling her arm away. I'm not quite able to stifle the growl that rises in me. Panos shoots me a glance, but no one else notices. They're too wrapped up gazing at each other.

"We're having a gala at the end of the week, to celebrate Aclines joining Ocron," the king says. "I'd like you to come. It would mean a lot to have a daughter of Aclines at my side."

Wren flushes. "Of course," she says.

He beams and then—still keeping eye contact—bows, and kisses her fucking hand.

Panos inserts himself between me and the king. "Shield Aris, it is always good to see you," he says before I can do anything stupid.

"Panos," I say through gritted teeth.

Wren walks past me, and I lock eyes with the king. I give him a bow—not a hairbreadth lower than required—and follow her out.

"Don't think that you're getting out of dagger practice tonight," I growl.

Wren acquiesces with a flutter of her hand, not fighting me. Clearly, her mind is on something or someone else. I don't want to know, really.

I leave her in our common room while I go strip off the stupid formal jacket Shields wear at court, and grab the pair of daggers I got from Aleka.

When I come back, she's sitting in one of the overstuffed chairs by the fire, her bare feet tucked under her, already sound asleep, a smile on her lips.

I stand and watch her for a minute, watch the firelight play across her face, lighting the curves and hollows. I should wake her up, make her practice. Her protection and well-being come before all else.

I let out a sigh.

I put the daggers down and scoop her up, and she curls into me, letting out a long sigh in her sleep. I put her in her bed, pulling a blanket up and over her. She looks so peaceful. I remember what it felt like to sleep beside her as a tiger, and I have to fight the urge to shift right then and there. She's so calm when she sleeps. I wonder if her magic is leaking out, if she's calling to the tiger in me even now.

I grab the spelled candle instead and settle down in the armchair for another vigil.

Chapter 33: Wren

The next day dawns pink and clear. I awake ravenous, and I'm halfway to the common room before I realize I'm still in the dress I changed into for dinner last night. I vaguely remember sitting down to wait for Aris, and then … what, falling asleep?

Aris isn't in my room. I change and then find him in the common room, waiting with a dagger in either hand.

"Good morning," he says, grinning wickedly. "Since you denied me practice yesterday, we'll do two hours today."

I roll my eyes, then ogle the plate of fruit and goodies someone's brought up.

"Can I at least eat first?" I say, grabbing a pastry. He was right—the magic practice is really sapping my energy, and I'm not even making anything much happen yet. I ate plenty at dinner last night, and when I think about last night, I think about Leo, and my eyes must go glassy or something, because I hear a thunk, and then there's a dagger embedded in an apple in front of me, the hilt still vibrating. Aris hurled it from across the room. I glare at him and take a big bite of my food.

"You could have hit me," I growl between bites.

He raises an eyebrow, as if to say, *Not likely*.

"Come on, princess," he says, rolling his shoulders, shaking out his arms, like he's getting ready for some big battle instead of simply teaching me. There's a glint in his eyes, and they sparkle like blue gems. He's in rare form today.

"A real knife today?" I say, looking down at it.

He snorts. "Dagger, Wren. Dagger. Not a knife."

I know. I just like to antagonize him.

"And no, you can't work with a real dagger today."

As he threatened, he puts me through two hours of blocks, blows, and stances, correcting me each time with an obnoxious attention to detail, and making me use the letter opener instead of one of the daggers he wears. I'm worn out by the time I get a note saying Panos is ready to meet with me, so I'm grateful for the reprieve. Aris has been restless all morning, and it's exhausting.

Aris walks me back to the room where I met with Ismini. Panos is there, with a shallow dish of water, a candle, a toy pinwheel, and a rock. It seems he's determined to get to the bottom of my lack of element today.

"I'll come back for you later," Aris growls. He sticks around for a while, though, like he wants to make sure I'm not going to light Panos on fire or anything.

I quickly get absorbed in Panos's teaching, and when I look back after a while, Aris is gone.

We spend hours with the things that Panos brought. We focus on one at a time. Each time, I envision my magic like a rope of shadows coiling away from me. And each time, nothing happens. By the end of the morning, I am frustrated and sticky with sweat.

"There's no rush, Wren," Panos reminds me. "Magic finds each in its own time."

"I wish it would hurry up," I grumble.

He smiles and changes tack. "Do you remember what you feel when your magic leaves you?"

I frown. "Sometimes nothing. I think I've been summoning animals, kind of controlling them." I don't like admitting this. The words come out in a jerky fashion. "I think that's been unconscious, really. It happens even when I sleep. Sometimes, though …" I stop.

Panos waits, patient as a glacier.

"Sometimes I feel a thrill, like a shiver down my spine," I say. "Is that normal?"

"Magic feels different to each," he says cryptically. "I feel it as a cool wave. I believe Mage Ismini senses more of a rumble. I was hoping the feeling of yours would point us in the direction of a particular element to focus on."

"Sorry. Not helpful," I say.

He gives me a patient smile. "In due time," he says, and pats my hand.

Then he stands, his old bones creaking and groaning. He offers me his hand, and when I stand, he loops it through his elbow.

"Come on," he says, and totters toward the door. "Let's take a break. I could use a walk."

Apparently, my training room isn't that far from the arena, so Panos takes us there first. There's a large courtyard set up similarly to the stadium at the school, with a sandy floor and racks of weapons. I spy Aleka shouting at a row of guards, making them jump to attention. Around the courtyard is a two-story walkway, with halls leading off toward barracks and a mess hall, and another toward the stables. It's easy to tell the Shields apart from the ungifted guards—they're taller, stronger, bolder, and the ungifted watch them with a mix of envy and awe. There are a half dozen of them training, along with two children, including the wolf-boy I saw earlier. I'm surprised to see children here, but they appear to be taking their tasks very seriously. They spar with wooden swords, while the older Shields bark instructions.

I find Aris doing a sort of exercise where he hangs from a bar and pulls himself up to it repeatedly. For some reason, this requires him to be shirtless, much to the enjoyment of the court ladies passing by on the walkway. He drops to the ground when he sees me, chest heaving from the exertion, chiseled muscles slick with sweat. I narrow my eyes at him, and he grins.

"Come to watch?" he asks, wiping the sweat from his face.

I shake my head, though I can't take my eyes off him. He knows it, and crosses his arms, which emphasizes just how perfect his muscles are. Arrogant bastard.

"Just stretching my old bones, Shield Aris," Panos says, patting my hand where it still rests on his arm. "You can join us, if you wish."

Aris grabs his shirt and follows.

Panos takes us through some passage through the Shields' quarters back toward the main hallway. Aris straps on his swords as we go. In the narrow passage, he smells of heat and metal, like the embodiment of a hot summer day. I shake my head again to clear it, but it doesn't really help.

"You seem to have a destination in mind," Aris growls as we make our way down the hallway.

Panos nods. "I'm expected in the throne room. The king likes to keep the court open so anyone can join in the discussion, and I like to hear what people have to say. Besides," he admits, his eyes twinkling, "it's a good excuse for me to sit quietly for a while, and sometimes take a nap."

The throne room is vast, larger than an entire barn, with sweeping columns ringing the periphery. At the end, on a raised dais, is a carved wooden throne with a gilded sun at the top, the rays framing the golden king. Leo sits thoughtfully, listening to a pair of men in dusty traveling gear. His eyes flick toward us, just for a moment, and I swear I see the corner of his mouth turn up. Panos guides us to a place conspicuously at the front of the room, past rows of festooned courtiers. A pair of them hastily make way for him. Panos leans heavily on my arm—more heavily than he was, though I'm sure just for show—and has me sit next to him, like I'm the one helping him. Aris fades into the shadows behind a column.

Panos sits back, his knees creaking, and settles the folds of his blue robe around him. I get a few curious glances directed at my plain robe, but I'm so busy looking around at everything that I barely notice. The room is full of nobles and guards and supplicants. Those wishing to speak form a surprisingly orderly line down the center of the room. The two men at the front are talking with Leo now. One is holding a battered hat and is running his hands along the brim, turning it over anxiously. He has a scrubby beard and a long leather coat. The other man is burly and has a bandage wrapped around his arm, stained rusty brown.

"They came out of nowhere," the hat man is saying, his voice hoarse. "Like mist, or smoke. We lost half our flock that first night, and the rest the second."

"Lost?" a noble asks—he is a thin man wrapped in a heavily embroidered coat and wearing garish pants.

"Slaughtered," the burly man croaks. "Carried off by bat-winged demons."

A gasp goes up from the ladies in the crowd, who begin fanning themselves furiously. A ripple of whispers echoes through the room.

"How do you know they went west?" the gaudy man asks.

"He likes to hear himself talk," Panos confided.

I stifle a smile.

"We followed the path of entrails," the burly man says, eyeing the gaudy man, who visibly pales.

The smile fades from my face.

The whispers intensify. I'm not sure what they're talking about, but they seem concerned.

"What's going on?" I ask Panos.

"Attacks. Things coming down from the mountains," he whispers back. "More every week." He looks at the line of supplicants, and I realize that the majority of them are also dirty and appear tired, like they've come a long way to ask their king for help.

I turn back to Leo, who's discussing something with a man at his side.

"It's them Black Water Witches!" one of the men in line cries, raising a fist. "They're the ones! Calling all kinds of foul beasts to their side!"

"Aye, the Black Water!" another exclaims, and shouts erupt.

I vaguely remember hearing about this mythical group at the school.

"I thought they were just a rumor," I say to Panos.

He shakes his head. "A cult of them found refuge up north, near Roallac. There's even a rumor that the Roallac queen herself is a convert, the queen of the witches," he whispers, but not softly. People around us swivel their heads to listen to him. "But they have no power over creatures such as this. They're a wretched band of mystics and fearmongers who desire power. They can cause little real trouble."

"I'm sure King Leonidas has a plan to help these poor men," a lilting voice is saying, soothing the crowd like a balm.

People begin to murmur in agreement.

The speaker is an elegant woman with long black hair piled high on her head and rows of blue gems around her neck. She preens at the attention, turning her gaze back to Leo. He watches her for a moment before clearing his throat.

"I have already dispatched teams to investigate," he says, raising a hand. "And a fleet of ships will be deployed within the week, with supplies to alleviate your need. You have my word."

"Thank you, sire," the hat man says, bobbing his head.

The burly man grunts but bows too.

The next group comes up, but the story is much the same. Attacks in the west—a pair of mountain trolls taking out a farm, a town torched by some fire-breathing beast. I struggle to sit still as horror after horror unfolds before us. The crowd also seems to be getting restless as Leo listens patiently, addressing each concern. The dark-haired lady is the only one who seems unperturbed.

"Lady Orothea," Panos says when he sees me watching her. "Daughter of a minor nobleman from the northeast. Family's been a loyal supporter of Estana for generations, up at the Roallac border. Easy to be calm when it's not your family on the front lines, I suppose."

"I see," I say. I fidget. I wonder how Leo can seem so poised, so patient. From time to time, I catch his eye and fight back a blush.

Panos begins to nod off. How he does this, I'm not sure—the crowd is getting antsy, wanting to know where the money to replace all these crops and defend the towns will come from. I see a pair of men in Aclinese black and green, whom I assume are governors or ambassadors. Their outfits are kind of bold, considering they're now technically a part of Ocron, but clearly, they have insisted on keeping their own colors, holding themselves apart. They argue that Aclines's treasury is being stripped to pay for things that aren't their concern.

"I think it's time we left," Panos says as the volume in the room increases, waking him from his nap.

I mutter my agreement and help him stand. I've never cared much for politics, so long as I was left alone in my lighthouse. I'm a lot closer to the center of things here, and I'm not sure my allegiance would go to Aclines instead of Ocron and Leo. I have to push through the crowd a bit as tempers rise—but then Aris is there, and the mob melts away around him. No one pushes a Shield around.

In the hallway, I feel like I can finally breathe again. Panos continues to lean on my arm, like all the strength has left him. We're followed by a stream of other people, who are chattering about the business in the west like they're discussing the weather—lightly, flippantly. One of the women breaks away from the group and approaches Aris with a sly smile.

"Shield Aris," she says in a husky voice. "So good to see you again."

Aris clears his throat. She runs a finger along his arm, tracing the black embroidery there. She's tall, with unnaturally red hair and a waist tightly cinched in by her gown. She's heavily adorned in jewelry, flashing from her fingers, ears, and wrists.

"Will you be in Estana long?" she purrs. "I hope we can see much more of each other."

I groan and roll my eyes.

Aris gently removes her hand. "Korinna. I'm busy," he says.

She pouts her bottom lip.

Aris brushes past her and doesn't look back.

"Honestly," I say as the three of us make our way back to the training room. "Have you ever had a relationship with a woman that wasn't sexual?"

"I don't have time for relationships, or friends," he says. "I have competition. And I have you. I have my duty."

I look back and see Korinna being escorted in the opposite direction by a gray-haired gentleman.

"Aleka," Aris says after a beat.

I turn back to him and raise an eyebrow. "What?"

"I am actually capable of talking to a woman without wanting to bed her," he says. "Aleka."

"She's like your substitute mother. That doesn't count," I say. "Name another."

We've reached the training room door, and Panos goes inside, mumbling to himself. Aris glares at me. I silently dare him to continue, to say the word on the tip of his tongue. It hovers between us, a threat—and a lie.

He walks away.

I work with Panos for another hour or so that afternoon, but it's futile, and nothing happens. I wait for Aris to turn up again, but eventually I get tired of waiting and make my way back to our rooms. The sun is still high, just starting its decline. I think about Aris and his interaction with the lady in the hallway—clearly, they have history. It bothers me more than I like. He was pretty cold to her, though, and she seemed surprised. I think about what he said to me afterward—or rather, what he failed to say. My face goes hot. Not that I've been imagining what it would be like for Aris to see me as a woman instead of a Mage. It distracts me so much that I don't realize that I'm turned around until I find myself in a dead-end hallway.

How has that happened? I look back and realize with dismay that the hallway I'm in looks identical to the hallway my rooms are on, but it's not the same hallway at all. My rooms should be here, but they're not. I rub the back of my neck and head back. If I can get back to the main hallway by the throne room, or the training room … but nothing looks familiar. I know I've never seen that tapestry of a one-armed knight before. Why can't the hallways have signs or something? I make a mental note to ask Leo the next time I see him—which raises a whole host of other warm feelings that I try to ignore.

Gods, it's hard to focus on these hallways. I'm used to living in a tower with one way up and one way down—this might as well be a maze. One of the doors is open, and there are luxurious rooms inside, sitting rooms and beds hung with velvet and gold. All right, so I've stumbled into some sort of residential hallway, like mine. I must be close.

I turn another corner and find the two governors from Aclines talking in angry but hushed tones. They look at me, glaring.

"What do you want?" one of them snarls. He has a hooked nose and a potbelly, and I frown at his tone.

"Just lost," I say. "Can you point me in the direction of the west wing?"

"You're the Aclinese Mage, the king's pet — the one who doesn't even have an element," the other man says. He's leaning over the potbellied man, one hand raised as if to strike him. He settles back now, straightening his jacket. The silver-and-black medallion on his chest gleams in the lantern light.

"The west wing?" I repeat, trying to sound bored.

"Why have you been so quick to ally yourself with that tyrant? Did Saroya use her mind tricks on you?" he asks.

Potbelly crosses his arms.

The hair on the back of my neck prickles. Their anger was directed at each other, or perhaps at Leo. Now it seems they've turned on me. *Great.*

"Never mind. I'll find it myself," I say, and turn back.

"Wait." The man grabs my arm.

I try to wrench free of him, but he's got a grip like the jaws of a shark, his fingers digging deep. I wish Aris were here. He'd rip the man's arm off.

"You're hurting me," I growl. "Let go." Now would be a really good time for my magic to appear. I have a theory about emotions triggering it. And my emotions are starting to get very, very heated. It would be a good time for this man to spontaneously combust. I think about what Ismini said, about looking down into my core, for tendrils of my power, but all I see is light.

And nothing happens.

"Now, little traitor Mage," he croons. "I just want to talk. Do you think it's fair, the way he's draining your home? The way your countrymen are being taxed after they bled to fight this man, to fund a western war that's none of their concern?"

"I think that you're a narrow-minded idiot," I say. I raise my other hand to pry him off me, but I find it's restrained by Potbelly. Somehow I've managed to get myself cornered by these two, in some random hallway, and my magic doesn't feel like playing today. *Great. Really, really great.*

"Be nice," the man says. He's close, and I can feel the heat of his breath against my cheek. "We can be good friends."

I'm starting to get nervous. I should have waited for Aris at the training room.

"You really think it's a good idea to threaten a Mage?" I bluff. "Do you have any idea what I can do to you? I'll turn you inside out, just for fun."

Potbelly blanches, but the other man just grins. His teeth are cracked and yellowed, and his breath is foul.

"Go ahead," he says, tightening his grip.

I flinch, and he cackles.

"Hmm," he says, and runs a finger down my cheek. "I wonder just how fond of you the king is. A king's ransom, now, that might just give Aclines the help we need."

I spit in his face.

His relatively good humor vanishes. He raises a hand to hit me, and restrained as I am, there's nothing I can do to stop it.

"If you wish to continue living, and with all your extremities still attached," a voice drawls, "I suggest you unhand my Mage."

The man steps back, and I see Leo standing there, arms crossed. Rage flashes in his eyes, but his pose is relaxed, at ease. Relief washes over me like a crashing wave. Two heavily armed guards are behind him, and they draw their swords. The clear ringing of steel echoes down the hallway. Potbelly quickly lets go of me and clasps his hands together behind his back.

"Sire," the other man says, bowing. "We were just having a chat with our fellow countrywoman here."

"I am no 'fellow' of yours," I say, wrenching my arm free. This time, he lets me go. I walk over to Leo, who scans me quickly.

"Are you hurt?" he asks. I look at my boots and shake my head, hot tears already springing to my eyes. I feel foolish.

He gently takes my chin with his fingers and raises my head until I'm forced to look at him, and I see the concern in his eyes. Concern that appears to be more than just that of a king for one of his subjects. Warmth floods through me, from the roots of my hair all the way to my toes. He seems convinced, at least, that I'm in no immediate danger and turns to his guards.

"The governors of Aclines are no longer welcome here," he says to them.

The guards clap their free hands against their chests. They sheathe their swords and leave us, heading toward the Aclinese men.

Leo puts an arm around my shoulders and walks me back down the hallway without another word. I glance back over my shoulder once, but my view of the governors is obscured by the veritable wall of metal that is the guards.

We walk in silence for a moment. It feels good, being held against him, and maybe I lean into the touch a little. His arm around my shoulders is warm, comforting.

"Thank you," I mumble after a moment.

His grip tightens a fraction. "Next time you'd like a tour, please allow me to accompany you," he says with a wink.

We pass an open door with a balcony, and he pauses a moment. The sun is dipping beneath the horizon, painting the clouds in blazing red and gold. The city itself glows too, the stone reflecting the brilliance of the sky. The roads spread from the palace like spokes in a wheel. Beyond the walls, nothing but mile upon mile of grassy plains and farms. In the distance, I even make out the dark, blocky shape of the Golden Crown Lodge, now truly glowing in the fading light. It's a gorgeous sight, and I feel all the fear from earlier, my inability to defend myself, just leaking out and away, dispersing into the oncoming night air.

"What will happen to them?" I ask.

Leo looks down at me. "They'll be stripped of their titles and sent home," he says.

Heat floods my face. Because of me. Their lives, their honor, ruined, because of me. They'll go home in disgrace just because I have no sense of direction.

"They didn't actually do anything," I mumble, embarrassed.

Leo purses his lips. "He was holding you against your will. I heard his threats. And I do not stand for an offense against anyone under my protection."

"Am I?" I ask, surprised.

He blinks. "Are you what?"

"Under your protection," I say.

The sun is nearly down, and a trail of stars is starting to blink against the darkening sky.

"Of course you are," he says softly.

His arm tightens around me, and I stare up at him a lot longer than is probably appropriate, my gaze lingering on his full lips, now quirking up at the corners.

He clears his throat. "As are all citizens of Ocron, of course," he says, smiling a little sheepishly.

"Of course," I echo, but I'm smiling too. I register only distantly the pounding footsteps coming down the hallway.

"Where in all the HELLS have you been?" Aris thunders, skidding to a halt in front of us. His eyes are wide, and he looks me over, confirming that I am in one piece.

Then he levels a glare at Leo. I've seen people nearly pass out when Aris looks at them like that.

Leo just looks right back, calmly amused.

"You were supposed to wait for me," Aris growls, fixing that stare on me now.

I swallow. *I* might pass out.

"I was tired of waiting," I say, but the words come out quiet. He's kind of scary right now, and I don't think I want to push him. His hands are on his hips, chest heaving as he fights back his anger. He looks upward, like he's silently praying to the First Shield for help.

"Why didn't you go to our rooms?" he says after a moment, in a surprisingly level tone.

"I got lost," I mutter.

Aris's gaze flicks again to Leo, to the arm that is still draped around my shoulders.

"How fortunate that the king found you," he says through gritted teeth. "Come on. It's time for training."

Chapter 34: Aris

"You didn't have to be so rude," Wren says as we make our way back to our rooms.

"Yes, I can see you had the situation well in hand," I say, and point to the statue that marks our hallway. "There's different art at each junction. This one is birds."

"Gray falcons," she corrects me. "What took you so long? I waited for you."

"I was … talking to someone," I say.

She stops and crosses her arms, waiting.

"Korinna," I relent. "I was talking to Korinna."

"Talking?" Wren asks archly, but at least she starts walking again.

"Yes," I say evenly. "Talking."

"About what?"

Honestly, the conversation with Korinna did not go well. My ears are still ringing from her screeching. I suppose that's what I get for telling her I won't be sleeping with her anymore—while she's standing next to her husband.

"Boundaries," I say after a moment. "I cannot afford distractions, not with you. I am your Shield. Your protection is my single duty, and so far I'm failing spectacularly at it."

"What are you so upset about? Leo stopped them before anything happened."

I stop.

Wren keeps going a moment before realizing I'm not beside her. She stops and turns, a questioning look on her face. "What?"

"Who's 'them'?" I ask, feeling my pulse start to speed up. "What happened?"

She looks at her boots for a second.

"Wren!"

She jumps, then glares at me. "I said nothing happened!" she says, and turns down our hallway.

I grab her arm, and she rips it from my hand. I let her.

"No!" she shouts.

A Fire Mage is passing and gives us a glance. "Everything all right?" he asks.

"None of your business," I growl.

Wren waves him off, and he continues down the hallway. She sighs, leaning back against the wall, and looks back up at me. She looks exhausted, like the whole ordeal drained her.

"I got lost. I ran into the Aclinese governors, and they were being stupid and rude. I tried to leave, and they grabbed me."

At this juncture, she looks pointedly at me. They grabbed her, like I just tried to. I acknowledge that and try to swallow down the rage building inside me. Every damn time I leave Wren alone, something happens. I should just sit through her lessons with her, every fucking day. My magic flares inside me, my muscles primed, ready for a fight, ready to tear something limb from limb if needed.

"Why didn't you use your magic?" I ask, my voice surprisingly steady.

"It didn't work," she says, shrugging. "So I spat in his face."

A laugh escapes me before I can cut it off. Gods, I'm going to have to give her a dagger to keep with her at all times and will just have to hope that she doesn't accidentally stab herself with it.

"He was going to hit me. Leo stopped him. He was walking me back to our rooms when you found us."

"Yes. You looked cozy," I mutter, though inwardly I'm still reeling from what she's revealed.

Wren raises an eyebrow at me and starts walking again.

"Wren," I say.

She looks back.

"Wrong way," I say, pointing down the hallway.

She throws up her hands and stalks off.

I continue in silence. If she finds this suspicious, she doesn't let on. I don't press her for any more details. I don't need to know any more.

After dagger training, once she's bathed and gone to bed, I get up from my chair. She's sound asleep, curled around a pillow, a smile on her lips. I lock the door silently as I leave the room—and go looking for the Aclinese governors.

Chapter 35: Wren

The next morning I spend with Panos again, without any further luck. We take a break, and then I spend the afternoon with Ismini. I was hopeful after that first initial flower, but I haven't been able to do anything since.

After a long afternoon of more nothing, we break, and I sip on some water as I wait for Aris. This time, I vow, I will not leave the training room until he arrives, so I make small talk with Ismini to pass the time. I feel embarrassed, but I ask Ismini what I should wear to the event that the king has invited me to. Would he expect me to wear one of those ridiculous gowns like the female courtiers wear? Or my Mage robe? I feel a little like a charlatan wearing it. I mean, I am wearing it right now, but that is different. I am actually training. Sort of. I am hardly a real Mage yet.

"Wear whatever you're comfortable in," Ismini recommends, which is less than helpful.

I am never really comfortable. Sure, I've gotten past some of my concern with exposing my skin, but not to the level that most of Ocron has. I'm not a full Mage, so I can't wear a solid-colored robe like they do, and conceal myself behind the folds of cloth. I'm not sure of my place in this country yet, exactly. I am now, as I always have been, "other." And this time there is no lighthouse for me to hide in.

I wrap my robe around myself like a blanket, glad for its comfort and warmth. When I first got the robe, unmarked and undyed, it felt like I'd failed, somehow. Like by not declaring an element, I was somehow lesser. Now, I realize it is exactly the opposite. In the way that sunshine can be fragmented into all the colors of the rainbow through the rain, so too can my gift shift into any element it chooses. I will wear the undyed robe with pride. Hells, maybe I'll even wear it to the ball, just to prove the point.

"Come on, princess," Aris says, nodding toward the door. "Enough play. It's time for lessons."

"We had two hours of lessons this morning," I say, waving goodbye to Ismini.

Aris and I head back to our rooms. He cracks his knuckles, and I note some broken skin there, some bruising. I guess he's been training hard with Aleka. A gaggle of court ladies passes us, their gowns whispering across the floor. They give Aris a series of raking glances that he doesn't seem to notice, but I do. I consider setting their dresses on fire.

Gods, I am tired. I cover a yawn with my hand. Aris gives me a pointed look, as if to say, *No excuses. You're not getting out of this today*. But I feel exhausted to my very bones, and I'm starving. The last thing I want to do is more exercise. I want sleep. I keep thinking about the Aclinese governors, though. When we enter our rooms and I'm still quiet, still thinking, Aris decides that the best way to break me out of my tired gloom is to impose more exercise. It might work for him, but I just want a nap.

"This morning was punishment for missing yesterday's lesson," he says. "You still owe me an hour today."

"Asshole," I mutter. Hunger is making me grumpy.

Aris cocks an eyebrow at me. "Oh? Have you suddenly mastered offensive and defensive magic and are no longer in need of my skills?"

"Fine," I say. I'm too tired to argue with him. "But let me …" I stare wistfully at the couch, so soft and warm by the fireplace. So comfortable. I could curl up there for just a moment, like a cat.

"Oh, no," he says. "Yesterday you sat down for a minute and fell asleep. We do this now. Come on. I have something for you."

Intrigued, I follow him into his room. We've only been here a few days, but the opulence of the place is already feeling normal. His room is tidy, bare; his bed is neatly made. He does have a beautiful view of the palace grounds, so I take a look while he digs for something in his pack. Elegantly dressed men and women promenade through the gardens, and dusk has fallen. It's a new moon tonight, and the sky is fading rapidly to black. In the distance, I see a pack of guards on massive warhorses, and I suddenly miss Obsidian. Maybe I'll go see him after my dagger lesson. Gods, that sounded exhausting, though.

"Here," Aris says.

I turn and find him holding a dagger out to me, hilt-first. It's the twin of the one in his other hand, one of the pair that he was using this morning. The blade is twice the length of my hand, and it's deceptively light. It's a plain blade, finely made. I take it, and the grip is warm from his touch.

"Try not to stab yourself with it," he says. "The king will have my head if you get hurt."

I try and fail to contain the heat that rises to my cheeks when he mentions Leo. Aris notices.

"Wren," he says, and his voice is almost gentle, "whatever … whatever you think is going on with him, remember that he's the king. A politician. It's his job to get people to like him, to follow him."

I frown, tightening my grip on the dagger hilt. I mean, I have to admit that I enjoy Leo's attention. The back of my hand still burns where he kissed it.

All right, fine, I have a crush.

"I know," I mumble. Aris is studying me, and I don't like it.

"Do you?" he asks, not giving up. "So you have a lot of experience with men like him?"

Arrogant asshole. I glare at him. I have little experience with men at all, but I don't tell him that. I don't need to, and that realization makes my cheeks burn even more. I have my back to the window, but I suddenly hear people shrieking as a freak rain shower pops up, drenching them all in seconds. I hold my head higher. I consider denying it. I consider changing the subject. But instead, my tongue seems to have a mind of its own, and words are coming out even before my brain registers them.

"Why, Aris, I do believe you are jealous," I say.

A flash of lightning illuminates the room, casting shadows over his hard face. His eyes stare right back at me, and he doesn't move, doesn't breathe, doesn't blink.

Oh my gods. He is *jealous*. For an instant, a thrill runs through me, and it's intoxicating. Is this a Shield thing? He can't have anyone touch his Mage?

"He's just using you," he growls.

"So are you!" I shout back at him—the thought that's been simmering for days, weeks, ever since that day in the arena when we agreed to work together. It boils over, escaping me like steam shrieking out of a teakettle. And in that moment, he's all Shield again, protecting what he thinks is "his." *Possessive asshole*.

I glare at him, my hands shaking. My vision blurs and my eyes burn, and I have to fight to keep the gathering tears from falling. I will not let them fall. I will not. If I were a reasonable person, I'd be terrified of him, of the way he's looking at me, angry and jealous and arrogant all at once, but right now he's pissing me off. Who does Aris think he is? He's only working with me to regain his precious honor, to be the hero everyone else wants him to be again. Nothing more. And I've had enough.

He blinks. Outside, the thunderstorm has intensified. Lightning flashes, flooding the room with green light, followed so closely by a thunderclap that the whole room shakes.

"Wren," he says, his voice calm. The mask is gone, the one he wears in Shield mode. He is treading cautiously now, and I like that a lot better. "Put the dagger down."

I look down at my arm and see it extended, pointing the blade at him.

And the blade is glowing jade green.

In that instant, I understand my magic. It doesn't operate with words the way magic does with others. It does operate with emotions, from my mind and my heart. It is not commanded—it flows. I feel it surge through me, filling me, making me powerful, unstoppable. Like I've been living through a drought and have just found a well that has filled me with strength—and magic.

All those days feeling like something to be feared, and maybe I am.

I laugh. I see a muscle flicker on the side of Aris's jaw, like he's grinding his teeth, but his voice is steady.

"Wren," he says again, his eyes flicking down to the blade. "Put—it—down."

Outside, the storm is raging. My storm. The windows rattle again in their frames, and thunder shakes the floors. I feel giddy, intoxicated. I can take on the world like this. I can take on Aris. I want to. I want to see just how far I can push, how far my power will go. I slash at the bedside table, and the corner comes off cleanly, with barely a ripple of resistance. I laugh, reveling in the power coursing through me, like lightning itself. I swing the blade, and a trail of light follows behind it. I did this, with my own power. I made light.

"Make me," I dare him.

All right, that was a stupid thing to say.

One minute I feel like I'm in some kind of enlightened state, and the next, I'm lying on the floor. Aris's hands are resting his full weight on my arms, pinning my wrists—and the dagger—to the floor in a viselike grip. I start to lose the feeling in my fingers, and the dagger clatters from them. I look at the blade—now colored like normal steel. My head throbs where it smacked into the marble floor, and I wonder if it's bleeding. I look back at Aris, and the look on his face—rage and maybe something else trying to break through his mask—brings my blood back to a boiling point.

I scream. I rage at him, at the audacity of him, thrashing, trying to push him off. How dare he?

And then I become acutely aware that he's lying on top of me, the full length of that hard body he's so fond of showing off pressed into me, molded to me, his knee resting in between my thighs. It's suddenly very hard to breathe, which has nothing to do with the weight of his strong chest on mine, heaving with mine.

Outside, the storm dies as suddenly as it sprang up. Starlight breaks through the clouds, washing the room in faint, watery light.

Aris doesn't move. His hair has come loose from its tie and falls around his shoulders in a dark veil. My fingers itch to touch it, but my hands are still locked in his, essentially bolted to the floor, which is probably a good thing. I don't know that I trust myself at the moment—not with magic, and not with him.

Aris lets out a long, shuddering breath, and the pressure on my wrists eases. He brushes a curl back from my face, the gesture surprisingly soft. My skin ignites where he touches it, my body responding to his in a way that I don't yet fully understand. But he does. I can tell he does. His eyes blaze like blue flames.

"You are mine," he says, and his voice is low, soft.

I feel the words vibrating through me, all the way to my core. And I can't help it—I shiver. It's like my entire body, my whole being, has come alive now along with my magic.

Aris's entire body stills against mine. He glares at me, clears his throat, and starts again.

"You are my Mage, and I am your Shield. I will protect you from everything, even yourself."

My gaze flicks down to his lips, which are slightly parted, like he's struggling for breath, and I ache to feel them on mine.

I feel the breath catch in his chest. I am a minute, a second, a breath away from doing something really, really stupid.

And then a glimmer, a glint of silver metal from the edge of the room, catches my eye.

My body goes cold and rigid between one heartbeat and the next. I reach up and shove him off me, scrambling up from the floor. He doesn't stop me. He knows what I'm seeing and doesn't try to avoid it.

His travel pack rests on a chair. I lift the flap, and my hand is trembling.

Inside, shining in the lamplight, are two slim silver circles.

My manacles.

He's kept them. Once they were removed, I didn't give them much thought. I didn't notice him taking them. Seconds ago, he talked about protecting me. At the time, it sounded … No matter how it sounded, it didn't matter. He kept the damn manacles because he was worried I was going to lose control, and then he'd cuff me, just like Darius, just like Saroya. Put the chains back on the monster. I wonder if he thought about doing it just now.

I turn to him. I have no words. He runs a hand through his hair, but he offers no explanation, no apology. There's no regret in his face; there's no remorse. Just … a sense of inevitability.

I leave his room. I don't stop until I'm in my room, with the door closed.

Then, and only then, do I allow myself to cry.

Chapter 36: Aris

One of these days, I am going to learn to stop fucking up the good shit in my life. Today, apparently, is not that day.

So on top of the fact that Wren can actually control the weather without conscious effort and make things glow, whatever that means, I've *also* managed to piss her off. I want her to be careful with King Leonidas. He's a good king—as far as kings go, I guess—but she's getting way too attached, too invested. We're going to be out on the road as soon as she's trained up. At the school, it would have taken two years. Here, with Ismini and Panos as her personal tutors, hopefully less. Saroya will have to grant her a Mage's robe if those two deem her worthy. And I don't want Wren thinking that being a palace Mage is a good idea. If I have to spend a lifetime watching her and the king make eyes at each other—or worse—I might seriously contemplate regicide. The sooner we get out of here, the better. No Shield ever made history sitting around a palace all day.

Not to mention her magic is way beyond what I expected, or even dreamed. I knew she'd be strong, whichever element chose her. I didn't even know her current magic was an option, whatever it is. It's like she's a little bit of all the elements all rolled into one glowing mess.

Being her Shield doesn't matter, though, because she is probably never going to talk to me again. I think about Odall. What would the First Shield think about me now? He would have been disappointed in me when I got Stefan killed—just like everyone else—but now? With my Mage unlikely to ever trust me again? I might be the fiercest Shield in a generation, but without a Mage at my side …

But she can't really blame me for keeping the manacles as a backup, not when she just casually created a thunderstorm and turned my dagger into a glowing weapon of doom. I wonder if she has any idea how she glowed when she was doing all that, how the green-gray of her eyes blazed with jade-colored fire. I've never seen anything like it, and I'm not sure if I want to ever again. She was terrifying. I leave the dagger where she left it on the floor. I don't want to touch it.

"Wren, don't make me break this door down!" I shout, banging on the door to her room. I don't really care if she forgives me, but she has to open this door. I have to be sure she is safe and not doing anything stupid inside—like accessing her magic again.

"Go away!" she roars back.

I hear something hit the door—it's probably a boot. Thank the gods I haven't given her any real weapons yet.

It's getting late. I end up not breaking down her door, though I contemplate it more than once. Instead, I shift. After all, my tiger form has a far better sense of hearing. I can feel the pull to her immediately once I've shifted, the unconscious magic she is using to lure me to her.

My ears twitch.

She's crying. I guess I expected she'd be throwing things or screaming or something. Somehow, listening to her quiet sobs is far worse. Crying like her heart is breaking.

I shift back, get dressed, pocket the manacles, and leave.

The palace is still lively. Some revelry is going on in the main hallway. It doesn't matter that it is late. It doesn't matter that Wren has revealed a glimpse of her true power. People drink and dance and laugh like the world is still turning, like nothing has changed. Gods, what am I going to do? If Wren doesn't forgive me, I'll never be able to show my face at the school again. I might as well have gone gray—it would have saved me a lot of trouble.

I leave the palace and head out to town, pausing on the bridge. It is quiet here, between the palace and the rest of Estana, like a pause. The sky is gray, a light drizzle starting to fall, making the lamps flicker along the bridge. I wonder if this is also Wren's doing, and I envision each raindrop as a tear. My chest aches. I'm not sure I actually want to go into town now. What would I do there? Find a tavern, do some gambling, find some other ways to distract myself from the buzzing in my head, the rage in my chest?

I stop and lean on the railing instead, looking down at the sluggish water of the moat. The water is as black as my mood, flat and still.

"Strange weather we're having this evening."

I don't need to look up. I know that voice.

My father comes and stands by me, leaning on the rail, like we are two old friends catching up, like he didn't smack me around last time we met.

Gods, this day really can't get any worse.

I have nothing to say to him, but he doesn't seem to notice, or care. He just stands with me while I silently fume.

"Everything all right with your Mage?" he asks.

Coming from anyone else, it would have been an innocent enough question. From Nestor, this is a probe, looking for a weakness to exploit.

"Fine," I say, though even to my ears the word sounds forced.

Nestor sighs and looks down, studying his hands. "It's a hard life, being a Shield," he says after a while.

I fight back a retort. No shit.

"It's harder still, watching my children go through it."

I'm sure I was less surprised by seeing him earlier than I am now. Nestor is not one for paternal fondness. I do look at him now, and there's a faraway look in his black eyes.

"I was like you once, trying to prove myself," he goes on. He looks down at his hands again—massive, scarred—and clenches them tightly. "But to what end? Thirty years of this, and I'm still penniless. My wife is dead. My Mage has retired. And I'm mucking out stalls in someone else's stables."

He hasn't mentioned my mother within my earshot in years. At times, I even wondered if he'd forgotten her name. Now, hearing him talk … well, if I could feel anything besides anger for this man, I'd be tempted to feel pity. But tigers don't have time for pity.

Nestor chuckles, a harsh, grating sound. "What do I have that you could possibly aspire to?" he asks me, but he's looking out at the moat.

I say nothing.

He lets out a sigh, leaning back. He's wrong. I don't want to be like him at all.

"Spyridon's been in the western mountains," he says.

At the mention of my oldest brother, I bristle. Spyridon could be our father's twin, in temperament and appearance. He's also the Shield to a very powerful Earth Mage, Stathis. When Stathis was found to have a particular knack for locating things like iron in the mountains, they were assigned there, permanently. I haven't heard from Spyridon in nearly a year.

"No glory in working the mines," he says wryly. "Not much pay either. Not that Shields are given payment worth a damn, anyway, not with the king throwing money away on worthless causes, like Aclines. Building them roads, thinking that will turn them into his grateful subjects. Bah." He spits into the moat.

I don't say anything. I mean, he's got a point. Shields are not paid much, but that's not why we do it. It's in our blood. I couldn't have been a farmer or a scholar. This life calls to us. It's all I've ever wanted, all I've ever known.

"They're talking about your Mage, you know," he says.

I grunt. People talk. That's nothing new.

"They're saying she's bewitching the king," he continues. "Enchanting him. That there's some kind of cult down in Aclines, like those Black Water Witches, except in this case they're being subtler, craftier. Sending your Wren in like bait."

I snort. I don't bother refuting his stupid story. Wren is a lot of things—stubborn, irritating, powerful. Tempting. She might be from Aclines, but she is not some kind of traitor. I know Wren. I know her as well as I know myself. Maybe better.

"Not good for a young ruler to be seen cozying up to the enemy," Nestor says, and he spits into the moat again. "Especially considering what happened to his father."

"Wren isn't the enemy," I say without thinking. "Or are you suggesting she was part of that assassination?"

King Leonidas II and his wife, Queen Katia, were murdered years ago in their sleep. The perpetrators, never caught. Of course, rumors abounded, just like now—some spurned lover of the queen's, maybe, or an assassin from the Isles, or one of the king's guards—the theories changed as often as the tides. Young Leonidas was thrust onto the throne at the tender age of twelve, and despite all that, he grew into a decent king. One I was proud to serve—once.

"Besides, Wren would have been, what, seven years old at the time?" I say.

"You could've claimed a decent Mage this time is all I'm saying," he says, eyeing me. "Even though you failed last time, you're my son and a decent fighter. Surely there was someone else who would have accepted your claim."

I stiffen, reminding myself that a physical altercation with Nestor has never gone in my favor. And Wren is worth ten thousand other Mages. I'll show him. Together, there won't be anything Wren and I can't do.

"Anyway," he says. And he leaves.

That's my father for you, always leaving, always stirring up trouble. No goodbyes, though, no nothing.

I stay on the bridge a long time. I pull the manacles out of my pocket and turn them over in my hands. They shine strangely in the dim lamplight, though they look pretty much just like ordinary silver bracelets otherwise, with a clasp and a hinge.

Wren has shown me what she is capable of tonight. Or at least a fraction of it. She was glowing—actually glowing—with power. What if she decided to aim that power against Ocron? Would anything honestly be able to stand against her?

I rub my fingers along the metal bands. Would these stand against her? Could these shackles do a damn thing anymore? They muted her power a bit, but that was before she was … whatever she is now. Before she began to understand her magic.

And could I really do that to her? Put her back in the manacles? Take away her power, even if the manacles did work? When she saw them, the light in her eyes sputtered and died. It nearly tore me apart.

When I first met her—well, the second time—I was so enraged at the way she'd been treated, like something to be feared and caged. How am I any better than Darius and Saroya, even if she is something fearsome? If I can't help her, as her Shield, who can?

The manacles glitter like two shooting stars, arcing away as I throw them into the moat.

Chapter 37: Wren

The one upside of crying yourself to sleep is that you're too exhausted to dream. If ever there were a night when I was going to accidentally burn the palace to the ground while I slept, this would be it.

Aris gave up after a while. I mean, it's not like he was trying to apologize. He just wanted me to keep the door open in case I did decide to burn the palace down. He knocked and yelled, but eventually, he left. Like everyone else. I'm sure that someone will be along in the morning to kick me out, just like Leo kicked out the Aclinese governors.

When I wake in the morning, my face feels sticky and swollen. A trio of mice has made it into my bed somehow, though they scurry back into some dark corner when I move. I splash water on my face and pick out a dress from the wardrobe. I'll be damned if I am going to train with Aris and his stupid daggers today. I want to feel good. The dress is much lower cut than anything I've ever worn, though I guess still modest by Estana standards, with ties up the back that take some intricate twisting and turning to figure out. The material is simple, fine, in shades of purple. I braid my hair, wrapping it up over my head, like a crown. I feel like I am wearing armor, like I am getting ready to go to war.

But when I unlock my door, Aris is nowhere to be seen.

Asshole. I've planned a whole speech to tell him off, but it doesn't matter. I doubt he'll want to be my Shield for much longer, anyhow. This realization stings, so I stand up straighter and head out of our rooms.

I find my way to the room I train in with the Mages. It is early, and not many people are out and about yet. I pass Tolis, who gives me a smile and a friendly wave.

Ismini is waiting for me.

"Want to talk about what happened last night?" she asks. She's sitting in a chair, sipping a cup of tea. She looks like someone who's just dropped by for a chat, rather than my teacher, rather than a Mage who can turn a mountain into dust with a word. As if to prove my point, she hands me a scone and pours a cup of tea for me.

"Why? Did Aris come talk to you?" I ask, munching on the snack.

Ismini raises an eyebrow.

"He didn't," she says. "Didn't need to. Panos spent most of the evening shutting down the storm you made before the winds blew the roof off."

I feel maybe a twinge of guilt.

"How do you know that was my fault?" I ask, swallowing the scone, which feels dry in my throat, like ash.

"The lightning was green," she says, "like you made at the school." She's not smiling.

I wonder if I'm about to be punished, clapped back in manacles or something. Maybe thrown into some dungeon. I look down at my shoes and scuff the toe along a vein of darker stone in the marble floor. I don't want to look at Ismini.

"Are you … going to punish me?" I ask. "Do you think I'm dangerous?" I want to hear her say it. Some twisted part of me wants her to.

"Of course you are dangerous," she says, unperturbed.

I look up.

She sets down her teacup. "We all are. You don't think Mages make mistakes in their training, that we don't sometimes get hurt? Or Shields, for that matter?"

I think about this for a minute, considering the implications. I expected more of a reaction from her.

"If I can keep you from going through that again, I will. Now, do you want to tell me what happened last night, what unlocked your magic?" she asks again, leveling her green eyes at me.

I can't help it—I wince. "Not really," I say.

Ismini keeps looking at me, waiting.

I want to give in. I think I want to tell someone, anyone, and she's the closest thing I have here to a friend now. So I relent, sagging into my chair.

"I … fought with Aris," I say.

She nods, waiting for me to continue.

"He told me the king was using me. And I know, yes, that's the whole reason I'm here, to be trained, so I can be … wielded. He was just so arrogant about it that I started shouting back at him. And then the storm just happened, and I was holding this dagger, and it turned green and—"

"The dagger turned green?" Ismini asks. She twists her lips, thinking.

I nod. "And sharp. I may have destroyed some furniture …" I wince again.

"Well, fights happen," Ismini says slowly. "Between Shields and Mages just like between family or friends or lovers. I can't tell you how many times I've shouted at Aleka, and vice versa."

"He kept my manacles," I spit out. Even the memory of those hated silver bangles makes me boiling mad. "He'll throw me back in chains whenever he feels that I'm out of control. How am I supposed to get past that?"

"Maybe you won't," she says, brushing her hands off on her skirt. "Maybe you will. We're still not sure what's going on with you, Wren. Not sure what you are. And whatever is going on between you and Aris, never doubt that your protection and well-being are his only concern. I know him well enough to tell you that."

But protection at the expense of my freedom? He might as well throw me into a cage, for now that I've tasted what my magic is capable of, there is no way I can do anything else but use it. I am no longer a lighthouse keeper. I am a Mage, and I have a role in this new country of mine, and I will seize it, with or without his help.

"Now," Ismini says, in that infuriatingly efficient, maternal manner of hers. She stands and gestures for me to get up too.

"What are we doing?" I ask.

"I'm going to the greenhouse," she says, ushering me out the door. "And as punishment for letting your magic get out of control last night, you're going to help me carry manure from the stables for compost. And do try not to turn any of my shovels green."

It's a long day, and by the end, my back is killing me from carting load after load of manure from the stables to the greenhouse, and I'm cursing the architect who put the structures on opposite sides of the palace. Not to mention I stink, and I'm not sure I'll ever get the stuff out from beneath my fingernails. Ismini either doesn't notice or doesn't care. She just cheerily directs me where to deposit each barrowload as she hums and waters her rows of plants. The greenhouses are beautiful structures, like miniature glass palaces themselves, with exotic plants and trees and flowers that I've never seen before. Ismini greets each one like a friend, though she is ruthless when it comes to pruning them.

This is the first day I haven't had Aris escorting me everywhere, the first day in a while without him. It should feel like freedom. Instead, it feels like I am missing something. I realize I'm looking for him around every corner. I guess I'm glad he's not here to see me sweating and stinking of horse manure, but I miss him all the same.

By the time I get back to our rooms, I am nearly faint with fatigue and hunger, and the sun has long since set. Someone has cleaned the rooms, made my bed—Aris's is untouched from the day before—and left food and juice for me. I take a bath, then a second one to make sure I get all the smell off me. I devour the food, grab a book, and settle into a couch by the fire. My glance catches on the letter opener, sitting on a side table. I glare at it. My magic is tied to emotion, or so Ismini says, and my emotions regarding this particular object are strong.

It melts into a streak of metallic goo, like ice melting under the sun. I smirk and return to my book. I glance up at it every few minutes, though. What else can I do? My fingertips tremble with anticipation.

A few hours later, Aris returns. He glances at me once, and he notices the cool puddle of metal burned into the table but doesn't comment on it. He looks like he's been training hard all day—he is covered in sweat and sand—and he heads right for the bath without talking to me. *Prick.* I wanted him to comment on the damn letter opener, to be in awe of me. I grumble to myself and go back to my book.

I definitely do not stare at him over the top of my book when he walks from the bath back to his room, a towel slung low across his hips. His tan skin gleams from the damp, which only highlights his scars. Thin white lines track along his torso, his arms, down his back, all marks from a lifetime of battle. I definitely do not notice the little dimples in the muscles of his lower back, just above the towel.

"Like what you see, Mage?" he says, cocking an eyebrow. He's stopped, amused.

I glare at him, wondering if I can set that towel on fire. Then I realize he'd be completely naked if I did. I swallow hard.

Gods, how can I be so pissed at him and still keep staring?

He lurks in the room the rest of the night, not talking, keeping his distance. I guess when I didn't immediately try to set him on fire or throw my shoes at him, he figured I'd calmed down a little.

So I read. But when I get ready for bed, I leave my door open. I can't really explain why. He settles into his chair, though, like nothing has changed, and I try to go to sleep. All evening, and not a word exchanged between us. His gaze followed me the whole night, like a tiger stalking its prey. I think, however, he's realized his prey might also have claws.

I sleep like shit. Aris doesn't talk to me the next morning either, though he is my silent shadow as I make my way to the practice room at dawn. He just drifts away silently once Panos arrives. I spend the early morning pulling water droplets out of the air, lighting candles, making the little wings of his paper pinwheel spin. These were things most gifted children could do, true, but most stuck with their element. Panos seems both pleased and perplexed by my ability to manipulate all of them. I'm unable to do anything bigger, though, and as the sun rises, I get worn out, and I can't even do the smaller magics anymore.

By lunchtime, I'm drenched in sweat and shaky from hunger. Panos makes me stop practicing and escorts me back to my room, chatting about the latest updates in his temple restoration as we go. I'm so exhausted that I don't ask too many questions, just nod along at his monologue.

Chapter 38: Aris

The daily training with Aleka is good for me, clears my mind. After our morning sparring session, I run and do all the other workouts that I missed on the road. It gives me a place to channel my frustrations—all my emotions, really. Some people meditate to clear their mind; I grind my sparring partners into the dust.

It is late by the time I make it back to our rooms. I lingered at the arena a little longer than necessary, admitting to myself it was because I didn't want to face Wren. At least she's allowed me to do my job over the past day, allowed me to be with her. If ever there had been a night for her to have bad dreams and blow up, it would have been the past few nights, but she didn't. The palace is having its big party for Aclines tonight, and I'll have to be alert, even if she seems to be gaining more control. I wonder if the fires before were just some product of her magic trying to leak around the manacles. I don't know. I'm no Mage, no scholar. But it seems like she is happier here—barring my own obvious failings.

Anyway, I make it back to our rooms, and she's already gone, didn't even fucking wait for me. A pair of lady's maids are cleaning up, taking away an empty box filled with tissue paper.

"Where's Wren?" I ask them.

They exchange a glance, a smile passing between them.

"Oh, Mage Verena just left with His Majesty," they say. "I believe they were headed to the grand ballroom."

My fists clench. As opposed to where, exactly?

I realize I can't show up to the big party the king is throwing for Aclines wearing my leathers and covered in arena sand, so I get cleaned up in record time, throw on that stupid embroidered jacket, and head out.

I realize then that her Mage's robe is balled up on the floor, discarded.

Chapter 39: Wren

The lessons today don't achieve much. I guess I'm distracted, and our training is cut short. Tonight is the celebration of the acquisition of Aclines, and I will be attending as the king's personal guest.

I get back to our rooms after Panos's afternoon lessons without getting lost, but Aris isn't there either. There is, however, a large box with a note in neat black ink and a single Tamdosan rose.

For tonight.
—Leo

I remove the fancy silk ribbon and open the box. The fabric inside is gorgeous, and I run a finger over it, my calluses snagging the smooth material. I can't keep a smile off my face. I planned on just picking something from my generous wardrobe to wear with my robe, seeing as I haven't yet taken Ismini up on her offer to go shopping.

This dress is gorgeous, loose and flowing, with a sash that can be tied around my waist. It will show off the skin of my arms, but at least the neckline is high. The color, though—this is not a dress for someone who wants to hide or blend in. This is something to be shown off, like I am worth showing off. Like Leo wants me to be seen. I clutch the dress to my chest for a moment, closing my eyes and imagining him picking this out for me, imagining what it'll be like to be seen in it. He said he wanted me to attend—I imagine catching his eye across the ballroom, and I wonder if I'll be able to steal a few minutes of his time tonight. I'd like that.

I bathe and wash my hair, letting it dry loose down my back. My daydreams are interrupted by a soft knock on the door. It's two girls wearing Estana's colors.

"Mage Verena," one says, curtsying. "The king sent us to see if you need any help getting ready."

"What kind of help?" I ask, curious. Do women here need help getting themselves dressed? That seems silly. What helpless creatures they must be. And dressing them is a full-time job for these women?

"Makeup, hair, clothing, whatever you need," the other says. She is a thin girl with pale skin and a red headscarf, and she eyes my hair appreciatively.

I might not be a particularly vain person, or even conscious of my appearance most of the time, but I am proud of my mane.

"What kind of makeup?" I ask. I am not about to let them turn me into a painted peacock like the women I've seen prancing about the palace.

"Why, whatever kind you like," the other girl says, producing a large, bulky bag. "We have some that can make your lips the exact shade of red as the roses outside, and combs made out of real snowflakes, frozen in time." She smiles. "Our small magics can be used for so much more than the academics that Mage Ismini will teach you."

I think for a moment. I've never worn cosmetics of any kind. I'm not sure how to maneuver around this new place I find myself in, with parties and kings. I don't even know if I'll like it—but I get a feeling that Aris won't. That makes up my mind for me.

"What would the king like?" I ask after a moment.

They exchange excited grins.

Chapter 40: Aris

The ball is a grand affair. I haven't been to many palace parties, but it seems like every royal and courtier in the country must be here tonight, fluttering between the ballroom and the surrounding corridors like so many giant butterflies. Music floats through the air, coming from a quartet of musicians playing stringed instruments. I'm taller than a lot of people, but it is so crowded I am having trouble spotting her. This makes me nervous. Where could she be if not here? Either she has been kidnapped, or she is entangled with the king somewhere. I don't want to think too much about it either way.

I make my way through the room. It's massive, larger than most buildings in the city, with wide columns around the outside, perfect for me to lurk behind and survey the room. I pull at the collar of my shirt. I don't like the formal attire that Shields wear on such occasions, but I want it clear that I'm here to do my job—despite the lingering glances some of the women are giving me. Another time, and I might have returned those heated looks. Unlike the king, I don't woo women. They come to me, always have, like moths to a flame. All except for one stubborn Mage with a fondness for thorny flowers.

The whole idea of this party grates on me. The undercurrent of the concerns from the west float through the room in whispers. It's like trying to hide a latrine stench with perfume.

Eventually, I spot the king. He's a tall man, and his guards have made sure that most of the crowd around him keeps its distance.

Most of the crowd, except for the woman on his arm.

I am no poet, but if I were, I would still be at a loss for how she glows, in a gold dress that moves around her like sunlight. Gold dusts her cheekbones, her eyelids, and when she smiles, all eyes in the room are on her, like she is the sun, and we are all mere plants stretching toward her.

It feels like I've never seen her before.

"Well, I see you're still thinking with your cock instead of your brain. At least this one's pretty."

My father has a way with words.

I stand on the periphery of the ballroom, watching Wren shine on the arm of the king. I wonder at the color choice—a symbol of unity, of Aclines and Ocron being together? The thought makes me want to gag. A show of dominance, then? An erasure of Aclines's identity, dressing her in his colors. Or maybe he just thought she'd look good in gold. Who knows? In that last case, though, he'd be right.

She's wearing her hair down—usually she braids it back, unless it's drying. I've never seen her wear it like this. There's still a braid, a small one looped across the top of her head like a crown. Otherwise, it forms a brown-gold cloud around her. I bet it's soft.

A servant passes by with a tray of drinks. I grab one and down it before I change my mind.

Nestor still stands next to me, watching the king and my Mage.

She doesn't need me at her side. I'm her Shield, so I do my job—I stay in the shadows, watching for trouble. The only trouble I see is next to Wren, in the form of an overly attentive king, who for some reason won't keep his hands off her. This has gone way past just simple manipulation. This is no longer just the words of a politician to get a powerful Mage as an ally. And Wren—she has no idea, but she's a butterfly caught in the web of a spider. And she's sipping from a glass of wine, her cheeks flushed under the gold dust. Gods, has she ever even had wine before?

"She's already got her claws in him, I see," Nestor says.

He's still standing near me. Doesn't he have anything better to do? Anyone else to antagonize?

"Anyway, I wouldn't have thought her your type," he continues.

I let out a huff. "She's not."

He looks at me, amusement glittering in his black eyes.

I feel the need to explain myself to him for some reason. "I prefer my women … experienced," I say. Wren is just so naive—I need to warn her. Men are never nice without a good reason—the gods know I'm not, not really. It's not my job to be nice to her. It's my job to protect her, and if that means protecting her from the king, so be it.

I grab another drink.

The king steps to the raised dais at the front of the room, keeping Wren at his side. If she's flustered or nervous, she doesn't show it. Quiet blankets the room, and all eyes turn to the king and the golden woman on his arm.

"Friends, thank you all for joining us this evening, for the celebration of Aclines and Ocron, together as one," he says, beaming down at Wren.

Something twists low in my gut.

"It remains my eternal hope that Ocron will bring peace and prosperity to our troubled continent," he says.

Wren is standing tall at his side, fearless and proud and glowing and out of my reach.

"To the king!" Lady Orothea cuts in, her clear voice ringing through the crowd. Her face is bright and flushed, and she raises a wineglass high.

"To the king!" the rest of the crowd thunders.

King Leonidas raises a hand, accepting their applause, and steps back down. The music strikes back up, though people are still intermittently yelling their good wishes and then downing their drinks.

From where I'm standing behind a column, the next few minutes pass in agonizing slowness. King Leonidas leads Wren to the center of the room, where couples are dancing. I can see the uncertainty on Wren's face, but he says something to her, and then her smile is like dawn breaking after a long night. I can barely take my eyes off them as they move about the floor—and I realize, neither can anyone else. The world itself has paused to watch them move and fawn over each other.

I can't stand it for a second longer.

Just when I think that I might have to do something drastic, the song ends, and the king is finally called away to do his kingly duties. He doesn't let go of Wren, though.

After a while, a couple of Mages approach her, and she wrenches herself away from the king long enough to chat with them. The king makes his rounds then, spending time with each of the nobles. He's a good king, really. I'm just not sure I like him as a man. Surely he could have his pick of any woman in the entire continent. Why Wren?

Something inside me twists again. I know why. I understand exactly what he's seeing, what he's feeling. I just don't want to admit it.

Wren finally catches my eye from across the room. I'm half-hidden in the shadows, but she finds me. She stops for a moment, the smile leaving her face—then she turns her back on me.

I want to punch something.

The king catches me glaring at him, and after a while, he approaches the column where I've been lurking. Nestor, fortunately, has gone away.

"It's good to see you, Shield Aris," the king says.

I give a bow. I'm no courtier; I have no talent with flattery or pretty words. He doesn't seem to mind.

"Sire," I say. He's the king; I'm just a Shield, even if I am a good one. He doesn't need to talk to me—unless he thinks I can give him some information about Wren, which I will do over my dead body.

He sees me watching Wren, watching her glow like a star. The rest of the women seem overdone in comparison, like they're all trying too hard. I notice that her dress is in the same style as the clothes of the new governors from Aclines—loose, flowing, instead of corseted. She's a column of golden fire.

"The court seems smitten with her," he says, like I don't already see that. "I must say, I never expected the scuffles over Aclines to yield up such a rare jewel."

"Mage Stefan died in one of those 'scuffles,'" I remind him through gritted teeth.

"Yes," the king says, unperturbed. His guards are hanging far enough back that I don't think they hear me, though they'd be fools not to think that I'd be a threat if I wanted to be.

"I've always been curious about the relationship between a Mage and their Shield," he says, sipping a glass of wine.

Bullshit. I'm able to hold back a snort of derision by some minor miracle. He's been around Mages and Shields since the day he was born.

"I've heard how you Shields can be, so protective of your Mages," he says.

I raise an eyebrow but don't otherwise answer. Of course he's familiar with the claim.

He continues, as calm as if he's chatting to me about the weather. "I hear the bond can be rather … intimate."

"It's not like that," I answer, far too quickly. I swallow hard.

"Oh, good," he says. "After all, marrying a girl from Aclines would be quite diplomatic of me, wouldn't it? Help me win over their hearts, as I've won hers."

And he walks off, sipping casually on his wine.

My blood runs hot and cold at the same time, the tiger within me roaring to be released. My fingers flex claws that aren't there. His confession has stunned me—people and music are still swirling around me, but I don't notice. The guards trailing the king strategically place themselves between us, but I'm not stupid. Furious, yes, but not stupid. Generally.

Chapter 41: Wren

The ball starts out like something out of a dream. I finish getting ready, and there's a knock on the door. Leo enters. The ladies with me fall into deep curtsies—I'm not really sure if I should do the same or not. I mean, I guess I should, but I can't take my eyes off him, and he doesn't seem to notice my lack of decorum.

Tonight he's in his full kingly regalia. He's still wearing polished black boots, a crimson shirt tucked into dark pants, but over this he's wearing a vest, and a black coat heavily embroidered with gold thread. On his wavy brown hair rests a tall golden crown set with rubies, the colors of Ocron. I can't help but notice that we're dressed to match.

"My little bird," he breathes, like all the air has gone out of his lungs. He takes my hand and bows low, kissing it, all the while fixing me with his gold-brown eyes. "You are breathtaking."

I feel the heat rise to my cheeks, and it's intoxicating. I feel … celebrated. I feel powerful, similar to the way I felt the other night when first channeling my magic. I am under a different sort of spell tonight.

"You could have picked a more muted color," I mutter, gesturing down at the gown. I am wearing gold, the color of Ocron, the color of the Golden City and its golden king. Gold powder dusts my cheeks and my eyelids. The maids have worked fragrant oils into my skin until it glows too. I love the way it all looks on me, so much so that I barely notice that my arms are exposed, that I'm showing more skin than I ever have before.

Leo is staring at me like he's under a spell himself. His eyes sparkle.

"Estana takes a lot of pride in its fabrics, silk in particular. The color was just a diplomatic choice," he says after a moment, airily. Then he rolls his eyes and grins self-consciously. "But … maybe I wanted to show you off."

He loops my hand through his arm, and he escorts me to the ballroom, where people are already gathered and waiting. They cheer as he enters the room, their glorious hero. We're brought drinks, and though he offers me water—I'm touched that he is so considerate, that he remembers from our dinner together—I do accept a glass of sparkling wine. He clinks his glass against mine, and we drink. I've never experienced anything like the light, bubbly taste of this wine. It tastes like magic itself.

I stand with Leo for a time, listening to him talk to the Aclinese ambassadors about the work he's already got underway improving the country's infrastructure. This is a man who really cares about others. My heart swells as we move from noble to noble. He introduces me to them all, but I can't keep all the names straight.

The evening is intoxicating. I don't think I can fully blame it on the glass or two of wine that I've consumed. The air is warm and heavy with perfume, and music floats through it, twining with the voices around me. Men and women glide through the room, dazzling in their jewels and richly colored outfits. I could never have imagined such a scenario in my wildest dreams. It seems that the nobles—and the Mages—are using this ball as an opportunity to showcase their "small magics," as my assistants earlier called them. Not everyone, apparently, is employed in great stations across the continent. Some have only minor magic—the kind that can keep your makeup from smearing all night, or your hair from going astray.

And then there are others. A tall Mage in a red robe, a Fire Mage, has added a short cape of flames around his shoulders that look like feathers and give off no heat, like my spelled candle. A noblewoman with rich brown skin wears a dress made entirely of leaves and flowers, which bloom as she dances. Lady Orothea is there, wearing a dress of shades like the sea, adorned with blue gems and pearls, holding court with the other noble ladies and casting shy glances at Leo. Another wears a dress that seems to be made entirely of frozen water droplets, shimmering like jewels themselves. I wonder at the concentration that someone is keeping to make sure the dress doesn't melt and leave her a walking scandal. A Water Mage with dark hair slicked back wears ropes and ropes of pearls around her neck, wound through her braids, decorating her fingers. It's a far cry from the mountain-moving, storm-raising magic I think I'll be learning, but it is very entertaining to see.

Leo turns back to me. He's been talking with another group of nobles. I've been watching the couples move on the dance floor—their steps are foreign to me, but they move easily, like they don't have a care in the entire world except dancing. One of the nobles Leo has been talking with sees me watching the dance and offers me his hand.

"Mage Wren, would you do me the honor?" he asks. He's older, handsome, with kind brown eyes that are twinkling with mischief and an orchid in the breast pocket of his jacket.

I put a hand to my cheek to cool it. "Oh," I say, looking back at the people dancing. It is a slow dance, but the steps look intricate. "I don't … I mean, I've never …"

"I think what my Mage is trying to say is that she promised the first dance to me," Leo says, the corners of his mouth lifting conspiratorially.

Oh, no. No, no, no. Bad idea.

But he takes my hand and settles it on his arm, confidently walking me toward the center of the room. People move out of our way.

I clutch at the thick fabric of his sleeve. “You’re going to regret this,” I warn.

He chuckles, and the sound releases something inside me. I realize it’s not about how well I dance—it’s about the fact that we’re doing this, together, in front of everyone.

“I’ve been dancing at these events since I could walk,” he says.

To prove his point, he spins me around until we’re face-to-face. He takes one of my hands in his—if he can feel it trembling, the cold sweat forming there, he doesn’t comment—and places the other on his shoulder. There remains half a foot of air between us, but it feels like nothing at all. All I can see is the dazzling man before me. The rest of the room has faded away. Even the music seems distant.

“Let me guide you,” he says.

I watch the words fall from his lips, watch his lips curve as he catches me watching them. He places a hand on my waist. The gesture feels so intimate—but then we’re off. A lifetime ago, I would never have imagined being touched like this, held like this. It takes a moment, but I relax into his grasp, and he moves through the music easily—proud, self-assured. His eyes are on mine, like there’s nowhere else in the world he needs to be right now. Like I am important, deserving of that attention. It is a heady feeling, and I melt into it. He doesn’t talk. We don’t need to. I know that, whatever happens, I will treasure this moment for the rest of my life.

The music ends too soon, and I am breathless, but not from exertion. Leo gives me a warm smile, and I feel my lips echoing it. I don’t want the moment to stop—Leo doesn’t seem to want it to either, but eventually someone calls to him, and the spell is broken. He loops my arm through his, and we go to greet the next group of well-wishers. I can’t focus on anything they’re saying—my world has narrowed, to the warmth of the man standing at my side, the heat of his hand over mine, still resting on his arm. Never have I felt so treasured, so adored. Every so often, he shoots me a glance or a smile, and I melt a little more each time.

Eventually, a couple of Mages approach, and Leo hands me off to them, again kissing my hand. It must be the drink, because I swear I felt that kiss on my lips too.

I turn to talk to the Mages, and I finally catch sight of Aris, brooding, hiding in the shadows at the edge of the ballroom. With him half-hidden like that, I can only clearly see his eyes, blazing blue like they're lit from within. He's wearing all black and blends into the shadows of the room, at odds with the splendor and color around him. Despite the warmth in the room, I feel a chill. Judgment is clear on his face.

I turn my back on him.

The Mages are very kind, introducing themselves, appearing very eager when I mention that I'd love to learn more, as much as possible. They trip over themselves offering their tutelage. I'm just telling them that I'll have to check with Ismini and Panos about their training plans when I hear a hiss from one of the noblewomen behind me. She's whispering, but not quietly—it's obvious she wants to be overheard.

"She doesn't look all that dangerous," she says.

There's little doubt that I am the "she" in question.

"I don't think she means to hurt anyone on purpose. She isn't malicious," someone else says.

I strain my ears to hear them, but the next words are clear, intending me to hear them.

"Neither is an earthquake. It can still flatten a city." This time, there is no mistaking the voice—it is coming from Lady Orothea, and her words strike me like a blow.

Here I am, all dressed up and pretending to be someone I'm not. I might have a better idea on how to access my magic, but I don't have control all the time, obviously. I wonder if she's aware of the thunderstorm the other day, if everyone knows that was me. I wonder if they saw me dancing with Leo, judged my ineptitude, saw how unsuitable we are.

Suddenly the room feels stuffy, like all the air is warm and thick and the scent of mingling sweat and perfume is overpowering. I have to get out. I wish I could shrink into oblivion, or just disappear altogether. The feeling intensifies, until it's hard to breathe, and I feel trapped.

I have to get out.

Chapter 42: Aris

I look up, and Wren is nowhere to be seen. My pulse hammers in my ears—*Not again, not again, not again.* Even here, in the relative safety of the palace, threats await. Where is she? Where did she go?

I burst into the corridor outside the ballroom and see her chatting with an Earth Mage, an old friend of Ismini's whom I sort of recognize. Wren sees me, and her eyes widen. She goes to turn her back on me—again—but I need to talk to her, even if she doesn't want to listen. I grab her arm, and she whirls on me.

"Careful," she says, her eyes flashing with jade fire. "I could incinerate you where you stand."

Gods, that look in her eyes nearly undoes me. How can I focus on external threats when I can't keep my own emotions in check?

"I need to talk to you," I say, pulling her down the corridor. I need to warn her about the king, really get her to listen this time. There are all kinds of dark spaces here, some of them occupied by couples locked in romantic embraces. I yank her into the space behind a thick column, which mostly shields us from the hallway. She yanks her arm away from me, and I let her.

"Let go! What is your problem?" she shouts.

"You are," I growl.

She leans back against the wall, raking me again with those fiery eyes. It's a bold look, one she's never given me before. She's drunk, or nearly. I can see it in the flush on her face, smell it on her breath. I want her so badly my hands are shaking, and I clench them tightly so she won't see.

"You know that you growl when you're angry, like a cat?" she says, and giggles, a sound I've never heard her make. "Do you also purr when you're happy?"

She turns, like she's going to leave me again, and I can't stand it. I slam a palm onto the wall on either side of her, caging her between my arms. And that's when I say something really stupid.

"Care to find out?"

Chapter 43: Wren

I have to get out before everyone sees what a fraud I am.

I excuse myself and slip into the hallway. More people try to talk to me, grab at me, and I just want out, just need a breath of fresh air. I think I'm nearly starting to panic—and then I see Aris coming at me like a thunderstorm.

He drags me down the hallway like some misbehaving child and stuffs me behind a column. It's quiet here, at least, and away from the crowd a little. I'd be relieved if he weren't looking like he'd breathe fire at me if he could. And when he growls at me, gods help me, I can't help but giggle. I don't usually giggle. I'm not that kind of girl—I'm not sure if it's the panic or the wine or what.

And then I find myself against a wall, pinned, his arms to either side of me, eyes glittering, scorching, heat rolling off him in waves.

"Care to find out?"

Gods, I am in trouble.

And yes, gods, yes, I care to find out. Thoughts of Leo battle with the emotions roiling through me now—the warmth of Leo, and the scorching heat of Aris. Between the two, I am completely aflame.

"You've been avoiding me," Aris says. He keeps his voice low, like he doesn't want to be overheard, but it rumbles in his chest when he does that, and that sends shivers down my spine that have nothing to do with my magic.

"I've been training," I say, lifting my chin—which is mostly true. And I remember that I'm mad at him, but gods, it's so hard to focus on anything right now. I need cool air. I need space. I need my mind to start working rationally again. "Now, if you're not planning on apologizing to me for being an ass, I'd like to get back to the party. Leo is waiting for me."

Saying his name was the wrong thing to do. Aris's gaze flicks to my lips, like he could make me take back the word. His breath heats my cheek, and I can't help but shiver. I smell the drink on his breath, warm and sweet. This is the first time he's had a drink since he claimed me—he didn't want to lose control, he said, didn't want his precious reflexes slowed or something. It seems that those concerns have been overridden tonight. I wonder if I would taste it on his lips too.

"He's using you, you know," he whispers, and the words register only dimly.

He bends then, like he's going to kiss me—and I lean toward him, like I'm being pulled. A thousand inappropriate thoughts slam through my mind.

Leo is not among them.

But Aris just presses his forehead to mine, letting out a sigh. I put up my hands, and when they touch his chest, he flinches, like I'm burning him. I'm torn for a moment between pushing him away and pulling him closer. I realize in that moment that I've wanted to touch him for so long—not as a tiger, but as a man—and that I've wanted him to touch me too. Heat rages through me, and I think that I really might burn him if I'm not careful. My hands slide to his flat stomach, feeling the hard planes of him through his shirt.

I make my decision. I bunch my fingers in the fabric of his embroidered jacket and pull him to me.

He doesn't resist. He leans into me, the way he leaned into me the other night on the floor. Each point of contact sears my skin like a flame. My body responds to him now as it did then—with more heat.

"I claimed you," he says, breathless, like he's been dying to say those words to me all night. "I claimed you, and you claimed me. No matter what happens between us, I will always put you first."

A pang spikes through my chest. I'm torn between the sheer physicality of him and the pain of our fight. I want to believe him, more than anything. I want to. I want to.

I can't.

"And the manacles?" I say, looking up at him through my lashes. Does he believe that deep down I'm the monster the others feared? Aris, of all people?

He lets out a breath, and I feel it shudder through him.

"Gone," he says simply.

Gone. He trusts me, or at least he trusts his own ability to calm me down when things get crazy. Either way, I'll take it over the shackles.

He raises his hands to my face, a thumb brushing over my lips before settling along my jaw, cradling my head in his calloused palms. His forehead is still against mine. My heart is fluttering in my chest like a bird.

"Tell me you hate me," he breathes. "Or tell me that I hate you, that I feel nothing for you outside of our bond, our claim. That you are my Mage and I am your Shield, and that is all. You have the power. *Make* me believe it. I can't focus, can't do my job when …" He trails off.

He's battling his inner demons, but all I can think about is the way he feels, pressed against me, and the heat racing through me. I want those hands on me, all over me. Now. I twist my hands in the fabric of his shirt. What he's admitting, what he's feeling, I can barely comprehend it.

"Why not?" I say, a whisper, a dare. Tension has been building between us since I first laid eyes on him in the arena. I barely understood what it was that I wanted from him—but here, now, in this moment, our actions could have repercussions across the rest of our lives. Aris is no saint—I'd have to be a fool to think otherwise—but I want him to be more than my protector, more than my Shield. He knows this—he must, from the way his eyes scan my face gently, like he's afraid he might break me—and to him, I must look so naive, so foolish. To him, a relationship between a man and a woman is a fleeting thing, something to be enjoyed and then discarded. Is it this attraction that he wants me to dispel, to save my poor little heart? Or is there something else, something deeper, that scares even Aris?

"I won't do it," I say. I will not do what he asks. I cannot. Even if I knew how to, I would not.

The words barely make it past my lips, but he hears them. He growls and releases me suddenly, then stalks down the hallway, shaking his head. All the air feels sucked out of the hallway, a great void where a moment ago there were flames.

"Good night, princess," he says over his shoulder. He does not stop. If anything, his pace increases.

I feel abruptly cold, like icy water has been thrown over me. He may not think I'm a monster to be caged, but for some reason, he can't bear the thought of being anything except my Shield. And he wants me to take away those thoughts, wants to keep our relationship professional. For what? His precious honor? Is he worried I'll jeopardize his status somehow, that I'm some silly girl who will lose her head over him and cause some scene, some drama, that keeps him from being the champion he's always dreamed of being? I want to yell after him, to throw something at him. I glare at him, hands clenched, daring him to turn back, to look at me. To see the fury on my face.

He does not look back.

Because standing there, watching both of us with wide eyes, is Leo.

Chapter 44: Aris

I can't be in this palace for another minute.

I don't trust myself with Wren, and I also don't trust her without me. And I don't trust King Leonidas with her either. Maybe I'll go find Aleka, have her fill in for me tonight, keep an eye on Wren while I sort this mess out.

Shit. Maybe I should have stayed by her side. I heard the king coming, calling for her as he left the ballroom. I could have moved then. I could have left.

Instead, I made sure he saw Wren with her hands bunched in my shirt, pulling me down to her, desire clear as day on her face. On mine too, probably.

It was a really shitty thing to do. Do I regret it? No. It had the intended effect. I wanted him to see that desire on her face, to see her acting on it, but that doesn't mean I am proud of what I did. The king would never propose to Wren if he thought she was … involved with me. That would start all kinds of rumors, the kind that a king can't afford. This will keep her out of his grasp, keep her safe, with me. Where he can't use her for his own political ends.

But gods, I didn't mean to say some of those things, to admit to them. She was just so distracting. Another minute, and I would have kissed her, and then I would really have been in deep shit.

I just need some air. Just a few minutes to settle my nerves. Then I will go back to my duties, back to guarding from the shadows, making sure she's safe. I can handle whatever it is that happens next. I am her Shield. It is my job.

A few deep breaths.

I go through the palace gates and stand for a minute on the bridge, halfway between the palace and the rest of the city. I look down at the moat, wondering if the glittering lights I see there are reflected stars or possibly the lights from the manacles I disposed of.

Those damned manacles. I never should have taken them. I don't often regret decisions I make—there's no room for uncertainty in the kind of life I lead. Now, tonight, I add two to that tally: one for keeping the manacles, one for wanting Wren. More than my honor, more than my reputation, more than being the hero, I have to be at her side. I will be the best Shield. And though she may think she wants me to be more than that … for all my teasing, I know I can't be the kind of man she wants. In my life, women come and go.

I look down into the moat, scrying for answers in the dark water. I have another kind of vision then, like I had in the library the night before the games. I see us, together. We'd be good, so good.

Gods, I want her so badly it aches.

But then it would fall apart, as those sorts of things inevitably do. And then what?

I don't know how to be the kind of man she needs—though I'll be damned to all the hells before I let the king have her. Seeing her on the arm of another man nearly killed me tonight. The thought makes my hands grip the railing so tightly that my knuckles throb with the effort. I do know how to be a Shield, though. That I can do, and do well. I can protect her from men—myself included—the same as from trolls.

I turn to go back in, not feeling settled but at least less likely to punch a king or tackle my Mage, but then a flash of yellow catches my eye.

I turn. Head Mage Saroya is … landing? She alights from the night sky, her slippered feet touching down lightly. Her dark hair is wind-whipped, forming a cloud around her face. She looks … haggard. Drawn. She still pulses with power, but it seems … tired somehow.

"Good evening, Shield Aris," she says, like she didn't just fucking fall out of the sky.

"Head Mage," I say. "You know how to make an entrance." I might be drunk or close to it, but my instincts are on high alert. This woman doesn't belong here. I had no idea she was coming. And how in all the hells did she get here, anyway? What, she can fly now?

Her mouth twists to one side, kind of like a smile, I guess, because my own jaw is hanging open.

"I am the wind," she says, like that explains anything.

She walks past me, into the palace. The guards at the gates do not try to stop her—not that they could even if they wanted to. I see the slack look on their faces and realize they saw her fly in too. If they hadn't, I might have thought it was all in my head. Some hallucination brought on by too much alcohol and too little sleep.

I follow her. I'm not sure what she's here for, but it can't be good. I stalk her from the shadows of the hallway, of which there are many. King Leonidas and Wren are talking quietly outside the ballroom, her hand on his chest, him bending down to touch her face. He turns, catching sight of Saroya coming, and he simply lifts a hand, as if to stop her.

I can barely conceal my shock when the woman actually stops. She's glaring at him, power folding around her in hot waves. The king turns, unperturbed, and takes Wren's arm—Wren is twisting around, trying to look at Saroya. He escorts her away from the ballroom.

Back toward her rooms. Our rooms. It seems the king is not going to give up on Wren so easily—and I'll be damned before I go back to the rooms and see what tricks he has up his sleeve next. My pride throbs like an infected wound. Do I really think she needs protection from him, or am I just jealous? Am I really worried about her innocence, her inexperience? Was I imagining the way she looked at me, when she's looking at him like that?

When did this get so complicated? I haven't felt this unsure of myself since I was an adolescent—me, Aris, tripping over myself for a girl. One that happens to be my Mage, and a rather unpredictable one at that.

There is only one thing I am certain of tonight—I do not want to be anywhere near that room.

Chapter 45: Wren

Aris leaves me.

My eyes burn. The lamps in the hallway flare briefly, flames leaping to ten times their usual height, before settling back down. I swallow hard, trying to force air past the lump in my throat. The flames return to their normal behavior.

Leo approaches me. He appears … cautious.

"Everything all right?" he asks.

Furious tears spring to my eyes, and I nod my head. "Fine," I say, but the word sounds pathetic even to my own ears.

He stares down the hallway behind me, where Aris went. I do not turn. He lets out a long breath and returns his gaze to me.

"It must be a lot to take in," he says, his voice calm, soothing. "Your whole world turning upside down. Learning how to wield your magic. Coming here. And then I drag you out to this ball and—"

"No," I say, putting up a hand to stop his words. He's too kind, too empathetic.

He takes my hand in his own warm ones and presses it to his chest, holding it there, holding my eyes with his. "I did not mean to overwhelm you," he says. His thumb traces a circle over the back of my hand, and I swear I feel it reverberate in my core. "Please forgive me. I was just … too enamored of the idea of having you at my side tonight."

What in all the hells do I say to a man like this? Warmth is building in my chest where Aris has left a gaping hole.

"You are forgiven," I say.

His smile grows, and I feel dazzled by it, by him. Aris wants me to forget him, make me hate him? That doesn't take magic. It just takes his own foolish actions. Standing before Leo, I think I'll have little trouble forgetting him.

"Would you like to return to your rooms?" Leo asks. There's another question there, in his words and in his eyes and in his hands, still holding mine. The unspoken question is this: would I like him to come with me?

"Won't you be missed?" I say, glancing toward the ballroom, feeling a little light-headed. I tell myself that I'm allowing him to touch me, flirt with me, because I'm pissed at Aris, but there's more than that. He is more. And his offer … Despite my anger, I feel a quiver of nerves in the pit of my stomach. Music and laughter are pouring out the doors, and revelers are cheering at something.

"They can spare me for a few minutes," he says, his eyes glittering.

And that's when I see Head Mage Saroya, yellow robe billowing in a wind no one else seems to feel, coming down the hallway like a hurricane. I wonder what in the hells she's doing here, and I can't help but think it must involve me somehow. I wonder if she's coming to try another set of shackles.

But Leo merely looks at her and holds up a hand. She stops in her tracks, a confused look on her face.

"Later," he says to her.

She glances toward me. While I thought she felt something like apathy toward me, or at most mild loathing, now her dark eyes glare at me, as hard and piercing as any knife. And Leo stilled her with a word. I like him more and more by the moment.

Leo turns and takes me with him. I turn and try to look over my shoulder at the Head Mage—she's still standing in the middle of the hallway, gaping at us. This is a woman who is not told to wait. People jump at her command, and here she is, being put in her place. I feel a rush of smug satisfaction.

Eventually, we turn a corner, and I return my attention to the man at my side.

"What is she doing here?" I ask.

"We're going to be discussing the school," he says. "I'm not exactly thrilled with her chosen methods of discipline. And the west continues to be a problem. The trolls are getting bolder, and other evil things keep coming down from the mountains."

It is about me—or at least partly. He's called her here because he's pissed that she put me in shackles. My heart swells to the point where I feel it's going to burst out of my chest and take flight. I don't even care that she's here, that she hates me—she can't touch me. I have Leo's protection. To him, I am worth protecting. To him, I am worthy. To Aris, I am a means to an end. The difference stings.

The walk back to my room isn't a long one. The halls are mostly empty but for a few servants, who give us curious glances but make themselves scarce. Everyone else seems to be at the party. The hem of my gold dress makes a soft scuffling sound on the marble floors. How in the hells have I ended up like this? A few minutes ago, I felt like a fraud, and now I am walking back to my room on the arm of the king.

I have a few ideas about what is going to happen next, each more thrilling than the last. Do I have experience with men? No. But I'm not an idiot. And I do have an imagination. A good one.

He stops outside my door. He doesn't open the door, doesn't ask to come in. He's the epitome of chivalry, though his brown eyes glow, the corners of his lips curving upward, ever so slightly, in a conspiratorial grin.

"You know," he says, tucking a stray curl behind my ear. His fingers graze my cheek, trail across my jawbone. My breath catches in my chest at his touch, his boldness. "I saw you when you rode into the palace grounds."

"Did you?" I breathe.

He steps closer. “Riding that war stallion with no bridle, no reins, just you. You sat tall and proud, without fear.”

I feel heat rushing to my face.

“You are fearless, my little Wren. And I think I already knew then,” he says.

He’s so close I can feel the heat of him radiating onto my skin, nearly singeing it. My head is spinning, but whether I can blame it on the drink, I’m not sure. All I can focus on is his lips, full and so close, as he speaks. This is a man who, like Saroya, is not used to being told no, to stop, to wait. But he is patient. He does not rush.

“Knew what?” I manage to say.

“Your Shield calls you ‘princess,’” he says, his lips lifting in a smile, and I try not to roll my eyes. It’s a ridiculous nickname. And it doesn’t escape me that he uses Aris’s title, not his name.

The next words that leave his mouth are spoken low, and he bends to whisper them into my ear. “I would call you a queen.”

A shiver runs through me, a thrill, which has nothing to do with my magic.

He pulls back, like he wants to see the reaction on my face. He doesn’t pull back far, and he must be pleased, because he leans down further and brushes those lips gently against mine. He tastes like wine and sunshine. I’m too stunned to move.

“Sleep well, little bird,” he says. He offers one final touch, one finger lightly stroking the side of my face, hovering at my lips, before he bows to me and turns to head back down the long hallway.

I watch him go until he turns the corner. My hand goes to my lips—and it’s shaking. I have no idea how those shaking fingers manage to unlatch the door handle, but they do, and I drift to my room in a daze, noticing that Aris isn’t there but not really caring.

I curl up in my bed. I’m not ready to take off this glorious dress, not ready for the night to end. I want to replay every moment in my head—except the ones with Aris. I realize that Leo must have seen him pressed against me in that dark corner, like a lover. And he must have seen Aris stomp off, spurned.

I don't want to think about Aris. He is my Shield, my protector. If that's all he wants, that's fine. Do I want more from him? Maybe. But if he isn't going to return my affection, if he's too afraid that I can't make my own decisions about my heart, then I will follow his wishes. I will make myself forget about him, without magic. It won't be hard, not with the golden king himself around. I thought Leo's interest in me was professional—that he saw me as a weapon to be honed and then wielded. Perhaps it was, at one point—but something has shifted. And I like it. I like it a lot.

I'm surprised at Leo, at his boldness, and simultaneously at his restraint. If he'd come in here, I might have done something really stupid tonight. Maybe he knew that, and that's why he stayed outside. I think back to my first kiss—a stolen one with Zacharias a hundred years ago, in the barn behind his house in Spit. Like I was something to hide. At the time, it felt like a thrilling secret. Now I see it for what it was—he was hiding me; he didn't want to be caught with me.

Leo has no such qualms. He was proud to be seen with me. I was a golden gem to be shown off, not hidden. And I wonder about Leo as a king. There must be noble women lined up for a mile to get his attention, and yet he is focused on me, the way the lens in my lighthouse would focus the flame and turn it into a brilliant beam. I wonder that he spoke to me so boldly—and yet I do not doubt his sincerity. No one who saw him in the ballroom tonight could. He spoke to all, listened to each courtier who approached, but he only had eyes for me.

It's enough to go to any girl's head.

Do I want to be a queen? It seems ridiculous to even consider. I am no one. I am the strange girl from the enemy country. The lighthouse keeper in a town called Spit, whom magic has apparently decided to infect, and the symptoms are not manifesting in the proper way. I'm an anomaly, a curiosity. I wonder if Saroya thinks I'm contagious, and the thought makes me giggle.

I cuddle up under my blankets, thinking about Leo, and definitely not thinking about a pair of blazing blue eyes and the sardonic, darkly handsome Shield they belong to.

Chapter 46: Aris

There are a lot of things that happen that night that I'm not proud of, the worst of which is leaving Wren alone. No Shield should ever leave their Mage unaccompanied—even though I told myself that she was in the palace, in the company of the king. Little could touch her there. And she's not exactly defenseless, even if she is still shit with a dagger.

I drown my emotions in ale and cards at a run-down tavern in Estana called the Cracked Egg and pour out my heart to a lovely, sympathetic ear before finding myself in her bed when the dawn light shines in through the open window.

I disentangle myself from her limbs and get dressed silently. She's not someone I've ever seen before. I can't remember her name, like the utter ass that I am, but now, in the light, I see round, smooth tan skin and long brown curls. The resemblance is not lost on me.

Rosa. Her name is Rosa. Or Rosanne. Shit.

I get the hells out of there before she wakes up. This part of town is not as glamorous as the main road—the streets are narrow and smell of piss and garbage. No, no, that's me. Gods, what got into me last night? I remember, with too much clarity, the events of the ball, the way Wren looked at me as she pulled me down to her, the way I wanted to respond … I remember leaving the palace, and after that, things get a little blurry. Cards, more ale, less clothing. My head throbs as I try to reconstruct the pieces of the evening.

I shift, leaving my ruined finery behind. As a tiger, I feel Wren's pull, like a silver bell ringing through a clear sky. There are some screams as I run toward the palace, and one little old lady actually tries to swat at me with a broom, like I'm some kind of errant house cat. I dunk myself in the moat to get the smell off before heading toward the bridge. The water helps a little, though even in this form, I reek, like ale is oozing out of my pores.

The guards on the bridge are trained in the shifting ability of Shields—and even if they weren't, what would a white tiger be doing running toward the palace in this corner of the world? They let me in, and I dash toward my rooms. Our rooms. Now that I'm going, I need to see Wren. The tiger in me is pulled to her, with a force as unstoppable as gravity. Most of the time, my own will dominates the tiger. But every so often—like when I was injured when Stefan died—the tiger takes over, and he's a vicious, territorial beast. I'm aware that if I find King Leonidas in the room with Wren, the tiger is going to need some serious restraining.

I get to our rooms and realize I can't operate the handle, so I shift back. I'm still damp from my improvised bath, water dripping down my back in freezing little trickles. I brace myself for whatever it is I'm about to see. There are no guards outside the door—if the king had spent the night here, there should have been guards.

My theory is confirmed when I enter. The living area appears undisturbed. Wren's door is closed, but not locked. I listen for a moment and hear nothing.

She's sound asleep. Gold paint is smeared across her cheeks, like she rubbed her eyes in her sleep. She's still wearing that gold dress that makes her look like some kind of sun deity, her hair strewn out across the pillow. She is luminous, like a sun on the verge of rising.

And she is alone. The other half of the bed is undisturbed. She slept completely alone last night, and I realize again what a complete ass I am for having left her, undefended, for hours. Vassilis would have had my head for such a lapse.

She stirs, so I turn and close the door. It's another day. Another chance. I don't know how many more I'm going to get, so I resolve to make the most of it.

Chapter 47: Wren

I feel Aris enter my room more than I hear him. I open my eyes just as he turns to leave.

He's naked, of course. The scars that were once red and puckered on his shoulder and chest are faded now, as if years have passed instead of weeks. And he appears to have tried to bathe—water drips from his hair, so long it nearly brushes his shoulders now, before funneling down the muscles of his back and … lower. But my gaze doesn't drop too much lower than his shoulder blades, where symmetrical rows of scratches in four parallel lines tell me exactly what my Shield was up to last night. Scratches his enhanced healing hasn't been able to erase just yet.

Prick. How dare he "confess" his feelings to me, jeopardize any possible future interactions with Leo, and then spend the night in the arms of someone else? I mean, not that I wanted him in my bed and—Shit. Yes. Yes, I did. Arrogant, stubborn, overbearing man-whore.

I rub the heels of my hands into my eyes, trying to block out the image of him with another woman. Of him touching, and kissing, and … My hands come away from my face smeared with gold, and I realize I'm a gilded mess.

I take a quick bath, but the cold water I dunk myself in does little to repel my bad mood. I find some pants and a shirt as black as my mood and put them on. The cold has left me chilly, so I put on my Mage's robe. I want to remind Aris—and myself—that I am his Mage. Until he decides otherwise. He is my Shield, my partner, my protector. But I can't help thinking, did he even mean it when he said he'd always put me first?

He's in the common room by the time I'm done, sipping something in a mug, glaring at me over the rim. I realize abruptly that I haven't thought of Leo once throughout my whole silent tantrum this morning.

"Good morning," I say briskly, helping myself to some breakfast. I pointedly ignore Aris, instead choosing to immerse myself in one of Ismini's books while I eat.

"Are you going to tell me what happened last night?" he says. The words are an accusation.

"You would know if you hadn't left me, Shield. I owe you no explanations," I say. Let him think what he wants. Let him think that Leo stayed with me last night. Let him think that I had a wonderful time without him.

He growls.

I glare at him, long enough that the tension sizzles between us. Then I change tack, giving him a sweet smile. "Unless you'd like to go first," I say.

He takes another sip from his cup. I guess it's coffee. Or that stupid ash water he likes. He's gripping it so hard I'm surprised the ceramic doesn't shatter, but he offers no explanation of his whereabouts, no apology for what he did. Not that it matters. I have no claim on him, other than his bond as my Shield.

I toss my braid back over my shoulder. "What's her name?" I ask, unable to bite my tongue.

He jerks his head up and glares at me.

"The woman you spent the night with. Is this going to be a regular thing?"

"Careful, Mage," he says.

I match his glare with my own, though I'm starting to get goose bumps.

He smirks. "Jealousy is not a good look on you," he says.

I finish my meal in silence. Then I read for a while in silence. And then I just glare at Aris. In silence.

"I'm going to see Ismini. Are you coming?" I ask. I had been expecting to hear from her by now, and I'm getting antsy.

He unfolds himself from his chair and follows me out, a silent shadow.

We meet Aleka in her fighting gear outside my training room.

"Good afternoon, you two. Ismini's running a few minutes late. She needed to stop by the greenhouses," she tells me. If she notices the ice between me and Aris, she doesn't comment on it. "You look like shit," she says, looking Aris over.

I decide I like this woman.

Aris rolls his eyes.

"Come on. Maybe that means I'll finally thrash you in the arena," she says, clapping him on the shoulder.

Aris heads out without so much as a glance my way. His movements are lighter, though, like the idea of some competition in the arena is waking him up more than the coffee ever could.

I head into the room and settle myself into a chair. I've just cracked my book open when a nervous-looking girl in palace livery knocks.

"Mage Verena?" she says, twitching like a scared rabbit.

I look up, waiting on her to say more.

"Um, Mage Ismini has been held up."

"I know," I say, not clear why she's here.

She swallows, her eyes darting around the room. Surely my reputation is not that terrifying. Yet.

"She suggests that you take a break from training this morning," she says. The words come out in a rush. "She recommends going for a ride. The weather will be fine today."

That's actually not a bad idea. I haven't seen Obsidian in ages, and the thought of going for a gallop outside the city walls, without Aris, makes me giddy. It would be wonderful to clear my head.

I follow the girl to the stables. Dozens, if not hundreds, of horses are here, from dainty ponies to massive workhorses to war stallions like Obsidian. They're grouped by purpose mostly, and I find Obsidian easily. He neighs and tosses his head when he sees me, pulling a lead rope through some poor stable boy's grip as he trots over to see me. The boy is chasing after him, red-faced, but he stops dead when he sees me.

Obsidian drops his huge black muzzle to my hand.

"Sorry. No treats today," I tell him.

He lets out a *whuff* of warm air into my palm. This was a really good idea. I feel more relaxed by the second.

"Not often you see a warhorse acting like a kitten," a voice calls. It belongs to a colossal man, probably close to six and a half feet tall, with short dark hair, glittering black eyes, and massive forearms. He looks like he could snap trees in half with his bare hands. There's no mistaking who this man is, not with that jawline, and I only wonder why I haven't run into him before.

"You're Aris's father," I say. I'm not really sure I know what to think—I'm pretty sure he and Aris had a fight when we arrived. They definitely have a tense relationship. Where Aris is graceful, this man appears as powerful as a troll. I vaguely recall someone telling me he worked with the warhorses, so I guess it's not a surprise he's here at this hour.

"Nestor Valorius. And you are Verena," he says.

"Wren," I correct automatically, realizing I'd never heard Aris use his last name—his father's name. As if he couldn't stand to be associated with the man.

He nods. "Can I help you with something, Mage Wren?"

"I'd like to go for a ride," I say, a bit sheepishly. I feel childish around this man, frivolous.

"The ladies' riding horses are on the other side of the stables," he says. "I can get someone to bring you one."

"Oh. I … prefer Obsidian," I say, and my face heats when he stares at me. "If that's all right, I mean." This man has me flustered. I don't like it.

But he just nods. "Need help with his tack?" he asks, nodding toward racks of saddles and bridles on the wall.

I shake my head awkwardly. "I don't need any."

He shrugs, like if I want to go off and break my neck, then I'm welcome to do so.

I recall Aris telling me that Nestor is better with animals than people, and I realize that so am I. I'm not sure how I feel about making this connection—then I recall how red Aris's face was after Nestor had struck him. Any connection I feel toward this man before me withers into loathing.

He pauses for a moment, studying me, like he's trying to figure out what to say to me next.

"All right. Just don't stay out too late, or you'll miss the festivities," he says at last.

I frown. "What festivities?"

"The king's announcing his engagement today," Nestor says. "Whole place is going to be buzzing tonight."

I startle. *What*? My face feels hot and then cold as I try to process this. What Leo said last night, that was a proposal? That's absurd—we barely know each other. The world spins around me, like I'm caught in a waterspout. He said he would call me a queen—his queen.

"Well, I wish him and Lady Orothea the best," Nestor says, brushing hay off his sleeve.

My heart stops. The world stops.

"What?" I whisper.

Nestor looks at me like he's afraid I'm going to shatter—or rather, like he's afraid I'm going to go into hysterics. He doesn't look like a man who tolerates hysterics. "Lady Orothea? He's been courting her for months," he says.

I curl my fingers into Obsidian's mane and press my face against his strong, warm neck. Gods, I am such a fool. Hot tears leak onto the velvet of Obsidian's coat. I feel the earth tilting under my feet. Aris was right—I am a naive idiot when it comes to men. I was just some amusement for Leo, some curiosity to pass the time with until his announcement. Thank all the gods I didn't let him into my room last night.

"Here," Nestor says, and a flask is thrust into my face.

I look up at him, wrinkling my brow.

He shrugs. "You look like you need it."

Well, he's not wrong. I take a sip—it's wine, sweet and cloying. I expected a man like Nestor to have something stronger, like the whiskey made in southern Ocron. But hey, I'm not the best judge of people, apparently. He can drink whatever the hells he wants.

I take a long tug on the wine before returning it to him. My head feels light; my toes and fingers tingle. I guess this is shock—maybe alcohol wasn't the best thing to mix it with, but I didn't drink all that much.

I take off Obsidian's halter, and Nestor gives me a leg up. Maybe he's not all that bad. It's not his fault he was the one to break bad news to me.

I thank him and turn Obsidian out of the stables.

Overhead, the fine day is turning cloudy and dark. Obsidian tosses his head, ready to go, and I let him. Together we thunder down the main street of Estana, narrowly avoiding trampling a few people, but I don't care. He gallops and gallops until we're free of the city gates, free of Estana. The wind whips through my hair, and I feel giddy, light, as if I might float right off his back like dandelion fluff, drifting up, up through the sky … The farther we get from the city, the more I feel like a tremendous weight has lifted from my shoulders, and I don't think anymore—I just let Obsidian run.

Chapter 48: Aris

I come close to getting my ass kicked by Aleka. Very close. Today a staff is her weapon of choice, and she delights in whacking it against my shins, my skull, and my back every chance she gets. Even with my healing abilities, I'm sure that I'll be splotchy with bruises tomorrow.

By the time we're done sparring, the sky is clouding up, and I'm panting heavily.

"You're slow today, kitten," Aleka says, tossing me a towel.

I wipe the sweat off my face. I'm never drinking again. My head is buzzing like a whole hive of bees has taken up residence in my skull, and my muscles feel slow to respond today, like I'm half-asleep despite the bees. It is not a good feeling.

"Rough night," I say.

Aleka raises an eyebrow, regarding me with narrowed eyes, like she can see right into my brain and pluck out the answer she's looking for.

"Mage trouble, woman trouble, or both?" she asks.

One of the things I like about her—she never beats around the bush, just gets right to the heart of the matter, even if I don't feel like talking about it.

I shrug, wiping sand off my arms from an earlier tumble. "Both," I mutter.

"I can't tell you how many fights Issi and I have had over the years," she says, pouring a pitcher of water over her head to cool herself off.

I run a hand through my hair, gathering most of it into a topknot. While long hair looks good on me, it does tend to get in the way. No wonder Aleka keeps hers cropped short.

"Each partnership is different," she goes on, wiping her face with a scarred hand. "But the most effective partnerships are the ones where both parties communicate, talk about what's going on. She's not a mind reader—you have to tell her what's going on in that thick skull of yours."

"I did. That's the problem," I growl, sitting down hard on a bench. I did tell her. I nearly poured out my gods-damned heart to her—right before I left her alone and spent the night with Rosa … or was it Rosemary? Also, somehow Wren knows about that tryst and is holding it against me. Which, I guess, I deserve.

"Look, something's different about her," Aleka says. I look up. She's regarding me, one hand on her hips. "Or you would have slept with her already."

"I'm going for a run," I say, getting up.

Aleka smacks me with her staff, knocking me back down, and I growl at her.

"Don't give me that snark, kitten," she says, raising a finger, "or I'll have you on double wall-patrol duty for a month."

"What can I possibly have to say to her?" I ask, not saying aloud that I don't want her with the king, but I can't be what she wants either.

"Ismini says she cares for you," Aleka says, with another smack. I groan. "So go talk to her. Be honest with her. This stupid dance you're both doing is giving the rest of us a headache."

Talk to her. Talk about *feelings*. Gods, I'd rather take on a whole clan of trolls.

But we can't continue to function as we are. I have to talk to Wren, and then let her make her own decision. I am faced with uncertainty, the fact that she may choose King Leonidas over me, and I don't like it. And if she chooses me? Damn it all to the hells. I'd have to find a way to be worthy.

I hate to admit it, but Aleka may have a point.

She knows it. She gives me a grin, and another smack across my shins for good measure.

It's late afternoon, so I head toward the training room to check on Wren. I'm about halfway down the hallway when I see Ismini heading toward the room with an armful of plants. I can't even see her face—it's totally obscured by leaves, and vines are reaching out to wrap around her fingers and arms. I follow her into the room.

"You wouldn't think that plants have emergencies, but they do," she pants, depositing the pots on a table. She shoos the vines off her arms like they're misbehaving pets. The leaves wilt and droop as they reluctantly let her go.

I look around—but Wren is nowhere to be seen. I see the book she was reading this morning, now discarded on a chair. But no Wren. Ismini peeks around me, like I'm hiding her behind me or something.

"Where's Wren?" she asks, arranging her pots.

"I thought she was with you," I say.

Ismini stops and shakes her head. "Haven't seen her all day," she says.

I frown. Wren was upset this morning—maybe she got tired of waiting around for Ismini and found something else to do with her time. My gut clenches when I wonder if she's with King Leonidas.

My fears are quickly alleviated when the king appears a few moments later, alone, but my relief is short-lived. He rushes into the room, instead of sauntering in his normal relaxed way. He's a man not easily flustered—and now I see the tremor in his hands, the wideness of his eyes. Something is wrong.

"Where's Wren?" I demand.

His gaze snaps to me.

I don't bow—I don't care.

"I was hoping she was here," he says.

"She's not. Obviously," I say.

Ismini gives me a stern look, but I don't look back at her.

I cross my arms. "Where is my Mage?"

"No one knows," King Leonidas says, and runs a hand across his face.

"What do you *mean*, no one knows?" I snarl. My pulse quickens. *Not again, not again, not again.*

"No one's seen her since earlier this morning," he says, and he swallows hard. "I came looking for her to … well …" He trails off.

"To what?" I ask through clenched teeth. *To pick up where you left off last night*?

"I don't have any meetings this evening, so I thought she might want to go for a walk or something," he says, not looking me in the eye.

Gods! My Mage is missing, and this man wants to take her out on a date.

I'll deal with him later.

"Who saw her last?" I ask. My hands reflexively go to the pair of gladiuses strapped across my back, reassured by the feel of their worn leather grips. Ismini is giving me a sideways look, though, so I don't draw them.

"A stable boy," King Leonidas says, eyeing my blades. "I asked after her when I returned from a ride earlier." He's standing straighter now, looking me in the eyes. The tremor has stilled.

"A stable boy," I echo. The stables. Sure, she could have gone down to see Obsidian. She's been talking about bringing him treats—turning that ferocious stallion into a pet. I almost grin at the thought.

And then I realize that Nestor is running the stables now. All my fears—the fear of losing a Mage again, the fear of losing Wren—come crashing down at once. Wherever Wren is, Nestor is sure to know, and I'm not sure that's a good thing. Panic floods my veins like ice, and visions of Stefan bleeding fog my vision until all I see is red. Would Nestor harm my Mage? He wouldn't dare—would he? Some twisted plot of his to leave me free to claim another?

I leave the room in a rush, a plan forming in my mind as I go. King Leonidas and Ismini chase after me.

"Where are you going?" Ismini asks. She's huffing a little, her face turning red, as she struggles to keep up.

"To find my Mage!" I roar.

I go to the stables, Ismini and the king flanking me. People trip over themselves getting away from us—whatever has managed to piss off the king, a Shield, and a senior Mage, they want no part in it. We find the stable boy who saw Wren last—one word from the king, and the others point him out, eagerly deflecting our wrath away from themselves. The boy's a nervous thing, and I think he might be about to piss his pants.

"Where is Wren?" I ask.

The boy flinches, shrinking back against a stall door, the freckles on his face standing out like blood on snow. "She went for a ride, on the black stallion, sir," he says. He gives the king a low bow and nearly falls over from the effort. Ismini catches him, a hand on his shoulder, which is the only reason he doesn't topple onto the stable floor. His face goes red.

"When?" I ask.

"Uh … about three, four hours ago," he says, scratching the back of his neck.

"Where is Nestor?" I say. By now, a crowd is starting to gather.

The nervous boy shakes his head, but someone calls out from the crowd.

"He left. I saw him heading out of the palace. Maybe a few hours ago. Left me to work the new colts by myself."

Shit.

What does Nestor want with Wren? I know the man hates me, but to go after a Mage is a crime unheard of among Shields. What does he intend to do with her? Is this some sort of retaliation against me, for picking a Mage he deems unworthy? For me not being the perfect son he wanted?

"Relax," Ismini says, putting a hand on my shoulder. "It's only been a few hours. Maybe she just went for a long ride, to clear her head. She's had a lot to deal with lately." She looks between me and the king.

The king has the grace to look a little embarrassed. I do not. I will find her, and I will not leave her side ever again. She can come with me to the training grounds, and I will sit in on her Mage lessons. I don't care if she does hate me. I don't care if I have to watch the king fall all over her for the rest of my life. Alarms are blaring in my head, like the kind the city uses when there's a fire. *Not again, not again, not again*. If I lose another Mage, if this bond is severed, I'm not sure I'll survive it.

The bond. I don't know why I didn't think about it before. I take a deep breath, fighting back panic, as a plan begins to form in my mind.

"I'm going to shift," I say, addressing Ismini. "I feel a pull to her when I'm in my other form. I'll be able to find her then, wherever she is."

The pull feels … thin. Like Wren is very far away, or very weak. The great silver bell that I'm used to hearing is no more than a faint chime. I swing my head from side to side, trying to figure out which direction the chime is coming from. I pace through the room. I can't pinpoint it in here. Plus the sensation of the bond feels … wrong. I'm reminded of the way the bond felt when Stefan was shot, the way I felt it twang like a popped wire. Resolve tightens in my chest—Wren's alive, at least. I can find her. I will find her. My claws gouge furrows through the stone floor, and my hackles rise. A growl tears from my throat as I shift back. Ismini hands me my clothes.

"Something's wrong. I can feel it through our bond," I say, struggling to keep panic from rising. "I'm going after her."

"I'm coming with you," Ismini says, her mouth a firm, hard line, her arms crossed. It is not a request.

"I … can't," King Leonidas says.

I roll my eyes. He might be able to keep up on horseback, but I doubt it. And even battle-hardened creatures like Flint don't like being around tigers for long. He couldn't—or wouldn't—abandon his duties, though, wouldn't put himself at any risk. Some part of me realizes that if something happened to him, it would leave the whole continent in an uproar—but right now, the only thing I see is incompetence. A man unwilling to fight to save the woman we both care about.

"Just … find her for me, whatever it takes," he says. He puts a hand on my shoulder, like we're friends, not two assholes going after the same woman, not a Shield and his king.

I shrug him off. "I will."

Ismini and I go to the arena. Aleka is nowhere to be found, so we send a messenger off to tell her what's going on. I grab a bag and fill it with weapons, a shield, leather armor, whatever I think I might need, and hand it to Ismini. She looks strange carrying it—she's a gardener, not a warrior. But I'm reminded that she also happens to be one of the strongest Earth Mages in a generation. As she walks, the very ground shakes in response to her rage. She hefts the bag over her shoulder, her eyes blazing as green as her Mage's robe. She gives me a nod. She's ready.

Ismini gathers my clothes and stuffs them into the bag, and then we're off. I'm sprinting from the palace, across the bridge, through the city, with the speed and agility granted to me in tiger form. I don't check to see if Ismini is keeping up—but then she's beside me. She's not running—she's not gifted with a Shield's speed and stamina. Instead, a roll of earth and stone is pushing her along, like a wave. Cobblestones clack and break as she speeds on, riding the wave of earth, just as fast as I am running, robe flapping out behind her like green wings. She leaves a trail of broken stone and earth in her wake. Whatever happens, whatever we encounter, I'll be thankful to have her at my side.

I roar at a group of people coming through the gates, blocking our path momentarily. They scatter, throwing themselves aside as we thunder through.

Before us, the hills around Estana roll like a dried green carpet in the fading evening light. The call is not growing any stronger. Either Wren's moving away from us, or she's fading.

I run faster.

In front of us, a storm is gathering. The clouds move slowly in the gathering dusk, but they are moving, massing into a growing thunderhead, turning darker every moment. It's centered over a small forest to the west of the city. That's where the pull is taking me. I have no doubt that the clouds are Wren's doing, her own beacon.

We tear across the plains, Ismini still riding her wave of earth, feet planted firmly. The clouds are starting to spiral, but it's a slow, lazy motion, like the clouds themselves are tired, worn out. My paws tear at the ground, eating up the miles.

A few miles out, we find Obsidian.

The stallion is dead. He fought. That much is clear. Blood is scattered over a wide swath of grass and dirt. The ground around him is torn up and covered with hoofprints, gouged deep into the soft earth. Someone has cut him several times along his flanks and stomach, and then at his neck, hard enough to nearly sever it. Great spurts of hot blood coat the ground, turning the soil into black mud. Ismini blanches at the sight.

I put a paw to the animal—still warm. We're not far now. Obsidian was a trained warhorse, devoted to Wren. He killed a troll for her with a single swipe of a hoof, caving in a skull like it was made of paper.

Whatever came for him this time was so much worse.

Chapter 49: Wren

I wake up to an intense feeling of wrongness.

My head feels heavy, my thoughts disjointed. My vision blurs as I blink awake.

Awake. Why was I asleep? My tongue feels thick and as dry as ashes in my mouth.

Obsidian. I went riding on Obsidian.

My thoughts clear slowly, like I'm walking through knee-deep mud. I try to wipe the dryness from my eyes, but my hands won't move.

They're tied up. I'm tied up? What in all the hells? I realize then that I can feel the abrasion of thick rope around my wrists, which are behind my back. And I feel something else—a kiss of ice-cold metal on my right wrist.

I realize why I feel so wrong, so out of focus. My magic is being blocked. Someone has put a manacle back on me.

The rage that flows through me at this realization clears my foggy head like a fire clears a dry grassy field.

I am seated in a thickly padded chair, my ankles also tied together. I don't recognize the room I'm in, which is large but sparse, and I don't recall how I got here. It doesn't feel like the palace—the colors of the stone are all wrong, and the floor is dirt instead of marble. I think I must have been drugged. I wonder how long I was asleep, or unconscious. I wonder if my healing abilities will metabolize this poison as fast as it healed that troll wound. One can only hope.

I wonder if Aris has missed me yet. Or Ismini, when she realizes I didn't show for her lessons. I miss them both with a ferocity I didn't know I possessed. When I see my Shield again, I'll let him know *exactly* how much I missed him.

If I see him again.

My nose itches. I wiggle it, but the sensation only gets worse. *Great.*

"Hey!" I scream. My throat is parched. The sound comes out raspy, but it's loud. The walls here are bare gray stone, so the acoustics make the echoes carry. It's a large room, maybe an abandoned barn or warehouse of some sort. I can see patches of dark cloud through holes in the thatched roof, far overhead.

Someone's kidnapped me. Right? That's what all this means. What in all the hells? I glare at the rope on my legs, willing it to disintegrate, for the plant fibers to burn and fall apart.

Nothing happens.

Shit.

I hear footsteps. Two pairs, one heavy and one very light.

Nestor comes in first.

Nestor. Of course. That wine he offered me—it was drugged. How could I have been so foolish? But what in all the hells does he want from me?

I struggle against my bonds, but the ropes are tight, and I'm unable to get up from the chair.

"Useful things, those manacles," he says lightly, and I realize that he wasn't present when they were removed. Someone must have told him about them. Aris told me the manacles were gone—I didn't realize that meant he'd given them to his father. A slick lie.

But I'd thought he hated his father. Why would he give the manacles to him, unless he and his father are in some sort of cahoots? Has Aris betrayed me, realized he'd be better off without me after all?

Gods, I must still be drugged. Who uses words like *cahoots*?

I must look bewildered, because Nestor laughs. It is a hoarse, deep sound. I don't like it. It makes the hairs on the back of my neck stand up.

"I know. No easy thing, getting them from the bottom of the moat," he says.

He assumes that I know something. What? That Aris put them there and that I am confused because he got them back? Aris said they were gone—so that means he threw them into the moat. He didn't betray me. Something inside me tightens and threatens to shatter. Aris. Gods, where is he? Is he all right? I wiggle my hands again, trying to slip one through the bonds. All I succeed in doing is somehow tightening them.

The second pair of footsteps, light and delicate, comes down some sort of corridor and then into my prison.

Head Mage Saroya.

I blink. She's still here, not a drug-induced hallucination. She enters the room swiftly, her yellow robe flaring out behind her on its own breeze. As she gets closer, I realize that the hem of her robe is muddy. Her ebony skin is matte with fatigue, her once-impeccable facade now tired, dirty.

"What in all the hells …?" I breathe.

She glances at Nestor, who drags a chair across the room for her so that she can sit across from me, like we're simply meeting for a friendly chat, like I'm not shackled and tied and drugged.

Bitch.

"I'm sure you have many questions, Verena," she says. Even her voice sounds tired. Not that I care—I am just noticing.

What has the Head Mage of all of Ocron so worn out? I guess I wasn't wrong—I am the reason she came to Estana. I wonder if something Leo said to her last night after he left me has pissed her off. But what would piss her off enough to kidnap me?

"A few," I spit. "Why don't you untie me, and then we can have a proper chat?"

The doorway they entered through appears to be the only exit from this place. I wonder if I could outrun her. Drugged or not, though, I'm certain I wouldn't be able to outrun Nestor. I wonder if he shifts to a tiger, like Aris, and can't repress the shudder that goes through me as I think of the damage those claws would do to me.

She shakes her head. "You are too dangerous," she says wearily.

I gape at her—she believes that. In the depths of her heart, she believes that I am dangerous. A monster to be chained after all.

"What did I ever do to you?" I scream. The light dims as the sky continues to darken.

"You? Nothing," she says. Her lips are a tight line. "You are … just a tumor."

"What?" I ask, taken aback.

"You are destructive, Verena. Invasive. Your influence will spread and grow until it chokes the life out of the entire continent," she says, her black eyes blazing.

"I haven't done anything!" I shriek.

"I believe that it may be unintentional on your part," Saroya says. She leans back, running a hand over her tired face. "A tumor doesn't realize it's a tumor. It just wants to grow. Your magic is the same. It is spreading from you, exerting a subconscious influence. Haven't you ever wondered why the king has taken such an interest in you?" She peers at me.

I fidget.

"As charming as I'm sure you think you are, your magic has been influencing him since you first arrived, attracting him to you like a bee to a flower. It would make you a queen, with dominion over us all."

I feel cold creeping up my neck. "What about Lady Orothea?" I ask.

Saroya arches an eyebrow. "Who?"

I look at Nestor, who shrugs when I mention Leo's queen-to-be.

"I made it up," he says.

"What … why would you …?" I sputter.

"Had to make you mad. We needed you outside of the city walls, where this would be safer."

"And so you drugged me," I say, glaring daggers at him. I wish my magic were back—I'd throw a big rock at his head.

Saroya apparently wasn't aware that this was part of his plan. She's frowning, the movement carving weary lines in her face I haven't noticed before.

"It worked, didn't it?" he says, to both of us, crossing his arms.

"So you're saying the only reason Leo ever took an interest in me was because I was subconsciously influencing his mind?" I say. It's hard to take, but that might be more because of pride than anything else. Of course I wanted him to like me. Why wouldn't I?

"The same way you influenced your horse to obey you, you've been influencing the king. It's a subtle kind of magic, one that only the most powerful Wind Mages have even attempted. As one well versed in mind control, I assure you, I was … impressed."

I hate this woman.

"And everyone else?" I ask dully. I'm not sure I want the answer, but I have to know. Ismini? Tolis? All those Mages who practically tripped over themselves to help me?

Aris?

Is he so divided because he knows in his heart he doesn't want to be with me, but my magic has just kept trying anyway? I knew he couldn't keep away as a tiger. Have I been so lonely, so desperate, that my magic just latched on to him?

"To varying degrees," Nestor says.

I sag, sitting back in the chair.

"There's more," Saroya says. "Things are stirring in the west, awakening. Things far worse than a stray band of trolls. Things older, fouler. Things that have heard your call the same way your horse did, the same way any Shield who's shifted has. Your power reaches across the continent for purchase. I cannot allow you to destroy us all."

I can't process what she's saying. I picture my magic like a light in a lighthouse, beam extending far beyond me, a warning—or a beacon. I thought maybe my magic was special, that I was special. And I guess I am—but not in a good way.

What if, in fact, I have been a monster all along?

"I'm not … I haven't …"

Saroya sighs. "I know," she says. She leans back in her chair, slumping, and runs a tired hand over her face. "Have you heard about Spit?"

A spike of cold fear shoots through me. I stare at her, but she just raises her eyebrows, waiting. Then she sighs and sits back up, leaning elbows on knees.

"Your lighthouse is gone, Verena," she says. Her voice is level, quiet, like she's telling me a loved one has died—which I guess in a way is an appropriate approach. The words hit me like a punch to the gut.

"What do you mean, gone?" I ask, though the words come out shaky. It's a three-story stone building. Those things don't just vanish into thin air.

"A ten-armed monster rose from the sea about two weeks ago," she says. "Each tentacle a hundred feet long. Tore your lighthouse down to the foundation."

"You lie," I say.

"Words have power, Verena—mine more than most. I cannot lie to you," she reminds me.

I slump back in my chair.

Gone. My home is gone. Destroyed, by some *thing*, presumably looking for *me*. I look from Saroya to Nestor, desperate, hoping to see a smirk or something that will tell me she's playing some kind of horrific joke on me, but Nestor just looks at me with his black eyes, an expression almost like pity on his face, if I thought the man capable of such an emotion.

"Was … was anyone in town hurt?" I ask.

Saroya shrugs. "Not to my knowledge," she says. "But I believe a number of them have left the area, in case the creature returns, looking for someone."

I shiver. That building was the pride of my family for generations. What she is saying is impossible—nothing has that kind of power. That lighthouse has withstood hurricanes.

"So … what? You're going to kill me in case something else wants to come after me?" I ask.

Nestor snorts. "Thought about it," he says.

Saroya glares at him again, and he shrugs. I believe him.

"Magic has been fading for years," Saroya says, changing the subject. "Fewer and fewer of us are gifted, fewer Mages and Shields every year. We've long feared an end to magic—and you, whether intentionally or not, are at best the harbinger of that end, the terminal illness that wipes out the last of us. At worst, you are a catalyst. A perversion.

"You'll see why, now, the manacle is necessary," she continues. "I am using my own mind control on you as well, inserted into your subconscious as you slept. It is … taxing. Once we have you controlled, we'll go back to the school, where we can study this more, where we can try to undo the damage you have done. It will be easier, of course, on all of us if you come willingly."

"Leo will never allow this," I mutter.

She raises an eyebrow. "The king will be informed about your manipulations, Verena, and then, yes, he will allow whatever it is I deem fit," she says.

She seems entirely certain of this, which sends a chill through me. Would Leo really allow me to be trussed up and carted off back to the school like this? Would Aris? Would he have to be restrained too, as he fought against whatever power I had over him?

I try to process all this, but it's taxing my drugged brain. The thoughts come slowly. If what Saroya says is true—and what possible motive could she have to lie about something like this, after the risk she's taken by kidnapping me?—then I really don't have a choice. I should go with her, voluntarily.

I should do everything in my power to help her figure this out. I have no idea what kinds of things are going on in the west—what kinds of creatures could be hearing my call, on their way even now. I think back to the supplicants in the throne room of Estana's palace, how they talked of great bat-winged beasts carrying people off. And this is somehow my fault?

If they have Saroya frightened, though, they must be formidable.

"I didn't intend to take you so … dramatically," Saroya explains. "But when I saw you with the king last night, I realized you were working far more quickly than we'd anticipated, your magic growing too fast. We had to act."

A tremor goes through me. Of course it had all been a farce. How did I possibly imagine that someone like Leo, or Aris, would ever desire me? I choke out a laugh. Stupid, naive little Wren. A common little bird after all. The trembling continues.

And that's when I realize the tremor isn't coming from me, but from the ground. The building is shaking as the earth rumbles below us. Nestor and Saroya exchange a glance. Thatch breaks free from the ceiling, showering us in dirt and mildewing straw.

And that's when the side of the building to my left explodes outward, leaving a giant, gaping hole. Dust billows in clouds, through which Ismini strides, eyes blazing, her green robe whipping around her.

And at her side, bristling with weapons, rage in his eyes, is Aris.

Chapter 50: Aris

The dust blows past us as a magical breeze clears the air. The breeze is emanating from Saroya, seated calmly in a chair. Nestor stands behind her, and in front of her—

Wren. My Wren. She's tied, bound to a chair. There's a strange look in her eyes when she sees me—it's not fear, or even rage.

She's sad. No, more than that—she's grieving. Relief floods through me—relief that she's here, alive, and doesn't look to be hurt. I nearly fall to my knees. And I have no idea why Saroya is involved in this mess, but I can't say I'm surprised.

Overhead, fat raindrops start to fall on the roof, through the holes, leaving circles on the dirt floor.

"You took something of mine," I growl at Nestor, and ready my gladiuses. "I want her back."

Whatever's going on here, whatever poison they've dripped in her ears, I'll deal with it later. Thick rope wraps her ankles and wrists—I flex my hands, feeling the tiger inside me roar. His claws and teeth would make short work of those bonds. Nestor rolls his eyes as he watches me—my glance darts between him and Wren. If he touches her again, I will end him.

"Relax, cub, we're not hurting her," he says, but he smirks. He crosses his arms and flexes his muscles, reminding me that he's much, much stronger than I am, just in case I'm thinking of doing something stupid.

I seriously consider patricide, but even with Ismini with me, I'm outmatched by him and Saroya.

It's a gamble I'm willing to take. We stare each other down, a cautious stalemate.

"Mage Ismini," Saroya says, breaking the terrible silence.

Ismini looks confused. She clearly didn't expect to find her Head Mage here, involved in whatever underhanded dealings are going on. "Head Mage," she says, with a little bow of her head. "I sure would appreciate an explanation as to why you've kidnapped my pupil."

"Ask her," Saroya says, pointing at Wren.

A tear falls down Wren's cheek. She looks … broken.

I clench my hands around the hilts of my swords, ready to draw, ready to fight. I want to run to her side, to cut the bonds—

"Don't," she whispers. The sound barely leaves her lips. Gone is my stubborn, feisty Mage. She sags against her bonds, her skin gray with dust.

And then she tells me what Nestor and Saroya have told her. Some nonsense about her being the herald of the end of magic, the bringer of our collective doom.

I don't believe a word of this shit.

Ismini, however, glances at me, nervous. "Do you think it's possible?" she whispers, leaning in.

We're here to rescue Wren—I was prepared to battle a hundred trolls, a thousand soldiers, but this? Wren doesn't even want to be rescued. She is ready to go with Saroya and Nestor, willingly.

"No," I say. I shake my head. "I don't believe it."

"Believe it, cub," Nestor says, and it's the gentlest I've ever heard him. I'd prefer it if he just punched me.

"Wren," I say, and I hate how my voice breaks.

Her eyes are filled with tears.

"Wren, don't listen to them. They lie," I say.

She shakes her head. "Aris, I've been controlling you from the beginning," she says, and she believes it. "When you were a tiger, remember? You couldn't stay away from me, even then."

Her heart is breaking in front of me. Wren—strong, beautiful, pain-in-my-ass Wren—looking lost and shattered. But they're wrong. They're both wrong about her.

"I'm going to go with them," she says.

The world may have stopped turning at that moment, and I wouldn't have noticed.

"No," I say, shaking my head.

She frowns, looking up at me with eyelashes rimmed with tears. "Come with us," she says.

Nestor makes a noise. It sounds approving.

I'm clenching my fists so tightly that my nails are breaking the skin of my palms, and I can feel a trickle of blood drip through my fingers. I nod, and she sags in relief. Of course I will. Where she goes, I go. It's a stupid-ass plan, but I'll worry about that later.

I approach her. No one tries to stop me.

I kneel in front of her, cutting through the thick ropes on her ankles, annoyed at how they've chafed her skin. I rub my thumb over the burns, like I can wipe them away. She holds my gaze for a long, long time.

"I'm so sorry," she whispers.

I look away, shaking my head. I cut through the ropes on her wrists—only to reveal the cold metal band there, glittering.

"Where did you get that?" I roar, wheeling to face Nestor.

He's leaning against a wall, totally unperturbed. He shrugs and saunters over, twirling the second manacle on his finger like a toy. In his giant hand, it looks laughably frail.

"Saw you toss them, so I fished them out," he says. He draws himself up to his full height, like he can intimidate me. It worked when I was a child. It does not work now.

"You should know," I say, letting my lips quirk into a feral grin. "One manacle is never going to hold her back. She's too strong." I mean this as a compliment, but I see her wince.

"Oh, it's not for her," Nestor says.

He grabs my wrist, faster than I can blink, and slams the manacle onto it.

Agony shreds every nerve in my body. I am on fire. I am fire. I am ice. I am rage and wrath and ruin. I roar, but the sound is muted, weak—even my vocal cords are straining. Every fiber of every muscle is atrophying at an alarming rate. My legs will no longer support me, and I fall, striking my head against the side of Wren's chair. The pain blooming in my skull pales beside the anguish racking my body.

No. This isn't possible. I am a Shield. I am Aris. I am the white tiger. I am strength and skill and speed incarnate. I feel a cold wave wash through me, and I realize this is fear. I am feeling fear, truly feeling it, for the first time, for myself. I try to scream, to give voice to my anger, but my lungs contract pitifully, the sound leaving my throat in a moan instead.

"What have you done?" Wren screams. She's kneeling beside me and cradles my head in her lap, her hands wiping away the tears that are streaming down my cheeks.

I don't even have the strength to stop her. I try to lift a hand, but my fingers cramp and claw, the muscles spasming, and my hand falls to the floor, a useless appendage.

"Had to be done," Nestor says in a flat tone. There is no remorse in his words, no regret. He's cut me off, eliminated a threat, the way one might sever a gangrenous limb to save a life. I've never before realized how deeply his hatred of me runs.

I lift my head to look at him, but my neck barely twitches—I feel … old. Weak. The strength, the power granted to me by my magic, magic I've known my whole life, is just … gone. My lungs burn, and I realize that the muscles controlling my breathing are also sputtering. I can't even tell Nestor what an asshole he is.

I look up at Wren instead. At the way her jade eyes are shining, bright in her dirty face. I should have told her everything. She touches my face gently, her fingertips shaking.

There is no wound for her to stitch up this time, no way for her to save me.

Chapter 51: Wren

"What have you done?" I say again as Aris's eyes flutter, threatening to roll back in their sockets. I want to scream it, but the words barely make it past my lips. Aris is like a puppet whose strings have been cut. In an instant, he seems to have lost half his body weight, the muscle bulk simply gone. The man in my arms is skeletal, gray, and barely breathing. His high cheekbones now shadow dark hollows, the vitality leached from him, leaving an emaciated echo of the Shield I know. Sweat gathers above his lip as he struggles simply to get air into his lungs, each breath a grunt of effort.

"What I had to," Nestor snaps. "He was too much of a liability. Your hold on him is too strong. Has been since you made him claim you in the arena."

His words sting, but I do not cringe. My fault. This is all my fault.

Ismini is at my side, incensed. "What, are you just going to slap manacles on everyone, then? On me? On the king?" she snarls.

"If I must," Saroya says. The words are delivered flatly, resolutely.

It is the wrong answer.

Ismini yells a single word, behind which I swear I can feel her throw her power. She's looking at Saroya with rage in her eyes. I can't imagine what conflict is raging inside her at the moment—her Head Mage, in whom her faith should be unquestionable, is … fallible.

"*Protect*!" she screams.

Stones and earth rise up with the swiftness of arrows, surrounding us before arching over our heads.

"*Light*," Ismini says, and in her outstretched palm is a small flame, burning emerald green. It illuminates our cave, our tiny shelter, giving everything an otherworldly glow. Outside, I hear gale-force winds battering the barricade, but Ismini does not relent. I see sweat beading on her forehead.

"Saroya is weak," Ismini says, the words coming out in a groan, like she's physically holding up the earth around us.

"She's doing something to my magic, cutting me off from it," I say.

Ismini nods. A drop of sweat falls from her chin.

I look down at Aris, his head still cradled in my lap. He struggles to sit up, and after a moment, he is sitting cross-legged, knee-to-knee with me and Ismini in the cramped space. He's panting, his eyes glazed. He looks ill, like he's caught a fever. The flesh hangs off his bones like he's aged a hundred years. His eyes are flat and ringed with purple. He's never known life without his power. He does not know what it feels like to be ungifted, and now the wear and tear of years has caught up to him.

I want to comfort him, but I don't. I don't know what to say.

"Not your fault," he grunts out at last. He lifts a hand with enormous effort, wiping dirt and sweat from his eyes.

"But it is," I moan, and the tears start falling like a flood.

He reaches out to cup my chin and wipe away the tears with his thumb. It must take monumental focus on his part. I want to stop him. I want to push him away. I don't want to influence him anymore, don't want my magic to force him to care for me, but I don't stop him. I can't. I let him touch me, and I savor it.

"Your power makes people like you when you like them? Like with the king?" he asks. Each word takes twice as long as it should for him to say, but they're starting to come a little easier, like he's settling into his new shape, his frail body. The breath wheezes from his lungs, crackling like dried tinder on a fire.

"Apparently," I say. I lean into his hand, wanting to cherish the contact, sure that he'll never look at me the same way again.

"You're not influencing me," he says.

"How can you be so sure?" I ask.

He doesn't move his hand.

Ismini grunts from effort but doesn't say anything.

"Because I've been mad at you plenty of times," he says, and a small smile lifts one side of his pale lips. "And I know you've hated me. I've given you lots of reasons to hate me. If you are influencing me, would we have felt that?"

"All right, hearing about how much you hate each other is very touching, but can we focus on what we're going to do now?" Ismini says. The earthen walls shudder around us, and she redoubles her efforts.

Aris looks at her. His body might be weak, but his mind is as sharp as ever. He will not give in to fear, to self-pity, to despair. He's analyzing our odds, strategizing. I realize that, despite everything, I feel … awe for him.

"How long can you hold out?" he asks.

She grunts. Her palms are in the dirt—she's sending her magic down into it, like roots, anchoring the structure. "A bit longer," she says. Her arms are starting to tremble.

I know her magical limit is deeper than most, but I worry she's using too much.

"We've got to get out of here," Aris says, looking at me. "We can figure the rest out later."

"Can you get our manacles off?" I ask Ismini.

She shakes her head. "Not without letting this spell go," she says. "And it would take time."

Overhead, the barrier shakes. Something has struck it, and strikes it again, ringing the cave around us like a muffled bell. It seems Nestor has joined the fight.

I look at Ismini, keeping us safe, her cave of earth protecting us from the tornado whipping past us outside as

Saroya's winds struggle for purchase. I think about her family—her husband, her sons. I think about what will happen to them if she burns out. To the families she supports with her farming. To Aleka, whose heart would break—before she went gray too.

I look at Aris, shackled but unbroken before me, his eyes blazing in the dark with the fury of a blue flame. I don't know if I've influenced him, if I've made him care for me more than he should, and it doesn't matter. I care for him. I will never, ever forgive Nestor for putting his own son through wearing a manacle, especially not on my behalf.

The cave begins to glow, and it's not from Ismini's emerald fire. It's from me, from my skin. And it's the green of jade.

"Give me your swords," I tell Aris.

Chapter 52: Aris

She's a little scary sometimes.

She's been drugged. She's been kidnapped. She's had venom dripped into her ears, making her doubt herself, making her doubt me, doubt us.

And now, she's pissed.

I almost feel sorry for Nestor and Saroya. Or I would if I had the strength to do so. My arms and legs are putty, barely responding to my commands. Even my tongue feels sluggish. My head must weigh a ton, judging by how hard it is for me to look at my Mage. My body is a wreck. The chiseled muscles, the vigor—gone, leaving me as decrepit as an old man. Worse than going gray. I can't bear to look at myself.

Wren's eyes glow jade green, like they did the night she found the manacles in my room. When she asks for my swords, I pass them over without a word. They are heavy in my hands and drag in the dirt.

The glow emanates from her, suffusing the metal in her hands. The blades begin to glow too, like fresh-forged steel, only instead of cherry red, they glow green.

The manacle on her wrist starts to blaze white-hot as she concentrates—and then it darkens, fading, blackening, until it falls from her wrist and shatters into black ash on the ground. Her face is blank, impassive. There is no room for doubt or fear. There is none of the triumphant pride on her face that there was the last time I saw her do this, no mocking, no jest. She might not believe in herself, but she believes in us, in Ismini and me, and damn it all if she's not going to go down swinging because of it.

Ismini's eyes are wide, from fear and from exertion. She grunts, shifting, like the weight of the cave is pressing on her shoulders. Sweat rolls off her.

Wren hands the swords back to me. Their grips are warm, but only from her touch. I swing them in my hands, the movement clumsy, slow. My reflexes are half what they were, and I nearly drop them.

I can see that Wren is thinking the same thing. She puts a hand on my knee, her other palm up, asking for mine. I slip my hand into hers, and she extends her index finger like she's feeling for a pulse - but instead, the fingertip contacts the manacle. A thrill races through me. It's not unpleasant, not like getting the manacle put on was. This is … like drawing poison from a wound.

She's panting from the effort, and a trickle of sweat traces down her neck. Ismini groans as another blow strikes her earthen shell. This startles Wren out of her concentration, and the flicker of jade fire in her eyes gutters for a second.

"I can do this," she says softly, and closes her eyes. If ever there were a time for her magic to work through her words, this is it.

For a minute, nothing happens. That minute drags into two. I'm not sure Ismini can hold on much longer, but I can't rush Wren either. The impotence is suffocating, but I wait as Wren wages some kind of internal war against her magic, bending it to her will.

The manacle disintegrates against my skin. A surge goes through me, and it feels like a wave, a swell, as muscles and bones and joints reconnect to the way they were always meant to be. The process takes less than a few heartbeats to complete. I take a deep breath, letting it out slowly, savoring the simple sensation.

I am whole again. I flex my hands, feeling their strength, rejoicing in the feel of the gladiuses. I could rip Nestor's head right off with this strength if I wanted to. And I really, really want to. The blades sing in my hands, carving the very air as they spin. The magic has honed their edges into something sharper than the sharpest blade, and harder than dragon-forged steel. With these blades, while the magic lasts, none can stand against me, not even Nestor.

Wren is still holding my hand, still glowing. She looks to Ismini, who nods.

"Ready?" Wren says.

The earthen cave around us explodes.

Saroya whisks away the dust with a word. She's shielded herself from the debris with a wall of air. Though haggard, she is unhurt by Ismini's barrage.

Nestor, though, is covered in dirt. I grin at him. I let him see me stand, my full strength returned. Let him see the green swords in my hands. Let him hear them sing.

Let him feel fear.

"We're leaving," I say.

"*No*," Saroya says.

Just one word, but I feel it pulse through me, and my feet stick to the earth. Shit. Ismini said she was weakened—apparently, not enough to keep her from using her mind control.

Wren walks on, though, unperturbed. "*Yes*," she counters.

My feet come unstuck, and I jerk forward, my arrested momentum catching up to me. Saroya's eyes go wide. I can see white all the way around her coal-black irises. Her gaze flicks to our wrists, now unshackled.

"Do not do this," she says. "Come with me. We can figure this out together."

"I will figure this out," Wren says, "with my friends." Her eyes flare, lighting up the space with jade fire.

Saroya flinches. "So be it," she says.

It's the opening Nestor has been waiting for. He comes at me, his favored battle axe raised high above his head.

Chapter 53: Wren

Aris raises his swords as Nestor's axe swings down. The shaft strikes the swords—and shatters into splinters, the axe head thudding to the ground.

Nestor stares down at it, dumbstruck.

"Yield," Aris growls. He's crouched, his dual swords pointed at his father. "Yield!"

Nestor tosses the broken handle aside. His hands hang at his sides, empty. He looks over Aris like he's assessing him, and finding him wanting.

The man roars, and the sound changes even as it reaches my ears, becoming wild, savage. He shifts into a dark-maned lion of impossible size. He's five feet tall at the shoulder, baring teeth as long and pointed as daggers.

He might have been unarmed, but a Shield is never defenseless.

I don't have the time to keep watching Aris and his father. Saroya is bearing down on me. Wind is whipping around Ismini and me, flinging particulates like arrows at us. She is not trying to kill me—she's aiming for my legs, my hands. She's trying to knock me off-balance, to sweep my legs out from under me with a flying chair. Ismini, though, Saroya is not being so careful about. Ismini is throwing up earthen shields, trying to protect herself and me.

I do not need her protection. The projectiles don't get within a foot of me before dropping from the air, like they've hit an invisible wall. I don't let them.

Saroya screams, any pretense at civility or poise gone. Her hair has fallen free from its restraints, forming a black nimbus around her head. Her fingers suddenly claw out at the air in front of her.

I can't breathe. I grab my chest, feeling my lungs scream for air, collapsing inside me. I open my mouth, but nothing comes out, no sound. And no air goes in. I look back at Saroya—her fingers are still clawed, pulling the air from my body. The green glow on my skin flickers as my vision starts to go dark at the edges.

Things are starting to blur, but I'm able to clearly make out the hail of pebbles being flung across the room by Ismini. The stones smack into Saroya's side and legs with a sickening thunking sound, burying themselves in flesh. Blood oozes down her legs, blooms on her yellow robe. I see Ismini, clutching her throat, draw a deep breath as Saroya's focus is lost from her onslaught. Air—blessed, sweet air—returns to my lungs, and my body soaks it in. My vision regains focus, though I'm panting heavily.

On the other side of the room, Aris is battling the massive lion. They circle and feint. There's dried blood on Aris's sleeve, the wound already stanched by his rapid healing abilities. He scores a deep cut along Nestor's flank as the great cat wheels away. Nestor bellows in rage, but the wound is already clotting, already closing. Aris has a chance, a window no longer than a heartbeat, to deliver a blow that will fell him.

He pauses.

The lion pounces, knocking him from his feet. I shout, and the air around me quivers. Aris's swords have been knocked from his hands, which are now pushed hard against the lion's chest, trying to keep those great jaws away from his face. Blood leaks from his arms, his stomach, where the massive paws are digging in.

And then the lion is being knocked back, thrown clear across the room, a massive brown shape plowing into him like an avalanche.

Standing over Aris is a great brown bear riddled with scars, immense and bellowing with rage. It's standing on its hind legs, each paw the size of my torso. Aris grunts, struggling to sit. I look over at Ismini, who's grinning.

"Aleka," she says, panting. Her Shield has arrived.

My attention snaps back to Saroya. The woman has come unhinged. She snaps out her hand, and bands of air wrap around Ismini, forcing her to her knees, wrapping around her legs, binding her arms to her chest, tightening around her neck.

I'm glowing green, but all I see is red.

"You will come with me," Saroya says. "Call off your Shield. Come with me to the school, and I will leave Ismini unhurt."

Aleka has turned her attention from Nestor. She roars with impotent rage but does not come within a dozen feet of Saroya.

We're at a standoff. Saroya has Ismini. I feel all the emotions from this horrible day all at once—fear, shame, pain, frustration, rage. They whirl through me like the winds of a hurricane. I can feel the sky itself answering my call, the night air whistling to my aid. Overhead, the wind howls as the clouds begin to spin. The roof—or what's left of it—is ripped off.

I return my gaze to Saroya. She tightens her grip, and Ismini gasps for air.

The earth begins to vibrate, little pebbles skittering across the ground around me before rising up, collecting, circling me. A bolt of jade-colored lightning flashes, bearing down on me before getting swept up into another spinning ring. Raindrops come to me next, forming another ring, weaving together all around me, leaving me the calm eye in the center of this swirling vortex of the elements.

I channel all my energy, every single piece that I can summon from that dark orb at my core. The vortex becomes a projectile, bearing down on Saroya in a single massive bolt of elemental force that has her whipping her hands up, freeing Ismini, and creating a shield. She barely does this in time. The power slams against it, pushes against it. She has her feet braced, but she's being forced back, her slippers skidding on the floor like it is made of ice. Back and back I force her, feeling the thrill of magic surge through me, all the elements at my command. I can feel her try to push back, her magic against mine, as fully as if it were her hand against mine.

Her shield begins to fray.

If I go gray from this, then so be it. I can only hope that Aris will get through it again, unscathed.

Ismini yells something, but I can't hear her over the screaming in my ears, the whistling of the wind and the crackle of lightning.

Saroya drops to one knee. She's panting, gasping. I see the fear on her face, etched around her wide eyes.

Unlike Aris, I do not flinch.

She shoves at my magic, one last, desperate punch. And I shove right back.

A crack like thunder booms through the room, rattling what's left of the walls, and the vortex is gone.

Ismini topples, and Aleka is at her side in a heartbeat. She's shifted back, crouching at her Mage's side. I tear my eyes away from the scars crisscrossing her pale, naked body and look at Saroya, who has been flung back against the wall.

Saroya looks dazed, her mouth slack. She slides to the floor like her legs don't work anymore. She looks … gray. Like all the color has leached out of her skin. She looks down at her hands, rubbing her thumb against her fingers.

"It's gone," she whispers. In the silence after the thunder, her words fall harshly, like rocks on a still pond.

I dread her next words, the feeling pooling in my stomach like ice.

"My magic. It's … gone," she says.

Ismini is sitting up now. Her nose is bleeding, and she's thrown her robe around Aleka, but otherwise, she looks all right. She glances from Saroya to me.

"She burned out," Ismini says. She stares at me.

I'm not burned out. I feel great. Powerful. But — maybe — a little regretful. The green glow on my skin flickers and fades.

Saroya's face crumples, and she tears at her hair, shrieking. "It's gone!" she wails before collapsing to the ground, battering it with her hands until I worry they will start to bleed.

I hear a grunt behind me and turn to find Nestor kneeling, naked, with Aris's green swords crossed at his neck.

"Yield," Aris says.

Nestor hangs his head.

Aleka goes over and binds Nestor's hands and feet before doing the same to Saroya, who does not protest. She doesn't even seem to notice. Her eyes are staring, unfocused, unblinking. A husk. A shell. She will never be what she was before. And I did that to her.

Maybe I am a monster.

Aris limps over to me, and my focus abruptly shifts. Dried blood coats his chest, his arms, and I can't tell if it's his or Nestor's. I push aside his shirt, frantically looking for wounds, but they're already healing, and a breath leaves me in a rush. Some of the wounds are already faint, puckered red lines; the bruises are already fading into the smooth tan of his skin, like melting snowflakes. I've never been so grateful for magic.

I realize then that after everything that's happened, I'm standing there with my hands all over him. I drop my hands, feeling heat rush to my face.

"Could you please wait to start undressing me until we get back to the palace? I don't like having an audience," Aris says, giving me a smug smile.

I narrow my eyes, glaring at him. "I was making sure you weren't going to bleed to death on me. I'd hate to have to train another Shield," I say.

He stares at me, those blue eyes boring into mine, and I never, ever want to look away again.

He reaches out and crushes me to him, wrapping me in an embrace so tight it knocks the breath from my lungs. I grab on to him like I'm drowning and he's the life raft that will carry me to shore, to safety. I bury my face in his chest, breathing in the warm strength of him, the earthy, piney scent mixed with sweat and copper and leather. I hold on to him with every ounce of strength left in me, too tired for games, too tired to keep on being angry.

"I am never letting you out of my sight again, for as long as I live," he breathes into my hair.

His grip tightens around me, and I realize the fight is leaving my body, the tension and adrenaline fading as I realize he's all right, I'm all right, I'm safe, I'm home.

Suddenly, I'm exhausted.

He pulls back and lifts a hand to my face, tracing my jaw, stopping at my chin. His eyebrows bunch, and he frowns.

"Careful, princess. You look like you're about to …"

Chapter 54: Aris

"… swoon," I say.

Well, the last word comes out in a rush, since Wren's eyes start to roll back in her head. I lay her down on the floor, and she passes out, like she did after the tornado incident at the school. I smooth the hair back from her sweaty face, check her pulse. She's breathing, and her pulse is strong.

"Oh gods," Ismini says. She rushes over and crashes to her knees at Wren's side. She lifts one of Wren's eyelids and checks her over.

I explain Wren's prior episode, that she seems to need an extended recovery period when using this kind of magic, but that she'll be all right. She has to be all right. Her breathing is steady, like she's in a deep sleep. I brush the hair back from her face again, and if Ismini notices my hand lingering, she doesn't comment. She's kneeling beside me, sweaty and breathing hard herself, and worrying over Wren, but Wren is flushed, her skin still a warm golden brown brushed with pink. Not gray. Not burned out. Not a husk.

Not like Saroya.

Somehow Wren pushed the strongest Mage on the continent into burnout.

Until recently, she couldn't even light a candle.

I have no idea what she'll be capable of in a month, or a year, but I won't let her face it alone. I hold her to me tighter, cradling her small warm body against mine.

Aleka's belted Ismini's robe around her, but it's comically large and drags on the ground behind her. She's allowed Nestor to get dressed, thank all the gods, and has him and Saroya tied to a shattered hitching post outside. Saroya doesn't even seem aware of what's going on around her. She allows herself to be led meekly, without complaint.

Aleka finds a pair of horses out back—a large brown stallion and a lighter riding horse. I climb onto the warhorse, and they hand Wren's unconscious form up to me. I settle her in the saddle before me, and she leans into me, like she's merely dozing. I wrap one arm around her and loop the reins around my other hand. The stallion prances like he's anxious to be out of here, and I don't blame him—the magical storm probably has most of Ocron on edge right now.

"Just get her to your rooms," Ismini tells me, patting the stallion's neck. "We'll be along soon enough. There will be time later to deal with the consequences of today."

Aleka makes Ismini take the gray mare, while she walks, tugging Nestor and Saroya after her like dogs on leashes. It will be a long, dark walk for them back to the city, but Aleka is strong, and Ismini—while tired—does not seem to be in imminent danger of collapse.

I turn the stallion toward the city, and we set off at a run.

As Ismini said, there are consequences. Wren sleeps through the first few days, and since I won't leave our rooms, we hold meetings in the common space. The king, to his credit, seems incredulous.

"So how much of that drivel do you believe?" he asks.

He's obviously happy to have Wren back, safe and sound. I'm too happy she's back to waste too much energy worrying over what he feels. We're sitting in front of the fireplace, sharing a pot of coffee while Ismini and Panos check on Wren. I can see them from where I'm sitting, because I insist her door remain open when I'm not in there.

Ismini called me a mother hen and flicked a towel at me to shoo me out when she checked Wren over—again—for any missed injuries. There hasn't been much change in the past few days—she just sleeps on, like she could wake at any minute. Her breathing remains calm, her pulse strong. She just won't wake. A niggling feeling in the back of my mind worries that she won't—that somehow the burden was too great, and Wren was too small. That she'll be stuck in some kind of limbo forever, neither awake nor dead, but somewhere in between. I haven't slept in days, just in case she wakes up and needs me. Even for a Shield, I am pushing it.

"I'm not sure," I admit to Leo. I move my mug to my right hand and shake out the tingling in my left. The battle with Nestor flared up my shoulder injury, and I roll my shoulder around for a moment until the sensation eases. "She said something about things—creatures—in the west, coming down from the mountains, waking up."

He nods, taking a sip from his mug as he thinks. He's leaning back into his chair, ankle crossed over his knee, as comfortable and at ease as if he were with a friend. "I've been getting word recently of some attacks on the villages out there. I sent a few Mages and their Shields about two weeks ago, and some ships with supplies. I'm hoping to have a report soon."

I stare into the flames. When I became a Shield, I pictured myself with my Mage off having brilliant adventures, fighting trolls and the like along the eastern coast. The west is a great unknown. Perhaps an even bigger challenge. I like a good challenge, but what this one will mean for Wren, I'm not sure. If she wakes. When she wakes.

My gaze settles on my helmet. Tulliano sent it up from the school—apparently, it was found in Aclines, so he won't have to make me a new one after all, he said in his note. Seeing it brought back memories of Stefan, obviously—but there was more. Like I became whole somehow. I know it's just a piece of armor, but I am glad to have it, to have its protection against whatever comes next.

"Do you really believe she's a harbinger of doom?" the king—who has started insisting that I call him Leo—says.

I shake my head. "A symptom of an illness," I say, thinking back to Saroya's analogy. "Something's going on with magic."

"I know," Leo says wearily, setting down his mug. "Fewer gifted every year. Saroya mentioned it last night."

We sit in silence for a while.

"Saroya still hasn't said anything since the burnout," he says into the stillness. "She just sits there in her cell, not talking, not moving."

"And Nestor?" I ask. I haven't heard anything about the man who sired me—I can't call him my father, not anymore. Though, to be fair, I haven't exactly gone looking for him since he stole my Mage.

Leo glances at me. "Awaiting trial. In the dungeons," he says.

I nod. I hope he rots down there a long time before he goes on trial. I hope he feels the rage and impotence and fear that I felt. He'll be judged by Shields—we handle our own justice. And it is not merciful. The law of the Shields is a harsh one, unforgiving. I have little doubt as to his fate when he is judged. I surprise myself by realizing exactly how little I care about that. I have no relationship with that man. I can barely claim my siblings—it's been years since I've seen most of them. With the exception of Spyridon, they will not shed a tear when Nestor is executed.

That man is too dangerous to be allowed to roam free—which, when I think about it, is exactly what he said about Wren.

"Do you really think she was somehow using her magic on you, to make you notice her?" I ask.

Leo looks at me strangely, but he's not offended.

Do I hope the answer is yes, that Wren *wanted* Leo to notice her, fall for her, and that she's then as dangerous as Saroya claims? Or do I hope that the answer is no, that their attraction was … natural? Mutual? I shift in my chair.

"Do I really think I was being charmed by a beautiful and exceptional woman? Yes. Yes, I do," he says, leaning back. "Do I think that there was magic involved? Not really. No more than the everyday kind of magic. Which, come to think of it, might be the most powerful kind of all."

I think about this for a while, drumming my fingers against the chair. Leo's much more flowery with language than I am, nearly a poet, but he does seem to have a point. I think about my own magic, about our bond, our claim. It is designed to make a Shield bond with their Mage, to better protect them. Stefan was my friend before my first games—afterward he was my brother. Could I blame this—whatever I feel about Wren—all on the claim? Shields and Mages are often intimate, true, but I've always thought that is due more to a kind of forced proximity, the long months they spend together on the road.

Can I blame what I'm feeling on Wren, on something about her magic influencing me to like her, a kind of supernatural persuasion so that I'll be a better protector? Like her magic is acting in its own self-interest, the way Saroya claimed.

I think about what Leo said, that there is magic here, with her, but it isn't the kind of magic that needs spells or books or years of study. It's everyday magic—which is somehow a lot more terrifying.

We sit in brooding silence for a while.

Leo is just opening his mouth again when Panos bursts into the room, as much as an old man can. He's breathing hard and braces his hands on his thighs for a moment to catch his breath. His face is red and shiny, and behind him come two Mages with armfuls of books and scrolls, equally unsettled. One of them drops a scroll, curses, and drops another while trying to pick it up.

Leo is up in an instant, as am I.

"What is it?" Leo asks.

Panos wheezes and holds up a hand. "Wren," he gasps. "I know what's going on with Wren."

Chapter 55: Wren

I wake up gradually, in waves, like my consciousness is having to swim up through water as thick as mud.

The first thing I notice is how much I hurt. Everywhere. My toenails hurt. My eyebrows are sore. Every muscle screams as I stretch. My eyes feel dry, sandy. And I'm starving. Seriously, I could eat for an entire day straight. I'd even eat Aris's barley gruel and ash water.

There's a healer in my room, a thin woman in a blue Water Mage robe, straightening something, and when she turns and sees me sitting up, she squeaks. The sound draws the attention of the two men in the sitting room—two men sitting quietly by the fire, drinking coffee and talking. Both stand, and I hear a clatter of ceramic against the marble fireplace.

They crowd into my doorway and stop, staring at me. My dark god, looking as sinful as ever, and my golden king.

"Hi," I croak. I clear my throat.

They're looking at me like they're afraid I'm going to break, like they have a million things they want to say—but maybe not in front of the other person.

"Let me get her cleaned and fed. Then you can talk," the healer says, crossing her arms.

I like this woman. They turn and go back to their chairs, like good boys.

I'm as weak as a kitten, and I'm glad to have the healer, Isobel, with me. My skin is marbled with bruises, including one spectacular purple mark down my left flank where

I guess I fell off Obsidian. I'm stiff, but everything moves like it should, and surprisingly, nothing seems broken. Isobel helps me bathe and wash my hair, then dress—honestly, I was flippant about lady's maids before, but she's a huge help. I'd do a sorry job myself right now, and I wouldn't dream of asking Aris and Leo to help me bathe.

I mean, I have dreamed about it, but the circumstances were very different.

Gods, how hard *did* I hit my head?

Isobel brings me food, and I devour it as she applies a salve to the worst of my bruises. It's cool and seeps into my skin, soothing the aches immediately. I can hear the men pacing outside my door, impatient. The bread catches in my throat. What do I even say to them?

It turns out it doesn't matter, because in a moment the door is flung open by Ismini. Her pale face is flushed, and she's panting, like she's run all the way here from … wherever she was. She ignores Isobel and instead runs to me, picking me up in an embrace as tight as a bear hug. The air leaves my lungs in a whoosh, and I swear I feel a rib under that giant purple bruise crack, but I hold on to her for dear life. Tears that I didn't realized I've been holding in start pouring down my cheeks, and before long I'm sobbing, and I'm having trouble breathing. I vaguely see Aris and Leo watching me with alarm, but Isobel waves them away again. Ismini sits on the bed with me and holds me and rocks me like I'm her own child. I never knew my mother, but I hope she would have been like Ismini. Ismini, who found me, fought for me, fought with me. I hope her boys know how exceptional she is.

She smooths the hair back from my face. Isobel is gone, off on some errand. The windowless room is filled with the glow of lanterns, so I suppose it's night.

We talk after a while. Ismini tells me that Saroya is locked up, but she's a husk. She doesn't speak, barely eats. People are known to die of starvation after a burnout, as they lose their will to keep living. Ismini's mouth is pinched as she tells me about her former Head Mage. I worry she feels guilty about her part in it—she was torn at the start, but then she fought against her as much as I did.

"What will happen to the school?" I ask.

Ismini shrugs. "I don't know. I'm sure they'll appoint a new Head Mage—and I'm sure King Leonidas will have a hand in it," she says, eyes twinkling. "He's become quite protective of you. He isn't happy about how you were treated there, and he wants to make sure no one else has to go through the same."

I bunch up the blanket in my hands, twisting it. "But that's just because my magic somehow influenced him, right?" I ask, looking up at her through my lashes. "Just like it's doing something to you, making you like me."

She looks at me for a long, long time.

"I've been thinking a lot about that," she says.

Uh-oh. Here it comes. I brace myself.

"It seems like magic is doing two different things to you," she says, smoothing the blanket under her fingertips. "You have elemental magic, which does seem to respond, at least a little, to traditional words or spells. Like what I can do, except you have some skill in all four elements. And then there's the other magic—the one that doesn't respond to the manacles' binding, that doesn't respond to the words, that flows through you like your own breath. We've seen it exert some control over animals, so when Saroya said that it was … awakening things in the far west, calling them to you, that I believe."

I swallow hard. *Well, shit*. So I'm some sort of beacon for monsters. All right. So no more will it be just groundhogs and screech owls responding to my unconscious summoning. What is it, exactly, that is "awakening"? That thing in Spit that destroyed my home? A shudder runs through me at the thought. Up until recently, I thought that trolls were imaginary, a bedtime story told to frighten young children into obeying their parents. *Go to sleep now, or the trolls will get you*! How many of the other creatures I thought were myths are now ambling about Ocron, causing chaos, because of me?

"And the rest?" I prompt.

"The rest?" Ismini says. "Do I think that you're influencing people the same way you influence animals?"

Her mouth is pursed. My throat constricts as I wait for her to speak.

"I don't. Your animal magic is pretty simple, just a sphere of influence that seems to grow in strength and size. Why would it then single out the king? We—King Leonidas and I—have been talking about it a lot. Panos too. We can't find anything in the library about that kind of control, so, basically, we think Saroya is full of shit," she says at last, and I snort at hearing her curse. It seems so out of character. Ismini likes this, and half her mouth pulls back in a wry smile. It fades quickly.

"You've somehow gotten tangled up in a mess here, Wren," she says, covering my hand with her own thickly calloused palm. "I'm not sure what your purpose is in it, whether—like she said—you're a harbinger or a catalyst. Saroya and Nestor think that magic is broken, fading, but we—that is, King Leonidas and Panos and I—feel that something new is being born. Some new magic is taking root in our continent, and it seems to have started with you. I'm not sure why, exactly, but I can promise you this: you won't need to face it alone."

She takes both my hands from the scrunched-up blanket now, warming them in hers. There's a warm earnestness to her face. I feel like I'm just waking up—and not just from my several-day slumber. She squeezes my hands after a minute. She has more to say, and I gather it's not something pleasant.

"What is it?" I ask.

She sighs. "Panos has a theory," she says. "About your magic. Why it acts the way it does."

"And … it's not something good?" I ask. My heart flips inside my chest.

"I don't know yet," she says. She reaches out and smooths my hair back from my face.

"Rest up," she says. "Say hello to the boys. Then we'll talk more."

After a while longer, after checking me over again, she stands. She leaves and sends in Leo first. I catch sight of Aris as Leo enters my bedroom, and as the door closes in his face, he looks like he's going to explode from glowering so hard.

Leo stands for a moment by the door before giving in to whatever emotions are warring within him, and he comes to sit on the bed with me. There's no kingly finery today, no crown. He could be anyone—a very handsome, very kind anyone.

I look down at my hands. I'm not sure what to say to him. The last time I spoke to him, he basically proposed to me. I pick at a scab on my left thumb—he's my king, and he can basically command me to do whatever he wants. Leave. Stay. Go back to the school. My future is in his hands—and yet I have no fear. Besides being my king, I realize this remarkable man before me has also become my friend, someone I respect. Whatever it is that he needs to say to me, I vow, I will do my best to be as honest and open with him as I can. Whatever is in his heart, I will pledge to work with him to the best of my ability, however that is.

He clears his throat. "How are you feeling?" he asks.

I look up and meet his warm brown eyes, full of concern. Lavender circles are starting to bloom under them, and I wonder how long it's been since he's slept.

"Fine," I say. "Did … did you hear what Saroya thought of me? Of … us?" I ask. Heat rushes to my face. There is no "us," not in that way, though I may have daydreamed about it, probably like every other foolish girl in this continent who's ever laid eyes on him.

"I did," he says, a patient smile on his face. "And I don't believe in her 'influence' theory for a single second."

We sit in awkward silence for a moment, and he picks at an invisible stray thread on the comforter.

"Can I get you anything?" he asks.

I shake my head. "Apparently, Panos has some ideas about my magic," I offer.

He nods, his lips a hard line. "Yes. He's getting some more materials and is going to meet us back here in a while. It seems," he says, and he takes my cold hand in his, "that you've managed to throw us all into a bit of chaos here."

"Sorry," I choke out, and offer a wry smile. I look down at our joined hands and take a deep breath.

"Did you know about the attack on Spit? On my lighthouse?" I ask. The idea has been worrying me, that he has been holding something back, but he shakes his head, soft brown waves of his hair falling out of place. I resist the urge to push them back.

"I just learned of it recently, after your … kidnapping," he says. He doesn't like saying the word, but he doesn't wince, doesn't cringe. His grip on my hand tightens. "How something like that could have happened to you, here, under my watch …"

I cover our hands with my other one. I wish I could take the guilt from him.

He offers me a sad smile. "There's more," he says.

Involuntarily my hands clutch his tightly. I realize after a second and relax my grip, but I've already left nail marks on his skin, little half-moons.

"Trolls attacked the Golden Crown Lodge," he says.

"What?" I breathe. "Were there … casualties?" I ask.

He meets my eyes, his own warm brown ones shining under his furrowed brow, and nods.

I bite my lip, hard, hoping the sting will keep the tears from falling. It mostly works.

Leo sighs and lets go of my hand. He raises his arm, resting it around my shoulders, and I lean into him reflexively, eager for the touch, his warmth. We sit in silence for a few minutes, and I feel his lips brush the top of my head.

"Do you … want me to send Aris in?"

"Yes," I say. The word comes out slowly.

He accepts this with a heavy nod and removes his arm from my shoulders. I realize belatedly that he was hoping that I'd say no. He pushes a stray curl back over my shoulder, sending a thrill through me at the touch.

"I hope you know," he says, looking me in the eyes, "that whatever you do, whatever you decide, you will always have friends here. You will always have me."

Leo stands to leave, and I walk him to my door. Night has fallen, and Aris is pacing the sitting room, drenched in shadows. I wonder if he's been pacing the entire time. It seems like something he would do.

Leo leans down and kisses my cheek, the stubble of his face gently scratching mine. I hear Aris growl from across the room and shoot him a warning glance.

"Goodbye, little bird," Leo says, cupping my cheek softly for a moment. Then he leaves. He gives Aris a pointed stare but doesn't say anything to him.

Now it's just the two of us, alone in our rooms, staring at each other. Gods, so many thoughts are going through my scrambled brain right now. How mad at him I was after I found out he'd kept the manacles, and after the ball with his stupid comments. How jealous I was when I saw the marks another woman had left on him. How relieved I was to see him when I'd been kidnapped—and later, after the battle, when I realized we'd made it through, relatively unscathed. My vain, sardonic, arrogant Aris. My fearsome protector.

I open my mouth to speak, but nothing comes out. He's waiting patiently, which is a first, though I can tell he's clenching his hands together behind his back. I bite my lip, trying to think about how to tell this man, my Shield, all the things I want to say. Instead, I meet his eyes, those glorious blue eyes, which claimed me the first moment I saw them.

Sometimes, words fail us.

He closes the space between us swiftly, the decision made. Before I can think, I'm reaching for him. His arms fold me into him, and his mouth comes crashing into mine, his lips bruising mine, claiming mine. He comes at me with such intensity that I crash into the wall behind me, the blow softened only somewhat by the cage of his arms, though I barely feel it. I wrap my arms around his neck, burying my fingers in his hair. It slides through my grasp like strands of heavy black silk, as soft as I thought it would be.

"I'm still mad at you," I manage to moan, gasping for air as his hands reach under the hem of my shirt, skimming over my skin, like he's desperate to make sure I'm all right, that I'm all in one piece. His calloused hands are cool as they rasp against my bruises, against my scorching skin, and little tingles spread out like cracks in ice with every touch.

"I know," he says between desperate kisses. "Just don't ever run off on me again."

I mold my body to his in reply, arching into him, delighted with how we fit together. He growls at the motion, bending to place kisses on my cheeks, my temples, to nuzzle the space where my neck meets my collarbone. Each kiss, each breath that skitters across my skin ignites something in me. I let my hands explore just as boldly, running down the sculpted muscles of his back, hooking into the fabric at his waistband, pulling him harder against me.

Eventually, he slows his frantic pace, satisfied that I'm not in immediate danger, and his breathing becomes ragged. He's running his hands over my face, my neck, my hair, like he wants to touch every part of me. That thought brings a fresh rush of heat into my face.

He lifts an eyebrow. "What are you thinking about?" he asks.

I glare at him. "Wouldn't you like to know," I say, breathless.

"Oh, I would," he says.

I squeal as he bends and scoops me up. Then he strides into my bedroom. I'm reminded of that night at the Golden Crown Lodge, but this time, he doesn't leave me. This time, he sinks into the bed beside me, his long body stretched out next to mine. He asks for nothing, expects nothing. He is content to lie with me, touching me, kissing me, claiming me. His hands run over me with care, skimming across bruises and scrapes. I think that they should be fading by now if I really do have some sort of enhanced healing like the Shields do, but then I am too distracted to spare another thought for it. I am content to stare at him, to lose myself in those blue eyes, to stroke the soft black stubble on his cheeks and the warm strength of his arms. To kiss those lips until I feel like I'm floating. I thought that after sleeping for days, I'd be wide awake, but his touches, his warmth, the happiness bursting from my chest soothe me in a way I've never felt before, and I fall asleep once more, curled in his arms.

Waking up is bliss. We're asleep in my bed, and Aris is folded around me, like he doesn't want to let me go even when he's sleeping. I've never slept with a man in my bed before—I think I could get used to it very fast, though. We explored this new thing between us with quiet touches and kisses, testing it out, relishing it. Gods, I could spend hours kissing him. I think I did, actually. My lips feel bruised, and as my fingers touch them, I smile.

Aris feels me stirring, and his arm tightens around my waist, though he's still sleeping. He takes a deep breath, and as he releases it, I can feel his chest rumble and vibrate against my back. The sound continues, filling the quiet room, and it takes me a moment to realize what it is.

Aris is purring.

Chapter 56: Aris

Later that morning, we gather in the common room—Wren, Leo, Ismini, Aleka, Panos and his two assistants, and I. The chairs and couch have been moved into a rough circle around the table, across which Panos has strewn charts and books. One diagram in particular catches my eye—six circles, in white, black, red, blue, yellow, and green. They form a rough hexagram, their edges just touching. I stand behind Wren, who's seated between Panos and Leo. Panos looks like he's aged ten years in the past few days. He looks like shit, but there's a manic gleam in his eyes too. A brightness. His hands tremble as he smooths out the papers in front of him.

"How much longer are you planning to keep us in suspense?" Leo asks. He's leaning forward, scanning the papers in front of him eagerly.

Wren has her hands clasped together in her lap, so hard that her knuckles have turned white. I rest my hands on the back of her chair, just close enough that my fingertips can touch her shoulders. She relaxes—just a little.

"Yes, yes, well, this is just … most unusual," Panos mutters, then seizes a scroll. He squints at it, grabs a quill, and holds it poised over an inkwell.

"Now, Mage Wren," he says, and all heads swivel toward my Mage. "Have you ever performed magic during the day?"

She blinks. "Of course I have," she says, frowning.

Panos shakes his head. "Not at sunset or dawn, not at night—during the day. At noon. Think, Wren," he says. A drop of ink drips onto his robe and rolls off it like water off a duck's back, finally finding purchase on a leather book cover.

"There was the tornado at the school—"

Panos raises his hand. "Dusk, on the day of the new moon."

"And … Saroya," she says, quieter.

"Also night. Think, Wren."

"The … fire," she says, and looks up at me. "Nighttime too, I guess."

Ismini is frowning. Aleka crosses her arms. She's standing behind her Mage too.

"What does this have to do with anything?" Aleka asks.

Panos is shaking with excitement, the scraggly hairs of his beard practically vibrating. "Wren is not a corruption of elemental magic at all, as Saroya believes," he says. "She is something entirely different, entirely new. Wren, your magic is a gift from the god of night himself."

The room goes still. Hells, I think maybe the world stops spinning too. Wren slumps a little, stunned. I rest my hand on her shoulder, but she doesn't respond.

"Explain," Leo says, and in the silence, his voice booms like thunder.

Panos clears his throat. "Well, yes," he stumbles. "You see, her magic is only accessible at night, or during the transition between night and day. I'd wager, too, that it's stronger on a moonless night, when the face of Lord Rigrasil is not reflected on the moon."

"Let's say you're right," Ismini says, leaning forward, raising a hand. "What about the fact that she can summon fire? Wind? She can grow plants and heal too."

"At night," Panos says, and shuffles some more papers. "And she only appears to heal on nights with a full moon, when Lord Rigrasil's influence—his healing power, like that of a Shield—is at its peak."

He looks like a man possessed, and it takes an interminable amount of time for him to find what he's looking for. Papers fall off the table, calendars and moon phases and star charts, and his apprentices hurry to scoop them up.

"There is an old passage, a theory, written by my predecessors back when magic was new and the gods still spoke to us. An excerpt I requested from my brothers in the west, from the Temple of Caladrius itself. It is a quote from the Book of Silver … Ah, here."

His voice takes on a strange quality, like that of a poet, or like the way priests recite prayers over the dead.

What is the moon but earth and rock?
What are the stars but fire?
What of all beasts that sleep, of the tides?
It is all of the god of night, Lord Caladrius.

"That's not possible," Wren says. Her voice trembles.

I grip the back of the chair tightly. My heart speeds up, like I'm preparing to fight, my whole body on high alert. I was always taught that the Book of Silver was a myth, nothing more. Now Panos is talking about it like it is a real thing, something to be read and studied and quoted, apparently.

Shields were given their gifts from the god Rigrasil, all those hundreds of years ago. Lord Rigrasil and Lord Caladrius ruled over everything, and always had. Between them, the day and the night, everything was their shared domain. The lesser gods gave their elemental gifts to the Mages, and in return the people worshipped them, raised temples, and burned sacrifices to them. But no one has seen or heard of the gods in ages. Their interest in the mortal realm has lessened, to the point where most believe they don't even exist, that magic is a natural phenomenon, like being born with a birthmark or something. The Shields still believe in Lord Rigrasil though, and most can trace their lineage back to Odall the First Shield himself. I've always envisioned Lord Rigrasil as a sort of doting grandfather, content to let his offspring settle their own messes.

But Panos believes that Lord Caladrius is now doling out magic and has picked Wren, of all people, to be his … what? His experiment? His prophet?

"Is that why the manacles didn't work well on her?" Aleka asks. "I thought they were just faulty or the spell was old or something, but it was because she just can't use her magic in the daytime?"

"Manacles work on Mages—on their elemental magic, from the lesser gods," Panos says.

I grunt. "They worked on me just fine," I say.

Panos shrugs. "It's just a theory. I don't have it all figured out yet," he admits. "They do seem to damper her magic a bit, like when she called the wolves."

"I see," Leo says, rubbing a hand on his chin. "Please, continue."

Panos nods his head and eagerly flips through books, shoving them in front of Wren and Leo.

"It all makes sense," Panos says in a rush. "The communication with beasts. The ability to manipulate all the elements in some way. Even the color of your magic. Look." He points to a passage.

I can't see it from where I am, but Wren draws in a sharp breath.

"The green fire that we see in the north, that lights up the night sky? That's his magic, Wren. That's your magic."

Wren is deathly still.

"Let's say you're right," Leo says, unruffled. "What does it mean? Are the gods among us again? Are we looking at a new era of magic? Is Caladrius bestowing gifts some sign that he's, what, bored? Or looking to make a move against his siblings?"

"I … don't know," Panos admits, letting out a fluttering breath. He sags into his chair.

"That's comforting," Aleka says.

Ismini shoots her a look, but Aleka just shrugs.

"So … I'm not a Mage?" Wren asks.

Panos hesitates. "Not in the way that Ismini and I are," he says carefully.

"You said these books came to you from one of his temples," Leo says.

Panos nods. One of his assistants, a mousy man in an Earth Mage robe, brings out a map of the continent and spreads it across the table so that it faces Wren.

Estana is a mere speck on the map, a gold crown signifying its position as the capital of Ocron, but it is obvious how vast and unexplored the continent remains, especially in the west.

"Here," Panos says, pointing to a black dot in the western mountains. "The oldest of Lord Caladrius's temples. The temple's caretaker, a fellow academic, has been able to send me communication over the past few days. He's been excavating the ruins there and believes there is much to be uncovered."

"If the trolls don't get him first," Aleka mutters.

Panos murmurs an agreement. "Yes, it's a particularly dangerous place to reach," he says. Understatement of the century there. "But it might be the only place where we can learn more about Lord Caladrius's will."

"I'll go," Wren says.

The room erupts, as do I.

"No," I say. No way. No way in all the hells am I letting her travel across the entire continent, toward the very things that are possibly drawn to her.

"Absolutely not," Leo says at the same time.

I glare at him.

"You heard Panos," Wren says, but she's turning toward me, looking up at me, her jade-colored eyes wide. "If I am some sort of beacon for those creatures in the west, then I need to leave Estana, draw them away from here. And if I can learn more about what's going on with me—and with magic—then that's where I want to go."

"To what end?" I ask. "Have your friend send his books and communications here," I tell Panos. "She doesn't need to go."

"I do," Wren says. "You've seen what the unrest out there is already causing. How can we allow any more delay?"

"Their safety is not my concern," I growl. "Yours is."

"But if I am not a Mage, are you still my Shield?" she asks softly.

I look down at her, at the trust and hope there, shining on her face. Like I have a choice.

"Where you go, I go," I say.

She lets out a long breath.

"Besides, I don't really want to go through the games again. It's not fair to the other Shields."

"No, it isn't," she says, but she's smiling, relieved.

I squeeze her shoulder, trying to reassure her. I don't like it, but if she needs to go west, then west we will go. I've fought trolls. I've fought wolves. I've fought men. I will fight whatever else comes our way. I am reminded of an age-old Shield saying, one my brothers recited often. *Aut inveniam viam aut faciam. I shall either find a way or make one.*

"Some of the new Mages and Shields have recently arrived," Leo says slowly, like he's still considering all the possibilities here. "If you do want to go west, you should have more than just your Shield with you for protection. I'll get you an entourage."

"She doesn't need anyone else," I growl.

Wren puts a hand on mine where it is still resting on her shoulder. "Not even you are invincible," she reminds me.

I think about the manacle, about how helpless I felt.

Fine. It will be a waste of their time, but as long as they don't slow us down, don't get in my way, then fine.

"So that's it? You're going?" Ismini asks.

Wren looks at her and nods. It is a simple decision in her mind—never mind the risk she's taking. "Yes," she says.

Chapter 57: Wren

A few days later, and I'm back at the stables. I miss Obsidian fiercely. Aris told me Nestor had killed him, which made me glad Nestor was safe in a dungeon and not around for me to pummel. I have a nice new horse waiting for me, though, a veteran bay gelding named Jasper. He wears a saddle, but only because I need the saddlebags to carry all the books Panos has given me to read on our journey. My education, he tells me, should not suffer just because I am on the road.

Ismini isn't coming with us. She wants to—she told me so with tears in her eyes. Having her and Aleka with us would be invaluable, but she can't leave her husband and her boys. I understand, I told her, though I don't like it. Aleka wants to come too, but she won't leave her Mage. Her knuckles are white as she clenches her hands together behind her back, and I realize she misses being out on the road. It's an odd thing, being one-half of a whole like we are, as Mages and Shields. In a singular way that blends fate and duty and the bonds between two people into a single gods-blessed creation. Whatever it was that made Aris claim me that day in the arena—or whatever fortune blew him my way when I was still a lighthouse keeper in Spit—I am grateful for it.

The wind is chilly today, and I wrap my arms around myself, wishing I had my robe. I haven't seen it since I was kidnapped, and I miss its weight, its reassuring presence.

Aris comes up beside me, leading Flint by the reins. The dappled gray tosses his head, like he's ready to be off adventuring again. Aris stands beside me, our shoulders just touching. I look up at him, and he offers me a small half smile, almost a smirk. In public, we maintain our professional barriers, mostly. I let Aris help me up into the saddle, and as I settle myself, I see Leo watching me from a window. He raises a hand, and I wave back. I'll miss him. He's a good man, a good king.

So I square my shoulders. We're going west. I'm going to keep working on my magic, as much as I can. And we're going to see exactly what is stirring out there. The Mages and Shields who were sent to scout the area have not returned, have not sent any messages back. At least things will be safer this way—if I stayed here, and if I truly am some sort of monster beacon, then I'd risk bringing all of that here, to Estana. To my friends. At least by my going west, they'll be safe.

It feels like we are on the edge of a storm, like the world is holding its breath, waiting for something. My dreams have been strange too. At first I chalked it up to post-magical-swoon delirium, but then they continued. Most often, they are of a winged man on a night-black horse, one who looks so like Obsidian it makes my heart ache. The man never says anything to me, just watches me. He moves like mist, like smoke—in a manner that is eerily graceful. It is always nighttime in my dreams. I'm not sure what to make of them. I told Aris about it one morning, and he grumbled that he didn't like me dreaming about other men. He then decided to take the dreams as a challenge and spent the better part of that morning teasing me with kisses and skillful touches, until all thoughts of anyone or anything else had completely left my mind.

"You are mine," he said later that morning, tracing circles down my arms.

I shivered at the sensation, gooseflesh pebbling my skin, before swatting his hand. He caught it and pulled me into him, wrapping me in a warm embrace. I laughed and laid my head against his smooth chest, listened to his steady heart beating, memorizing the sounds and the heat of him. I'd never felt so safe, so whole in my entire life. He held my hand there against him, as content as I'd ever seen him.

"You are mine," I whispered back to him after a moment.

He looked down at me like he was surprised, before settling back again, his eyes closing. "I am yours," he agreed.

Now, it seems those quiet, lingering mornings might be a thing already of the past. I finger the dagger that Aris has given me, now sheathed at my belt. While it seemed I was able to summon all four elements before, I've not been able to do so since fighting Saroya, not even at midnight. Ismini mentioned that perhaps some lingering effects of the drugs or the manacle or the full moon or Saroya's own influence were still hampering me. Until I can access the magic at will, I'll keep practicing with the blade—though both it and Aris's swords have remained the normal gray of steel.

"What are you thinking about?" Aris asks.

The horses are restless, ready to be off. Jasper is prancing, his massive hooves ringing against the cobblestones. I pat his neck absently.

"It's just … I haven't been able to make so much as a Tamdosan rose since …" I give him a bright smile, one that I don't feel. He isn't fooled. "I guess you'll have to be the brawn for now."

He nods. The twin swords across his back glitter with the movement. "That's all right. You just bloom. I'll be your thorns," he says.

And I believe him. I believe in him, in us. We will figure all this out. His confidence bolsters me, and I leave doubt behind. Aris has his helmet sitting on the back of his saddle—it's a gorgeous thing, the roaring mouth of a tiger wrought in steel, its wicked jaws open. Long canines extend to either side of Aris's face when he wears it. I'm glad he has it back—I have little idea what we'll be up against, and I couldn't bear it if he were injured. The sight of him wearing the manacle will haunt me the rest of my life.

We hear more voices enter the courtyard, and turn. Four people—two Mages and their Shields—approach, leading their own horses. They're wearing traveling clothes, and I suppose this is the additional support that Leo mentioned we should take with us.

It's not until they get closer that I recognize some of them.

"Mariana," I say, surprised. She leads the pack, pulling a white mare behind her. Her blond hair is done back in an intricate braid, and it shines against her blue Water Mage robe.

Aris makes a choking sound, then comes to stand by me. He crosses his arms, flexing the muscles intentionally.

"I want it made perfectly clear that this was not my idea," Mariana says, raising a finger. "But the king has commanded the very best to protect his Night Mage, so here we are."

"Night Mage," I echo. I'm still getting used to the name.

Mariana shrugs. She gives Aris a long look, then walks past us, pulling her mare behind her. It seems that she hasn't gotten over Aris picking me over her at the games.

I wonder how differently things might have turned out if he had picked her. Would I still be back at the school, still shackled and ignorant? I brush my fingers against the back of Aris's elbow, grateful that he chose me, that we're here, despite the dangers ahead. A muscle tightens along his jaw.

"Caelus," Mariana's Shield says abruptly, by way of greeting.

I vaguely remember the man from the games—he's the one who reinjured Aris's shoulder. His eyes gleam strangely yellow, almost glowing. He's tall and lean and weathered, with slightly elongated canine teeth that glint in the light. His gladiuses are sheathed on his back, his shield hung on his horse's saddle.

"At your service," he mutters, dipping his head.

"I'm Rafael," another man says, at Caelus's side. He's a tall, handsome man with shoulder-length blond hair and a red Fire Mage robe. He has intense golden-brown eyes, dark brows, and a strong profile. He offers me his hand to shake.

"I'm excited to be traveling with you, Night Mage. I'm sure that we'll have much to teach each other along the way."

Aris makes a growling sound, and Rafael's charismatic smile broadens. I note a network of waxy burn scars on his hand, which is still holding mine, and a flicker of scar up the side of his neck.

He notices my gaze. "When you play with fire, sometimes you get burned. Isn't that right, Aris?" he says, and claps Aris on the shoulder.

Aris doesn't budge. He might as well be made of stone.

"What is it?" I ask him as Rafael trails after Mariana and Caelus.

"I'll … explain later," Aris says through gritted teeth.

The last Shield, a woman, approaches. She's slim and beautiful, as graceful as a cat. She has smooth olive-toned skin, a cloud of dark hair, and an aquiline nose that has probably been broken a few times. Somehow it only adds to the aura of strength that she projects.

"I'm Dimitra," she says, and shakes my hand. She gives a meaningful look to Aris, who rolls his eyes. "I'm sure this is going to be a very interesting trip."

Dimitra passes us too. The four of them wait at the exit, mounting their horses and not talking. Aris is looking back at the window where I saw Leo. I swear I see the king smirk at him before he vanishes.

"Friends of yours?" I ask Aris.

He grumbles. "You could say that."

Ismini brings me a robe as we line up our horses. It's night black and made of wool lined with silk, woven so finely that it seems to float on the slightest current of air. Leo mentioned the superiority of silk in this city, and as I touch the fabric, letting it glide like a whisper across my fingers, I believe it. Practical it is not—how will silk hold up against the journey ahead?—but it is gorgeous.

"Only fair to have a robe to match your magic," Ismini says. A tear spills from her eye. "Panos and I put every protective spell we could think of on it. It will keep you warm and dry, of course, and deflect most spells and weapons."

"Thank you," I say, and I throw my arms around her neck, squeezing her hard.

She squeezes me back just as tightly, holding me for a long minute before letting go, cupping my cheek with one calloused palm.

"Be safe out there, Night Mage," she says.

I nod, my throat suddenly choked with emotion.

Aris takes the robe and helps me fasten it around my neck—though his touch lingers on the base of my throat, and his eyes darken to the color of sapphires, nobody notices but me. He helps me mount Jasper, and then we head out of the city. We are a silent procession, each of us locked in their own thoughts.

The sun is shining down on us as we leave Estana and head into the west.

The End

www.ingramcontent.com/pod-product-compliance
Lightning Source LLC
Chambersburg PA
CBHW020247030826
48979CB00030B/2639/J
* 9 7 9 8 2 1 8 0 7 3 5 4 1 *